THE IMMORAL REVEREND

THE IMMORAL REVEREND

A NOVEL BY
ROBERT H. RIMMER

Prometheus Books
Buffalo, New York

Published 1985 by
Prometheus Books
700 E. Amherst Street, Buffalo, New York 14215

Copyright © 1985 by Robert H. Rimmer

All rights reserved

No part of this book may be reproduced or transmitted in any form or by any means, electronic or mechanical, including photocopying, recording, or any system now known or to be invented, without permission in writing from the publisher, except by a reviewer who wishes to quote brief passages for inclusion in a magazine, newspaper, or broadcast.

Printed in the United States of America

Library of Congress Catalogue Card No. 85-43080
ISBN 0-87975-299-8

The time frame of this story is not today. It might have begun with "Once upon a tomorrow." Some of the historical roots concerning people and institutions in Adamsport, Massachusetts—including my presumption that the Adamsport First Parish Meeting House is the final resting place of the Adams family, or that the Godwin family and the Godwin Shipyards exist in Adamsport—require a willing suspension of disbelief. On the other hand, since "coming events often cast their shadows before," there's always a possibility—at least I hope—in the many stories I have written, that one day a reader may exclaim: "Good Lord, I read about something like that in a book once, a long time ago."

Part One

I rejoice that in this blessed country of free inquiry and belief, which has surrendered its creed and conscience neither to kings nor priests, the genuine doctrine of only one God is reviving; I trust that there is not a young man now living who will not die a Unitarian.

Thomas Jefferson

1

Until last summer, when he was arrested for mowing his front lawn stark naked—not even wearing sneakers and oblivious to the fact that he might lose his toes in the whirling mower blade, and while a half-dozen giggling kids watched, and their mothers rushed out of their homes to see what was happening and stared in silent horrified awe at his penis waving merrily at them from a forest of grey and black pubic hairs—until last summer very few of the hundred thousand or so people who lived in Adamsport, Massachusetts, had ever heard of Robert J. Lovejoy.

Most of his neighbors thought that Lovejoy was retired. He probably wasn't a millionaire, but he was rich enough to afford a Cadillac and a kidney-shaped swimming pool in his half-acre back yard, which was enclosed by a seven-foot-tall cedar fence. Very few of his neighbors were readers, or they might have known that Lovejoy was the author of many science fiction novels. Unfortunately, his books were not so well known as those written by Robert Heinlein or Frank Herbert or Ursula Guin. Some of his neighbors suspected that Lovejoy didn't depend on writing for his income. But, on the other hand, what he earned must be moderate, else why would he and his wife, Emily, have settled in the Happy Shores section of Adamsport and stayed there for many years?

Unlike most residents of Happy Shores, the Lovejoys came from Protestant backgrounds, so they did not attend mass at St. Joseph's, the only church in Happy Shores. Most of the Lovejoys' neighbors were children of Irish immigrants. Long ago their fathers and mothers had been lured from Ireland to work in the promised land of textile mills or to become servants in the mansions of proper Bostonians.

In those days Boston was known as "the Athens of America." But today most of the Irish and Italians who have overflowed into Happy Shores and Adamsport don't give a damn about, or a second thought to, their Greek and Puritan forbears. Nor are most of them aware that the land they live on had once been forests and rolling meadows owned by men like John Adams, John Hancock, and Josiah Quincy.

Today, Adamsport is not a rich city. Except for the Godwins, the Inches, and the Motleys, very few millionaires still live there. Most of the wealthy have moved to Milton or Brookline or Newton, or south to Scituate or Cohasset. Rumors constantly circulate that when the Godwin Shipyards, which built aircraft carriers and cruisers during World War II, completes its contracts for liquefied natural gas tankers, it may close its doors. If that happens, Adamsport would become a financially distressed area, because more than 20 percent of the population, directly or indirectly, depend on the shipyards for their income.

But should that occur, in all probability a certain well-known United States senator would introduce a bill into Congress to subsidize the shipyards with some kind of naval contract. Lovejoy had suggested to Emily that instead of building destroyers and cruisers and LNG tankers, which could be quickly bombed out of existence in the event of war, the Godwins should build floating hotels. Designed to accommodate five hundred or more Americans in their own kitchenette apartments, the vessels could be launched and towed to major harbors all over the world. Accessible from airports, they could offer timid Americans low-cost, romantic escape environments in foreign countries with all the safety and amenities of living at home. Lovejoy was sure that although such hotels, manned by foreign nationals, might not improve the American image abroad, they would be preferable to Coca-Cola and short-range missiles.

After nearly forty years of marriage Emily Lovejoy had learned to listen to her husband's eccentric ideas with a tiny grin and a helpless shrug of her head. She knew that his novels were filled with even crazier proposals. Behind a typewriter, Roje was even better with words. But he was aloof with strangers. Only a few people were aware of the nickname that Emily had given him. "Roje" was a contraction of his first name and Jesus, a middle name inherited from some long-dead relative who believed in such miracles.

By contrast with Roje, Emily was a friendly person who would bring a homemade cake or a ham to the home of a neighbor whose relatives had passed away. Despite her age, she was still very pretty with laughing blue eyes, tinted blonde hair, an affectionate way of embracing strangers, and a physical shape that made many men, who might range ten years younger or older than she was, wonder what she would be like in bed.

Even though she could trace her Protestant lineage back to the first Daughters of the American Revolution, she believed in the free exercise of religion, and she therefore tried to ignore the electronic church bells that some pious Catholic had given to St. Joseph's, only a street away from the Lovejoys' back yard. Roje was not so tolerant.

The bells tolled the half-hours as well as the hours. He telephoned Father O'Leary and told him that those damned bells were measuring his remaining hours on this earth very belligerently and that they were invading his privacy.

But to Roje's surprise, Father O'Leary was equal to the attack. "Being aware of your mortality, Mr. Lovejoy, should give your futuristic novels a more heavenly dimension."

It developed that Father O'Leary was one of the few people living in Happy Shores who had actually read a Lovejoy novel. A few of them were still on the paperback shelves of the larger bookstores in the Portview Mall, but from month to month they stayed there, and it was just a matter of time before a more popular author whose last name began with *L* replaced the pockets that held Lovejoy novels. Roje had no illusions about his fame as a writer. As he saw it, his novels were too sexually mature for pimply-faced, computer-oriented high school male readers, and were not romantically provocative enough to appeal to their mothers. So, Roje couldn't afford to lose a reader—not even a Catholic priest who didn't worry about for whom the bells tolled.

The Adamsport *Daily Chronicle* printed an enlarged Polaroid shot of Roje in his birthday suit that some neighborhood kid had taken. It was airbrushed, of course, and Emily tried to cool the situation by telling reporters, "I'm sure that my husband really intended to put his shorts on when he finished mowing the back lawn. Our back yard is totally fenced in, you know. No one could see him out there. But lately, I'm afraid that he's getting a little absent-minded. When he's working on a book, he's not always living in the here and now. He probably forgot that he was even mowing."

"Like hell, I forgot," Lovejoy told Judge Gravman, who fined him fifty dollars for lewd and obscene behavior. "I did it because of those bells. They're driving me crazy. Since Father O'Leary insists on reminding me of my approaching demise, I am simply pointing out to him that if he can invade my privacy with his bells, I can invade his with my balls. Actually, my genitals are a more important fact of religious life than his mechanical bells. Thanks to our Puritan forbears and the sanctimonious Irish who have taken over where they left off, the younger generation of kids are growing up ashamed of a man's balls and prick, not to mention the glorious female vagina where they find repose."

Roje then tried to convince Judge Gravman that the bells might be tolerable if they were hung in a steeple where they could be rung by some unemployed Quasimodo. "The trouble is, these bells are simply electronic noisemakers," he insisted. "If they don't stop ringing them, I may picket St. Joseph's naked, or maybe I'll go all out. My sixty-fifth birthday is next week. Maybe I'll drive to Boston and take the elevator to the top of the Prudential Life Insurance building. Prudential is always advertising that it is stronger than the Rock of Gibraltar. When I come down and the elevator opens, I'll be wearing my birthday suit showing my rocks—which may not be as impregnable as the Rock of Gibraltar but may have more local interest. If I decide to do this, you can call it Lovejoy's Return to Sexual Sanity, or The Rebellion of the Last Puritan."

It was fortunate that Emily was in the court. She ushered him quickly out before he could continue with his analogies. Judge Gravman had been momentarily too shocked to hold him in contempt. But he did mention that if Roje decided to appear naked in public again, he would recommend that Roje be put under psychiatric observation as a potentially dangerous flasher.

The truth was that none of the reasons Roje gave for his neighborhood appearance in his skin were totally true. Emily was sure, although Roje refused to admit it, that the reason he was suddenly acting like a hippie left over from the sixties was that no one was reading the words of wisdom in his many novels. But Emily didn't appreciate Roje's problem. Deep down he was angry with himself. At his age many men no more brilliant than he were still running the world in ways he did not approve. Even worse, lately he could no longer talk to Emily about childish sexual things, like romance and falling in love, or futuristic things that he wrote in his novels, like going to bed with a total stranger and discovering what she was really like in bits and pieces as they undressed and saw each other naked for the first time and made love.

After years of listening to Roje talk such silliness and reading about it in his novels, and knowing that her husband had, in the past, both extolled and experienced the joys of loving more than one person at the same time (herself being one of them), Emily had found a new lover. At least Roje was sure that she had. Not that she was any less affectionate with him. But only a romantic lover could have turned a sixty-year-old woman into a songstress who was suddenly singing all the current romantic songs like *"Cheeseburger in Paradise,"* buying rock records, dancing happily around the house, and acting sillier and laughing more than most women, young or old, ever did with their spouses of many years.

Roje didn't ask Emily who her lover might be. During the years of their long marriage and the raising of three children (who had long since scattered to their occupations and professions in various parts of the country), the Lovejoys had been intimately involved, in different periods of their lives, with some of their closest friends. They had spent many delightful hours in various beds, in their own homes and the homes of others, with spouses other than the one they had promised eons ago to remain faithful to, to love, honor, and obey until death did them part.

But the Lovejoys did not think of themselves as swingers—a word used to characterize the amorphous sexuality of less discriminating Americans. Their particular extracurricular in-bed activities had always involved a considerable amount of loving, caring commitment to specific extramarital partners. Both Emily and Roje agreed that brain-swiving with a friend was a joyous *sine qua non* of genital swiving. Of course, it took more time than swingers usually allotted to their multiple one-night penile-vaginal explorations, and occasionally their wandering eyes created little jealous traumas, but in the long run it was much more satisfying.

One reason that Roje didn't ask Emily who, besides himself, she might be currently enjoying in chest-to-breast encounters was that he was sure she would eventually tell him. At the moment, he guessed, Emily might be a little embarrassed, because she knew that for some time now Roje had been monogamous. He hadn't discovered any other lady whom he really cared to snuggle with. Former friends, as old friends often do, had moved away, or passed away. But the real reason that Roje hadn't asked her was that he was afraid that Emily's new lover might be one of his own peer group at the Adamsport Country Club, where Emily—not Roje, who hated the game—played golf twice a week, spring, summer, and fall.

With an eighteen-hole golf course built through former woodlands on the western edge of the city, two huge swimming pools, tennis courts, a four-lane bowling alley, and a billiard room, the Adamsport Country Club had not been designed for lower-income families in the area. The membership fee was $4,000 a year. Dinner for two—who must be members—could run close to fifty dollars. The club offered all the luxuries for those who enjoyed this kind of escapism, but, sadly, Roje wasn't a golfer. Worse, he wasn't a man's man. He preferred women, and not all of them, either. Roje enjoyed women who were aware of their femaleness, women who talked both with their mouths and bodies and smiled at him with happy little sexual come-ons flickering around their eyes and mouths. Roje tried to convince Emily that he was not the kind of man who needed the pseudo-identity achieved by membership in clubs or associations. As far as he was concerned, belonging to organizations contributed nothing to his life; and he really didn't care if his obituary notices were expanded beyond the simple fact that Robert Lovejoy had disappeared yesterday and probably wouldn't return for another hundred years.

But as Emily pointed out to him, they didn't have many friends and they could afford the country club. Moreover, if Roje insisted on vacillating between being a hail fellow well met some of the time and a misanthrope the rest of the time, and if he was so sure that the rest of humanity's brains weren't equal to his own, that was Roje's problem. Emily liked people. She enjoyed them all, the long and the short and the tall.

Actually, Emily's summary of Roje's feelings was a little unfair. Roje had simply told Emily that the Adamsport Country Club was like every organization he had ever been associated with. It was run by noncommunicating factions whose greatest joy in life was gossiping about each other's peccadillos. At the Adamsport Country Club these factions were further subdivided by income levels. People like Irene and Matt Godwin, Rebecca and Henderson Inch, Henrietta and John Motley—a combination of shipyard, banking, and real estate money—were always friendly with the lesser income members of the club, like the Lovejoys, but were, for the most part, careful to circulate only with members in their own income group. It avoided financial embarrassment on either side.

As a compromise, Roje had agreed to join Emily once a week for dinner at the club. Roje did enjoy dining on the window-walled verandah. Far off in the distance you could see the gangling weighs of the Godwin Shipyards and the bulbous domes of the liquefied natural gas tankers under construction, as well as the curving coastline of Happy Shores. Far beyond, over the horizon, there was Europe from whose shores the ancestors of these strangers in paradise had migrated little more than three hundred years ago. Roje enjoyed the wine and cuisine at the club, but he carefully avoided invitations to join mixed or, worse, totally male golf foursomes. Roje knew that wacking a golf ball up and down the steep hills of the eighteen-hole golf course would never make him feel at one with the world or his competitive companions. Despite their once-a-week methodical hill-trudging exercise, as Roje delighted in pointing out to Emily, many of the members still owned thrusting, pugnacious bellies. Privately he hoped that whoever Emily's lover might be, he wasn't one of these club bon vivants. He was sure that some of them probably hadn't actually seen their own cocks beneath their curving extremities for years. Their idea of a nice Saturday or Sunday at the club was a round of golf, showers—segregated by sex, of course—followed by plenty of booze, thick steaks or lobsters, and much talk about baseball, football, the current state of the stock market, or goddamned radicals who believed that things like the Equal Rights Amendment should be passed, thus creating the final indignity of co-ed toilets.

Roje had to admit that Emily often could see good things in morons' minds that he had completely overlooked. Emily was sure that there were many male club members with whom he could identify. And not all of them were golf enthusiasts. There was Matt Godwin, for example. Matt was one of the rich Adamsport Godwins. Emily played golf with his wife, Irene, occasionally. Irene had told her that when Matt was in his middle twenties, nearly eighteen years ago, he had been a minister in some small town in northern Maine. That was before his father had convinced him to go back to Harvard and get a master's degree in business. Irene had intimated that Matt had very socialistic ideas about women, if not business. According to Emily, rumor had it that Matt was currently involved with some Jewish woman in Adamsport and his wife was not very happy about it.

The only time that Roje remembered talking with Matt at the club was more than a year ago. Matt had been standing at the bar. Roje couldn't have sworn to it, but he was fairly sure that Matt was more than a little drunk. Staring down from his six-foot height, he was either trying to focus Roje or hypnotize him. With grey-blue eyes, the color of a stormy sea, set wide apart in a massive skull, and high cheekbones that gave his face an almost emaciated appearance, he reminded Roje of a quotation from Shakespeare: "Yon Cassius hath a lean and hungry look; such men are dangerous."

To Roje's surprise, Matt knew who he was. "Been publishing any more of your science fiction daydreams, Lovejoy?" he demanded.

Before Roje could answer, Harry Holman, a big-bellied member of the club who, Emily had told him, was one of the club's top golfers, squeezed next to them at the bar and asked Roje if he would like to join a foursome tomorrow. Roje was sure that Emily had put Harry up to it. "Not unless I can play with a croquet mallet," Roje responded, and he noticed that Matt was grinning. "It's the only club I own."

"There's a challenge for you, Harry," Matt laughed. "If Lovejoy will play eighteen holes with a croquet club, I'll be your caddy. Of course, he'll have to give you a handicap."

Holman didn't think that was very funny, especially when his wife, Bee, joined them and with twinkling eyes said, "Matt, what's this thing you have about being a caddy? I heard that you had offered to caddy one of the ladies' foursomes." She paused for effect. "But only if you could do it bare-ass." Bee's grin indicated that she wasn't adverse to the idea even if her husband was.

"I just thought the ladies might find it more inspiring to keep their eyes on their Daddy's balls rather than golf balls," Matt replied, edging away from them with two scotches in his hands. "Unfortunately, I haven't been able to convince Irene." He smirked at Roje. "I'm afraid, Lovejoy, that you and I will have to grow up. Life is real, life is earnest. At least my Daddy tells me so."

Roje's naked lawn-mowing escapade reminded Emily that Matt was still offering to caddy for his wife in his birthday suit. In addition, recently Matt had startled several club members by suggesting that at least once a month, to pep things up and to make the club less boring, the manager could offer nude couples splash parties in the pool and nude couple bowling.

"Matt Godwin sounds almost as crazy as you are," Emily scowled at Roje. "Why is it that men are so anxious to expose their genitals to the world?"

"Not to the world," Roje assured her. "To show women . . . and to be praised for their cocks, of course. If men had feathers like a male peacock, they'd ruffle them instead."

Actually, during his brief encounter with Matt and Harry, the squirmy thought had crossed Roje's mind that Harry Holman might be Emily's new lover. If so, he hoped that Emily wouldn't try to pawn him off on Bee Holman. Harry's belly was big enough, but Bee must weigh at least two hundred pounds. How she managed to play golf was a wonderment to him. With her blue-rinsed hair piled high on her head, she reminded Roje of a bluejay. She wasn't the kind of woman that he could imagine himself cavorting in bed with. Hopefully, the Holmans dissipated their sexual energy together on the golf course. Not that Roje couldn't enjoy a plump lady in the sack, but he abhorred cooing ladies who waddled like pigeons.

Although Roje's encounter with Judge Gravman had not been reported in the *Chronicle,* Sylvanus Williams heard about it. Many of the Adamsport Country Club members didn't like Williams or tried to ignore him. Some insisted that, despite his name, he was the club's only token Jewish member. He owned the notorious Silly Willy's, a sexy strip club located on a main artery, cluttered with fast food franchises, that cut through Adamsport from Boston and filtered traffic south to Hingham and Cape Cod. A deeply tanned man in his middle sixties with a frosting of white in his otherwise black hair, he was tall and coldly handsome. Conspicuous on the third finger of his left hand was a huge sparkling diamond in a heavy gold setting. Roje, who had rarely spoken to Sylvie, told Emily that he looked like a gangster left over from the 1930s.

Now, to Roje's surprise, he had suddenly acquired a new friend. Uninvited, Williams dragged up a chair. Emily and Roje were dining at their usual window table at the club. Before he sat down he bussed Emily's cheek and shook hands enthusiastically with a bewildered Roje.

"I've played an occasional foursome with your wife, Lovejoy." Williams beamed lovingly at her. "Emily's a great golfer. I had no idea that her husband was such a rebellious character. You're a man after my own heart, Lovejoy." For a moment Roje was afraid that this handsome stranger was actually going to hug him, but Williams restrained himself. "Ferris—you know Tom? He's a member here. Ferris was in court the other day when you told Judge Gravman off. Tom is one of my lawyers." Williams shrugged. "In my business, if you want to survive you have to have several law-boys on the payroll. Unfortunately, they eat up most of the profits. Anyway, Tom told me that you were absolutely great. You plan to restore sexual sanity to Massachusetts by walking around the Pru bare-ass? My God, Lovejoy, that's fabulous! It restores my faith in America to know that there's still a few American Puritans left who aren't afraid to challenge King George."

Roje knew that "King George" was a reference to George Gallagher, who had been recently elected mayor of Adamsport, partially because of a campaign promise that he would eliminate smut and pornography from Adamsport—particularly Silly Willy's, where naked female dancers appeared at lunch time and entertained males from Adamsport and surrounding communities with intimate views of their behinds, breasts, and genitals. Except for Wednesdays. Then Silly Willy's offered male ecdysiasts for matrons young and old who arrived by the busloads to scream their enthusiasm at the flat-bellied male dancers shaking their "goodies" at them.

"I told Chuck Simpson—Chuck is the club manager—that I want to sponsor a testimonial cocktail party for you here at the club," Williams said, ignoring Roje's rather pursed-lip look. "Matt Godwin's wife Irene heard me and she tried to squelch the idea. But Chuck says it's my money. If you can wait a couple of weeks for the first open night, he'll set it up. At my expense, of course. On the other hand, Lovejoy, if you'd like to carry your rebellion a little further and appear at my club any Wednesday, just give me a ring. We pay porno ladies like Juliet Anderson and Annette Haven three grand a week. You're in pretty good shape, Lovejoy; you should be worth a couple of thou."

Roje was sure that Williams was trying to aggravate him, but before he could respond sarcastically that Sylvie, as Emily called him, wasn't getting the message, Williams was paged for a telephone call. "Damn it," Roje told Emily after he left, "I think I'm batting my head against a wall. He doesn't have sense enough to realize that if the average guy could watch young ladies like Annette Haven mowing their lawns naked, they wouldn't *pay* to see them, not even when they bend over with their ass in the air like they do at Silly Willy's."

"I'm sure Bee Holman will be happy to oblige you. Why don't you invite her over for a naked swim in our pool?" Emily asked and grinned at Roje's sour look. "Anyway, don't put Sylvie down. I know most of the people in this club detest him, but he's a laughing man. The trouble with most WASPs is they have forgotten how to laugh. And Sylvie's a good golfer." Emily told Roje she had heard rumors that Williams was a millionaire several times over. "When Doris Tilburg and I played golf with him and Tom Ferris a couple of weeks ago, he told us that he's starting a new business. He plans to franchise it nationally." Emily laughed. "Wait until George Gallagher hears about this one. It's called the Water Brothers Corporation. He's going to offer Soaky-Pokey franchises nationally, and he's planning to open a couple of test ones right here in downtown Adamsport."

"Are they dance studios?" Roje asked.

"No, honey, you're thinking of the hokey pokey. Soaky-Pokeys will be places where you can rent a hot tub by the hour to share with your friends. Sylvie's lawyer is a little afraid of them. Rooms will be available with both tubs and air mattresses for relaxing." Emily gave Roje a searching look. "If you had a lady friend, you could rent one by the hour and soak and poke."

"Alas, I don't," Roje said, happy that Sylvie had left. He couldn't picture him as a friend with whom he might share philosophical discussions about the future of the world. But he had to admit that Williams had been friendlier than most of the club members, who either ignored him or, after his recent escapade, acted as if he were some kind of extraterrestrial who had suddenly moved into the neighborhood.

Roje was just about to tell Emily that he had had enough of the Adamsport Country Club for one night when Sylvie suddenly reappeared.

"That was Sam Early," he said, referring to his phone call. "Local gossip has it that old man Godwin, Ike, Matt's father, is returning to Adamsport with a new child bride. The old man is about seventy-five. Rumor has it that his new wife is young enough to be his daughter." Sylvie looked at Emily questioningly. "You play golf with Irene Godwin occasionally, don't you? I wonder how Matt feels about that?"

Emily shrugged. "I'm sorry, I'm not friendly enough with Irene to share confidences. As some writer once said—was it Fitzgerald, Roje?—'The rich are different from us.' Maybe Ike Godwin will lend you money for your new business."

"Not likely," Sylvie laughed. "But maybe Roje—you don't mind if I call you Roje, do you?—maybe Roje and Matt Godwin might be able to help me some day." Noticing the suspicious, I'm-not-getting-involved expression on Roje's face, Sylvie diverted the subject. "You know Matt Godwin, don't you? He's a member here. He's kind of a rebel, too. I hear that he's going to preach a sermon after Labor Day and his father is none too pleased." Sylvie shrugged. "The three of us do have something in common. We all enjoy bare skin."

"Not exactly in the same way," Roje said coldly. "I don't approve of selling the privilege to see it."

"Makes no difference. You're as much a persona non grata as I am." Sylvie grinned at Roje. "Anyway, Sam Early just told me that he thinks there's something unusual cooking at City Hall. Rumor has it that Ike Godwin is going to offer a redevelopment plan for downtown Adamsport. I'm sure that our pudgy mayor, George Gallagher, doesn't approve of you anymore than he does me, but momentarily he may need a Jewish UU to help him."

Sylvie evidently thought Roje knew what a UU was, but Roje didn't. A few people were dancing to syrupy music on tape provided on Sunday evenings by the club. Sylvie asked Emily to dance, and Roje forgot to ask him what a Jewish UU was. Actually, he didn't give a damn, anyway.

2

In Los Angeles, only a few hours after Roje had been talking with Sylvie, Jack Handley, senior pilot for Controlled Power Corporation, was piloting the company Grumman jet down the runway at Los Angeles Airport. As the plane reached a safe altitude he grinned at Joe Wagner, his copilot, and said, "I wonder if the old man will try to knock off a piece tonight in the aft cabin with his new wife." Jack chuckled. "He's got five hours to get it up." He gestured toward the rear of the Grumman jet. "It isn't often we have a pretty lady like that aboard. She may be forty something or other, but she's a real sexy-looking doll. I'll bet that she's only a year or two older than Matt Godwin's wife. And she's even prettier." He looked at his watch. "It's one o'clock. My guess is that within ten or fifteen minutes they'll be in the sack. If you take a walk back, you may catch a glimpse of her in her birthday suit."

"No thanks," Wagner shook his head. "I don't think Big Daddy would like that."

"How would you feel if your old man married a woman thirty years younger than he was?"

Wagner laughed. "If Big Daddy wasn't up to it, I'd have to take charge of my new mommy in the sack—what else?"

Handley grinned. "Not Ike Godwin's wife you wouldn't. He'd cut your balls off."

Back in the cabin of the high-powered jet, Isaac Zachary Godwin was holding hands with Gillian Marlowe Godwin. He was still unable to believe that this woman had finally agreed to marry him. Knowing that he was acting like a naive teen-ager with his first love, he couldn't help himself. He kissed Jill's long neck and shoulder that was partially revealed by her low-cut blouse. It formed a lovely bow between her shoulders. Then he pointed out of the window at the disappearing lights. "We've got six hours before we land at Logan. Do you want to lie down and get a little sleep?"

Gillian shook her head. "Not right away. I know it's silly, but I'm suddenly feeling quite nervous, Ike." She squeezed his hand. "It's one thing to spring a new wife on your children, but how are they going to react when you tell them that we may be living permanently in Adamsport?"

"They'll be in a state of shock probably, particularly my son, Matt." Isaac grinned at her. "He'll be jealous when he sees how beautiful you are."

The Godwin-Marlowe wedding had been nothing to write home about or invite relatives to—none had been invited. But with two marriages behind her, Gillian really didn't care. The two-hundred-thousand-dollar diamond sparkling on her finger was resplendent proof that Ike Godwin loved her. The only relative who had appeared at the wedding was Ike's youngest daughter. Sally Godwin lived in California. She was thirty-two.

"Momma was forty-two when I was born," she told Gillian and hugged her. "Proves that you'd better not take chances." Sally felt an immediate affinity with Gillian. "Daddy's quite a picker," she said. "You look young enough to have a few more kids. You'd better be careful. Big Daddy loves to play God. He may want to create a few more Godwins in his own image." Sally laughed. "Outside of my sister Becky he hasn't succeeded too well, thus far."

Sally had flown down to Los Angeles from Big Sur, where she had her own studio overlooking the Pacific. She told Gillian that when she wasn't painting—and supporting herself very well, thank you, without her father's help—she cohabited with two totally different males.

"I like variety," she admitted, already comfortable enough with Gillian to know that she would never share Sally's confidences with Ike. "One of them wants to marry me. Right now he's an occasional weekend companion. If Daddy knew who he was, he'd shit his pants. Gus is chief cook and bottle washer of Infinity Corporation, a company that Daddy took over last year. There's no love lost between the two of them."

Sally warned Gillian that her sister, Becky, who lived in Adamsport, was quite New England stuffy and that Henderson, her husband, was a faithful old prune. "Good for your bowels, but not ecstatic to eat," she said. "The only one in our family who is any fun is my brother, Matt." But according to Sally, Matt's wife had a tight leash on him.

The weekend three months ago when Gillian Marlowe had decided to stay overnight and go to bed with Isaac Godwin, she had no intention of ever marrying him. Ike had bought a lavish eight-room condominium in Beverly Hills a few weeks after Controlled Power had finally taken over Infinity Corporation. In the wake of a bitter proxy battle, it became apparent that the final merging of the companies would require the watchful eyes of the top brass of CPC for a year or two.

Ike told her that he bought the condominium nearly a year ago, before Sarah died. Sarah had flown out to look at it but had refused to move to California. Though she had visited California often in her youth, she told Ike that Beverly Hills was too luxurious for her blood and she could never learn to drive on the freeways. She preferred their ancestral home in Adamsport. She couldn't imagine living in a world where it was impossible to walk from one place to another, where there were no well-defined seasons, where Unitarian ministers swaggered into a pulpit on Sundays and preached their sermons wearing sport shirts and blue jeans.

No one could do any serious work in a world where the sun always shone. Sarah was always "waiting for winter" to get things done. She didn't mind the bleak New England winters. She often trudged from the Godwin estate, on a hill overlooking Adamsport, down to the First Parish Church, even through snowdrifts in February. The Big House, as it was known, had twenty rooms, but it was a cozy place with real fireplaces that smoked and burned real wood. There were no fake gas logs that burned endlessly without sputtering or crackling and never left any ashes to pick up. Winter in New England made one really appreciate the first sweet breath of spring. And the sticky days of summer made you look forward to a crisp and invigorating October. She told Ike that since he already commuted between New York, Los Angeles, and Boston, at least once a month, she'd keep the home fires burning in Adamsport until Controlled Power had digested Infinity Corporation.

The first night Gillian snuggled against Ike's bony chest she told him that she wanted to be honest with him. She had been married twice. She had two children with her first husband, who couldn't understand her need to be not just a mother and housewife but an actress to boot, and a good one. Her son, Chuck, was an actor, still paying his dues, appearing mostly in summer stock and with a repertory company in Indianapolis in the winter. Wendy, her daughter, had married a stockbroker and was enjoying upper-class affluence. Gillian had divorced her second husband three years ago. He was an actor who spent most of his time not on the stage but in the beds of ingénues, bewailing his failures. Since the divorce she had had a few itinerant lovers.

She had told Ike that she would never marry again. "It's not your age," she said, hugging his lean body when he first voiced the idea. "I really like you. But I'm sure that your daughter Rebecca and your son Matt wouldn't approve of a new mother their own age." Ike had told her that his elder daughter, Becky, was a proper New Englander who had married a Bostonian, Henderson Inch. The Inches could trace their lineage back to the *Mayflower*. Henderson, eight years older than Matt, had become like an older son to Ike; he had been remarkably cooperative when Ike had made Matt manager of the Godwin Shipyards instead of him.

Gillian feared that Becky and Hendy would be certain that she was a gold digger. "And from what you told me about Matt, he'd resent my taking Sarah's place."

"My daughter and Hendy won't be your problem," Ike had insisted. "But Matt is another cup of tea. I don't know whether he's actually been unfaithful to his wife, but I have a feeling that they've been close to divorce."

Gillian noted that whenever Ike mentioned his son, his jaw twitched. "The trouble with Matt," Ike continued, "is that in the past few years he has acquired some very strange ideas about marriage and fidelity. I don't think that he wants to separate from Irene, but he thinks that he can have his cake and eat it." Ike kissed Gillian possessively. "If he tries his seductive ways on you, you'll have to make it clear that from now on you're monogamous." Ike had laughed when he said it, but he stared at her a little anxiously and said, "Despite your two marriages, you really are monogamous, aren't you?"

To Gillian's surprise, she gradually discovered that it was certainly not a case of like father like son. During his forty-five years of marriage Ike had never been unfaithful to Sarah. Ike believed that if you slept with a woman you should marry her. In truth, a man shouldn't want to sleep with a woman until he was prepared to marry her. "I am very much in love with you, Jill," he told her, "but I really don't feel right about sleeping with you until you're really mine."

Nervous though the word "mine" made her and knowing that she was not about to be owned by any man, Gillian had finally capitulated. Most of her friends believed the only reason she would agree to marry a man twenty-six years older than she, was to eventually inherit some of his millions. But the truth was that she liked Ike. His driving need for success paralleled her own. At seventy-two Ike was thin and wiry with the ageless appearance of a tough New England sea captain. Gillian was sure of one thing: enjoying Ike's remaining years with him would be far more interesting than bucking the tide. After twenty years on the New York stage, she had finally made one movie. But she was no longer a femme fatale. She had played a character part: the mother of a much younger woman. She wouldn't look forward to winning an Oscar if, like Bette Davis or Joan Crawford in their later years, she had to play nasty old lady parts for the rest of her life. She told Ike quite honestly that she actually didn't want to give up the stage, or the possibility of making another movie, and she admitted that by marrying him she could happily tell her agent to go to hell. She'd be in the driver's seat; she could pick and choose her roles. Ike had agreed enthusiastically. "You are the epitome of Controlled Power," he told her, chuckling. "I have faith in you. Pick your play or film, and I'll finance it. Then I'll watch the audience, and anyone who isn't cheering or applauding you will get tossed out on his ass."

As for sex with a senior citizen, Gillian had discovered the first night, and practically every night since, that Ike was part satyr in bed, and she happily responded. He thoroughly enjoyed what he called her "middle-aged nymphomania." Her carefully role-played, in-bed capitulation and submission to him delighted Isaac and thoroughly eroticized both of them. Gillian hadn't dared to ask him if he had been so sexually driven with Sarah. Probably not. She wondered if, when she was in her seventies as Sarah had been, she would finally be a sexually cooler woman. But that would be almost thirty years from now. By then either Isaac or she would most likely have gone to their maker. One thing was sure and she didn't need Sally's advice. She took her pills on schedule. She wasn't going to give birth to any more Godwins—not for all of Ike's millions.

Jill discovered that during the Godwins' long marriage, Ike and Sarah had developed very divergent views on both politics and religion. Sarah had been a far-out, left-wing Democrat. Ike's heroes were Nixon and Reagan and, of course, the man who Ike Godwin considered the best president of all—Ike Eisenhower. While Isaac was by no means a fundamentalist, a Jesus-will-save-you kind of person, he had been brought up on high church principles. Until he met Sarah he had never known what he called anti-trinitarians. He had been brought up an Episcopalian. Like most sound American business and political leaders, he knew that Jesus Christ and God were synonymous. He also knew that hard work was man's route to salvation. Jesus Christ had shown the way. As far as Ike was concerned, he personally didn't need to get mixed up in church affairs and politics.

Although they had been married in the Adamsport Episcopalian Church and Ike continued the Godwin tradition of giving the church $10,000 a year, he and Sarah had only appeared occasionally for Sunday services—but always on Easter, Thanksgiving, and Christmas. Then, to his shock, a few years after they were married, Sarah, whose family were active Unitarians, told him that she really couldn't stomach Jesus idolatry.

Before he was fully aware of what she meant, she began attending the First Parish Unitarian Church regularly. "I should have put my foot down," he told Gillian, "but most of the time I wasn't in Adamsport on Sundays, anyway. Then I discovered the kids were going to the First Parish Church Sunday School. Sarah never stopped trying to indoctrinate them, especially Matt. She told him the Godwins had enough money and they didn't need any more businessmen in the family. When he finally went to Harvard she encouraged him to major in philosophy. She kept telling Matt that like his grandfather—her father—someday he might become a man of God."

Ike shrugged. "I'm glad that you're not a church do-gooder, Jill. The UU's are the worst of the lot. Why Sarah was so intrigued with them is beyond me. Most of them haven't got a pot to piss in. They're practically pagans. They think that Jesus was on a par with Buddha, or Mohammed. They don't really have much faith in God, either. Instead of putting their shoulders to the wheel, they're so damned busy picketing nuclear power plants, fighting against the development of nuclear energy, fighting anti-abortion bills, or trying to socialize the country that they don't care whether God's in his heaven or not. The truth is, Jill, that Sarah got worse as she got older. Being a UU wasn't bad enough; she became an all-out feminist. Margaret Sanger was her heroine, and after her Betty Friedan and Gloria Steinem. To her dying days Sarah was writing, talking, and actually donating thousands of my hard-earned dollars to try and get the Equal Rights Amendment passed."

Isaac had grinned at her. "Don't get nervous, honey. I'm not against equal rights for women, but I don't think women should wear pants or work in my foundaries or fight in wars." He laughed, "And I don't want to find some female using the public hopper when I want to use it."

Gillian didn't agree with Ike, but she didn't challenge him either. She had learned years ago that the easiest way to control a man was to play the female game. As an actress she had perfected the gentle art of seduction, and did not believe that it demeaned women to use their sexuality. It simply added spice to life. Nevertheless, she was jittery about meeting Matt and Becky for the first time and sleeping in the Godwin mansion. According to Ike, his home had at least ten rooms ready for them in the west wing. When Becky and Henderson got married they had moved into the east wing, and later Matt and Irene had taken over the carriage house. Jill hadn't made an issue of it yet with Ike, but she was certain she wasn't going to sleep in some family heirloom bed that once had been occupied by him and Sarah.

Isaac had told Jill that Sarah's personal estate had been over two million dollars, but he hadn't told her, or his children, that Sarah had written him a letter a few days before she died in which she requested that her money be equally divided between the First Parish Church and the Unitarian Universalist Headquarters in Boston. Ike was sure that such insanity had been motivated by Reverend Littlejohn or his predecessor at the First Parish Church, Moses Fletcher. When Fletcher had died ten years ago, although Ike had been very reluctant, Sarah had established a two-hundred-fifty-thousand-dollar Godwin Trust Fund for the church in his memory. Sarah had never personally earned or inherited any of the money; it was mostly in stocks and bonds that he had transferred to her over their years of marriage. So Ike wasn't happy about letting Godwin money disappear into the UU sinkhole of iniquity. Especially so now. Before Sarah died, Becky had transferred her allegiance to the Congregational Church where she and Henderson had been married. Matt continued to be a Unitarian but attended church infrequently. There really was no further need to underwrite the UU's—especially so because if his plans worked out, within a few months Controlled Power would own the First Parish Church building and would be tearing it down.

3

Lying beside Jill in the private bunk area of the Grumman, Ike kissed her closed eyes and she opened them with a tiny loving smile on her face. Jill had shed her dress and was wearing only a bra and panties, but although he was tempted to make love to her, he resisted. Now was not really the time or place. His thoughts wandered back to the directors' meeting of Controlled Power, ten days ago. He knew that he'd have to fly back to California for at least one more meeting in January, but if everything fell into place, by the end of the first quarter of next year he'd have CPC relocated in the East. When he had started building the multi-billion-dollar company on the foundations of the Godwin Shipyards, he had promised himself and Sarah that one day he would return. Fifteen years later Controlled Power had become one of the top hundred in *Fortune* magazine's listing of the billion-dollar companies.

He had assured Jill that he wasn't just thinking of his own convenience—or of building a monument to the Godwin family. If Controlled Power Corporation actually built a new thirty-story headquarters in the center of downtown Adamsport, it would help restore a city that had fallen on hard times. All the big retail chains had moved to the Portview Mall. The only hope for Adamsport was to remodel it and re-create it as a new suburban business center. Adamsport could offer better parking and lower taxes and rentals than the city of Boston, which was only a few miles away. A week before the CPC board meeting, he had telephoned George Gallagher, the mayor of Adamsport. "It's not for publication, George," he told him, "and it may not happen, but I want to know how you feel about Controlled Power relocating its headquarters in Adamsport."

If Gallagher could have reached across three thousand miles and hugged Ike, he would have. It was well known in the city that the Godwin Shipyards desperately needed some new contracts. While it still offered employment to several thousand Adamsport families, there was no certainty that it could stay open. The shipyard was now only one small division of Controlled Power Corporation, but if Ike Godwin was planning to relocate CPC in Adamsport, that meant that the shipyard was once again going to get his personal attention.

"You could build your building out near the yard," Gallagher told Ike. "But I have got a better idea for you. How would you like to locate right across the street from City Hall? The First Parish Church is on its last legs. It needs at least a quarter of a million dollars to keep it from falling down. I know your wife left some money to the church, but the sad truth is, there aren't enough Unitarians in Adamsport to support the place. I've heard rumors that the church board—the people who run the church—think the only solution is to sell the building. I think you could pick it up for a song. Your problem would be sentimentality. As you well know, the Adams family are buried under the portico. A lot of people think it should be a national monument, but unless the UU's move out, the National Park Service refuses to take it over. If you could figure out some way to relocate the Adamses' tombs, I'm sure the city council will go all out to help you, taxwise and any other way."

Ike was immediately enthusiastic. "You don't have to worry about the Adams family," he said jovially. "Old John may have been a Unitarian, but he didn't publicize it. John Quincy most certainly wasn't a Unitarian. Originally the First Parish Church was a Congregational church, and it still was when the Adamses were alive. No one seems to know how or when it finally became Unitarian Universalist. Get me some photographs of the church and the whole area, George. I'll have some tentative architectural drawings made, and don't worry about the Adamses—we won't neglect them."

Convincing the Controlled Power Board of Directors hadn't been easy. Since the takeover of Infinity Corporation, Ike had inadvertently acquired two new board members who up till now challenged more than they ever confirmed his leadership. Before CPC moved in, Gus Belshin and Hank Crowell had been their own bosses at Infinity, and they were Californians by birth. Most of the directors had been certain when Ike had purchased a condominium in Beverly Hills that eventually CPC would move out of their rented headquarters space in Los Angeles and build a high-rise office building downtown or in San Francisco.

But carefully pursuing his dream, Ike had pointed out the tax advantages of relocating the company's headquarters in a suburb next to a large metropolitan city. "Not a city like L.A. or New York," he told the directors. "We don't need a high density corporate environment. We've built the better mousetrap."

Then Gus Belshin had inadvertently played into his hands. "Why not Adamsport, Massachusetts, Ike?" he had asked sarcastically. "You could build your own monument right next to your shipyards."

Ike had acknowledged the general laughter with a genial wave of his hand. "It's not so far-fetched as you might think, Gus. While Infinity has added close to a billion dollars to our corporate sales, most of our revenues still come from eastern divisions of the corporation. In this computerized, fast-communication age, we can keep in the middle of things no matter where we're located. But I personally think CPC headquarters should be in the East." Ike grinned craftily at Crowell and Belshin. "You personally don't have to relocate. We need you right here in Los Angeles. Top management would be out of your hair on a day-to-day basis. Only two of the twelve of us would have to fly cross-country for meetings. My son, Matt, couldn't make this meeting, but I'm sure he'd agree."

Actually that wasn't true. Ike had telephoned Matt last week and told him: "You can skip this meeting. I've been talking with some of the top brass in the navy, and they're about to make some important decisions on their Sealift plans. It's just as well that you stay close to home base."

Ike purposely hadn't told Matt that he was planning to bring up the relocation of CPC headquarters or that he was going to nominate Matt for president of Controlled Power, thus letting himself move up to the vacant office of chairman of the board. He hadn't told any of the directors either that in his various phone conversations with his son, Matt had made it abundantly clear that he didn't want to move to California. And whenever Ike brought up the subject of the presidency of Controlled Power Corporation, Matt had blocked the conversation, protesting that there were many people in the company who were more qualified than he was for the job. Convincing Matt that he could skip the meeting made it possible to steer him in the direction that he must go. Matt might object, but in the long run it was for his own good, and Ike was sure that Matt would someday thank him for it.

Later when Ike telephoned Irene, she had been a little hysterical. "Matt's going through another one of his wishy-washy midlife crises," she told him. "He's wondering why he ever left the ministry. I think you are going to have a hard time convincing him he should be president of CPC."

Ike told her curtly that he wasn't going to tolerate another round of bull shit from his son. "He has no choice, Irene, he's got to move up in CPC or get out. Henderson should have taken over as manager of the yard five years ago. You've got to convince Matt that he's not cut out to be a preacher. Deep down he knows it. I saved him from God twelve years ago when he was making an ass out of himself in Maine. The Godwins—not God—put the frosting on his cake. As you well know, Irene, Matt enjoys the frosting as well as the next guy. But by God he's going to earn it. I'm not handing the cake to him on a silver platter."

Manipulating his only son and manipulating the board of Controlled Power were all in a day's work for Ike. Of course, as a major stockholder and creator of the conglomerate, Ike held all the high cards. The board had unanimously elected Matthew Godwin president of CPC, effective at the beginning of the coming corporate year, January 1, when it was assumed that the final location of the new headquarters would have been determined. And Ike would finally be chairman of the corporation he had created.

Now, Ike was suddenly aware that Gillian was watching him. She patted his cheek affectionately and asked him why he wasn't sleeping. Ike gave her a big hug. He knew that at seventy-two he shouldn't be getting a hard-on every time he touched Jill, but he really was delighted with his latest acquisition. He undid her bra strap and kissed her breasts. "I'm too excited to sleep," he said. "I was wondering why my son Matt couldn't be as lovable as you are." He smiled happily at her. He didn't quite dare to ask if she'd like to have him come inside her.

"That's easy," Gillian grinned at him provocatively. "A good wife obeys her husband and does what he wants her to do. Sons never do that." She kissed his cheek, and teased him. "But you should keep in mind I never promised you that I'd be a good wife all the time."

Listening to her, Ike knew that he had to be careful. For the first time in his life a human being, a woman—it had never happened to him with Sarah—could manipulate him. With a nice sprinkling of white in her black hair, big myopic dark brown eyes in her lean, high-cheekboned face, whether she knew it or not (and she probably did), Jill released all his pent-up protective instincts. He was an unconquerable white knight ready to slay dragons for his lady. And if there weren't any around, he'd be happy to create a few.

"I'm not sure how Jack is planning to arrive when he comes into Boston," he said, happy to discover that Jill was aware of his engorged penis and was holding it tenderly. "Sometimes we fly in over the shipyard. If we are further to the west you can see the Godwin estate. I think I told you, we have about thirty acres overlooking Adamsport. Becky and Hendy live in the east wing of the Big House with their kids; Sarah and I lived in the west wing. The house was completely remodeled about fifteen years ago, along with the carriage house, when Matt and Irene got married. They turned it into a charming ten-room home. Most of the estate is fenced in and includes greenhouses, a bird sanctuary, gazebos, and even an abandoned granite quarry. My grandfather Zach built it in the early 1900s. He was quite a guy. During the First World War he broke all shipbuilding records and turned out destroyers from keel to launching in forty-five days. He was eighty at the time. If Matt had just a little of his drive, there's no limit to what we could do."

Jill grinned at her craggy-faced husband. "You'd better come inside me. But no yelling climax, please. I'd be embarrassed if your pilots heard us." When she was on top of him she laughed, "Good Lord, I'll never assimilate all the Godwin family history." The thought had flickered through her mind more than once in the past few days.

As if he guessed her thoughts, Ike told her that she'd have no problem with Becky, Irene, or Hendy. "They think like you and I do," he said. "We live conservatively. We don't flaunt our wealth. We don't advertise our religion or our politics, and we try to maintain a low profile." He scowled, "But Matt is a horse of another color." He tried to explain to Jill, as he had several times before, that Matt was his *bête noire*. It was really all Sarah's fault.

From the time Matt was a kid, Sarah had created a kind of no man's land between them. Sarah had taught Matt to read fluently, even before he was five years old, but then she cluttered his mind with a never-never land of fairy tales. Ike accused her of making her son think like a woman. Long before Matt was a teenager his only friends were girls. Instead of playing football and baseball with the boys, Matt was always "playing house" with the daughters of friends of Sarah. Once Ike had caught Matt with three of them in a back parlor of the house. None of them was much older than ten or twelve, and one was Sally. The girls' panties were on the floor, their dresses in disarray, and Matt's trousers were unzipped. Sarah had shrugged and told him that it was quite natural for children to examine each other's genitals. He didn't have to worry. The girls were too young to get pregnant.

Playing doctor was one thing; Ike accepted that. But it wasn't natural for a well-developed boy to be reading poetry or crazy oriental philosophy. When Matt was fifteen, with Sarah's help he had discovered a swami (long dead, fortunately) who called himself Vivekananda. According to Sarah, Vivekananda had been Mary Baker Eddy's inspiration for that crazy Christian Science religion in which no one ever really got sick but was simply invaded by something called "error." Sopping up such stuff, Matt coolly told his father that everything in the universe, including bugs, the leaves on the trees, the food they were eating, his cat and dog, and even Matt himself, was God. What's more, God didn't just have one son—he had billions of sons and daughters. They were everywhere.

On top of that, Moses Fletcher, pastor of the First Parish Church, told Ike after one of the holiday services (which he had attended to please Sarah) at that damned Unitarian Church, that Matt at seventeen had read the Old and New Testament. Matt could quote much of it chapter and verse. "If he believed in the Bible," Moses had beamed, obviously thoroughly happy that Matt didn't, "Matthew Godwin could out-quote Billy Graham or Jerry Falwell."

When Sarah first hinted that perhaps Matt should be a minister, Ike hadn't listened to her. He had been aggravated that neither Sarah nor his useless brother, Matthew Samuel Godwin, seemed to care that Ike was spending every minute of his time rescuing the shipyards from a postwar depression and using family-controlled stock in a very clever recapitalization that would eventually underwrite a billion-dollar expansion far beyond shipbuilding. Ike was furious when Matt, after majoring in psychology and philosophy, told him that he had been accepted to Harvard Divinity School.

"He had just graduated from Harvard with high honors," Ike

reminisced to Jill, happy to feel her flesh against his and pleased that she seemed to enjoy his passive love-making. "Standing there in the Harvard yard with his cap and gown, he dumped that one on me. I told him to stop spouting his mother's insane ideas. 'Sure we have enough money to afford a minister in the family,' I told him, 'but you're the only male heir to a huge corporate enterprise. You'll never be happy wasting your life trying to figure out how many angels can dance on the end of a pin. You're going to Harvard Business School. I know Dean Whitaker personally, and he assured me that with your marks you'll be accepted. Don't worry, you can still save mankind. You can help provide a couple of hundred thousand of them with jobs. Keep one thing in mind, son. No man loves God very much on an empty stomach.'"

Telling Jill about it now—for what he realized must be the third or fourth time, but it was important that she understand—Ike shook his head grimly. "I couldn't stop him. Matt refused to apply to Harvard Business School. I told you that Matt had met Irene when he was working one summer at the yard. He didn't really want to work, especially at the shipyard. But I warned him and Sarah that if I was going to subsidize Matt's heavenly nonsense, I'd go just so far. He'd have to learn the value of money. I'd pay his tuition and room and board at Divinity School, but he had to earn his own spending money. And since Matt supposedly loved mankind so damned much, he'd better sweat a little with them. When he did, he'd soon be thanking God that he hadn't been born to a poor man." Ike shrugged. "Of course, I didn't expect that he was going to jump into bed with one of them."

He squeezed Jill's hand and winked at her. "The first thing I knew, he was dating Irene Ferruzi. Irene was and still is a very luscious-looking woman. Hendy, my son-in-law, had hired her as an assistant in the planning department. She had just received her bachelor's degree in business administration from Boston University. When Hendy married Becky, he invited Irene to the wedding. That's when Matt met her. Irene is Catholic. First I thought that Matt was going around with a damned pope-lover just to spite me, but it turned out that I can relate to Irene better than any of my family. She may be Catholic but she's saner than those damn UU's. Irene has both feet on the ground. She withdraws from all our father and son battles, but afterwards she's on my side and she tries to make Matt see the light." Ike shook his head and sighed. "At least they were intelligent enough not to try and convert to each other's different religions. Irene goes to mass regularly. Father Timothy of St. Margaret's is one of her best friends. Irene even plays golf with him."

"Did he marry Irene when he was studying for the ministry?" Jill asked.

"Not until he was ordained." Ike shrugged. "Matt's first and only church was in a depressed little town in Maine—Sweetwater. It's filled with a lot of hard-headed, sour-mouth Down Easters. Matt tried to convince them that God never had a son and Jesus Christ was just another prophet no worse or better than Mohammed or Buddha . . . plus a lot of other nonsense like man is really God. He had learned all that nonsense from those Eastern religions that Sarah was always studying. Matt soon found out that his parishioners were really Congregationalists, not UU's, and they didn't want to stray too far from the Good Book. Irene finally convinced him that he wasn't getting anywhere—and they certainly weren't living in the style she might have expected by marrying a Godwin. So at twenty-nine, after wasting six years of his life, Matt finally got the message. He applied to Harvard Business School and was accepted." Ike laughed. "He finally learned to preach where the money is—and it's not in a collection plate on Sunday."

4

Roje's midsummer afternoon madness never made the six o'clock television news nor any of the national news services. Consequently, it did not transform him from a "has been" to an "is now" status. But it did have one interesting result. He was discovered by another UU. He still didn't know who the UU's were nor did he give a damn, but this one was intent on educating him.

It began rather benignly, a few days later, with a phone call. Emily was playing golf, so Roje reluctantly abandoned a rather sexy scene he was writing and answered it.

"Mr. Lovejoy? I hope I'm not interrupting anything important," a female voice said huskily into his ear. She was. But the reality of her come-hither intonation was better than any words Roje had been trying to put on paper. He acknowledged that her time was his and even gave a little prayer that the voice emanated from a body which reflected the same "me Jane—you Tarzan" quality that he was hearing.

"Oh, Mr. Lovejoy," she breathed into the phone, "I love you." Then he heard her sigh. "Alas, my husband, Saul, doesn't love you. He thinks you're probably an old goat. But being Jewish, he doesn't mind if I fall in love with an author. Of course, this time, it's different. It's the first time it ever happened to me."

For a moment Roje wondered if he was the lucky recipient of an obscene phone call from a female. Hope springs eternal in male authors' fantasies. Even if Roje weren't the most popular author in the

United States, over the past years he had occasionally been lucky. When he met a particular woman who had read all his books and told him that she loved him, at least one in ten times she was pretty, too. Fortunately, men never told Lovejoy they loved him. Men aren't so open about loving strangers as women are, but, as Roje well knew, women read most of the novels written, anyway. So the percentage was in favor of women.

"My name is Mary Stein. I've been in love with authors before," Mary bubbled, "but I never met one, and I never realized until yesterday that Robert Lovejoy actually lives in Adamsport. Practically next door to me. I've read all of your books, Mr. Lovejoy. Are you really in your sixties? Somehow, you don't write like a man your age—or someone who lives in Massachusetts. Oh dear, I'm so thrilled. Just think! I could jog over to your house in less than ten minutes."

Lovejoy scowled into the phone. A woman jogger! My God, she was probably musclebound, and a feminist to boot. "But Saul wouldn't want you to," he said a little fearfully into the phone, wondering how he was going to terminate this verbal relationship before Mary Stein arrived on his doorstep in person.

"Mostly Saul is good-natured," she responded, but she sounded a little doubtful. "A long time ago he agreed with me that we don't have to like each other's friends."

"Well, that's nice," Lovejoy told her amicably. He hoped that if Mary was going to thrust her friendship on him that she didn't weigh three hundred pounds. That would be more friendship than he could bear. Then a thought occurred to him that he couldn't restrain. "Mary Stein? Is that really your name?" He was grinning. "Mary is a strange name for a Jewish girl."

"I'm only partially Jewish, Mr. Lovejoy," she giggled. "My mother was a WASP. Her maiden name was Peachy. It became my middle name. I'm sorry I was so formal with you. Actually, from the day I was born everyone, including my mother and father, called me Peachy instead of Mary. Do you have a nickname, Mr. Lovejoy?"

Peachy? Roje was sure that he was in trouble. He had an immediate vision of a big-busted, blue-eyed, corn-fed, scatterbrained highschool cheerleader. If her friends still called Mrs. Stein "Peachy," she probably looked like a turnip.

"My wife calls me Roje," he said gruffly. "My middle name is Jesus." He hoped that might slow Peachy down. And it did. But only for a moment.

She burst into a gale of laughter. "Oh, no, it can't be!" she gasped, finally catching her breath. "The reason I'm telephoning you, Mr. Lovejoy, is that we really need men like you. But please don't tell any of them your middle name. We're not Jesus savers, as you may know."

Now it's coming, Lovejoy thought. Peachy had read the story about him in the *Adamsport Chronicle*. She was probably trying to raise money for some cause or other. "Who is we—and them?" he demanded.

"The UU's, Mr. Lovejoy. Someday I hope I may call you Roje. After reading the write-up about you in our daily blab sheet, despite your middle name, I assume that you aren't strongly affiliated with any local church. Since you've lived in Massachusetts so long, I'm sure that you must have heard of William Ellery Channing or Ralph Waldo Emerson. They were both Unitarians. About twenty-five years ago the Unitarians joined with the Universalists. They all believe that Jesus was a very nice man, but not actually the Son of God. Since you seem to be a very free thinker, I was sure that you must know a little about Unitarian Universalists."

Roje wasn't sure that he did. Listening silently, he knew it was time for caution. This Peachy UU was obviously going to try to convince him to go to church. Listening to ministers, who often sounded as if they ran a funeral home on the side, exhorting their parishioners with chapters and verses from the Bible, whether they believed in Jesus or not, was not his idea of an escapist Sunday morning. "I'm familiar with King's Chapel in Boston," he said coldly. "I've walked through the building several times, but I have never been to any Unitarian services. I prefer to go sailing on Sunday."

"That's no problem. We close down for July and August," Peachy said cheerily. "Since the Adamsport First Parish Meeting House occupies nearly three acres in the center of Adamsport, I presume that you know where it is."

Roje knew the church. No one passing through the center of Adamsport could ignore it. Built entirely of Adamsport granite more than one hundred and sixty years ago, it was an interesting architectural merger of the Greek and Federal styles that had been popular around the middle of the nineteenth century. Four twenty-five-foot Doric columns cut from solid pieces of granite supported the pediment, from which rose a thirty-foot-high gold-domed steeple. Though he had never visited the church, Roje was aware that John Adams and his son John Quincy Adams, the first and third presidents of the United States, and their wives were buried in the crypt.

But if anyone had asked Roje which religious denomination supported the church, he, like most Adamsport residents, would have to admit he had never noticed the sign on the front lawn. Shrugging, he would have replied, "Protestant, I guess."

An architectural survivor from another era, the church fortunately still occupied enough space, with green lawns and trees around it, to maintain some of its bygone dignity. But now it was surrounded by traffic lights, bargain emporiums, fast food chains, pizza and hamburger parlors, and a half-mile-long uninspiring row of small store fronts occupied by hardware, clothing, sport, music and video stores, bakery shops, barber shops, repair shops, women's weight-loss clinics, toy stores, card shops, an office equipment store, cafeterias, countertop restaurants, one rundown movie theater, an imposing granite city hall, and a bank that had once been the tallest building in town (thirteen stories high) with wedding-cake style architecture that was popular when it was built in the 1930s. The bank was now overshadowed by a modern office building, squatting belligerently in the middle of the square and proclaiming its twentieth-century stone and glass efficiency to all beholders. Several barrooms flanked the extremities of the main street, catering to the late afternoon overflow from Godwin Shipyards—men who prolonged the moment until they must inevitably return to their cooped-up wives and battling children.

While this picture of downtown Adamsport, which he rarely visited, was flashing through his mind, Roje was telling Peachy: "To be honest with you, Mrs. Stein, any interest I might have once had in religion has long since disappeared. My mother was a Catholic; my father, who rarely went to church, was a Protestant. When I was a boy they sent me to Christian Science Sunday School. The teacher was very nice and tried to answer all the questions a curious kid could think of, but I thought of so many I asked myself right out the front door. Neither God nor Jesus nor any of their stand-ins on earth really interest me. To tell you the truth, I don't believe in one God. I prefer lots of them. As for church activities and fellowships and all that organized religious crap—it bores me!"

"Then you will like UU's," Peachy laughed. "We're totally disorganized. We need men like you, Mr. Lovejoy, men who aren't afraid of their convictions. Men who dare to challenge the world and stand united with others who dare to question the old ways."

"You mean that UU's will defend me if I go swimming naked in Adamsport Bay? Or if I decide to picket St. Joseph's in my birthday suit?" Roje knew this conversation was getting ridiculous. If it hadn't been for the sensation that Peachy was caressing him with her voice, he would have politely said, "Good-bye."

"I'll defend you," she replied emphatically. "I've been doing my student internship as a future minister with Reverend Paul Littlejohn. I go to all the meetings of the board of governors of the First Parish Church. Of course, I can't speak for all the members of the church. Some of them are old New Englanders and they are really Congregationalists at heart. But I was talking with Matt Godwin yesterday. He's a UU. He thought the story about you in the *Chronicle* was very amusing."

Peachy Stein had told Matt Godwin yesterday that she was going to telephone Lovejoy. "Someone has to wave the flag," she said. "I love you, Matt Godwin, but I'll love you better if you'll get off the sidelines and help save your church. With you and a man like Lovejoy, we could stir things up. We could increase the membership and put the First Parish Church UU's back in the headlines."

Actually, Peachy knew that she had been getting much too involved with Matt. A little extracurricular hugging and kissing really hurt no one; in truth it could add a nice romantic dimension to a rather placid life with Saul. But yesterday when Matt had popped into the church, obviously to see her and not Reverend Littlejohn, and they had begun discussing Lovejoy—like herself, Matt had read most of his novels—Matt had become so intrigued with her happy laughter and the thought of Lovejoy forgetting to put his pants on when he mowed his front lawn that he told Peachy: "Good Lord, you look so pretty, I can't help myself. I need to kiss you from head to toe."

Before she could protest, or admit that she needed to hug him, too, he had scooped her full breasts out of her low-cut dress, and, oblivious to Reverend Littlejohn, who was in his office behind a closed door, there they stood in the deserted Parish Hall with Matt's hands happily exploring her bare behind while he kissed her tits. All the while he was muttering, "Maybe unknown to yourselves, you and Lovejoy are telling me something. The world needs female ministers, and you're a heaven-sent intermediary."

"Telling you what?" Peachy had sighed. She could feel his still contained erection pressing against her mound.

"Telling me to hell with it. I should take up arms against a sea of troubles. Telling me to stop talking and start acting. Dare to! Dare to do what? Ah, there's the rub." By this time Matt was kneeling on the floor murmuring into Peachy's vulva. "Really, it would be simpler to return to the womb."

Fortunately, before Matt could try to return any farther, Reverend Littlejohn had opened his office door. Seeing Peachy, who had heard him coming, desperately trying to reorganize her disheveled clothing, he prudently closed it. Matt had only grinned at her dismay. "Don't let Little Johnny frighten you," he told her. "A minister will never expose another minister's indiscretions lest his own pop out of the closet."

Before Peachy, her heart threatening to jump out of her mouth, finally shooed Matt out of the church, he said, "If you telephone Lovejoy, tell him that I'm glad to hear that he hasn't grown up either. Maybe someday we'll get together at the club for nude bowling or nude croquet."

Peachy grimaced at him. "That would be a lot safer than making love to a future minister in the sanctuary."

For the hundredth time, Peachy wanted to ask Matt why, at this stage in his life, he couldn't make up his mind. Why was he so afraid of his father? Why didn't he tell the old buzzard that he wasn't cut out to be an organization man? The problem was that Matt needed reinforcement. Someone to help him to stop wavering. During their brief affair—which Peachy knew from the beginning she had engineered and probably would proceed to an in-bed consummation—they had never discussed their spouses as sexual companions. But it was apparent that Irene Godwin and Saul Stein were much more constrained by middle-class conventions and sexual beliefs that Matt and she were. Peachy was sure that Irene was still conditioned by her Catholic upbringing. She had been one of the ten Ferruzi children, a poor Italian family who lived in a tenement "three decker" area of Adamsport. According to Matt, Irene was sure that their marriage had been "saved," not only from divorce but from a life of starvation in the ministry, by Matt's father. "Irene should have been Ike's wife," Matt told Peachy with a pixieish grin. "They really think alike . . . I'm the wayward son who is constantly screwing up their well-ordered lives."

Before she telephoned Lovejoy, Peachy wondered if he might be the kind of person whom Matt could relate to, someone who might encourage him to return to the ministry where he really belonged. But now she doubted it. Lovejoy's novels might indicate that there was a radical thinker hidden somewhere between the lines, but she was getting the impression that actually he was an armchair liberal—a talker, not a doer. Nevertheless, she decided to give Lovejoy one more opportunity to show his true colors. She repeated Matt's invitation to join him in nude athletics at the club.

"I'm sorry, Mrs. Stein." Roje knew that he should have terminated this phone conversation some time ago. "But I don't have a martyr mentality. From now on I may never appear naked again except in my own back yard where I'm protected from human eyes oozing horror at the sight of a penis and testicles. Anyway, I'm sure that despite Matt Godwin most of the UU's are probably just as conservative about showing their genitals to God as our neighbors in Happy Shores are."

"Didn't I just tell you, Mr. Lovejoy, that we are practically neighbors? My husband and I live on Cherokee Street. It's only two streets away from your home."

Roje frowned. This really was too close for comfort. If he weren't careful, he might be invaded by a bubbling two-hundred-pound matron intent on converting him to UUism. "You're not facing reality, Mrs. Stein," he said curtly. "The sad truth is that until a few days ago most of the little girls and boys in Happy Shores had never seen a man's balls or cock unless they spied on their daddy through a keyhole in the bathroom door. Now that so many have seen mine, our neighbors are not very happy with me. Do you have any children, Mrs. Stein?"

"Yes. My daughter is twelve. David is eleven."

"Have they seen Saul's balls?"

Roje hoped that Peachy would gasp. Instead she chuckled. "Maybe, but not for casual observation, Mr. Lovejoy. You see, Saul is Jewish. Not orthodox, thank God, but on the conservative side. He does go to shul on all the holidays and Saturdays when he feels the need. Occasionally, he even comes to church with me. Of course, many Jews are Unitarians at heart. But Saul is a little embarrassed about his body. He's not like me—Cheryl and David have seen me naked plenty of times." Peachy was getting a little annoyed at Lovejoy. Her voice was no longer seductive. "Really, Mr. Lovejoy, I didn't telephone you because you mowed your lawn naked, or because I want to see your balls. I just thought you might be the kind of person who would enjoy the fellowship, occasionally, of some thinking, caring people."

Roje suddenly was afraid that Peachy would hang up. Emily was playing golf. When he put the phone down he had one of two choices. He could go back to writing one more book about a world of sweetness and light sometime in the year 2050 or try to make one now. It was a dangerous way to eliminate momentary boredom, and Mrs. Stein—Peachy—no matter how much she weighed, was obviously a church-fair do-gooder. But if he never saw her, he still had an author's prerogative. He could create her in his own most desirable female image. He could imagine that her caressing voice breathed from beneath equally soothing and nubile breasts. Her children weren't in their teens yet. That meant Peachy was probably still in her thirties. Roje knew that any fantasies he might have about her were equivalent to cradle-snatching, but it was an amusing way to pass the moment.

"I think you should understand, Mrs. Stein," he said, "despite the story in the *Chronicle,* I'm not a proselytizing nudist. Nor do I worry about God much, one way or another. I simply think that if God exists he would be very pleased if people would pause for a moment in their bathtubs or when they walk outdoors naked in his sunlight or his moonlight, and they should thank him and tell him how amazed and pleased they are that he gave them such nice and efficient and erotic skin and blood and muscles and bones and bowels and genitals."

"Oh, Mr. Lovejoy, I really do love you," Peachy almost sobbed into the phone. "You sound just like Matt. You and Matt really do have one thing in common. He's not afraid to run around in his skin. Rumors are that when Matt preached his last sermon to a very startled congregation in Maine, many years ago, he threatened to undress as he preached it. He wanted to make a point about the emperor's clothes, I think." Peachy giggled, "Not with his penis, of course."

Roje was afraid that if he kept probing too much he might never get rid of Peachy, but her voice was an aphrodisiac; and he was surprised, though he remembered vaguely that Sylvanus Williams had said something about Matt preaching, that Matt Godwin had been a minister. "Godwin seems to be a rather unlikely person to be managing a shipyard," he said, wondering if Peachy was more involved with Matt than she was admitting. "At least, the Godwins must be an excellent financial resource for the church."

"Matt's mother, Sarah, was a pillar of the church," Peachy sighed. If Roje could have seen her face he would have seen tears flooding her eyes. Peachy was afraid that trying to explain the Godwin family and Matt's father's antipathy to UU's might convince Lovejoy that he was better off not getting involved. But Lovejoy's silence indicated that, although he might not be sympathetic, he was still listening.

"Unfortunately, Sarah Godwin died last April," she continued, "without leaving a will. As you probably know, the shipyards are only a small part of the Godwin empire. Matt's father, Isaac, is very wealthy—he's president of Controlled Power Corporation—but he rarely comes to the First Parish Church. He insists that if Godwin money goes to a church, there should be a cross over the altar, even if Jesus isn't hanging on it. Fortunately, Sarah didn't listen to him."

Peachy knew she sounded lugubrious. "What I'm really trying to tell you, Mr. Lovejoy, is that you'd better be careful. Ike Godwin and a lot of other people in Adamsport don't appreciate people who go skipping around bare-ass. A lot of them would be happy to tar and feather you and run you out of the city on a rail. There's only a very few of us left in the world who really dare to say, or do, what we believe, or defy the Ike Godwins. We really should all stick together.

"I know that it was kind of crazy to telephone you," she continued, wondering why Lovejoy wasn't responding, "but the truth is, despite Sarah Godwin's endowment of $250,000 to the church many years ago, the interest income nets us only about $22,000 annually. Together with Matt's personal contribution of $5,000 a year, it represents nearly one-half of our annual income. The rest of the parish averages only about $200 a year per family, in pledges. And you have to understand that until his father dies, and maybe not even then, Matt Godwin is not a rich man. Matt and his father have always been at sword's point. When Isaac dies, Matt may inherit some money, but most of the Godwin millions will probably end up in the Godwin Foundation."

Roje tried to tell Peachy that he really wasn't interested in the Adamsport First Parish Church's monetary problems. But he was still reluctant to say good-bye, so he listened to her ramble on: "The truth is that our entire church income from all sources is under $75,000 a year. As you must know, the building is very old. It needs repairs that will cost over a half-million dollars. To add to our problems Reverend Littlejohn is a very nice person, but he has already told our board of governors that he has an offer of another job and can't survive on the $28,000 a year that he is now paid. Before we adjourned for the summer, he told the board that he needed at least a 20 percent increase in pay. We can't possibly give it to him and heat the church during January, February, and March—not without increasing our operating budget $25,000 more than our projected income. I know all of this sounds like poor-mouthing to you, Mr. Lovejoy." Peachy's laugh, a low alto trill, made Roje feel like reaching through the phone and hugging her. "It may even sound to you as if I am asking you for a donation, but really I'm not. We're only a small congregation—fifty active families, 135 members. The truth is that we need members more than money."

Despite his romantic feeling toward this stranger, Roje was sure of one thing: come hell or high water he was not going to get involved in the problems of the Adamsport First Parish Meeting House. But a thought did occur to him. "It seems to me that your best solution would be to ask the United States government to help you. The Adams family are buried in the crypt, aren't they? I believe that should qualify the church as a national monument."

"We went down that road many years ago," Peachy said. "During the Carter administration the church was accepted, following an act of Congress, for takeover and administration by the National Park Service. Unfortunately, some politician discovered, belatedly, that this could be in conflict with the Constitution. You know, the separation of Church and State. We were given the option by the National Park Service to be good guys. If we moved out and gave the church to them, they'd be happy to maintain it. But we'd have to find some other place to have our services and continue our fellowship. You may be sure that the UU's would never accept that alternative. The Adamsport Meeting House is a million-dollar building, and it's sitting on a million-dollar piece of real estate. Can you believe that for chutzpah? The United States government wanted it for nothing."

At that price, Roje wanted to suggest to Peachy, the congregation should vote to sell the church, but he suspected that would only lead to further conversation. "I'm sorry you have so many problems, Mrs. Stein. It's been nice talking with you, but I'm really not the church type. I'm sure that whatever God may exist in the cosmos, he doesn't give a damn what happens to the Adamsport Meeting House and particularly whether I go to church there or any other church on Sunday."

"I'm sure that you're right." Peachy couldn't conceal the irritation in her voice. "UU's don't go to church to meet God. They go to church to meet each other. We don't have much money, and we're probably the smallest religious minority in America, but we care about people, Mr. Lovejoy, and we care about what is happening to our world. Right now there aren't many people like that left in Adamsport or in the world. We're an endangered species, Mr. Lovejoy, and so are you! For your own self-protection I think you should come to church—we re-open the Sunday after Labor Day—and get acquainted."

5

Ike couldn't sleep. He looked at his watch. It was five-thirty in the morning, and he knew they would be landing in Boston within an hour. Trying to decide exactly how he should confront Matt without precipitating an explosion, he kissed Jill's cheek. Curled on her side, she murmured sleepily to him that he really should try to relax.

Ike had told Jill that when Matt was studying for his M.B.A. at Harvard Business School, Irene had been so happy with him, because he had given up the ministry, that she had practically studied all of Matt's courses with him. In addition, she not only typed all his papers but she had also fulfilled her role as dutiful wife and devoted mother.

Although Ike's son-in-law, Henderson Inch, had been in line for the job, Ike put Matt in charge of the shipyard. And then to Ike's surprise, up until the past six months Matt had actually buckled down and proved that whether he was in the pulpit or on the other side of a customer's desk, he could be a hypnotic salesman. While they could rarely talk together without being on opposite sides of the fence, Ike had had no complaints about his son's business dealings. Matt had helped close contracts with foreign governments for liquefied natural gas carriers (LNGs) that had kept the shipyard humming for quite a few years.

But now, according to Irene, actually since Sarah had died in April, Matt had been going through one of his regular, moody reappraisals of his life. In one of her weekly telephone calls to Ike, Irene had said, "He's not very easy to live with, Ike; he's always sailing against the wind. Yesterday he told Henderson that the whole capitalistic system is in the process of self-destruction. Matt thinks that people like you and a lot of others who head up the largest corporations aren't creative any more. You're not interested in seeding new industries or creating new jobs. He thinks that the people who run the top companies are all engaged in a power orgy. Instead of putting money into finding new sources of energy or creating new products, they spend all their time merging into huge do-nothing monstrosities. He tells everybody the only people who benefit are do-nothing stockholders."

Irene didn't tell Ike that Matt was determined to find a way to put a spoke in the wheel of power-hungry people like his father who were really barnacles on the ship of capitalism. Matt hadn't been laughing when he said it.

"Matt is still living in the fairy-tale world that Sarah imprinted on his childish mind," Ike told her. "He hasn't learned that it's a grow or die world. Sarah and her damn UU religion is a good example. It should do some creative merging before it disappears." Ike told Irene not to worry. "I'll straighten Matt out," he said. "It's not for publication—

I'll tell Becky and Matt about it when I arrive—but Jill and I are moving to the East Coast. If things work out, I may have an even bigger surprise for you."

"I think Matt's biggest problem is that he's feeling guilty," Irene told him. "He was Sarah's boy, you know, and he thinks that he let her down." Irene really wasn't sure how Matt felt about his father getting married again—only four months after Sarah's death—so she spoke cautiously. "Matt thinks he should have been more involved with the UU's. He knows it would have made Sarah happy if he had preached a sermon there once or twice a year. You know she asked him more than once. Reverend Littlejohn was agreeable, but Matt always put it off. At the very least, Sarah wanted him to become a member of the church board, but Matt refused."

Irene sighed. "I hope you realize that it's not my fault, Ike. I never kept Matt away from his church. I know that he didn't approve of the boys having their First Communion, but I never told him that he couldn't take them to the UU Sunday School if he wanted to." Ike could hear Irene suppress a little sob. "I'm afraid that Matt thinks that he should never have abandoned the ministry and particularly Unitarianism. If he had kept at it, he thinks, he could have given the UU's a totally new perspective on religion. He thinks he could have shown them how they could become a major religious force in America. Now Reverend Littlejohn is going to leave the church for a better paying job, and some of the members are trying to convince Matt that he could fill in two or three Sundays a month—free, of course—and thus improve the church's budget."

"Don't let him get involved with that damned church," Ike had snorted over the phone. He didn't want to tell Irene yet, or Matt, but he suspected that Matt wasn't going to be happy when he discovered that Controlled Power Corporation was going to offer to buy the First Parish Church and tear it down. As a businessman Matt should understand that the UU's would be a lot better off accepting hard cash than hanging on to a dilapidated building that they couldn't possibly afford to repair or modernize.

"Just remind your husband," Ike told Irene, "that the UU's may be damned near pagans, but they aren't as far out as he is. Twelve years ago, when he was preaching his return-sex-to-religion crap up in Sweetwater, Maine, before I rescued both of you, his congregation was nearly ready to make a new Jesus Christ out of him. If he hadn't resigned, they'd have nailed him to the cross that they still have over their altar. I'm sure that when push comes to shove the UU's in Adamsport are no more considerate of the other guy's philosophy than the Jews or Romans were."

Jack Handley's voice on the plane's intercom interrupted Ike's thoughts. "We'll be flying over the shipyard in about twenty minutes,

Mr. Godwin," he said. "I'll drop down so Mrs. Godwin can take a look."

Jill pushed Ike out of the bunk. "My God, we're nearly there," she said. "Get out of my way, lover, unless you want me to arrive bare-ass."

As she disappeared into the toilet, they both could feel their eardrums tightening as the plane slowly lost altitude. When she reappeared, radiant and smiling, Ike told her to look out the window. A few thousand feet beneath them she could see a one-hundred-and-fifty-ton cargo sphere suspended momentarily by a Goliath crane. Below the crane was a huge steel dragon superstructure supporting two ships under construction. "My God," she gasped. "What's inside those big plastic bubbles?"

"They're not plastic," Ike laughed, "They're steel containers to hold liquefied natural gas. That's one of them on the crane, being lowered onto the deck." He was grinning proudly at her. Watching any of the Controlled Power properties from the air made him feel like a creator himself. "In a few months those babies will be on their way to Africa—Algiers probably—to bring home natural gas. They pump it into the ships through underwater pipe lines while they stand offshore. The gas is immediately frozen to condense it for transport." Ike squeezed her arm affectionately. "Wasn't that a sight? But the yard's got problems. When those ships are finished we are going to be down to a couple of small navy contracts. The simple way would be to close the place, but the navy has some big plans for deployment ships, and, despite their vulnerability, I'm betting that with our new increased defense budget there'll be more nuclear warships built." He bussed her cheek. "My great-great-grandfather, Isaac Matthew Godwin, after whom Matt is named, must be smiling down from heaven. In 1847 he launched the last clipper ship built in America from the old yards. We use that area for storage now."

"My God!" Gillian exclaimed. "Does your family go back to the *Mayflower?*" She was feeling a little like an Ellis Islander. The Marlowe roots were still on the surface; her father and mother had arrived in America from Sweden only a few years before she was born.

Isaac laughed. "The Adams family beat us by about one hundred years. The Godwins didn't get here until 1842. Isaac Matthew was an apprentice shipbuilder in Glasgow. His daddy, Thaddeus, my great-grandfather, built the first naval destroyer in the yards in the late 1890s. It was sunk in the Spanish-American War. I told you about my grandfather in World War I. My father, Zachary Matthew, was a whip-lashing old-time patriarch, if there ever was one. In the 1940s, with a work force of over 40,000 people, Zach built more than 350 warships of every kind, from LSTs—Landing Ship Tanks—to aircraft carriers. He died, a year after my mother, in 1949. I married Sarah during World War II. I was an ensign on a Godwin-built aircraft carrier."

"Tell me about your brother," Jill said. "Does he live in Adamsport?"

"My brother, Matthew, is a playboy," Ike scowled. "Presumably he's in charge of our European operations, but he spends most of his time arranging and attending parties with assorted jet-setters. He's been married a few times but has no children." He shrugged. "In the long run it doesn't matter. I am sure of one thing: even if I don't live to see it, and even if I have to boot my son out on his ass, it's not the end of the Godwin line. Irene won't let Ink or Able become ministers or priests. You can bet on that! Henry Ford outlived his only son, Edsel, and finally his grandson, Henry, took over." Ike laughed harshly. "You never can tell. I'm a tough old cookie. I might outlive Matt."

"Ink and Able?" Gillian asked, thinking that she really should have questioned Ike more about his family before she married him. "Are they really your grandsons' names?"

Isaac grimaced. "It was Matt's crazy idea. I should have known it was a straw in the wind. Matt has always defied conventions, and Irene had no choice. She had to go along with him. Never mind, we retained the family names as middle names, so now we have Increase Matthew Godwin and Amicable Isaac Godwin. If you and I end up living in Adamsport, I'll make sure they learn to fly right."

"Will Matt be waiting for us at the airport?"

"I doubt it, Jill. Matt is a very obstinate man, though if he wants to be, he can be quite a charmer. You've got to help me convince him that taking over as president of Controlled Power is a step in a direction that he really has to go. I keep telling him that if he'll work with me, before he's fifty—and after a few years at the helm of CPC—I'll back him for political office. I'll help him get elected senator from Massachusetts. Getting rid of a Kennedy is a better way of saving mankind than praying for them every Sunday." Isaac brushed Gillian's cheek with his hand. "Maybe you can find out what makes Matt tick. Just don't fall in love with him."

Gillian smiled. "Seems to me that Matt is still fighting the classic oedipal rebellion against his old man. Maybe one day he'll discover that both of you, in your own ways, are trying to save mankind."

Ike chuckled. "The problem is, I believe in the Ronald Reagan trickle-down-the-wealth economic method. But Matt hasn't learned that the workers would be a hell of a lot better off if they'd only get off the backs of those who are willing to bust their asses to save them— not by deeds, but by giving them work to do that puts money in their pockets." He grinned at her. "Tell me, Jill, would you have married me if I had been some half-ass preacher?"

"Not likely, Big Daddy. I probably would have never met you. I've never been the churchgoing type. Getting married in a church by a minister last Saturday was your idea."

The plane was now skimming the surface of the runway. The wheels kissed gently without vibration. "Welcome to Boston and Adamsport, home of the *God*-wins," Ike said. "As is his custom, I'm sure that Henderson Inch, and not my son, will be waiting to greet us and drive us to Adamsport in one of the shipyard limousines."

6

When Jack Handley buzzed the shipyard, Matt Godwin was standing near a picture window that flanked one wall of his mahogany-paneled office. Five floors below him, hundreds of men were organizing tons of steel, pipes, valves, and wiring, inching them toward completion and transforming them into monster hulls with superstructures that looked as if they were conceived on another planet. One day they would miraculously float and be driven across the oceans by huge, throbbing engines.

Although the shipyard activity often turned Matt into a philosopher—wondering about men's drives and goals and their need to control their environments—this morning he wasn't feeling quite so profound. He recognized the Controlled Power jet when it flew over, and he knew that within the next hour his father would be sitting behind Grandpa Zach's huge mahogany desk and he'd be on the other side listening to Ike and staring at the carved, open-mouthed, snarling lions' heads that glared at visitors from either corner of the desk. And Matt knew that he would be trying not to get angry with Ike, who, as a matter of policy, never poured oil on troubled waters. He was sure that right now, a few minutes after leaving Logan, Ike, Gillian, and Hendy, all three of them sitting democratically in the front seat of the Cadillac limousine, would be discussing the problem: "How do we get Matt to straighten up and fly right?"

Yesterday Sally had telephoned him from Big Sur and asked if he had hired a brass band to meet Daddy Ike and his Jill at the airport. Except for wondering why an attractive woman like Jill would marry their cantankerous father, Sally assured him that he would like her, and perhaps she might even soften up the old buzzard. "Especially so since I hear he's coming home to roost," Sally said, and she was surprised that Matt had not heard the news. "Controlled Power is moving its headquarters back East," she told him. It hadn't been decided yet, but she had heard that Daddy Ike wanted to build in Adamsport. "I don't envy you living that close to Daddy Ike," she said, "but congratulations, anyway. I hear that you have been elected president of CPC."

Matt was listening to her in disbelief and semi-shock.

"Who in hell told you all this crap?" he demanded.

"Gus Belshin. He used to be top dog at Infinity Corporation before CPC took them over. Now Infinity has two seats on the board of directors of CPC and Gus is a thorn in Daddy's flesh." Sally's voice sounded very chipper and almost giggly. "Keep in mind that I'm not married; I don't have to be faithful like you do. When Gus wants to get away from the business world harassment and his wife, he calls me up and spends a weekend up here in God's country. Didn't Daddy Ike tell you about your promotion?"

"I told him flatly that I didn't want the presidency," Matt said angrily. "Especially with him standing over me as chairman."

"I'll bet your wife knows. You better watch out or Daddy will make Irene president. All he really wants is someone with the Godwin name running things." Sally laughed, "You and he should switch wives. Irene is much more his style than Gillian."

Sally told Matt that she missed him, and before she said "goodbye" she sounded very nostalgic. "You're my one and only favorite brother," she told him softly. "Yours is the first jamoke that I ever saw and held in my hand. I love you, Matt-so. Why don't you remind Daddy Ike that your initials are I. M. and that *you* are God—not him!"

Matt didn't tell Irene about Sally's phone call until the morning of Ike's arrival. He knew that she often talked with Ike, and he guessed that, if Sally had told him the truth, Irene had decided to stay out of the fray. Her policy always had been that if the top was going to blow off in the Godwin family, she wasn't lighting the fuse between father and son.

Matt wasn't really angry with Ike. The world was composed of the jugglers and those who were juggled. But this time he was going to toss all the balls into the air at once. If Ike wanted him involved with CPC, it was going to be on his own terms. Something new was going to happen in Adamsport. Instead of sitting in the pews on Sunday morning, Matthew Godwin, Doctor of Divinity and a Master in Business, was going to preach from the pulpit. Matt couldn't help grinning at the thought. In America, business was a religion for millions of people. Why couldn't a new, celebrating, joyous religion become the core busy-ness of life?

Years ago when he had allowed himself to be juggled—give up the ministry and apply to Harvard Business School—he had been more or less a passive patsy for Ike and Irene. But even after fighting a totally turned-off father for four years and marrying Irene—who went along with his crazy ideas but never really believed in them—Matt knew that his strength and weakness, both in business and in religion, was his belief in human perfectibility.

As a minister in Maine, he had expected to find a small group of believers enthusiastically cheering the spiritual insights of their new leader. But his congregation consisted of sixty-eight UU's, most of whom had lived fifty years or longer. Another dozen or so younger ones had been attending off and on for years so that their kids could get some religious training, but most of them were still too suspicious to "sign the book" and thereby automatically become UU's and members of the Sweetwater Church. His ministerial compensation, which was only slightly above the national poverty level, included residence in a crumbling parish farmhouse with ten acres of forest, enough of which was cleared so that he and Irene could plant a necessary-for-subsistence vegetable garden. Their first son, Increase, had been born in Sweetwater, and, as they say in old New England, their second, Amicable, was in the oven.

After two lonely Maine winters, during which Irene and Ink were often "summering," as they called it, with Sarah and Ike three hundred miles south in Adamsport (sometimes for two weeks at a time), Matt slowly discovered that most of his parishioners were not charmed by his weekly blend of heavenly and far-out sexual wisdom. Reluctantly he threw in the towel and applied to Harvard Business School. Being accepted had been equivalent to Alladin rubbing the magic lantern. Ike even made sure they had Oriental rugs in their off-campus apartment in Cambridge. But even then Matt warned Irene: "Just because I may eventually become one of the chosen with an M.B.A., you have to face reality. I probably never will be God's gift to General Motors or the Godwin Shipyards, either." Matt would have included Controlled Power, too, but at the time Ike hadn't named the new baby he was carefully creating.

Turning the pages of the morning *Globe* while Irene sipped her coffee, Matt coldly reported Sally's phone call and demanded to know why she hadn't told him a week ago about the CPC directors' meeting in Los Angeles. Irene was fidgety, but she denied knowing anything about it. "Ike doesn't tell me everything," she said. "But he did tell me he was going to have some nice surprises for the whole family." Irene tried to counteract his dour expression with a bright smile. "Your promotion must be one of them. You should be jumping for joy. You've been telling me for months that you were bored with the shipyard."

"That doesn't mean that I'm getting ready to jump from the frying pan into the fire." Matt scowled at his cereal. "And it doesn't mean that I'm going to spend the rest of my life in Adamsport trying to please Ike. It could mean that he and I have come to the parting of the ways—for the second time in my life."

"Maybe you can convince him to relocate the company nearer

New York City," Irene said. "Anyway, I'm sure that Ike won't be in your hair. He and Gillian will be traveling. You should be happy to have him home. After all, he isn't going to live forever."

"Yes, he is," Matt said, grinning sourly. "He's planning to outlive me and marry you, too. Then he'll have two adoring wives."

Irene scowled at him. "That's stupid talk. I don't really understand either of you. During the past year you have talked with your father at least once a week, but you still play cat and mouse with each other."

Matt shrugged. "Ike and I never discuss our private lives. He didn't even tell me that he was playing Jack to some Jill for the past six months. Last time we talked, I told him he should be very happy; profits are about the same at the shipyard this year, and sales are 15 percent ahead of last year. His response was that he was counting on a 25 percent increase and the yard needed that much to give CPC stock a goose upwards." Matt shook his head gloomily. "The truth is that Ike is planning to offer CPC stockholders a stock split. Having more stock, he can continue to move CPC onward and upward to his heaven where all the streets are paved with gold."

He glared at Irene and knew that she was trying to avoid his eyes. She often told him that sometimes he was much too intense. He had a way of staring at a person that made them think he was seeing their brains in action and hearing all the things they left unsaid. Finally, he said, "The trouble with our marriage, Irene, is that we never really communicate with each other." Not even when we're screwing, he thought, but he didn't say it. For a moment he wondered how she would respond if he just suddenly grabbed Irene, yanked open her robe, and started to make passionate love to her. But after fifteen years he knew without trying. Instead of happily surrendering as he explored her lush breasts, she'd pull away and ask him if he had gone crazy. In her world sane people didn't make love at the breakfast table. In bed, on her back, she never refused him. But she was embarrassed by spontaneous sex. She was distressed if he put his hand on her ass in public, and although she dressed to display her good physical shape, she never used her body to tease him or any man. Irene believed that men were compelled to initiate love-making and women shouldn't.

"You'd better understand how I really feel," he said. "I'm not a bit happy with Ike's end run. I'm perfectly capable of running CPC and following in Ike's footsteps, but I'm not going to! What have you been telling him about me?"

Looking at him over the rim of her coffee cup, Irene didn't answer for a moment. "I told him that I love you but I still don't know what makes you tick. Practically any top executive in America who's in his forties would sell his soul for the job." As soon as she said the words, Irene knew she shouldn't have.

"That's it exactly!" Matt said coldly.

"I'm sorry. I didn't mean it that way. I was simply honest with Ike. He had never heard of him, but I told him that you had visions of being the successor to Bhagwan Rajneesh."

Matt laughed. "Ike probably would love Rajneesh. He keeps at least twenty Rolls Royces at his headquarters out in Antelope, Oregon, and I heard that he now controls the whole town. He's something new in the world—a religious capitalist. His business director is a woman, Ma Ananda Sheela. Sheela tells his followers all over the world just like it is: 'Religion can only be for rich persons. When you're hungry you can't think of the divine. When your stomach is full and you don't know what else to do, you think about art and God.'"

Irene couldn't tell whether Matt was serious or was teasing her.

"Bhagwan has the answer for the poor," Matt continued. "'Get off your ass and start working! Life offers everyone what is available. It's up to you to take advantage.' That's Ike's old philosophy. He should send Rajneesh a good donation. They speak the same language."

"He really sounds ridiculous," Irene said.

"Not really. He's emulating the pope. Only Protestants believe that their ministers should be ascetic. Harvard Business School should give the Bhagwan an honorary degree. And just for the record, I'm not in love with him, but in many ways he's a very wise philosopher. He's written millions of words showing that all religions—Zen, Tao, Tantra, Vedanta, Yoga, Sufism, Hasidism, Buddha, Mohammed, Confucius, you name them—are all searching for ways for men and women to live beyond their human illusions." Matt grinned at her. "Rajneesh even extols screwing. According to him, when you've finally had an orgasm that lasts three hours, you achieve Samadhi and never need to fuck again. Thus far it hasn't happened to me."

"Not when you're making love to me, at least," Irene replied sarcastically. She knew that Matt had been talking on the phone with Reverend Littlejohn. Matt often went to lunch in downtown Adamsport. No doubt he had stopped at the First Parish Church and seen Peachy Stein. To smoke him out she tried a carom shot. "I suppose you know that Sylvanus Williams is planning a 'Let's Celebrate Robert Lovejoy Cocktail Party' at the club. You can invite Ike and Gillian and Becky and Henderson. We can all have a family reunion." Irene sounded grim. "Afterwards, I'm sure Lovejoy would love to join us for a little nude bowling. Peachy Stein will probably be there. I'm sure you must know that Silly Willy is her father."

Matt shrugged. "Peachy and her father don't get along. As for Lovejoy, I scarcely know him. I've read a couple of his novels, and we seem to be on the same wavelength, but Silly Willy's celebration isn't my idea. It's his bash and he's paying for it."

"But you encouraged him with all that nonsense about nude bowling."

"Why not? In ancient Greece, in Sparta, all the athletic contests were held with naked contestants. It's really quite a sane idea. It would add a more interesting dimension to bowling or golf or even tennis," Matt chuckled. "You're really very tense this morning, Irene. What are you worrying about? You know it isn't going to happen. The members of the Adamsport Country Club are very conservative citizens."

"But you shouldn't give Sylvanus Williams credibility," Irene said. "You know damned well that he owns that degrading strip joint on the Cape Artery. I really don't think you should associate with him."

Trying to get Irene off the subject of Sylvanus Williams and his daughter, Matt replied, "You still haven't told me what you and Ike really talked about."

"You know that I call Ike once a week. And I never call him to talk about you. This time I called to congratulate him and Jill on their marriage. You should have called him, too. They sound very happy. Jill has a very friendly voice."

Matt didn't answer. He was reading the business section of the *Globe*.

Irene wondered if she should tell him that she had told Ike that, on top of everything else, she was sure that their marriage was in trouble, too. Although Matt hadn't said anything or given her any indication that he didn't still enjoy her as a bed companion, she was positive that the sudden rebirth of his religious insanities could be traced to Peachy Stein.

The few times that she had gone to services at the First Parish Church with Matt, when Sarah was alive, that damned Stein woman had always been mooning around Matt. Matt thought it was great that Peachy had been studying for the ministry and that she might even take over for Paul Littlejohn after she completed her student internship and was ordained.

Irene was well aware that Peachy had cornered Matt at Sarah's funeral and tried to convince him that even though he had given up the ministry, he should actively support his mother's church. Monetary pledges were one thing, she told Matt while Irene was listening, and the Godwins had been very generous—but the UU's needed men with ideas, men who weren't afraid to tell it like it was. Irene was sure that Peachy was speaking for herself more than for the members of the church. Irene was also aware that Peachy had told Matt that she was in a kind of "open marriage." Exactly what she meant and whether her husband, Saul, approved or not, Matt didn't seem to know, and he seemed very reluctant to discuss Peachy with Irene. But Peachy had told several members that as far as religion went, she and her children were on their own. Saul didn't mind if she became a minister; he was sure that she could never become a rabbi. After spending Saturday morning at Temple Hillel, Saul didn't feel the need for more religion, even if UU's were closer to Jewish than to Christian thinking.

During the early years of their marriage, and particularly a few weeks after he had been ordained, Irene had been shocked to discover that Matt had some very strange ideas about monogamy and his religious thinking was even farther removed from her Catholic beliefs than she had imagined. She knew before she married him that UU's weren't exactly Christians, but as she told Matt, "I'm sure that they aren't old-time Mormons either."

Then he told a parishioner and her husband, who had come to him for advice about their marital problems, that they probably would be much happier over a long marriage, if they dared to risk themselves and their privacies and enjoy an occasional intimate adventure with friends of the other sex. More than a little shocked, Irene questioned whether that applied to their own marriage, and his grinning "Why not?" did nothing to assuage her doubts.

Word got around the congregation about Matt's "open marriage" advice, and the older members began to label him a damned California UU who pretty soon would be inviting gays and blacks to join their church. One woman—Irene remembered her name, Clara Witty, and she was sure that Matt had ultimately capitulated to her—invited Matt to her farmhouse when her husband was away in Portland. Matt told Irene that Clara, who was in her forties, had greeted him wearing only a bathrobe. "My husband, George, is a once-a-month man," she told him, letting her bathrobe fall open to display her lush body.

"The poor woman needed some loving," Matt told Irene later and admitted that he had been tempted. He tried to explain to her that he could have actually made caring love to another woman and it was a rare man who could forsake all others. Fortunately, a few months later Matt was safely enrolled at Harvard Business School. Rather than contest his ideas, Irene had learned to smile and take the path of least resistance. Like a benign mother, she refused to challenge him, particularly on such insane ideas as sex worship and extramarital adventuring.

The truth was that she might even have agreed with Matt that after several years of marriage, going to bed with a strange man might be an interesting experience. But he didn't understand that for her it could only be a fantasy. She didn't need any such adventures to improve her marriage. She reminded him that in her religion, marriage was a sacrament, and for better or for worse she and he were in it till death do us part. Anyhow, the whole idea of secondary relationships was silly. She scarcely had time enough for Matt and their two boys, let alone another man. Although Irene enjoyed sex with Matt, she admitted that she was not like many of the women she knew: she was never, to use a silly male expression, "horny." If Matt didn't take the initiative, she never felt deprived. She could go for months at a time without sex and not feel neglected. But women like Mary Stein—Peachy, what a god-awful name—who were overtly sexy toward men made Irene feel very uncomfortable to the point of anger. Women like Peachy were dangerous. Irene was sure that if Matt had told Peachy some of his crazy theories, she was obviously the kind of woman who would be only too willing to experiment with him . . . even if she were married. Which she was. Had Matt been to bed with Peachy? It wasn't the kind of question that Irene would ask him, but if she had asked and he answered yes, could she tolerate it?

Matt finally returned to reality from his newspaper reverie. "If I don't get to the office soon, Ike will beat me there," he said. "I still can't believe it. My father with a child bride! I'll give him credit for one thing, the old goat can still get it up. But I can't see why any woman would want to go to bed with him. If I were a woman, I wouldn't—not for all his millions!"

"Jill's no child," Irene said. "She's your age. Two years older than me. She's probably one of those women who always had a father complex. You have to give Ike credit. He has just what you need—a new, young, adoring wife."

"You're young enough," he smiled. "But thanks just the same. What I really need is a loving friend, and she doesn't have to adore me."

Matt knew the second he uttered the words, he shouldn't have. The truth was that from the first day when he lusted for Irene's twenty-one-year-old body (and only after months of pursuit had he managed to get his hands on her full breasts and pear-shaped behind and explore the soft hairy black triangle growing just below the warm flesh of her stomach), Irene and he had never really been friends. When his beautiful Italian Catholic girl friend, with the classic madonna-shaped face of a Renaissance artist's model, had finally surrendered her virginity, her tears were for God, not for Matt Godwin. Although the sin had been quickly rectified by marriage, Irene had never really surrendered or responded to him with a passionate enthusiasm equal to his own. Matt blamed her Catholic conditioning and told her that if she wanted to hang Jesus on the cross over their bed so that Jesus could watch them screwing, she could. That had made her very angry. "You might be a much better lover," she told him, "if you loved God more than me."

Now Irene was looking at him bitterly. "It seems to me that you've found the loving friend," she said. "Just be sure and keep her informed. Your loving wife isn't about to share her husband. I don't believe in your multiple-loving philosophy."

"If you're referring to Peachy Stein . . ." Matt grinned at her and for a moment he looked just like Ink or Able when she caught them doing something they shouldn't have been doing (like yesterday when they tried to fly a kite from the captain's walk on the Big House, hoping it would divert low-flying aircraft going into Logan and make them take some other direction). But right now she didn't like what she was hearing.

"You should get better acquainted with Peachy," Matt told her. "She's only a couple of years younger than you are, and she also has two kids and a loving husband."

"That doesn't mean she's a loving wife," Irene said, staring coolly at him. "Every time I've seen her talking to you in church, she looks as if she's going to jump in your arms and moan at you: 'Oh Matt, Matt, when are you going to fuck me?'" Irene's voice was suddenly tearfully shrill.

Scowling at her, Matt looked toward the stairs that curved into the dining room. "Where's Ink and Able?"

"They never get out of bed until you're gone." Irene tried to regain her composure. "Don't worry. They're not listening. And if they were, they would have heard you say 'fuck' a few minutes ago." She stared at him angrily. "If you don't like the word, change it to 'copulate'. Have you obliged Peachy yet?"

"Haven't we made love twice this week? Wasn't it nice?"

For a moment Irene looked bewildered. "What kind of answer is that?"

"That you're not being deprived," Matt grinned, trying to divert her. "The truth is that Peachy is more interested in Unitarianism than she is in me. I just hope that you haven't told Ike that I have agreed to serve on the church board or that I am going to preach the first Sunday after Labor Day. I might even fill in once a month until the selection committee finds someone to replace Littlejohn."

"You know that they aren't going to find anyone to replace Littlejohn," Irene said. "The reason he's leaving is that the church can't afford him. You told me so yourself. Obviously your loving friend Peachy has convinced you that you can be the savior of the First Parish Church."

"I suppose you told Ike that."

"Are you crazy? That's your problem. But keep one thing in mind. Hendy says that more than 80 percent of the employees of the shipyard are Catholic, and the rest are Protestants who still believe that Jesus died to save them—as I do most of the time until you get me confused. I'm sure Ike won't be happy that the top manager of the largest employer in the area is preaching in a church that not only denies the divinity of Jesus but is filled with feminists fighting for equal rights, including abortion rights, and doesn't believe in censoring pornography, gives its blessings to homosexuals—who actually run some of the UU churches—and worse, preaches the kind of things I've heard you preach. Ike believes that a sound businessman should keep a low profile and not publicize his religious preferences." Irene sighed. "Keep in mind, I never repeat this kind of conversation to your father. I did tell him I thought you were probably feeling a little guilty because you hadn't been more active in the church while Sarah was alive."

7

As usual in his discussions with Irene there had been a superficial honesty but no real attempt to be the other person or try to understand his motivations. Matt used the pronoun *his* rather than *hers* because he was sure that he often attempted to see himself through another person's eyes and brains. He knew that he was a continuing enigma to Irene. Basically, her Catholic childhood conditioning made her put up roadblocks against, or completely reject, the freewheeling situation-morality of Unitarian Universalism, which she felt put more emphasis on fellowship than God. The best two years of their marriage had been at Harvard Business School. For the first time, as Matt tried to reorient himself in an entirely different world, they had something in common. With an undergraduate degree in business administration, Irene could often guide him in the continuous case studies of business situations, and, he discovered, she could make hard-nosed decisions on business problems and come up with solutions and profit-making approaches that reflected the kind of answers his professors were seeking. She particularly enjoyed courses in business policy and management that gave students the illusion that they were actually running a particular company.

But even though Matt continued to read beyond the confines of business literature and argued with Irene that much corporate problem solving and management was moronic and one-dimensional, she never seemed to realize that the entire Harvard Business School experience was fueling his rebellion. He disagreed so fundamentally with what he called the insane motivations of competitive capitalism that it kept him studying continuously. He was determined to understand every nuance of business economics and morality. When he challenged Irene or his classmates in "bull sessions," Irene couldn't tell whether he was playing the devil's advocate or really believed what seemed to her to be far-out "leftist" thinking.

After Matt graduated and began working at the shipyards, they slowly lost intellectual touch with each other. Bringing up the kids, united in the conviction that Ink and Able should excel in whatever they might do in life, had catalyzed their joint lives. But they both knew that their divergent ideas on the meanings and purposes of life would ultimately confuse Ink and Able. Eventually, the boys would become aware that their parents were often at sword's point, and they'd have to choose sides. Like Sarah and Ike, he and Irene had boarded the same train but didn't realize they were headed for different destinations until it was too late.

Or was it too late? Amusingly—and amazingly—since Sarah's funeral in April, when he had met Peachy Stein and talked with her at some length, for the first time he had been completely honest and able to communicate what Abraham Maslow might have called his basic "higher needs." With Peachy he revealed a more intimate, truly laughing-man aspect of himself than he had ever dared to with Irene. He was sure that Peachy realized that the playful word game between them, their challenging mental interplay, must finally express itself in the ineffable joining of their bodies. A sexual conclusion? No, *conclusion* was the wrong word. Although it had never happened to him before, Matt felt confident that he could blithely slalom through the continuing interpersonal consequences of a sex life with more than one woman. But could Peachy? . . . or could Irene, if she suspected? And Irene obviously already did suspect.

Unable to concentrate on the in-progress construction reports on the LNG carriers that Hendy had left on his desk, Matt flicked his intercom and asked Mrs. Toomey, his efficient, if somewhat owlish, secretary, if he had any messages—particularly from his father, who should be here by now. Before she could answer, Isaac, followed by Henderson Inch, opened his office door and walked in exclaiming heartily, "Good to see you, boy. You're looking fit as a fiddle."

Matt stood up and tried to embrace him. After all, though they had never seen eye to eye on practically anything, Ike was his father. But the old man pulled back suspiciously and thrust out his hand. Scotchmen of his generation never hugged another man no matter who he might be.

Glancing around the office, before he sat down in the chair behind the Godwin ancestral desk that Matt ordinarily occupied, Ike beamed at him. "Glad to see that you haven't changed the place. Mahogany paneling and Oriental rugs give an office character. Makes customers and prospects aware of roots and stability. It's good to be back in New England—not like California, which is covered from one end to the other with tile and plastic and broadloom."

"Sorry that we haven't made contact since your wedding," Matt said, surveying his father coolly. "Congratulations. I heard rumors that you had a girl friend, but Irene didn't tell me that you were so smitten. I understand that our new mother is quite charming."

Ike scowled at him. "Technically, I suppose, Jill is your stepmother, but I don't picture her in that role. I'm hoping that you and Becky will go all out and make her feel like a sister. We all know that no one will ever replace Sarah in this family."

Ike stared grimly at Matt. "I don't know about your generation, son, but I can assure you there was no other woman in my life when your mother was alive." Getting no reaction from Matt, he changed the subject. "We dropped Jill off at the house. Irene and Becky are taking her to the club for lunch." Ike looked at his watch and shook his head, "I can't believe that it is only 11 A.M. Last night after we took off from Los Angeles, Jill and I stretched out on our bunks. When we awoke at five the sun was rising and we were practically home. I have a meeting with your new mayor, George Gallagher, this afternoon at City Hall, but first I want to have a good talk with you." Ike shook his head at Henderson, who murmured that he and Matt might want to talk privately. "You're part of this family, Hendy. There's nothing I have to say to Matt that you shouldn't hear. I want you to know everything that's happening."

"I presume that you already do," Matt said coolly to Henderson, who responded silently with a quizzical look and a shrug of his shoulders.

"What do you mean?" Ike demanded.

"I'm sure that Hendy is well aware that, responding to your desires, the board of directors of CPC has elected me president. I also assume that Hendy knows that he's going to take over the management of the shipyard beginning January first."

Ike smiled approvingly. "You do keep your ear to the ground, don't you? I suppose Irene told you."

"No. She insisted that she didn't know."

Ike frowned. "I damned well would like to know who did tell you. The board understood that there were to be no leaks—no advance publicity. We're not announcing any executive changes to the business press till everything is in place."

"You mean that you are prepared for me to resign as president before I actually take office?"

"Resign? What the hell are you talking about?" Ike demanded.

Matt shrugged. "I haven't said that I am going to. I said that I might. Keep in mind that I didn't seek the job. From now until January is a lame duck session; you are still in charge." Matt couldn't conceal a furtive smile. "Uneasy ducks often fly the coop before they become sitting ducks."

Ike leaned back in his chair and stared at him with ill-concealed anger. "Let's cut out the crap with each other, son. You can't afford to fly the coop. The presidency of CPC, with bonuses, pays close to a half-million a year. Three times what you are now earning. You could be a rich man in a few years."

"As Sarah used to ask, how rich must you be?" Matt could see that his father's face was flushed, and they were well on their way to one of their usual showdowns. He couldn't stop himself; he threw a match on the oily waters. "Anyways, your estate must be close to three hundred million. I'm sure that if you die before us, Becky, Sally, and I could enjoy life on our split, even after taxes."

"You'd better be very, very careful how you talk to me." Ike's voice was almost a soft growl. "I'm not too happy with you or Sally. I didn't create the Godwin fortunes single-handedly. I built on very solid foundations that my father and his father before him erected. I'm not interested in money per se. Money is a tool for builders, not wasters like your Uncle Matthew. But I am interested in Godwin family continuity. If you're not, and if you're planning to go back to shirtsleeves in the typical three generations (and as far as I'm concerned, a minister's robe is just a covering for poverty), then I can promise you—and my will is already written to that effect—the only Godwin money that you'll ever spend will be doled out to you by your wife or children." Ike stared at him coldly. "I hope that you get the message."

"Clearly," Matt said calmly. "But I'm not compromising my beliefs for a fast buck. I told you last year when you and Hendy unleashed your new marketing and development plans to help the navy with their Sealift program, I am totally against building ships to deploy American troops in foreign countries to fight wars on foreign soil. Not only that; I'm totally shocked that Controlled Power has become so dependent on the Pentagon and military contracts. I can't convince myself that Controlled Power, or Boeing, or Lockheed, or any of a hundred companies who depend on military contracts for survival have the welfare of the American people at heart. Their bread is buttered with the blood and gore of war, and they thrive on it."

"I don't give a shit what you personally believe," Ike exploded. "But you damned well better keep your mouth shut. Army and navy contracts represent more than a third of our gross sales. My family motto is: God can only win over the Devil by continuously fighting back. Are you trying to tell me that you don't give a damn if the Soviets take over the world?"

"I believe that the military one-upmanship between the United States and Russia must stop and that our leaders should take the initiative, not by trying to effect a bilateral freeze on nuclear weapons, but by withdrawing our military forces from around the world." Matt stared back directly into his father's eyes. "That, incidentally, will be one subject of a sermon that I'm going to preach a week from Sunday at the First Parish Church."

"No employee of Controlled Power is going to preach such insanity." Ike's voice was steely. "If you shoot your mouth off with such nonsense, you're finished here, and with me. And you'd better wake up to reality. Your life in Adamsport will be totally untenable. The shipyards support more than 25 percent of the people in this city. Some of them may be on committees to stop production of nuclear weapons or nuclear power plants, but if push comes to shove and we have to announce that the shipyards will close because we have no contracts, they'll be writing their congressmen telling them to build nuclear bombs right here in Adamsport, if that will keep them employed."

Ike stood up. "Right now, son, I suggest you do some deep thinking. You've got a family to support. If you think your UU's will be on your side, you'd better give it some second thoughts. I'm sure that quite a few Unitarian families who still live in this city earn money directly or indirectly from the yard. As for the First Parish Church, forget it. If things work out, before snow flies we may be tearing it down."

Matt couldn't conceal his astonishment. "What the hell do you mean?"

"One of your members, Sylvanus Williams, told a friend of his on the city council that if the price were right, he believed the members of the First Parish Church would vote to sell it. It's either sell the place or watch it cave in."

"You'd better be careful, Ike," Matt said grimly. "Williams is a very personable fellow, but he's not your type. He may be on the board of the church, but most of the members wish that he'd go back to Temple Beth Hillel. Unfortunately, Rabbi Greene doesn't want him either." Matt suddenly remembered Ike's pronoun. "Who the hell is 'we'?" he demanded.

"I guess you haven't heard all the news," Ike said triumphantly. "CPC is going to relocate its headquarters. We're considering Adamsport. If the price is right, I can't think of a better location than on the grounds of the First Parish Church. George Gallagher told me all about this character, Williams. He runs an unsavory sex club out on the Cape Thruway. Gallagher promised if he got elected he would run Williams out of town, but Gallagher knows the score. If Williams comes through for us, we'll show him how to clean up his act. You can't always choose your friends." Ike scowled at Matt. "Or your relatives. You should be pleased. If you're determined to go back to the ministry and if the UU's hire you, which I doubt, they can build another church or take over an abandoned store front. At least they'll have enough money to pay you. I understand that Littlejohn has quit. He can't afford the luxury of his integrity."

"How much are you offering for the church?" Matt was sadly aware that there was some logic in Ike's proposal.

"As little as we can get it for. That's going to be a subject for discussion between the church board and the incoming president of CPC."

"You couldn't replace the building for five million."

Ike shrugged. "Back in the 1800s it was built for $35,000. Unfortunately, it would take a quarter of a million to fix the roof, repair the bell tower, get the bell ringing, and bring the heating system up to date. Even if the UU's could afford all that, they still couldn't pay the oil bill to heat the entire church. As you very well know, they don't use the sanctuary during the winter."

"The church is a national landmark. The Adamses and their wives are buried there. What are you going to do with them?"

Ike laughed. "No problem. Hendy will show you an artist's drawing of the redeveloped downtown area. It includes the new thirty-story CPC headquarters and a small memorial chapel on what is now Hancock Boulevard. If the city is agreeable, we'll redivert the Boulevard—move the tombs over and build a small chapel which would accommodate about fifty people. That's more than ever show up at any one time now to commune with the Adamses' bones. On either side of the chapel will be fountains and green lawns and a walkway from the lobby of the CPC building. I am sure that the Adamses' heirs will be very happy. And don't try to tell me that the Adamses were Unitarians. The world hasn't changed that much. No one, now or then, can get elected president of the United States unless they believe in Jesus. That eliminates Unitarians and Jews."

8

The day after Ike's return, Matt moved out of his office. Actually, it was big enough for both of them. Ike had told Henderson to have another desk moved in for him, but Matt refused. Ike was king of this jungle and Matt had no desire to contest with him on his own territory.

"You have to understand," he told him, "I'm not your style business executive. As president of Controlled Power I would run the company with a management team. It wouldn't be a one-man show. This would give me time for other interests." Matt knew that he was treading on dangerous ground, but he persisted. "I'll give you one example. In my opinion, for the next few years this company needs to consolidate and shake out some of the unprofitable divisions that you have put together over the past fifteen years. I am well aware that CPC wouldn't exist if it hadn't been for the shipyard, but year after year the shipyard is depressing our overall profits. I think we should sell it or move in other directions that free us from a dependence on navy or government contracts."

"I'll never sell the Godwin Shipyards," Ike responded curtly. "And I'm not going along with your insane belief that you can function as a part-time radical minister and manage a business of this size at the same time. Get it out of your head! No president of CPC is going to undermine the work that I've personally done with the navy or jeopardize future contracts. This shipyard will be here long after I'm gone. If you can't run it properly, I'm sure Hendy can."

Sitting behind his grandfather's mahogany desk, Ike stared at Matt coldly. "I know that you are committed to deliver a sermon at the First Parish Church. That's all right with me. But I'm warning you, don't make it a way of life. And confine your sermon to God and not the Godwins. If you don't, and if you don't inform your religious friends that in the future you're sorry but you can't mix business and religion, then I can assure you the directors of CPC will rescind your election. It will be no problem since you don't take office officially until January."

After Ike's "words to the wise," although they passed each other daily in the corridors of the Administration Building, conversation between them had been replaced by glum stares.

In tears at his refusal to play ball with his father, Irene told him that, whether he came with her or not, she was accepting Becky's invitation to dine at the Big House for the next few weeks to visit Ike and get acquainted with Gillian. Matt passed the days walking the floor of his new office (empty except for a desk), staring out the window at the yard, and occasionally jotting notes for a sermon. He knew that his refusal to meet Gillian was adding insult to injury, but the alternative was more angry confrontation with Ike, which he was sure wouldn't make Ike's new wife very happy either.

That first evening he ate alone the dinner that Mrs. Goodale, their cook and housekeeper, had prepared for him. When Irene arrived back at the carriage house with Ink and Able around nine o'clock, she greeted him perfunctorily. He suggested that they should talk, but she responded angrily. "Go talk with your Peachy Stein. I'm sure that she'll have an orgasm in the pew when she listens to your sermon next Sunday."

Irene agreed with Becky, Hendy, and Ike that Matt was not only playing a losing hand, he was also jeopardizing their security. "Your father means it when he tells you that he'll cut you off without a cent," she said bitterly. "Keep in mind that you have two boys to support—not to mention a wife."

"We're not exactly poor," Matt reminded her. "We have close to a million dollars in sound investments. They generate nearly a hundred thousand a year. If worse came to worse," he grinned, "I could donate my services to the First Parish Church. They still own the parsonage, and Littlejohn has moved out. We can live there. We probably couldn't afford a housekeeper and a nanny, but I'm sure we could get along."

Matt didn't tell Irene how deeply involved with Peachy he really was. Peachy was confident that he could become famous as a businessman preacher. She would never have agreed with Irene, who insisted that at the advanced age of forty-two Matt was belatedly responding to his own "ego achievement needs." Peachy insisted that he was still a young man and it certainly wasn't "too late" to change careers. She told him that if he could make his new kind of UU church a reality, he would need plenty of ministerial assistance, and she was available. She offered the moral support of a fellow daydreamer. Matt had read her an article from the *Wall Street Journal* that revealed the many professionals who had given up law degrees and even medical degrees to seek a more fulfilling life in the ministry.

Peachy agreed. "There is no reason why a minister with vision couldn't become very influential in this country," she told him. She backed up her enthusiasm with a very erotic, squirmy hug and said, "I can see you now—Matt Godwin, advisor to the president of the United States."

Matt tried to explain to Irene that as manager of the shipyard, or, if it finally came to pass, as president of Controlled Power, there was no way he, or any businessman, could really stick his oar in the water and help create a new, vibrant America.

But Irene wasn't convinced. "Ike keeps telling you that eventually he'll help you get into politics," she said. "Your problem is that you are too radical. You couldn't be elected dog catcher. You seem to forget that the UU's in Sweetwater, Maine, who are a good cross section of middle-class America, weren't jumping on their pews and cheering your religious philosophy or your wild ideas on how the country should be run. From what I've seen of UU's here in Adamsport, the members of the First Parish Church won't be very enthusiastic about your new moralities either. I really don't understand you, Matt. If you were born in a poor family like I was, you'd be happy as hell to have what you have now. You're a very fortunate man. You have a three-generation family. You have everything that money can buy. All of us are in good health. You've proved that you can run a big company employing several thousand people. There are very few Americans who wouldn't be happy to change places with you. Why must you be *famous?*" Irene wished she could erase the rueful expression on his face and hug him, but that wasn't her style.

Matt shrugged. "Being famous—being locally or nationally known, recognized, applauded—is the basic motivation of everyone who runs for public office. Many politicians spend millions to get elected. But very few of them are leaders who have any historical perspective, or have the faintest idea how to resolve the insidious democratic and ethnic separation and disintegration that is inevitable in a democracy of this size. I don't believe that entropy is the nature of things. We can wind up the system again, remold it, and give a majority of Americans a real sense of national purpose. We can blend thousands of various pulling-and-hauling factions and groups, and millions of new Spanish-Americans, into a proud new style of American."

"What makes you think the country is going to be happy with you playing God?" Irene demanded. "I know that you don't think much of Him, but keep in mind what happened to Jesus Christ."

"Jesus wanted to be crucified. Like Socrates, he chose the spectacular-death route to fame." Matt laughed, "If the bug bites you, infamy will do. In the words of Antonio, 'How I found it or came by it, I know not.' But Antonio was talking about his sadness, and I'm talking about joy and wonder.

"You don't seem to understand," Matt mused aloud for Irene. "I can't escape my parental indoctrinations. In different ways both Sarah and Ike wanted me to achieve the immortality that escaped them. When I was about fourteen, John Adams's diaries were published, and Sarah immersed herself in them. John went to Harvard at fifteen. After teaching school in Worcester he began to study law. He was determined to be famous. He asked friends how to achieve fame and greatness—and he agonized over his shortcomings. He wasn't particularly proud of the 'petti-foggers', as he called some of the Boston lawyers, yet he asked himself, 'Should I exert all the soul and body I own to cut a flash, strike amazement, catch the vulgar . . . should I make one bold determined leap into the midst of fame, cash and business?'" Matt shrugged. "Sarah used to read me stuff like that with tears in her eyes. But her real hero was Henry Ward Beecher. Have you ever heard of him?"

Irene shook her head. "Was he related to Harriet Beecher Stowe?"

"She was his sister." Matt was thinking it was just as well Irene didn't know too much about Beecher. She most certainly wouldn't approve of Beecher's extramarital life. "Before the Civil War, when he was very young, he became a revivalist preacher. Then at the age of thirty-four he was offered the pulpit of the Plymouth Congregational Church in Brooklyn. He became so famous that eventually the members, following his desires, remodeled it so that he could preach his sermons surrounded by his congregation, which he did, off the cuff, without notes. At the same time he was editor of the *Brooklyn Independent*. During the Civil War, some people were sure that he was advisor to Abraham Lincoln and forced Lincoln to deliver the Emancipation Proclamation. After the war, when Lincoln was asked who was the greatest of his countrymen, Lincoln replied, 'Beecher!'"

Irene shrugged. "So, Beecher proves what I've always told you. Fame is fleeting. A hundred or so years later, who cares? I think people who spend their whole lives looking for public affirmation and applause, or trying to be remembered by posterity, are really afraid of dying." She smiled tentatively, knowing that she was probably irritating him, but was unable to resist the challenge. "Good Catholics realize that this life is simply a preparation for the next. They don't spend their entire lives recording every action or thought the way John

Adams did, as a good example. So, he was second president of the United States. Two hundred years later, who really cares? There probably aren't ten people in the whole world in any one day who give him a second thought."

Matt grimaced. "Daddy Ike is one. If he succeeds in buying the First Parish, he'd better build a new tomb for the Adams family or the Department of the Interior will get in the act." He laughed. "People might not give much thought to the Adamses, but, despite Ike, I haven't heard anyone suggest that we rename the city Godwinsport."

9

Trying to decide whether a showdown with Ike would cause open warfare between himself and Irene, and wondering if as president of CPC he still might finally put some substance to his daydreams, Matt telephoned Gus Belshin at Infinity Corporation. Belshin was coolly cordial. "To tell you the truth, Matt, you were elected president over my dead body. But congratulations, anyway. I met your sister Sally a few months ago. I feel like one of the family now."

"Did you want the job?" Matt asked.

"Hell no, not with your old man still at the wheel. Enjoy the driver's seat in good health."

Matt told him that he wasn't afraid of the presidency. He could handle the job, but he wasn't going to live, breathe, and eat CPC twenty-four hours a day. Matt laughed, "I'm not like my father. I don't believe in one-man rule."

"That will be a pleasant change," Gus said. "On the other hand, there can be too many cooks in the kitchen." Gus chuckled. "Sally told me that you are planning to tell Congress how to run the country and become, according to the newspapers, the great god Godwin. She thinks at heart you are really a wild-eyed leftover hippie. It doesn't bother me. The directors may stick by you if only to irritate your old man. It may take a bit of doing, but I'm sure that you can serve two masters—most of us do. Mine are more simple than yours. There's my wandering prick and the bottom line. But as much as I adore the former and try to please him, the bottom line comes first with me, as it does with the rest of the board of directors. So watch yourself, chum."

In other words, Matt could play with fire just as long as CPC didn't get burned. "If worse comes to worse, you don't have to worry," Gus said. "One of these days your sister Sally may decide to marry me. Of course I'll have to divorce my wife first, but if she does, I could become a Jewish Godwin by penetration. Anyway, if, by chance, I should end up running things, I promise we'll keep you on the payroll. Controlled Power Corporation needs to maintain some contacts with God."

Matt had no sooner hung up than Becky was on the phone. "You can stop being a spoiled, nasty little boy," she said. "Gillian really wants to meet you. There's no damn reason why you have to eat alone every night."

Becky confirmed that Ike and Jill were going to live in the west wing of the main house until a final decision was made on the location of the CPC headquarters. She told him that her two girls, Rachael and Dorothy, who were in their early teens, had agreed to eat dinner earlier with Ink and Able, and they all would be supervised by their respective nannies, Mrs. Delaney and Mrs. Richards.

"Just keep one thing in mind, Matt Godwin," she said belligerently, "we're a family and you're the one who is screwing things up. It makes me very uneasy to know that you're sitting down the road a quarter of a mile from here eating all alone. And it's embarrassing to try to explain your behavior to Jill. She's sure that you think she's a gold digger. She's not, Matt. She's a soft-spoken, well-educated woman. You'll really like her."

"I'm sure that I will," Matt said. "I'm not angry at her. I'm happy the old man has a loving bed companion."

"So get your head on straight," Becky said. "Ike is really right, you know. There's no damn reason why you have to shoot your mouth off at the First Parish Church. You can back down a little. Be grateful that Ike has faith enough in you to want you to be president of CPC. If you love that UU church so much, save it some other way. If you play your cards right, you can probably convince Ike that some other location in Adamsport would be just as good as the First Parish Church for CPC." Becky tried to sound cheerful. "You should be happy. It's a damn sight better location than Boston or New York City. You could even walk to work."

"There are three things that you, Hendy, and Irene don't understand," Matt said. "The main reason I want to preach Sunday is to save *myself*. Second, I want to discover if there is anyone left in Adamsport, or in the United States, for that matter, who dares to challenge the negativism of the Protestant fundamentalists and the other-worldliness of Catholics. Someone who dares to offer a new kind of religious humanism. And please don't tell me that I have suddenly become a Mr. Hyde. I'm not like your husband; I haven't spent the last twelve years thinking of nothing night and day but the shipyard. I know that you and Hendy and Irene all think that I'm a utopian daydreamer—"

"Why don't you write a book about your mad utopias," Becky interrupted him. "You can call up that crazy old man who lives in

Happy Shores. What's his name? Lovejoy something or other? He'll probably be glad to help you. What's the third reason?"

"To do what Sarah would have done had she lived: try to save the church for her and John Adams, who she loved, and Abigail, who she tried to emulate."

"That's only the tip of the iceberg, Matt," Becky snorted. "If you're trying to save yourself, why don't you be honest with yourself? Your problem isn't business or religion. It's a piece of ass five years younger than Irene's. It has magnetized your prick. My advice to you is to decunt before you lose your wife. If you don't, and if you don't want me to declare war on you, too, then you be here tonight at seven."

Walking up to the big house on a tree-lined road on a deeply wooded section of the Godwin estate that dated from Zach Godwin's time and had been preserved as a bird sanctuary, Matt had fortified himself with three scotches. He was erotically aware of Irene's behind, controlled from its natural sway by her plasticized panty hose. "You have a very pretty ass," he said, watching her a little tipsily. "But it would be a lot more inviting if you'd let it undulate." He grinned at her, and before she could stop him, he slipped his hand under her skirt and clasped her nylon encased buttocks. "We're early," he said, ignoring her startled what-the-hell-do-you-think-you're-doing? "I think we should walk up to the gazebo and make love."

"For God's sake, Matt, grow up. Let go of me and stop being ridiculous."

"I'm not ridiculous. I'm a horny husband. You should be happy. After almost fifteen years, I still crave your body."

"You may prefer to screw swinging from the trees, but I don't." She could feel her panty hose slipping down on her calves as she tried desperately to wiggle out of his embrace. "Stop it! I don't intend to arrive at Becky's all sweaty and smelling of sperm."

Irene's resistance was making him more excited, but he was aware that she was frozenly tense in his arms. "Come on," he whispered in her ear. "Do something crazy for the first time in your life. You can sit on my prick for ten minutes and give me big romantic kisses. I promise you, I won't climax."

"Damn you. If you don't stop, I'll scream."

Reluctantly, Matt let her go. "Just once I'd like to see you respond to me spontaneously." He grinned more seriously at her. "Okay, you've won the first round, but later, around ten, when we are walking back home, you can take the curse off the evening. We'll go swimming bollicky in the quarry." Matt ignored her frown. "Even Becky did it once when we were kids, and Sally probably lost her virginity up there."

"You are crazy," she told him grimly, "I don't even let the kids go near that place. Your grandfather might have thought it was great, and fenced it in on the grounds for his children, but I don't believe in suffering. We have a perfectly good swimming pool."

"Great!" Matt slapped her behind enthusiastically as they arrived on the front porch of the big yellow house. "Tonight, after this ordeal, when we are walking home, my wife is going to fling off her clothes, jump into my arms naked, wrap her legs around me, scream her delight as I enter her nest, and then, hugging me ecstatically, she'll climax as I jump with her into our moonlighted swimming pool. In the morning we'll be discovered floating on the surface—drowned literally and figuratively in each other's love. Irene and Matthew, a legend to equal Romeo and Juliet or Heloise and Abélard or Daphnis and Chloe."

"Stop being idiotic," Irene hissed at him, then yelled through the screen door, "Hi! We're here!" She glared at Matt. "You're shut off. No more booze."

Becky led them into the living room. She nodded coolly at Matt but couldn't escape his older-brotherly embrace. "The prodigal son returneth," he said, "seeking mental reinforcement from his father and a little cuddling on his sister's tits."

Jill appeared with Ike behind her. "I was afraid that you were angry with me," she said, extending her hand to him as Becky extricated herself from Matt's arms.

"That's silly, Jill. I love you." He grabbed her around the waist and bussed her cheek. "Daddy and I don't agree on much," he said, still holding her and examining her body and face, "but I'm sure that my father and I agree on you." He hoped that she was aware that he was being quite honest. Women like Jill who signal their total femaleness to a male at first glance appealed to him.

"Unfortunately," he continued, "Irene and Becky think I have an Oedipus complex. They're wrong. I never wanted to marry Sarah. But you're a different cup of tea."

Jill wondered if Matt were trying to hypnotize her. She knew she felt an immediate rapport with him, and her brains were swimming loose in his bold stare.

Ike saw the interchange and frowned grimly at Matt. Fortunately, he had never paid any attention to Freud and knew nothing about sons destroying their fathers to take their places in their mothers' beds. During dinner Becky and Henderson managed to steer the conversation into the calm waters of the Godwin children and Gillian's career on the stage.

Later, in one of the downstairs living rooms, Gillian told them about her opening night experience in several theaters in Boston. Neither play had lasted long on Broadway. She smiled at Matt. "I've never been a churchgoer, but I suspect that actors and preachers have a lot in common. They must capture their audiences and get them to believe, at least momentarily. Ike tells me that preaching is still in your blood." Jill suddenly realized that she was walking on thin ice. She looked at Ike, who was pouring himself a healthy snifter of Napoleon brandy.

"If Matt would get up in the pulpit and preach a sound religious philosophy, I wouldn't give a damn," Ike said. "In fact, if he preached John Calvin style and told his parish that work was their salvation and not try to massage them with Emerson and Thoreau's Unitarian nonsense, CPC might endorse him. America got where it is today by believing in a God who expects man to earn his daily bread."

"Tell Matt what happened at the Rotary meeting today," Henderson said, obviously trying to divert the conversation to less fractious grounds. "Ike's dreams for a new headquarters may be the best thing that ever happened to the Unitarians of this city."

"It was the biggest turnout the Adamsport Rotary has had in years," Ike beamed at everyone, including Matt. "Hendy gave a little speech and told them if CPC built its headquarters in downtown Adamsport, we would be seeding the future. The city has to forget its former basis as a retailing center. We're living in an information-based society. CPC will resurrect the city with a white-collar management at its center and robot computerized manufacturing on the periphery. We'll not only provide employment but also give the city a broader tax base. Even more important, with CPC's top brass living and working right here in the city, we'll solve the problem of what the shipyard is going to be doing when we finish building the last LNG carrier next year."

Ike was exuberant, knowing that he had captured his wife's and his children's full attention. "When we showed them the drawings of the redeveloped downtown and told them that we were prepared to negotiate with the members of the First Parish Church for a healthy sum for the property—more than enough to help them build a new church building—everyone stood up and cheered. Sylvanus Williams and quite a few Unitarians were there."

"Poor Sarah," Matt said gloomily as he refilled the bottom of his brandy glass. "She and John, John Quincy, Abigail, and Louisa must be restless in their graves."

"That's bullshit, Matt," Ike said angrily, "and you know it. John Adams didn't give the land to build the first meeting house. The town of Adamsport did. When John died he left the trust fund to help build the new church, but he was just as interested in setting up an academy for young men. Old John was long dead when the church was finally completed. It was his son John Quincy Adams's idea to stick his father's and mother's bones under the present building and make it a memorial to his father. But once the present church was completed, no further money was given. All money from the trust fund went to Adams Academy, which was John Adams's dream more than the church. When it comes right down to it, the Godwins have probably given more money to the First Parish Church than the Adamses ever did. I checked with Williams. He doesn't think we'll get any flack from any of John Adams's descendants. Most of them aren't even Unitarians."

"There must be some rich Adamses around?" Gillian interjected.

"Maybe there are, but they don't live in Adamsport." Ike stared sourly at her. "Matt will tell you. Reverend Littlejohn has a hard time convincing the Adams Trust Fund to wash the plaques and busts of John and his son that flank the pulpit. A few years ago when members of the church finally convinced Congress to pass a bill making the church a national monument, they didn't get much of any help from Adams's twentieth-century relatives. They're usually conspicuous by their absence." Ike laughed. "Believe me, two hundred years from now the Godwins will be better remembered in this town than the Adamses."

"I'll toast to that." Matt stood up, waving his glass in the air and ignoring the frozen look that Irene gave him. "You have to understand, Jill, our family has an immortality problem. My father wants to build his own monument while he is still alive." Matt grinned at his father. "And so do I! But your initials are wrong, Ike. You're I. Z. Godwin and I. M. God-win!"

"I think God is drunk," Ike said sarcastically. "You'd better take him home, Irene. He may be in heaven, but all is not well with the world."

10

Tuesday, after Labor Day, Robert Lovejoy had merged any lubricous fantasies he might have had about an unseen telephone lady with a come-hither voice into a female character in a futuristic novel that he was working on. Peachy Stein's conviction that he was a latent UU, and her concern that he should come to Sunday services at the First Parish Church to hear Matt Godwin preach, had been of so little import in his life that he hadn't even reported the telephone conversation to Emily.

As for his front yard, nude lawn-mowing fling, fame was fleeting. If it hadn't been for Sylvanus Williams, who was still trying to arrange his "Let's Celebrate Lovejoy Cocktail Party" at the Adamsport Country Club (Williams had apologized to Lovejoy that so much time had elapsed), Lovejoy would have vanished into his familiar obscurity.

Actually, Lovejoy didn't give a damn. He was aware that some people at the club were sure that Silly Willy's motives were not altruistic. Offering a testimonial to a senior citizen who had exposed his naked body to his neighbors was probably Sylvie's left-handed way of reminding Adamsport ladies that every Wednesday night was ladies' night at Silly Willy's, where they could let go of their repressions and watch younger male genitals with far greater potential than Lovejoy's dangling in the breeze.

Floating naked on an air mattress in his back yard swimming pool, which he would soon have to drain for the winter, Lovejoy was only dimly aware that it was a very warm day for September. Actually, he was working, trying to decide whether some interesting sexual reflections going on in the mind of one of his female characters would slow up the story action of his novel in progress.

After all these years, Emily still didn't believe that anyone could work while lying on his back, but she had kissed him good-bye and gone to the club to play golf with Doris Tilburg and any other two, preferably male, whom they might inveigle into a foursome for the afternoon.

The screened patio doors to the back yard were open. When Lovejoy heard the front door chime, he was determined not to answer it. But whoever was repeating the few notes of Beethoven's *Eroica*—his choice of door music—was as insistent as he was. After the fourth serenade he gave up. Groaning, he docked his mattress and slid into an abbreviated bathing suit. Yelling to the unseen ringer, "For God's sake, don't leave now, I'm coming," he pattered through the living room.

Opening the front door, he stared in astonishment at a perspiring woman, her hair tied in a bun, wearing white shorts cut high on her tanned thighs and a halter that contained her breasts but didn't stop them from jiggling as she jogged in place on his front doorstep.

"If you weren't going to answer, I didn't want to lose my rhythm," she said, and though she was gasping a little, Lovejoy recognized her voice. It was Peachy Stein. Rivulets of sweat trickled down the cheeks of her oval-shaped face. With laughing, wide apart almond-shaped eyes, a small and slightly Semitic curve to her nose, she exuded a Mediterranean female flavor that instantly eroticized many Anglo-Saxon males who were bored with their fairer-skinned counterparts.

Roje stared at her euphorically for a moment. "I know that your wife isn't home," she said, still jogging but more lanquidly now. "So I thought I'd give you one more try. Matt Godwin is preaching Sunday, and you're just the one to hear him." She stared at Roje conspiratorily. "Matt is going to blow the top off of Adamsport. Do you have a shower? If I can cool off, I'll tell you all about it."

There were two bathrooms in the house with shower stalls and an outdoor shower beside the swimming pool. Never having had a female visitor who wanted to wash herself, Roje mumbled that she could have her choice. "Oh, the pool shower will be fine," she said. Following him through the living room into the back yard, she was ecstatic when she saw the pool. "Could I swim in it?" she asked, dancing toward the outdoor shower on the other side of the pool.

Roje was about to tell her that he was sorry, there was a cabana but he was sure that there were no female bathing suits that would fit her full breasts or pear-shaped behind. But before he could get the words out, Peachy had stripped off her shorts and halter, gingerly peeled off adhesive bandages that covered her nipples, explaining that if she didn't do that they would become chafed, and under the shower she was soaping her underarms and bushy vulva with great thoroughness.

"I hope you don't mind," she laughed, "but I'm not afraid of exposing myself, either." She handed him the soap. "Take off your bathing suit. You can wash my back." Roje stared at her dubiously. Women as lovely as Peachy didn't float into a senior citizen's back yard and shed their clothes. He was sure that he was dreaming. "Maybe all that stuff you told Judge Gravman was just bullshit," she said as she walked out of the shower, wiped the water from her skin, and held her arms up in the air to dry. "I don't think that you'd ever really dare to walk around the Pru bare-ass."

"I hadn't planned to do it with a naked sexy young female." Roje was trying to keep his eyes focused on her face. "The problem, as you are probably well aware, is that I have an erection."

Peachy grinned at him. "That's a compliment, Mr. Lovejoy. Give it some air. I enjoy seeing a man's penis, especially when it salutes me." She walked out on the diving board. "Don't worry, it won't last. They never do," she said, and she dove gracefully into the pool.

Deciding that it was the better part of valor, Roje wiggled out of his suit and dove in beside her. Sputtering as he surfaced, slithering for a moment against her body, he couldn't help laughing. Playing naked with a live female was a hell of a lot better than writing about it. He wondered briefly if their nudity might lead to sex. But he quickly extinguished a brief daydream of himself slowly entering Peachy's body. He should be thankful for little things. After all, even in his novels young women didn't capitulate to men old enough to be their fathers—but, on the other hand, such a fantasy might be worth a chapter or two.

"How did you know that Emily wasn't home?" he asked her, treading water as she floated face up on the air mattress a few inches away.

Peachy laughed. "Because she's playing golf with my father. When I telephoned you, I didn't know that he knew your wife. As a matter of fact, Sylvie told me that Emily Lovejoy was just about the nicest person and the best female golfer in the Adamsport Country Club."

"Sylvanus Williams is your father?" Roje asked, surprised. "I can't believe that Sylvie has a daughter who is about to become a minister." Nor who is as pretty as you, he thought but didn't say.

He wondered if Peachy might be one of the local housewives who, rumor had it, occasionally stripped at Silly Willy's to supplement their family income.

"I thought everyone in Adamsport knew," Peachy shrugged apologetically. "Keep in mind, I'm not responsible for him." She sighed, "The truth is that I'm ashamed of him. His damned club is disgusting. He makes sex objects out of women."

"But you obviously don't object to women running around naked."

Peachy grinned. "Of course not. I told you that I agreed with you. Like now—right here—being naked is nice. But I'm not on a stage with a hundred guys peering at my cunt. I'm Peachy Stein with a potential friend. Friends, young and old, can play naked together and it's totally different. My father *makes* women do it."

Roje laughed, "Well, not exactly makes them; he pays them."

"You know damn well poor people are for sale," Peachy snorted, "especially if you pay them enough." She rolled off the mattress into the pool and swam to the opposite side where she hoisted herself up and sat dangling her feet in the water. Treading water, Roje was on a level with the fluttery-butterfly opening of her vagina. He tried not to look and resisted swimming closer to her, but he had a strange feeling that if he did, Peachy might have opened her legs farther and even rested them on his shoulders while he kissed her vulva.

"You'd better call me Roje." Roje hoisted himself up and sat beside her on the edge of the pool. "You must be very happy that your friend Godwin is going to preach. He should attract a lot of people to the church."

"I am and I'm not," Peachy said. "I haven't read Matt's sermon— according to him he only speaks from notes—but if he blasts off with some of the new moralities that he is proposing, I'm afraid that he'll not only alienate his father and his family but most of the Unitarians in this parish as well. The Unitarian Association may even disown him. Matt doesn't like it when I tell him, but he has a little bit of a messiah complex. He told me that he's going to propose what amounts to a new religion. I'm his press agent. So far, I've invited Boston television, Community Television, and the Christian Broadcasting network to video tape him. All the news services will have reporters there. Keep in mind, they might not pay any attention to any ordinary minister, but Matt is manager of the shipyards, and he's informed the press that he's been elected president of Controlled Power Corporation. My father, who's on the board of governors of the church, is fascinated with him. I rarely see Sylvie, but yesterday he was on the telephone, trying to find out from me exactly what Matt is going to preach about in his sermon. He told me that he had a great idea. Matt should buy the church, not his father."

Peachy shook her head. "Getting involved with my father won't do Matt any good. The Jewish community in Adamsport is very unhappy with Sylvie and wishes he would go away, and so do I. Before he opened Silly Willy's, he ran porno movie theaters in Boston. My mother divorced him when I was twenty-five. That was two years after I had married Saul. Saul thinks my father is an evil man. Mother is married again. She lives in Newton with a totally monogamous man." Peachy was absorbing Roje with an affectionate expression that wasn't at all filial and they both knew it. She laughed, "I really shouldn't criticize Sylvie too much. In some ways I guess I take after him. I find it hard to be faithful."

"You seem to be quite taken with Matt Godwin." Roje couldn't believe that she was trying to seduce him, but he decided that as an author, given this kind of provocation, he could fish a little. "Are you in love with him?"

Leaning back on her hands to give her breasts the benefit of the sun, Peachy smiled teasingly at him. "I told you on the telephone, I'm in love with you. But I'm in love with Matt, too. And I'm in love with Saul. But each love is quite different. Actually, although I've lived in Adamsport all my life, I never knew Matt very well until last April, after his mother died. I knew that he was going through some kind of emotional crisis. He was surprised to discover that I was going to graduate from Divinity School in June. He had come down to the church to talk with Reverend Littlejohn several times, but when Paul wasn't there, he'd talk with me. He was at sixes and sevens in his life. I don't think he has ever felt totally comfortable in the business world. Matt's a lonely man." Peachy smiled. "Not sexually; he's married, you know. But mentally. He didn't blame his wife or his father, but Hamlet-style he questions his lack of decisiveness. I guess we untied the knots in each other's brain. After that we managed to see each other at least once a week." Peachy smiled blithely at Roje. "It's been a long courtship. We've fooled around, touched each other, but we've never gone all the way. Not because Matt hasn't wanted to . . ."

Then, to Roje's surprise, she kissed his cheek. "Your poor cock is drooping—sympathetic to my sorrow, no doubt. Are you going to make love to me?"

Roje stared at her, speechless. "You mean right out here with God watching?" he finally asked.

Peachy reached over and took his penis lightly in her hand. "God is watching. I'm God. You're God. That's what Matt believes, and God is love . . . and loving." She grinned. "But I hope that your neighbors can't see us." She corraled the air mattress that was floating near her foot and lifted it out of the pool. "If we go over there," she said, pointing to the far end where the cabana provided visual protection on three sides, "and if you believe God out there is watching, then only She can see us. We have about an hour and a half before my kids come home from school, then I must jog back home." She tossed the air mattress down near the cabana and stretched out on it, leaning her head on one elbow. "I hope that you're not a fast lover, Roje."

Standing over her totally relaxed, flowing flesh, Roje couldn't help laughing. "No, but I am a bewildered lover."

"Why?"

"I've never had such a delightful invitation, and from a minister, no less! Why are you so generous to me? You just told me you are in love with Matt Godwin but you won't make love with him. Even though you say you love your husband, I presume that he wouldn't be happy with you if he could see you right now."

Roje sat on the air mattress next to her. Peachy's eyes were closed. He kissed her breasts gently and tasted her erect nipples. She pulled his head down to her face and gave him a hundred little kisses on his mouth, nose, and cheeks. "Those are an old man's questions, Roje," she chuckled. "A young man would ravish me and ask questions afterwards. I really do love you, and I'm not quite so promiscuous as you might think. I have an advantage over you; I've read all of your books. I have a pretty good idea of what goes on in your head. Making love to you is equivalent to making love to a mature version of Matt Godwin. I'm pretty sure that having sex with you won't disrupt your life as much as it would Matt's."

"What about yourself? Won't you feel guilty?"

Peachy was leaning over his penis, laughing as she gave it a very lengthy sensual mouthing. "I've always been very honest with myself. I would only feel guilty if I made love to a man I didn't love. Anyway, I'm hooked on you. I love to make love to a man who never stops asking questions and wondering."

"Wondering about what?"

"About both of us wondering. About our necessities to merge with another person. About the leaves above us that are getting ready to die and won't be born again until next April."

"Your husband doesn't wonder about such things?"

"Saul is a good man, but he's an accountant, and he never asks any questions except about the figures that he feeds into a computer."

After Peachy had gone, Roje wondered if he had dreamed her. He had explored her body hungrily with his mouth and hands, marveling over her flesh, until she begged him: "Come inside me—ever so slowly . . . make it a sweet agony." Undulating like a tiny wave in a light breeze, with one hand she moved his glans against her clitoris, and with the fingers of her other hand clutched deep into his buttocks.

Their merger seemed like infinity, and even after it was completed their heartbeats and blood flow were synchronized. After a long, whispery mental and sexual surrender, which Roje realized later had lasted close to an hour, she laughed happily and rolled on top of him. Still joined, she brought herself and him to a screaming loss of their selves.

Still naked he had followed her to the front door. Dressed once again in her jogging clothes, her eyes sparkling, she said, "I hope you realize that I don't usually recruit UU's this way. And you should also understand it wasn't all love. It was a trade off. I expect to see you in church Sunday. And, if I can arrange it, Tuesday night I'd like to see you at the finale, which will be our last UU board meeting. That's when the contestants are supposed to bid for the First Parish Church."

"For heaven's sake," Roje scowled at her. "You can't leave me dangling like this. I still don't know how Godwin is planning to blow the top off of Adamsport."

Peachy laughed. "Neither do I. I told you, Matt never writes his sermons. It kills spontaneity. He knows where he is going and roughly where the middle and end will be. His father warned him and even quoted Jesus to him: 'No one can serve two masters; for either he will hate one and love the other or else he will be loyal to the one and despise the other.' Ike didn't finish the statement, but Matt did: 'You can't serve God and Mammon.' He told his father that, in case Ike didn't know it, Mammon for Jesus meant 'riches' and that obviously Jesus had been wrong. Neither Ike nor the pope has taken a vow of poverty, and they both think God loves them."

Peachy patted Roje's bare behind. "The nitty-gritty of the matter is that Isaac is determined to erect CPC on the bones of the First Parish Church. Tomorrow the *Adamsport Chronicle* will publish the artist's drawings of a new downtown Adamsport. Occupying the space of the First Parish Church will be a thirty-story tribute to Mammon—the new Controlled Power Corporation headquarters."

Peachy fished in the pocket of her shorts and handed Roje a slightly damp paper. "I don't know whether it's going to be a rerun of David and Goliath, but Matt is responding with his slingshot. Here's a copy of the full-page advertisement which will appear in the *Chronicle* both Friday and Saturday." Peachy brushed her lips against Roje's. "Hope you like it; I helped Matt write it. See you in church. And don't tell your wife about this afternoon." She grinned at him. "Not yet, anyway; not until she tells you what she's doing with Sylvie, besides playing golf."

Roje stood staring at the door for several minutes after she had gone, then finally remembered the paper in his hand. In bold type it proclaimed:

THE SUN SHINES TODAY ALSO

Why should we not enjoy an original relation to the Universe? Why should we not have a religion by revelation to us—and not a history of theirs? Let us demand our own works and laws and worship.

You are cordially invited to hear a sermon by
I. Matthew Godwin, D.D., M.B.A., newly elected President of Controlled Power Corporation, at the First Parish Church

To consider proposals for new approaches to sacramentalizing human sexuality and celebrating a loving God who manifests Himself in human loving and caring, together with a proposal for a new

CHURCH OF MODERN MORALITIES
BUILT ON THE FOUNDATIONS OF UNITARIAN UNIVERSALISM

A church which will be led by a business-oriented male and female clergy seeking to merge Church, State, and Capitalism in a new relationship that will give Americans a new sense of national purpose and sane moralities to live by.

As President-elect of Controlled Power Corporation, Matt Godwin, as he is known to thousands of Adamsport residents, will also offer several alternate proposals to save the First Parish Church and rebuild it physically with a vibrant new leadership and activist members who could provide future direction for America and all American churches and synagogues.

Services at 10:30 A.M. Sunday

Roje couldn't help smiling as he recognized the Emersonian influences. The opening fall Sunday services at the First Parish Church sounded more exhilarating than walking around the Prudential Tower bare-ass. For the first time in several years, living life promised to be more interesting than writing about it.

11

Inching through heavy three-lane traffic into downtown Adamsport, Paul Littlejohn grew increasingly nervous. Many of the cars were filled to capacity with well-dressed people. Usually at this hour on a Sunday morning, twenty minutes before services started, there were plenty of parking places left. But not today. Cars were double- and triple-parked in the circular square created by the First Parish Church. It was obvious from the crowd standing on the front steps that the sanctuary, capable of seating at least seven hundred people, was already jammed to capacity.

During his eight years as minister of the church, except for Christmas services, Littlejohn had never preached to a congregation exceeding one hundred and fifty people. Most of the diminishing membership of the church were well over sixty years old. A small contingent of young parents rotated Sunday religious education of their fifteen or twenty children among themselves.

Entering the rear door of the Parish Hall, Littlejohn tried to be cheerful. He hadn't seen such crowds in a church since the Vietnam War. During those terrible days he had offered a church in New Jersey, of which he was pastor, as a refuge for draft protesters. But crowds like that spelled disaster. Conflict between the police and the young people broke out at a blink of an eye. Littlejohn sensed that it could happen here in Adamsport if the people—most of them weren't UU's—were sufficiently antagonized. He knew that most of them hadn't come to church because of any sudden religious sentiment. They had read Matt Godwin's full-page advertisement in the *Chronicle,* and the rumor had quickly spread throughout the city—especially after the editors had run a story that Controlled Power might want to buy the building and tear down the church—that there was a Godwin family dispute in the making. Many people who had talked to Littlejohn were sure that Matt and Becky Godwin were shocked that old Ike had got himself a sexy bed companion young enough to be his daughter.

Littlejohn nodded at several women in the Parish Hall who were preparing coffee and setting out cakes and cookies for the after-services social hour. Amanda Brackett, a very voluble member of the church's board of governors, greeted him. "If you're looking for Matt Godwin," she gestured disapprovingly at the minister's office, "he's in there with Peachy Stein. He told me that we shouldn't bother to make coffee. He's personally hired a catering service. Presumably, he's paying for it himself. But if all the people out there try to cram in here after the services, there won't be room for anyone to bend their elbows, let alone drink their tea or coffee." She looked at Littlejohn tearfully. "We all wish that you could have stayed with your flock, Paul." Then she moved closer to him, "And you can take it from me, even though Peachy Stein has practically got her divinity degree, we don't want her in this parish."

Littlejohn had told the congregation at the last service in June, before the regular closing during July and August, that even though he had accepted a slightly higher paying job at UU headquarters in Boston, if they couldn't find a replacement, he'd be happy to fill in occasionally. He was certain that whether Peachy Stein got the position or not, the new minister would be female. He silently agreed with

Amanda that even though the ministerial robes would cover her voluptuous body when she preached, Peachy was altogether too sexy for the staid congregation of the First Parish Church of Adamsport. While Littlejohn certainly championed equal rights for women, he was positive that a female, like Peachy Stein, could never provide the kind of leadership for a congregation that a male could. What man in the congregation would come to Peachy with his marital problems for counseling, for example? Unless, of course, the petitioner hoped that the female minister might assuage him in the sack. Most of the males in the congregation would agree that Peachy was a delectable little dish. Although she had never made any advances to him personally, he wasn't too sure that she wouldn't do exactly that with a particular male—Matt Godwin being a good example—if the mood seized her. Maybe he was getting too old. You couldn't stop progress such as it was. Already more than half of all UU ministers were women. They could afford to work for lower wages than a man, who was most likely supporting an entire family. Nevertheless, Littlejohn could not adapt himself to the idea of a female God, let alone a female preacher.

And if progress came in the form of Matt Godwin, it was obvious that he couldn't stop that either. Last spring when Matt had offered to preach a sermon at the fall reopening, Littlejohn had been a little apprehensive. He was sure that Peachy Stein was responsible. She obviously had more influence over Matt than his mother ever had, and Littlejohn had no doubt that Peachy's interest in Matt had passed beyond the bounds of her present role in a student minister internship. In any event, it was questionable whether UU headquarters would recognize Matt's right to preach after so many years and whether he was the kind of man any divinity student, male or female, should intern with. But Littlejohn really had had no choice. If Matt didn't give the opening sermon in September, then he personally would have had to preach yet one more sermon. Peachy was still a good year away from ordination even though she was the only preacher the First Parish Church could afford.

Anyway, at the time when Matt asked him, it had seemed for the best. After Sarah died it appeared unlikely that Matt or any other Godwin would ever take an active interest in the First Parish Church. Even if Matt only preached one sermon, it might help to increase the cash flow from the Godwin family. He might even become more active. John Codman hoped to persuade Matt to become chairman of the board of governors next May. One thing was sure: if Matt Godwin really got involved in the First Parish Church, the Godwin family could resolve its financial problems and not even miss the money.

But all that thinking had preceded Matt's advertisement in the *Chronicle,* which Littlejohn had read with a sense of foreboding. He had no idea that Matt Godwin was such an out and out radical, though he had heard rumors. During his short sojourn in the ministry up in Sweetwater, Maine, young Godwin had evidently been a hippie-style minister. But that was long ago. Or was it? Evidently Matt was still a rebel, temporarily wearing the sheep's clothing of a conservative businessman.

When Littlejohn and his wife had moved to Boston in August, most of the members of the church had located his new address. His phone had been ringing continuously since Friday evening. Some members were obviously delighted that the Godwins were at war with each other. A surprising number seemed resigned to selling the "leaking ark" and building a church that they could afford. But a few like Amanda Brackett and Moses and Annie Belcher, who had built their retired life around church activities, along with Dorothy and Henry Hancock, were incensed.

"They can't sell this church," Henry Hancock had almost been yelling into the phone when Littlejohn answered. Hancock was related to one of the original pastors in the seventeenth century. "It's a national landmark," Hancock stormed. "Let the goddamned Godwins build their headquarters near the shipyards. There's plenty of room down there."

But John Codman, vice president of the Adamsport National Bank and chairman of the board of governors of the church, was enthusiastic. "I don't care what the Belchers think," he told Littlejohn. "Just remind them that a few years ago when St. Paul's and St. Andre's Church in New York City was declared a national landmark by the New York State Landmark Committee to try to prevent its sale, the church members sued the committee for $30 million."

Littlejohn tried to tell Codman that he had already said a reluctant good-bye to the church in June. He was really no longer active, and he could not appear at board meetings unless he was invited. "You're invited," Codman said positively. "Sylvanus Williams wants to have Matt Godwin come to the first meeting after Labor Day, too, but I'm not in favor of that. There's quite a few people on the board who think Godwin is interested in a full-time ministry. That's the second subject we have to discuss next Tuesday, and Godwin shouldn't be around when we do it. I've talked to Matt occasionally at the club." Codman's voice had a negative tone, and he obviously wasn't very happy with Matt's advertisement in the *Chronicle*. "For a man running a business as big as the shipyards, young Godwin has some pretty far-out ideas. I talked to his father, and Ike thinks he's going to use his sermon to screw up the sale of the church. You know damned well, Paul, that it's too late for sentimentality. I don't care if the church can't be duplicated for several million dollars. It was originally built for $35,000. Ike told me confidentially that he might offer up to $400,000, but no more. With that kind of money we could build a small wooden classic New

England church and still have a hundred thousand dollars or more left over. That would solve our financial problems."

Inside Littlejohn's former office, Matt Godwin had already donned his grey ministerial robes with red trimmings. He greeted Paul with a big grin. "Peachy did it. The place is bursting at the seams. She convinced Fred Ames, he's the boss over at Community Television, to broadcast the sermon live. Channel 5 has their camera in the opposite aisle. They're taping for possible national distribution. There's a good chance that the sermon may be rerun on Sunday morning network television in the next month or so."

Peachy, as bubbly as a new bride, was checking the snaps on Matt's robes. Littlejohn wondered aloud whether her husband was coming. "Not today," Peachy shrugged. "Saul thinks when ministers or rabbis become too business oriented, they aren't spiritual enough. I told him that after living with him so long that maybe I will try to become a rabbi instead of a minister. I'm really more Jewish than he is. At least I'm not afraid to promote a good thing. I convinced Bill Walsh of the *Chronicle* to tape the whole program. Old man Walsh doesn't love me very much, but he admitted that the *Chronicle* may print the entire sermon in the Monday edition." Peachy laughed. "He'll probably call Matt's father and ask his permission before he does it. Did you see the speakers attached to the front columns? I rented them just in case. Don't worry, Matt's paying the rental cost. Lucky I did. It's such a balmy day, I'm sure there'll be several hundred people sitting outside listening." Unable to restrain herself, Peachy kissed Matt's cheek. "Matt's going to give Adamsport its first revival meeting in a century!"

Littlejohn knew that he should have asked Peachy to participate in the service. It was expected as a part of her student training program. But he was sure that would be tossing gasoline on the fire. Although Irene Godwin seldom came to church, she surely would come today and she certainly wouldn't approve of Peachy. "I hope you realize, Matt," he said, "there's a lot of people out there who are pretty conservative. It's one thing for you and Peachy to try to blow the minds of a UU congregation, but today you've got a cross section of Adamsport. I know for a fact that your wife's friend, Father Timothy Sullivan, is coming, and so is Rabbi Goldman." Littlejohn raised his eyebrows. "I guess he's a little puzzled by a future UU minister whose name is Mary Peachy Stein. Some of the local Protestant ministers might even show up, since, from the looks of things, their own churches will be deserted. And don't forget, Matt, many of the people in Adamsport are Jesus lovers. A lot of them are fundamentalists, like Jerry Falwell, and they're convinced that the UU's and everyone they call humanists are trying to destroy the country."

Matt patted Littlejohn's arm soothingly. "Stop worrying, Paul.

You're not responsible for what I'm going to say. I'll make it clear that UU's aren't either. Today I'm going to propose a new style religion. UU's can either accept or reject it, but it could stand on its own, anyway. I am sorry about one thing. Last spring, when I offered to preach, I know that you had no idea that Ike and I might finally confront each other, especially over my belief that a business-trained person can function effectively in the rare climate of theology. But the larger issue is that I am searching for a new approach to religion. Actually, I think a new kind of religion with a complete spiritual dimension could couple this with celebration, entertainment, and an exciting, viable morality for the world as we know it today. I believe that kind of religion can get people out of their homes, not just on Sunday, but other days of the week as well. I think we can create a religious environment that will be more popular than movie theaters. In addition, it would be a kind of religion that would build people up, something that they could look forward to every day of their life."

Matt laughed at Paul's bewilderment. "But I'm not going to preach my sermon here. From the sound of the organ, the time has arrived. The curtain is rising." Matt kissed Peachy on the mouth. "See you later. Go sing with the choir, and if you see anyone about to assassinate me, yell so I can duck."

Following Littlejohn, who had put on his robe and had opened the door into the sanctuary, Matt could hear the whisper of excitement rising in volume over the organ music. Close to a thousand people, many with smiles of recognition, were packed six abreast in the pews. Sitting under the high domed ceiling, most of them were unaware of the sexual overtones of the plaster lotus blossoms that circled the ceiling fifty feet above their heads and culminated at the top center in an open blossom. He reminded himself to tell them about "the jewel in the lotus."

Matt had agreed with Paul that they should not immediately ascend to the mahogany pulpit, which stood fifteen feet above the floor of the sanctuary and obscured anyone who sat behind it. First, Paul would lead the services through the call to worship, various readings, and the offering, the basic structure of the Sunday service, including prayer and meditation, after which he would turn the pulpit over to Matt for a half-hour sermon.

Watching the congregation watching him—remembering the old Spanish proverb: "Who watches the watcher?"—Matt only half-listened to the unison affirmation, a reading that reflected Unitarian Universalist beliefs and a philosophy which he was sure were quite unbelievable to many of the congregation present today. Knowing that the sermon he was about to preach would be blasphemous, shocking, and even disgusting to many people, Matt wondered about his own crazy compulsions. Was he suicidal? Why did he want to challenge the religious beliefs of staid New Englanders? He remembered Michael Servetus, who, nearly five centuries ago, had tried to correct John Calvin's theology. Servetus was burned at the stake. Wasn't he playing an equally dangerous game?

Irene was sure that he was, and Ike's response to his advertisement had been swift and grim. Shaking the *Chronicle* at him as if he'd like to smack Matt across the face with it, Ike told him angrily, "If you deliver this sermon of yours, don't come to the yard Monday morning. You can dictate your resignation over the phone to your secretary. I'll also tell Gus Belshin to poll the board as quickly as possible and withdraw your election as president of CPC. And I warn you, if you try to mix sex and religion and politics in Adamsport, which is equivalent to fouling your own boat, I won't be the only one in Adamsport who will be happy to pull the plug on you."

To Matt's surprise, Gillian had tried to mollify Ike. "Don't you think you should wait and hear what Matt has to say?" She smiled tenuously at Ike. "It would seem to me that the Godwin family should present a united front. At least in public."

Ike shook his head vehemently. "You don't know this man, Jill. He's always tried to bite the hand that feeds him. I don't intend to sit in the First Parish Church and listen to my son defile Christian moralities. Most of the people who live in this town are like me. They believe in Jesus Christ, and they believe that he was the Son of God and sacrificed himself on the cross to save all of us. And they believe in monogamy, and the right to life, and most of all they believe in spending money to prevent the godless Russians from taking over the world. I'm not stupid. I have a pretty good idea what Matt is going to say, and if he does, he's giving me no choice. I'll disassociate the Godwin family from what amounts to devil worship."

Last night, during a tearful, screaming discussion as they were getting ready for bed, Irene told him that he was sabotaging their marriage and making fools out of her and their children. Choking with self-pity and rage, she sobbed, "I'm sorry, Matt. I've tried to be a good wife. I've listened to your insanities for years and even tried to shrug when you inveigled our friends into mad discussions and tried to convert them. But I'm not going to stand by while you go public and ruin all of our lives with this kind of ego mania." In her nightgown, she left the bedroom. "I'm sorry. Tonight I'm going to sleep in the guest room. I don't want you near me and maybe I never will again."

Listening to Littlejohn's words of welcome to the congregation and his wistful hope that this might be the beginning of a new era for the First Parish Church, Matt suddenly recognized Gillian and Irene. They were sitting in the middle of the sanctuary, and, to his surprise, next to Irene was Father Timothy Sullivan. Irene was staring rigidly at Matt. But a tiny smile was flickering on Jill's lips, and Matt was sure that she knew he had recognized them. What had possessed her to defy Ike and come hear him? Probably the only reason Irene had come was because Jill had persuaded her. The first evening that he met Jill at the Big House, there had been an unspoken rapport between them. Now, Matt grinned at her. The old man might have become a rejuvenated lover in bed with her, but Matt was sure that Jill would relate to the son better on the meanings and purposes of life.

As the choir sang once again, Matt watched Peachy in the front row of the balcony. She was radiantly pretty and singing just to him. He was sure that today of all days Peachy wanted to go to bed with him. Perhaps in another century, a man could ask his wife's permission and a woman could ask her husband's. Why not a blessing for a little joyful dalliance? Matt suppressed a little chuckle. It was one of the messages of his sermon, but he doubted if he'd live to see it become a way of life.

Letting his eyes wander over the pews, he picked out John Codman sitting in a pew with George Gallagher, and several other men who, Matt knew, were city councillors. Then he spotted Sylvanus Williams sitting with a heavily made-up young lady who Matt suspected was one of the dancers at Silly Willy's. She was sitting between Williams and Robert Lovejoy, who had evidently given his wife, Emily, an unmatrimonial place on the other side of Williams. Lovejoy was watching Matt with the amused, detached interest of an author trying to fix the moment forever in words.

Whenever Matt spoke in public, he always made it a point to catch the eyes of a few people in various sections of the audience, especially those who he was sure, from the expressions on their faces, were identifying with him. It also amused him to pick out a few sour-faced listeners like Amanda Brackett, who, he noted, was crammed into a pew with the Belchers and Hancocks. These people he often fixed with what he called his Bela Lugosi stare—and many people who were thus transfixed had told him afterwards that they thought he was trying to hypnotize them and that they had seen the Devil burning in his eyes.

Peachy had mentioned briefly, this morning, that she had been playing her own seduction game with Robert Lovejoy. She hadn't gone into details, but she told him she had jogged over to Lovejoy's house and challenged him to swim naked with her in his swimming pool. Peachy had laughed, "The poor man was really quite shook up."

But just before Littlejohn had arrived, Peachy told Matt that she was feeling a little jittery. She had had a strange telephone call from her father. "Sylvie kept pumping me. He was trying to find out what you were going to say. He told me that he really wants to talk with you and Robert Lovejoy. He asked me to invite you to his house after services and told me I could come along too." Peachy had been helping him to get into his robe. Touching his trousers, she giggled. "Do you always get an erection when I'm talking to you?"

"You're not talking," Matt had grinned at her. "You're rubbing. What did you tell your father?"

Peachy laughed. "That you were going into competition with him. That you were going to offer nude adorational services at the First Parish Church. Actually, I told him to get off your back. Did he telephone you?"

Matt nodded. "Yesterday. He told me that I know damned well that the only solution for the UU's in Adamsport is to sell the church. He tried to convince me it doesn't matter what I preach today. I'm not going to compete with Billy Graham, Oral Roberts, or Jerry Falwell; I'm not going to open up the mail next week and find a million dollars from enthusiastic supporters to save the First Parish Church." Matt had scowled at her. "Obviously you must have told him that I am going to try. Otherwise why in hell did he ask me if I want to buy the church? I told him that he was talking to the wrong Godwin. Only my father could afford philanthropy on that scale. He told me that I wouldn't have to use my own money. If I were interested, he'd help me outbid my old man. 'I'm not talking philanthropy, either,' Sylvie told me. 'I know that morality is your subject, but if you'll come down to my house after church, I'll introduce you to a more practical kind of morality.' For some reason he wants Robert Lovejoy and his wife to hear what he has to say."

Peachy shook her head. "I don't know how much money my father has, but most of it he probably didn't get legitimately. Don't get involved with him, Matt. He might understand your morality, but you won't understand his."

"I don't understand yours either," Matt said. "You know damned well that for the past four months you have been giving me continuous let's-go-to-bed signals. But when I try to get through to you, you run like a scared chick."

"The problem is I'm not sleepy," Peachy laughed. "But if you're going to see my father this afternoon, I think I'd better come along and make sure that he doesn't seduce you first."

12

After inviting everyone in the church to the social hour following the sermon, Littlejohn smiled at the thousand or more attentive faces below him. "Thanks to our guest of honor, the church is filled to capacity. Strangely, although UU's don't revere Jesus, this usually only occurs on Christmas and Easter. This morning I am happy to turn this pulpit over to Isaac Matthew Godwin, a member of this church and a citizen of Adamsport. As some of you may know, Matthew was an active Unitarian Universalist minister many years ago. I'm sure he has a provocative message for all of us."

Matt rose from behind the pulpit and stared thoughtfully at the congregation for a moment. It was an act of absorption and blending with the sea of minds and faces, representing many different cultural and ethnic origins, that were solemnly concentrating on his face.

"Good morning. I love you. As loving creatures, individually and collectively, you and I are God. The only God we will ever know. Indivisible and rejoicing, we can experience Him in every moment of our lives in the many aspects of ourselves and others. That is religion—no matter by what name it may be called.

"I am happy to be here in the 348th year of the First Parish Church and on this, our opening Sunday, on such a summery day in September. In New England, despite rumors, the days never 'dwindle down to a precious few.' There was a time when Unitarian Universalist churches did not close for the summer, and in the winter the congregations did not have to move out of their sanctuaries into the parish hall for services. More people came to church, and the cost of heating the church was apportioned over many more parishioners.

"During this coming winter, if by some miracle we could fill the sanctuary with as many warm bodies as we have today, and if the minister would give sermons to heat our minds, we might solve some of the financial problems of this church. We might not have to burn oil at all, especially if the congregation would agree to wear several layers of clothing, as our ancestors did—or thermal underwear. The members might even agree to modify the pews and make them more comfortable. If they did, we might restore the old New England custom of bundling.

"Why not?" Matt knew at that moment that he had captured his audience. He grinned infectiously and specifically at Jill, who, he noticed, was smiling at him. But Irene, sitting beside her, did not seem amused. Here and there, he recognized a few other women who, despite their spouses' cooler expressions, seemed to be on the same wavelength as he was. In the balcony he could see Peachy, grinning and making transcendental love to him.

"Why not?" he repeated. "God is Love. Why can't we have churches where we can worship Love? Most Christians agree on one thing. God is Love. Even Ike Godwin, my father, who prefers Episcopalian theology, would agree that God is Love." Matt smiled serenely. "Unfortunately, like many Americans, my father finds it embarrassing to talk about human loving in public. He believes that love of God should be a kind of spiritual love. Philosophers call it 'agape.' Most ministers, priests, and rabbis would agree with him. They feel uncomfortable with the human aspects of loving. They can't believe that God can be lusty, erotic, laughing, and loving, too.

"If you want eros in your life, you have to read *Playboy* or watch Music Television or go to clubs like Adamsport's notorious Silly Willy's." Matt grinned at Sylvanus Williams, whose mouth dropped open in surprise at this sudden recognition. "During the next half-hour, I want to suggest that the Western world may be ready to embrace a new kind of God. A God who never intended to maintain a separate existence from his creations. A God who can't believe that He has created men and women who aren't fully aware that He and they are one and the same. An erotic God, a dancing God, a God who needs no Christ or Messiah, because He is continuously giving birth to Himself. A God who loves you very much, especially when you dare to be naked with Him, physically and mentally, and when you are celebrating His and your interdependence in the act of loving in all of its manifestations.

"Before I explore this new kind of God and a religion which exalts Him and You and I simultaneously, I want you to know that when I originally offered to deliver this sermon, I planned to do it in memory of my mother, Sarah Godwin. Many of you knew her personally. During the past years she asked me many times if I might ever return to the pulpit. Sarah taught me, from my first years, the I/Thou relationship with life and with death. But I wasn't, in my own mind, sure that a man who had given up the ministry for the world of business could straddle two worlds. After much thought and study, I am convinced that today, more than ever, we need a common unity between the Church, the State, and Capitalism. We need a new understanding of the meaning of the separation of Church and State. We need to understand that in America, at least, Capitalism is one economic method for men and women and society to function together, but it is not so all-powerful that it can function without moral guidance provided by the Church. We need a new understanding of our Constitution and a recognition that in a vibrant nation, the Church and State can never be independent of each other. They must work together to give all men and women a sane perspective on themselves as a nation and a sense of national purpose which can be accepted by the majority of people. The Church has a moral duty to keep the State in a continuous process of re-creation for the benefit of its citizens. We need a new understanding of our national motto In God We Trust. As God, you and I must never lose trust with ourselves.

"Today the First Parish Church in Adamsport represents the Church in microcosm. Within the next forty-eight hours, the board of governors of this church must call a meeting of the members to decide whether to sell this building to Controlled Power Corporation. If the members decide *not* to sell the church, then they have to resolve the problems of how a small congregation of Unitarian Universalists in Adamsport can continue to worship here and provide the necessary money for repairs to the roof, the belfry, and the obsolete heating system. The problems of this church are not unique. All over the United States, Catholic and Protestant churches and synagogues, with insufficient parishioners to support them, have been sold to real estate developers. Neither the church nor the synagogue plays an important part in the daily lives of most Americans.

"But for many centuries the Church and the State were indistinguishable. Some philosophers like Karl Marx called religion the opiate of the masses. Opiate is the wrong word. The Church and its ministers and priests dramatized the bewildering interplay between good and evil in everyone's life. There were few books, no radio, no television. The Bible was the medium and the message. It offered a thousand stories of man's inhumanity to man and seasoned them with the hope of better things to come. Religion, the Church and the Good Book, provided an escape route, fearful at times when it was populated with purgatory, hell, and evils, but always fascinating.

"Today, the masses in Western countries have other opiates and endless escape from realities. Most of our gross national product is not for the creation of food, clothing, and shelter, but rather it is a reflection of our increasing ability to be able to play instead of work. Automobiles, television, radios, books, magazines, newspapers, video cassettes and discs, video games, motion pictures, dining out, spectator sports, vacations all over the world, alcohol, and our never ending fascination with our own sexual compulsions are some of the ways we divert ourselves. Escaping boredom, we often act as if we were God, but in the process of celebrating ourselves and our achievements as God, we forget the more important celebration of ourselves as Gods of Love and Wonder.

"Today, no society, no nation, no group of people believe in the Church or the synagogue enough to devote their entire lives and incomes to the kind of religious thinking that once dominated the civilized world. God is a handkerchief we keep in our back pocket to wipe away our tears and blow our noses should the need arise.

"If you read the invitation in the *Adamsport Chronicle* to hear me this morning, you may have detected an underlying note of heresy. My feeling is that now, as never before, the Church and God need heretics. Religious men and women who dare to chart new courses and abandon outworn theologies. What is heresy? It has nothing to do with being right or wrong in the conventional sense. If everyone believes that there is a God and I say that there is no God, that there never was one, then I am a heretic. I am reviling God as Exodus warns both Jews and Christians not to do. Actually, you may believe that by telling you that you and I are God, I am reviling God. Many Jews and Christians would consider this blasphemous. I am happy to be a blasphemer. They forget that Jesus reviled God. He declared that he was the Son of God, and long before Jesus was born, Jewish law made it a crime for anyone to claim that there might be other gods besides Yahweh. A Son of God, as every human father well knows, could destroy the father and become God himself.

"Punishment for blasphemy was stoning, not crucifixion. That was Pilate's choice. Had Jesus been left to the Sanhedrin, the Jewish trial lawyers, he would have been stoned to death. Obviously that kind of death would not have been so dramatic as the crucifixion. In contrast, the fate of heretics was usually burning at the stake or, if they were lucky, banishment.

"In his fascinating book titled *Heresies,* Thomas Szasz reminds us: 'Just so long as there is tension between the individual and the group of which he is a member there will be heresy whatever it might be called.... The individual must think for himself. More than anything else that makes him an individual. The group, on the other hand, must want its members to echo its beliefs. ... It follows then that if the group is held together by the ideals of Christianity then heresy is a deviation from the official beliefs and dogmas of the clergy. But when people and societies are held together, as many are now, by the images of science and technology, then heresy is a deviation from the official beliefs and dogmas of scientists and doctors.'

"This morning, as I try to convince you that you and I are God and that we should return to the religion of awe and wonder that inspired our remote ancestors before Christianity, I'd also like to revive a long forgotten word, *antinominy,* and remind you that antinominiasts, who in the early seventeenth century were considered blasphemers and heretics, actually erected the foundations for the religious and political liberty that we in America—less than three hundred years later—consider our rightful heritage. Antinomianism means being against the moral law and specifically, in history, that under the gospel, dispensation of faith alone is necessary for salvation.

"Actually the first antinominiasts, or heretics, just a few years after Matthew, Mark, Luke, and John, were writing gospels of their own. They defined the Christian religion for Catholics and most Protestants today. Some of the first Christian heretics were called Gnostics, from the Greek word meaning 'knowing.' They claimed that they really knew the truth about Christ and the Apostles Peter and Paul, and they derided the Scriptures as we know them. They were unhappy that Luke, by insisting on the actual physical resurrection of Christ, was establishing the groundwork for the Catholic Church and Apostolic succession resting in Peter, the first of the Apostles. Since Peter was the first witness to the resurrection, ultimately the pope, the bishops, and the priests, whose spiritual and political power came directly from the Scriptures, would trace their lineage to Peter.

"If you study the history of the Christian religions, you quickly discover that the Church and the State were synonymous. Questioning the Scriptures, right through the seventeenth century, was equivalent to questioning the leaders of the State, whether they were kings or popes, bishops or priests. Questioning the leaders could lead to imprisonment, death, or banishment.

"The first Unitarians were antinominiasts. Followers of a man named Faustus Socinus, they disavowed the deity of Christ, the doctrine of original sin, and the Christian belief in atonement. The Anabaptists also rejected much of the Scriptures and believed in the guidance of an inner light derived from God and one's own conscience. The early Quakers likewise believed in the 'indwelling light of Christ' to such an extent that every man and woman was the Son of God. Quakers got their name because they trembled and quaked at this revelation. One of the first Quaker leaders (a man more daring than George Fox), James Nayler, proclaimed: 'I am the Son of God, but I have many brethren,' and he told the House of Commons when he was on trial for blasphemy: 'I wonder why any man should be so amazed at this. Is not God in every house and in every stone, in every creature . . . If you hang every man who says Christ is in you, you will hang a good many.'"

Matt paused for a moment. "They didn't hang James Nayler for blasphemy. Under the English blasphemy laws, which, incidentally, have never been repealed, the House of Commons decreed that Nayler should be whipped with 300 lashes, put in a pillory for many hours, have his tongue bored through with a hot rod, and he should be ridden through the city naked, facing backward on a horse.

"That was in 1656. A few years earlier, across the Atlantic in this city, John Wheelwright, the first pastor of the original church on this site, was declared a heretic and banished from the Massachusetts Colony. The original church was called the Meeting House on the Mount—a Chapel of Ease. Permission to build it was given by the General Court of Massachusetts so that the few farmers who lived in this area, who could not easily travel back and forth to Boston for religious services, could have a place where they could commune with God."

Matt was happy to note that he had the full attention of the Belchers and the Hancocks, who appreciated church history. But he was sure they wouldn't like what he had to say next. "Unfortunately for Wheelwright, he got mixed up with a woman, Anne Hutchinson, his sister-in-law, who was America's first feminist. A very well educated woman, she dared to accuse Boston ministers of not properly understanding the Bible. She convened weekly sessions which were attended by nearly a hundred Boston women—keep in mind the church and religion fulfilled the lives of our forefathers—and she tried to convince these women that the Boston preachers weren't sealed ministers of the gospel. A forgiving God had given men and women a Covenant of Grace. Wheelwright agreed with her. He preached a sermon which aroused all of Boston. In chapter 3, verse 15 of Genesis, he told his congregation, God had actually given Adam a second covenant. The first covenant was that they must suffer and work to achieve salvation for their sin. The second was that there was a divine spirit dwelling within you, and if you recognized it, saint or sinner, you could achieve Grace.

"I'm sure that Anne Hutchinson would have agreed that the Covenant of Grace is not only the recognition that God is Love, but that Man-Woman is God. All we have to do to discover the truth is to transcend our petty egos and blend ourselves with the ebb and flow of the universe.

"Incensed with their heresy, John Winthrop, the governor of Massachusetts, and John Endicott brought them to trial. But they refused to admit their errors and they were banished from the Colony—Wheelwright to New Hampshire and Anne to Rhode Island where, according to the Pilgrims, she received her just punishment and was scalped by the Indians. Think about this. John and Anne were banished by a civil court, a court composed of people who had fled from England because they were considered blasphemers themselves and had refused to use the English *Book of Common Prayer* in their churches.

"In God We Trust. Just so long as your concept of God is my concept of God. Centuries before Wheelwright lived, Michael Servetus, who many think of as the first Unitarian, challenged John Calvin about the nature of God. Servetus insisted that God has only one identity and can not be both the Son and the Holy Spirit. Servetus was burned at the stake in Geneva, Switzerland."

Matt beamed at the congregation and noted happily that both Irene and Jill were following him intently. "In those days the true meaning of heresy, which is from the Greek word *haresis*, 'to take a choice', was corrupted by church leaders and applied to anyone who denied church doctrine or intimated that there might be other choices than those decreed by the church fathers. Sociologist Peter Berger has pointed out that 'in the ancient world man had limited choices—fate and the gods determined what happened in his life. Modern man and woman by contrast have almost unlimited choices in many aspects of their lives. Thus, for pre-modern man heresy was a possibility, but usually rather remote; for modern man heresy typically becomes a necessity. Today modernity creates a new situation in which picking and choosing becomes an imperative.'

"I have given you this background on heresy and blasphemy because today I'm asking you to join with me in a reverse kind of heresy. Separation of the Church and State in this era of total overkill, nuclear war, and confused moralities has gone too far. The theory behind constitutional doctrine is that religious leaders, Catholic, Protestant, or Jewish, are supposed to take care of the spiritual and moral concerns of their believers and not shoot their mouths off when political and economic decisions impinge on moral beliefs.

"In recent years the National Conference of Bishops and the U.S. Catholic Conference have rightfully offered official church pronouncements on many aspects of politics and economics that in some cases even go counter to normal Catholic moral beliefs. *Time* magazine made the statement: 'It almost seems as if the world's Roman Catholic bishops have set themselves up as a new branch of government. In country after country they are measuring specific government programs and issuing moral report cards on what they see.' In agreement with Moral Majority, the Catholic bishops have demanded tuition tax credits to help private schools, demanded prayer in public schools, come out against mercy killing and sex on television. In Canada, the Bishops Commission rejected Prime Minister Trudeau's economic proposals as immoral. They accused the government of deliberately encouraging unemployment and of aiding the rich at the expense of the poor.

"The Catholic church has taken moral positions on crime, housing, national health insurance, world food policy, the Panama Canal Treaty, the Palestinian State, Israel's right to exist, and even the redistribution of economic wealth in the United States. For the first time, not only Catholics but ministers and rabbis are questioning the nature of war and whether any form of nuclear warfare can be moral in any circumstance.

"Politicians, who believe the province of the Church is simply spiritual leadership and evangelism, deplore what they call the secularization of the Church—and they insist that the Church is losing sight of its essential purpose, to preach the gospel. But they are wrong. While I don't agree with many Catholic moralities, including their uneasy stance on nuclear war, the bishops have as much right to present their moralities as the elected politicians and the media. In the last few years of the twentieth century, priests, ministers, and rabbis have much less influence on moral conduct and leadership of this country than the *Wall Street Journal, Time,* or *Newsweek*—none of which hesitate from one issue to another to proclaim the moralities of their editors. An excellent recent example was *Time* magazine's reportorial weeping over the herpes explosion. In a kind of reverse morality, they recognized it as an over-due call for a return to monogamous morality. In *Time's* view, herpes is God's judgment on you for premarital and extramarital sexual encounters.

"After Breshnev's death both *Time* and *Newsweek* in supposedly reportorial stories advised our national leaders how to deal with the Russians. Not a week goes by that the editors of the *Wall Street Journal* don't moralize over particular economic and political decisions of our nation's leaders.

"At the same time the media and the politicians excoriate the intervention of the Church, and try to convince you that the Church is losing sight of its essential purpose, to preach the gospel, but they are wrong. This morning, as you will discover, my first heresy leads to many others.

"I believe that we must create a modern merger between the church, the synagogue, the state, and business in America, and we must offer a new kind of moral leadership. Although, in the beginning, religious leaders and sects may not agree on any particular set of moral beliefs, our combined goal should be a morally mature America. In the process we must till the fields and sow the seed for a new kind of religious leadership in America. We need religious leaders who will gradually establish sound national purposes and will make it possible for the vast majority of Americans to live joyous, self-fulfilling lives.

"In 1982, both the House of Representatives and the Senate passed a resolution requesting the president to declare 1983 the 'Year of the Bible . . . in recognition of both the formative influence the Bible has had on our nation and our national need to study and apply the teaching of the Holy Scripture.' In my opinion, using the Bible to provide moral leadership for America so that we can muddle through into a Golden Age is equivalent to the ostrich burying its head in the sand. The old-time religion might have been good enough for Daddy, but Daddy is dead. He doesn't live here any more.

"Pope Pius XI suggested, 'Today we are all Protestants.' But the Pope and Protestant leaders alike are all bogged down in biblical word games that ultimately demand 'a leap of faith.' They are simply unaware that You and I, being born, living, procreating, and dying— You and I surrounded by myriad forms of life carrying out the same process—You and I *are* God and the only God we ever need to know and love.

"No papal guidance based on biblical teachings has had much effect on moral behavior over the past two thousand years. If every American devoted himself or herself to a study of the Bible, we'd still have abortion as a method of birth control. We'd still have prostitution. We'd still have adultery and pornography and drug abuse and murder and theft, and we'd still have leaders of nations mobilizing their people to fight the peoples of other nations."

As he spoke Matt was aware that many of the faces watching him had a glazed, rejecting look. Many minds were hearing but not processing such sacrilegious thoughts in the synapses of their brains. "Before I continue," he said with a warm smile, "I want all of you to know that you should not feel obligated to hear me through to the end. On the other hand, if you are secure in your religion, your vision of God, and your moralities, I am sure that you will be able to cope with what is to come. More than a hundred years ago, Emerson asked the question for the twenty-first century: 'Why should not we also enjoy an original relation to the universe? . . . Why should we not have a religion by revelation to us? Let us demand our own laws and worship.' My belief is that all men and women are essentially religious creatures, but millions of us have lost sight of our basically loving and caring natures. We have been buried in the debris of outworn creeds and negative moralities.

"So today I am proposing to Unitarian Universalist leadership that it broaden its vision and create a Church of Modern Moralities. A transformed UU church could attract millions of Americans who no longer identify with the creeds and the music and the rituals of our ancestors who lived in an entirely different kind of world. We must provide new moralities for what is now an information society. We may never become a moral majority. Fundamentalists may denounce us as humanists, but hopefully, many million Americans will hear my words. You are aware that this sermon is being televised. It is my hope that video tapes of today's service will be shown nationally at some later date. Not only can this historic building be saved from the wrecking hammers of Controlled Power Corporation and the decision of the Godwin family, including myself, to build an office building on this site; but I am proposing to Americans everywhere who hear this sermon that we need a few million of you who are not afraid to help create an exciting new world. A new world where *God as Us* is a vital part of our daily life.

"If you send your contributions to the First Church of Modern Moralities Building Fund here in Adamsport, Massachusetts, I am hoping that we can create a new, morally mature church on these ancient foundations. We can dare to proclaim that God really does exist in this world and that He is in constant communication with us. But only when we recognize that He is You and I. I am Thou. You are Thou. Together as God we are in a continuous process of creation. Together we as God have a choice. We can recognize this joyous gestalt and flow with Him in the joy and wonder and the eternal mystery of Us, or we can deny Him in hateful and degrading interpersonal interactions, which is equivalent to denying ourselves.

"We don't need magic or symbols or Bibles or Talmuds that obscure the absolute wonder and miracle of life and procreation and death. We don't need to legislate our behavior with negative moralities. Rather, we need a church that offers new, modern moralities, with leaders and a fellowship of human beings who recognize that our reach exceeds our grasp. Leaders who remind us to wonder . . . to wonder at the miracle of the human brain and heart and blood and our power to re-create and transmit this miracle with penises and vaginas to future generations.

"I am well aware that many Unitarian Universalists will not agree with the kind of leadership that I am advocating. Jack Mendelsohn, a much admired UU leader, stated UU philosophy as follows: 'We are believers, but beliefs centered in method, a process of religious life, rather than the closed articles of faith. We have no creed. . . . Our churches make *no* official pronouncement on God, the Bible, Jesus, immortality, or any of the other theological questions which are generally answered with unabashed finality by more traditional religious groups.'

"In my opinion, Mendelsohn's kind of hands-off religious theology and philosophy, which is reflected in the purposes and principles that Unitarian Universalists are still trying to define for themselves, denies every sound principle of lasting organizations and sound business principles. It is equivalent to writing an obituary for a religion or a nation or any association. Right or wrong, lasting societies of any kind are organized around a well-defined set of beliefs on the meanings and purposes of life. Keep in mind I am a businessman. I am proposing that the new mixture of business and religion would provide a new yeast—a new kind of manna from a heaven of our own creation. In a sense this sermon is a trial balloon. I am not seeking self-aggrandizement. Churches with only one guru tend toward dictatorships and were the reason that our forefathers legalized, in our Constitution, the separation of Church and State.

"But today the churches and synagogues of America need hundreds of men and women like myself. Not just one lone individual shouting in the wilderness, but a Council of Moral Stemwinders to set the human clock ticking again. Unitarian Universalists, humanists, feminists—though we are probably less than two hundred thousand in number—together we should merge and create a Council of Moral Stemwinders. Men and women who dare to propose a new moral structure for this country and offer moral direction that deals with current realities. Instead of the kind of divisive democracy that now exists in a thousand UU churches, we should become a unified Church of Modern Moralities that doesn't hesitate to use the advertising weapons of the capitalistic system to attract millions of new members. Our goal should be to meld Church, State, and Capitalism into a revitalized America.

"This morning, therefore, I would like to provide guidelines for a Committee of Moral Stemwinders. I would like to suggest that the UU's announce nationally that they have decided to phase out biblical sexual morality and return religion to its origins. Let's create a religion that is unashamed that all religion originated from sex and fertility worship. Let's dare to proclaim one basic truth. If men and women have any purpose on this earth, it is to perpetuate themselves, within limits, and make this spaceship a happy, self-fulfilling place to live.

"Such a religion will not be hung up on the old rituals of any religion. During the past quarter century, beginning in the 1960s, in what was then called the Human Potential movement, there has been a growing awareness of the joy and wonder possible in human sexual merger. Total sexual loving and religion are perfectly compatible. Sex is sitting on the doorstep of churches and synagogues, waiting to be invited back in. Sex worship can be both a laughing experience and a humbling experience. Millions of men and women will be charmed to rediscover that the very beginning of religious beliefs proceeded not only from fear—fear of misunderstood phenomena such as earthquakes, hurricanes, volcanoes—but simultaneously from wonder and awe, the wonder of the sun and the moon, the tides and menstrual cycles, and procreation and the recurring birth and death of all life.

"Instead of degrading human sexuality, we need to exalt it. Instead of compartmentalizing our sexual lives and coming to our churches and synagogues like creatures who copulate with one another because we are forced to by sinful compulsions, we should make sex and sex-making a sacrament. Sexual repression and sexual sickness are man-made diseases. For nearly two thousand years Christians and Jews have been guided by a craftily contrived sexual morality. The first pornographers were the male leaders of the tribe. Determined to gain power and hold it over their people, they invented Eve who tempted Adam. After eating of the tree of knowledge of good and evil, not only were Adam and Eve ashamed of their nakedness but somehow they had sinned against God, who had warned them not to eat the fruit of this tree. If you want to repress people, you must make them feel guilty. Whoever wrote Genesis laid the foundation for Christian guilt. Most of the people listening to me today probably do not really believe that God created Adam and made Eve from one of his ribs, or that Eve, with the help of a serpent, tempted Adam. But sexual temptation and the essential nature of woman as seductress and women as temptresses have been processed into the male psyche by centuries of indoctrination. Male prophets and theologians of the Middle Ages warned men against women. Man's compulsion to merge his body with a woman's and impregnate her was evil, unless it occurred within the sacrament of monogamous marriage performed by power-hungry priests who claimed their authority from God.

"For more than a thousand years nude men and women—glorified in Greek art and sculpture—with the exception of Christ on the Cross, disappeared from European painting and sculpture. The prophets condemned the human body and its pleasures. Art critic Robert Melville has pointed out: 'When the nude finally did appear in Christian art, the body had ceased to be, as it had for the Greeks, a mirror of divine perfection. The naked body had largely become an object of humiliation and shame.' Using the medium of woodcuts, engravings, painting, and sculpture, artists were permitted to show not vice itself—not the actual sex-making—but the punishment for sexual sinning. Eves and Liliths and their female descendants became witches and seducers of men, who consorted with devils and snakes, and the artists of these centuries proved it by painting pictures of snakes and toads eating female vulvas and breasts, or by picturing lascivious women copulating with goats and women who could only be satiated by the permanent erection of the Devil himself.

"Today, nearly two thousand years later, millions of men still regard a woman as a temptress. Men still fear her control over him and retaliate by degrading her and making her a sex object of his lust. Today, young men grow up seeing photographs of women naked and lascivious, their legs spread-eagle, exposing their vulvas, opening their labia with their fingers so that a man can't resist them and must thrust his swollen penis into them. And when he has ejaculated into this anonymous woman he feels empty and futile, but he continues to exist on frustrated sex in all sizes, shapes, and colors. And men profit from each other by commercializing the forbidden sight of women's breasts, vaginas, anuses, and buttocks, or, if you prefer the common vernacular, catering to the vacillating attraction and repulsion of women's tits, cunts, assholes, and asses—all existing in some forbidden land extraneous to the person herself."

Amanda Brackett suddenly stood up in the middle of the congregation and shouted, "This is disgusting! Matthew Godwin, I won't listen to it another moment." She edged out of her pew and walked out of the church, followed by a scattered clap of hands.

Matt watched her leave. "If there are any others who would like to join Amanda now or at any time during the rest of this sermon, which I assure you may be more shocking to Christian sensibilities than anything you have heard thus far, please feel free to leave." He looked at the congregation with a sad smile. "If you need to save yourself from the power of mere words, for some of you it may be even easier to make the sign of the cross.

"After centuries of sexual repression," he continued, "and sexual frustration created by ministers, priests, and rabbis, and tight-lipped, tormented men like St. Augustine, who was shocked by his sexual compulsions, few people could believe that men and women could transcend their egos or find God in their own joyous physical merger—whether they were married by a priest or not.

"Denying our God-given sexuality, we have created a joyless sex world. A world of the sex tease, a sex-drenched society where the illusion of sex fulfillment replaces the reality. We have the strange phenomena of magazines, designed specifically for men or women, that capitalize on the frustrated misunderstandings of our mutual sexuality. They sell millions of copies as they try to explain the drives and needs of men and women to each other. Many of these articles and stories, and much of the advertising in these magazines and on television—which the average American watches six to eight hours a day—exploit a supposed continuing adversary relationship between men and women. They try to convince us that men and women have different needs and compulsions and can only coexist together as if they lived in an armed camp. They ignore the truth. The adversary relationship is not real. It is built into the male and female psyche from childhood by parents, teachers, and religious leaders who are guided by sex-negative biblical moralities.

"A Church of Modern Moralities will not moralize *post facto* on moral problems. Rather, it will lead the way. It will, for example, agree that premarital and extramarital sexual caring and loving are inevitable in many situations and that caring is not evil but rather is a reflection of ourselves as loving gods.

"A Church of Modern Moralities would propose new educational and postmarital structures which would offer all men and women, in their late teens and before marriage, the opportunity to experience caring sex with more than one person of the other sex. A Church of Modern Moralities would accept the fact that in many cases an additional caring sexual commitment can coexist with the original marriage pair bonding and not destroy it.

"A Church of Modern Moralities would propose a new right to life morality. It would insist that one of the most immoral things any man and woman can do is create a life they cannot, because of their youth, or will not, because they feel no human obligation, be responsible for.

"A Church of Modern Moralities will insist that the right to create life is a social privilege given not by a single God but by men and women who are God and recognize their responsibility as creators.

"A Church of Modern Moralities, recognizing man as God, would insist that an individual man or woman has the right to terminate his own life whether it be because of debilitating illness, old age, severe depression, or simply a desire not to cope any longer with the problems of the world. The church would demand that simple medical means be provided, in a hospital-controlled environment, for this form of suicide.

"Moral Stemwinders will insist that every man and woman, from the age of seventeen until they draw their last breath on this earth, has the right to experience a full and responsible sex life. To accomplish this, a Church of Modern Moral Maturity would incorporate sexual teachings and responsibility into its Sunday School teachings and sermons. It would also advocate state-licensed prostitution in homes run by husband and wife teams who arrange appointments with sexual surrogates, male or female, who could offer caring sex with regulated fees for millions of those who cannot, for one reason or another, enjoy a caring sexual relationship in their daily lives.

"A Church of Modern Moralities would bring human nudity and human loving into the church sanctuary and, using modern visual techniques, explore the long history of man and woman's quest for love and understanding of their sexual drives and compulsions. At some services, members of both sexes would reenact religious stories and dramas and rituals from all religious traditions. A Church of Modern Moralities would propose that we change city and state laws to permit men and women to be naked in public, where it is convenient for them to be naked."

Matt grinned at the surprised faces of Robert Lovejoy and Sylvanus Williams. "Thus it would be unnecessary to arrest a citizen for mowing his front lawn naked or to close up clubs like Silly Willy's, which exist only because we are so prurient about showing ourselves as naked children of God. The truth is that in a new, morally mature environment, when the beaches surrounding Adamsport are filled with young men and women frolicking naked in the sand and water and when there are naked acolytes in the church sanctuary—then magazines like *Playboy* or clubs like Silly Willy's will cease to exist.

"A Church of Modern Moralities would advocate the nationwide voluntary dispersion of black people and Spanish people and those of Asian origin—de-ghettoizing America and relocating these people in the white suburbs of America. It would propose zoning that would welcome black people and those of Asian or Hispanic descent into the white suburbs, but would prevent ethnic concentrations from dominating any particular area. Homeowners would be compelled by state legislation to apportion small percentages of apartments and private dwellings in various geographic areas of these cities to help these people to disperse into the mainstream of America. The survival of America depends on a melting pot that keeps melting and will produce incoming generations of a unified people with common goals.

"A Church of Modern Moralities would advocate the legalization of marijuana and cocaine and make hard drugs such as heroin available in state-controlled drug centers at nominal prices. It would advocate that marijuana and cocaine be sold commercially under the same kind of laws that govern alcohol. At the same time it would continuously teach and sermonize that in a sexual caring and loving society, trying to escape from life by using chemically induced means is sick and immoral behavior.

"To help eliminate the multi-billion-dollar crime-controlled drug traffic, a Church of Modern Moralities would advocate the total legalization of gambling. The income from gambling would be controlled by city-licensed gambling corporations with profits and taxes regulated by individual states. This dual control would gradually eliminate criminal involvement in gambling profits. Ultimately, legalizing and bringing human needs and compulsions into the light of day—compulsions such as gambling, prostitution, the use of drugs, pornography—would minimize or eliminate the seedbeds of crime in this country. Instead of inveighing against human immoralities, a Church of Modern Moralities would guide people into more satisfying ways to express their insecurities, fears, and loneliness, and need for love.

"A Church of Modern Moralities would underwrite these new freedoms with very harsh punishment for crimes with victims. It would advocate the death penalty, with absolutely no extenuating circumstances, for anyone directly responsible for killing another person.

"A Church of Modern Moralities would advocate the right to bear arms, but not small arms. Small arms have no other purpose in this modern world except to kill another person.

"A Church of Modern Moralities would advocate nationwide experiments to rehabilitate criminals, with sentences under ten years, in former military installations to eliminate prison overcrowding. Prisoners would live in barracks, be given army-style physical training programs, disciplined work projects, and disciplined vocational training in service related jobs. Prisoners would be forewarned that escapees, or those sentenced again for any crime, would have their original sentences doubled and would serve their remaining time in regular prisons.

"A Church of Modern Moralities would propose that in the age of nuclear deterrence and possible nuclear war, there is no need for American soldiers ever to fight again on foreign soil, and that it is immoral to build ships here in Adamsport, or anywhere else, for this purpose or to deploy American troops on foreign soil. A Church of Modern Moralities would advocate a defense policy for the North American continent based on long-range, highly mobile, land and sea nuclear missiles which can destroy an enemy just as effectively as short-range missiles or weapons of conventional warfare. Such a policy would allow us to withdraw our soldiers and close our military installations everywhere except in the Northern Hemisphere and advise European countries that it is not, and never will be, America's intention to fight a territorial war on someone else's soil. Such a moral policy would immediately put the spotlight on potential Soviet aggression in Europe and in Third World countries. If such aggression continued, the American people could warn the Soviets that they could not achieve world domination at our expense, or on the backs of other nations, and that if they continued to do so, they would be inviting long-range nuclear retaliation as well as our total military cooperation with any threatened nation.

"A Church of Modern Moralities would encourage the formation of a College for Modern Moralities to be underwritten by Protestants, Catholics, Jews, Mohammedans, and other religions of the world to study, create, and revise moral attitudes in any areas that would help all men and women to live in closer harmony with their own realities."

Matt was well aware of the growing shock on the glazed faces of many of the congregation. He saw Jill shake her head in amused wonder. He saw Father Timothy touch Irene's shoulder, whisper something in her ear, and then, as more than a dozen others had done, edge out of the pew. Followed by Irene, Father Timothy walked out of the church.

But like a man standing on the parapet of a building, Matt knew it was too late. He had to jump. The final plunge might be to his self-destruction, but it was impossible to pull back.

"To create the environment for this modern morality and build a new kind of church which could weave spiritual and secular concerns into a meaningful tapestry, a Church of Modern Moralities should go back to our origins and return sex worship to the church. God isn't dead! God isn't moribund! Like His creatures, during the past two thousand years God has been growing, too! Let's worship Him as Ourselves! Let's create a sex-positive religion—not just for the young, but a lifelong religion where penile-vaginal penetration, or a loving kiss, or the touch of caring minds and bodies, and the adoration and wonder and the miracle of our flesh and blood and bones is the kind of sacrament a twenty-first-century God would appreciate.

"A return to sex worship would need a new kind of liturgy and eucharist. Human beings need symbols in their lives and easily graspable ritual ways of defining experiences and emotions that are beyond words. Thousands of sexual symbols and myths that have been purposely buried by Christian fathers need to be exhumed and revealed in their true origins. A Modern Moral congregation would delight in the simplicity and relevance of these early creations for our lives today.

"Above you, the dome of this church is circled by closed lotus blossoms culminating at the peak of the dome in an open lotus blossom. Was the designer of this church aware that the open lotus blossom is an ancient Indian symbol for the vagina? Did he realize that 'the jewel in the lotus' is a metaphor for the human sexual merger? Behind me is a cross without a plaster Jesus nailed to it. Regardless of its meaning for Christianity, a Church of Modern Moralities would rediscover and rejoice in the original meaning of the cross, which was also a symbol of the penis penetrating the vagina.

"In the ancient Hindu religion the lingam standing upright in the yoni was an object of veneration. Sculptured and revealed in new idealistic stylings, we should exalt human sexuality and ourselves as God with similar modern religious symbols that encourage every man, woman, and child in our new moral church to grow up fully aware of the imagery and the exaltation of life processes reflected in these never changing fertility symbols. In such a church, men and women sermonizing on love and God and human loving would reveal the origins of phallic worship common to all religions. Our ministers, priests, and rabbis would be unashamed of the original concept of the Trinity, which is symbolized by three separate parts of the male genitals. Two testicles and one penis together form a T which is another form of an ancient sexual cross. So sacred is this symbol in some ancient religions that the Assyrian gods Assur and Anu and Hoa were simply names of the penis and the right and left testicles.

"In our Church of Modern Moralities we won't hesitate to explore the thousands of aspects of human sexuality revealed in the original books of the Old Testament. Our modern congregation would be delighted to know that in a male-dominated society the family jewels were so sacred that in the twenty-third chapter of Deuteronomy, Jehovah advised his people: 'He that is wounded in the stones, or hath his privy member cut off shall not enter the congregation of the Lord.'

No man could possibly be a religious leader if he were shorn of any part of his testicles. In chapter 25 of Deuteronomy you will learn that, 'If two men fight together, and the wife of one draws near to rescue her husband from the hand of one attacking him, and she puts out her hand and seizes him by the genitals: then you shall cut off her hand: you shall not pity her.'

"Is it any wonder after thousands of years of such dictums—even if a woman is saving a man from his enemy, she can't kick his enemy in the balls or, worse, yank them—is it any wonder that even today many women are reluctant to touch their husband's penis? By exploring early sex worship we can reorient it for the twenty-first century, which has only recently discovered that the female body is better designed for survival and nonstop loving than the male body. And our new Moral Stemwinders would never run out of interesting sermons on the origin of sex worship, because there are literally hundreds of thousands of sexual meanings preserved in visual art and words. Not just from the past two thousand years but from thirty thousand years of known human history and long before Christ was ever dreamed of. And the congregations would discover that the morals of these early people, who never heard of Jesus Christ as their savior, were just as good as, or better than, the morals of latter day saints and prophets.

"Our Church of Modern Moralities would restore the original meaning of the Ark, which was the divine symbol of the earth, and hence the female principle. The Ark contained and succored the germ of animated nature. Properly understood, Noah's Ark and the Ark of the Covenant are sacred receptacles symbolizing the vagina, the divine wisdom and power, and the Great Mother from which all things come.

The Ark of the Covenant contained not only the Table of Laws but also Aaron's rod, which sprang to life and budded, thus symbolizing fertility and making the Ark the repository of the creative deity. And our sex worshippers should discover how this symbol developed in a different but similar way in the Roman Catholic pyx, the holy receptacle of the Body of Christ, and in Mary, who became the tabernacle of God.

"Amazed at the wonder of our sexuality, our new moralists would explore other religions. In Egypt, they would discover, the Ark again contains the most universal religious symbols. The Triune commences with the male testicles and harbors a phallus, an egg, and a serpent. In pre-Christian days the phallus often represented the sun—the male generative principle, the Creator. The egg represented the passive female principle; and the snake was both the destroyer and the creator. Understanding Egyptian mythology would give our modern moralists a very different interpretation of the story of Adam and Eve, which was written much later. Or compare this sexual trinity to the cylinder on the altar of the Hindu temple. Here the pedestal is the symbol of Brahma, the creator of all that is in the universe. The vase (the vagina) stands for Vishnu, the preserver, the female principle. The cylinder within the vase represents Shiva, the Destroyer, the male God—also the lingam or penis. Now compare this to Adam and Eve and the serpent, or the Father and Son and the Holy Spirit, and discover that in many respects the snake has meanings equivalent to the Holy Spirit. In either case they were recognized as the spirit of love between man and his Creator. And our modern moralists would discover that in primitive religions where symbolism is more apparent, the snake is actually a throbbing penis in the anomalous position of creating both life and the suffering and evil attendant upon it.

"The ministers in our new Church of Modern Moralities will remind those who are about to be married that the wedding ring put on the bride's finger is really a symbol for the vagina, which only begins to function when the bride has inserted her finger through it in the act of marriage. Thus a double ring ceremony has a reverse and equally lovely sexual significance. When sex and religion are integrated into the realities of human sexuality, think of how much more fun and joyous the celebration attending a wedding service will be. Instead of worrying about sexual sin and a God who forgives sin, you will find a new loving God who equates human loving with divinity. You will be able to release your natural eroticism, sing hymns to your sexual self, and discover that our real problem as interacting individuals and as a nation is that we refuse to recognize our basic interdependence, sexual and otherwise.

"When that happens we'll sing new hymns, and Walt Whitman's poem, which was being written when the cornerstone of this church was being laid, will be etched on the front door of every church:

> I too, following many and follow'd by many, inaugurate a
> new religion. . .
> Each is not for its own sake,
> I say the whole earth and all the stars in the sky are for religion's sake.
> I say no man has ever yet been half devout enough,
> None has ever adored or worship'd half enough,
> None has begun to think how divine he himself is, and how
> certain the future is.
> My comrade. . . share with me two greatnesses, and a third one
> rising inclusive and more resplendent,
> The greatness of Love and Democracy, and the greatness of
> Religion.
> I say that the real and permanent grandeur of these States
> must be their religion.

"On June 11, 1827, when the cornerstone of this church was laid, Adamsport had 280 dwellings, occupied by 827 males and 798 females and 13 coloreds. (In those days black people were listed with other chattel.) One of the benefactors and prominent members of this church, a man named Thomas Greenleaf, wondered, in his cornerstone laying speech, about the future: 'In looking forward to the period when another temple shall rise upon the ruins of this one, we are naturally led to reflect upon what will be the nature of society here. How vastly improved! How far surpassing us in intellectual and moral excellence will be the generation then existing. Today, our hearts rejoice in the contemplation of the increasing virtue and wisdom of the world. . . .' "

Matt smiled at the numbed congregation. "Let's rebuild this monument and prove to our forefathers that a Church of Love and Modern Moralities can point the way to moral excellence. Thank you. We'll sing hymn #230 in the Blue Book: 'Let Us Now Sing the Praises of Famous Men.' Appropriately, the words are taken from Ecclesiasticus 41, one of the Apocryphal books of the Bible."

13

Ordinarily after the "Closing Words," a UU minister shakes hands individually with his congregation. With more than five hundred people surging toward the Parish Hall, both Littlejohn and Matt realized that this was not practical. They led the way, followed close on their heels by the people from the first row of the pews, who were suddenly relaxed and chattering noisily.

Peachy was reaching for Matt. "Get up on the stage where they can see you," she said. "There's a microphone attached to the podium."

"Limit it to a half-hour," Paul said nervously. "There's a lot of unhappy Christians out there. If they were lions, they'd probably reverse roles and toss you to them."

"See if you can find Gillian," Matt told Peachy. "She was sitting with my wife and Father Timothy. I saw Irene leave with Tim before I finished."

Peachy shook her head. "Sorry, chum, I wouldn't know Gillian from Eve. If she still loves you, maybe she'll get through the crowds to you." Matt noticed tears in her eyes, and he guessed that she wanted to hug him. "It was great, Matt," she said, "but I'm probably one of the few who think so. Take my advice. Give them only fifteen minutes to rip you up. Then leave by the side door. I'll wait for you there and drive you to my father's house."

Matt had forgotten that he had promised to talk with Sylvie. "I'd prefer to fall into bed with you," he said. "I think the time has come."

"Sorry," Peachy smiled sadly at him. "Not today. I told Saul that I'd be home by three, but I'll take a rain check."

By this time the Parish Hall was jammed. A few hundred had managed to get coffee or bouillon, but it was impossible for the rest to get near the serving tables. Mashed together they were arguing with each other or staring with astonishment or grim faces at Matt and Littlejohn on the stage. Over the roar of conversation and shocked emotions it was impossible to sort out any particular conversations.

Turning up the volume on the microphone, Littlejohn tapped on it to get attention. "I doubt if anyone in Adamsport has ever heard a more provocative sermon," he said. "Matt Godwin has raised questions and issues that we could spend the whole afternoon discussing. Before you get too angry with him, I hope that you'll keep in mind that he has offered a proposal for a new religion that is really a kind of Third Force, standing somewhere between our political leadership and Catholic morality as well as Protestant morality as it is reflected particularly in fundamentalist beliefs. You may prefer the Moral Majority. You may not believe in Matt's Church of Modern Moralities, but he is not denying God. Rather, he is offering a belief in a new kind of God and a religion for secular humanists."

"It's a religion for pagans!" a man shouted. "You'd better reread the Gospel of Matthew. 'Away with you Satan! For it is written. You shall worship the Lord your God and Him only shall you serve.'"

"I am serving God, by loving all of us as God." Matt smiled. "I love the sheer wonder and mystery of Us. I'm in awe at the fourscore years or more your heart and mine will circulate our blood. I'm astounded at the miracle that our brain correlates and remembers. I'm amazed that our mouths eat food and drink and our stomachs process it for our nourishment and our bladders and intestines defecate and urinate the portions we don't need for survival. Above all I delight in one-to-one sexual communication during which a man and woman can transcend themselves and re-create themselves literally and figuratively. You are God. But I refuse to suffer for your sins, or Adam's and Eve's, and I don't need a Son of God or a Mary or a Holy Spirit to save me. I can save myself by celebrating with God in this amazing Hall of Mirrors where all we can ever know or see are His reflections. You and Me and all of Us."

"Are you a man or an animal?" an elderly woman who was waving her hand demanded.

"I am God's animal, but I'm not confined to a rutting season," Matt laughed. "I can make love with my penis or with a caring touch and caring words every day of my life."

"You say you love everybody," a man in the back of the hall shouted. "What about your old man? From the looks of things, you don't love him."

"Loving a person doesn't mean controlling him or trying to make him believe as you do," Matt said calmly. "I refer you to the Gospel of Matthew and you'll discover even Jesus accepted the inevitable. Some people would not believe that he was the Son of God. He told them to turn the other cheek and love their enemies. Maybe it's you who thinks they are your enemies and not them."

Matt acknowledged Dorothy Belcher, whose anger bubbled in her words as she spoke. "There are a great many people here today, Matthew Godwin, who are not Unitarian Universalists, and I want them to understand that although most of us do not believe that Jesus was the Son of God, we do live by the principles of Jesus Christ. We certainly don't approve of your 'free love' philosophy, or running around naked, or most of the other things that you call modern morality."

"That's your privilege, Dorothy. Fortunately we live in a country where the government gives us the freedom to follow our religious beliefs whatever they may be."

"Running around bareass and going to bed with your neighbor's wife aren't religious beliefs," a grey-haired man standing just below the stage shouted at him. "It's sick and even Jesus Christ says so. You're a sex pervert, Matthew Godwin. I'm not a member of this church, but I've lived in this city all my life. If you try to preach that kind of evil, Godless thinking, if you try to turn this church into a pornographer's paradise, we'll turn the city out against you."

Matt shrugged. "I won't ask you who 'we' are," he said. "But being naked or not being monogamous and sleeping with more than one woman have been incorporated into many religious beliefs.

The Arabs have long permitted harems for those who can afford them, and many wives assured a Mormon's entry into heaven. In Canada there used to be a religious sect called the Doukhobors, who attended their religious services naked."

"In this crazy country," a woman who had been waving her hand said, "I'm sure that you'll attract plenty of followers. When do you invite them to Guyana and feed them all poison like Reverend Jones did?"

As she spoke Matt noted that Sylvanus Williams and the Lovejoys were leaving by a door on the far side of the hall. At least fifty hands were waving frantically in the crowd. "I'm sorry, but that's the last question I can answer. I'm not a Reverend Jones or a Reverend Moon. Hopefully, if a Church of Modern Moralities was born here today, it will be because there are a lot of Moral Stemwinders out there who believe that we can prevent even more senseless deaths than occurred in Jonestown. Interpersonal suicide and self-destruction is now taking place in this country at an unbelievable rate simply because most people have not evolved new moralities and a new religious way of life that works for them. They are strangled by the chains of sins and evils and repressions which were cooked up for them by a generation long dead. All that I am saying is that we need a new kind of believer. If you believe that you are God and you really accept all the joy and obligation that go with being a deity, you'll live a much happier life and you will never die in the conventional sense."

Part Two

No one born of God commits sin: for God's nature abides in him.

I John 3:19

To the pure all things are pure.

Titus 1:15

14

Peachy was waiting for Matt at the side door of the church. She squeezed his arm. "My car is on the next street. Run for your life." Inside the automobile she kissed him, but when he kissed her back more passionately, she pushed him away. "Oh dear God," she said, "I really do love you."

He stared at her. "Then why are you rejecting me?"

She grinned at him. "You may be God," she said, "but I'm not wholly convinced that I am—or as God that we can get away with it."

She drove her Chevrolet down Adams Boulevard toward a peninsula beyond Happy Shores that extends to the Atlantic with the Adamsport River on one side. "I don't know what my father is up to," she said, "but I don't trust him. He probably wants to have you put the Godwins' stamp of approval on Silly Willy's."

"I can do better than that," Matt said. "If the UU's would appoint me minister, I'd invite his strippers, male and female, to put on one show a month in the church. Properly handled, we could probably increase the revenues of the church so much that the members would never have to sell it." His hand was between her legs. Surprised that she wasn't wearing panties, he quickly cupped her vulva.

"Stop it," she gasped, "or God will be dead when I hit a telephone pole. Do you want me to drive right off the road?"

"Sure, pick a good spot. I'd rather make love to you than listen to your father's insanity."

"I told you, we don't have time."

"Why aren't you wearing panties?"

She laughed. "Because I had hoped we might have time, but alas, as you can see, we don't." She pulled up to a curb in front of a large new wooden house on a hill overlooking the Adamsport Bay. It was built Victorian style with attic cupolas and filigree adorning the gutters. "The Lovejoys are here already." She pointed to a Cadillac in the driveway. "The Mercedes sedan belongs to Daddy."

Sylvie met them at the front door. "Your sermon was terrific, Matt. Better than I had hoped for. Come on in. Roje and Emily are out on the verandah having a drink. I just told Roje that if the three of us can work together, within a year you could become the most famous preacher in America."

He led them through a broadloomed living room that had been recently remodeled. With white and gold modern furniture and framed prints on the walls, it lacked a woman's touch and gave the feeling of an expensive hotel lobby created by an interior decorator.

"Do you live here alone?" Matt asked.

"Hell no. It's a boarding house." Sylvie grinned. "At the moment I only have a couple of boarders. They're both on the strip circuit. They show their tits and pussies at Silly Willy's for ten days, four times a day, and then they move on to another city. I brought one of them, Milly the Dilly, to church to hear you this morning. Right now both of the gals are at the club getting ready for the Sunday afternoon show."

Drinks in hand, Roje and Emily were sitting on a glass-enclosed porch that gave a breath-taking view of the Atlantic and the skyscrapers of Boston, eight miles away, etched against a clear sky. Peachy shook hands with Roje and gave his fingers a special squeeze. She smiled at Emily. "It's nice to meet you, Mrs. Lovejoy. I'm sure that your husband thinks I'm a terrible pest, but I really am glad that you both came to church this morning."

Trying to erase a vision of Peachy sitting naked on his stomach, Roje congratulated Matt but also warned him: "Adamsport is not a free-thinking community. Irish-born Catholics, who dominate this area, have been brainwashed. They know they aren't God, and they are damn sure that you're not. I realize that you are challenging your old man, but do you really want to take on the whole country?" Roje grinned. "It's one thing to do it the way I do. If anyone gets shook up by the novels I write, I quickly tell them they must remember that it is all fiction. My stories take place sometime in a future that may never happen, and usually I don't do as my characters do."

"Mowing your front yard naked must have been oversight," Matt said with a twinkly smile. "Or maybe the real you took charge for a moment. But to answer your question. Someone has to be active in this passive world. Maybe I'm the last heretic. The sermon was a trial balloon." He laughed. "But I agree with you, I can't keep it floating and full of air all by myself. I need disciples."

"You're not going to get them in Adamsport," Emily said. "You're a very charming man and a very persuasive speaker. I'll wash your feet anytime. Younger women, and a few women my age who still think young, will love to play Goddess to your God or Mary Magdalene to your Jesus. But older women and most men will hate you. You make them feel insecure."

"Agreed," Matt said, "but I didn't specify the age or sex of my disciples."

Sylvie gestured to a bar at one end of the porch. "Help yourself. A little alcohol will get you in the mood to hear a strange story I want to tell you. It won't take too long." He smiled at Peachy. "It's a fairy tale—one I never told you when you were a wee lass. Like all fairy tales, it happened long ago in another land."

Plopping into an old-fashioned rocking chair while Matt poured himself a vodka and Peachy a glass of white wine, Sylvie began.

"Unlike most fairy tales, if you really believe this one, it could come true." With a quizzical half-smile Sylvie's eyes wandered from face to face as he spoke, trying to gauge his listeners' reactions. "Once upon a time, nearly fifty years ago, during World War II, in what was known as the CBI—the China-Burma-India Theater of War—there was a young, very brash lieutenant colonel. Coming up through the ranks as a career army man, he was a master sergeant when World War II broke out. He had trained in army finance, which is basically the process of paying the troops and meeting army payrolls. Within a year after Pearl Harbor, Sergeant Gamble became Lieutenant Colonel Gamble. He was attached to the Air Transport Command, a division of the U.S. Air Force, which had established supply bases up and down the Assam Valley. Assam is now called Bangladesh. Operating under a joint command with the British, the generals were planning on a very long war with Japan. Japan had already moved across China and occupied Burma, and was knocking on India's back door. In the event that we couldn't defeat them in the Pacific, the plan was to fight the Japanese all the way across the China mainland.

"One of the Chinese leaders who was very famous at the time, Chiang Kai-shek, convinced the Americans that a well-supplied Chinese army could defeat the Japanese without involving American troops too much. In typical American fashion, when we get involved in other peoples' wars, we backed the wrong horse. After we defeated the Japs in the Pacific—and not in China—another Chinese leader, Mao Tse-tung, as you well know, finally drove Chiang Kai-shek into the Pacific and on to the island of Formosa. But, for at least four or five years before that happened, our generals were convinced that, even though it might be a Thirty Years' War, we had no choice but to help Chiang Kai-shek. So for several hundred miles along the Indian side of the huge Himalaya Mountains, we, along with the British, established a chain of supply bases and airstrips to fly soldiers and equipment into China. Every day, for many years, army airplanes known as C-47's, which had two fans (propellers), flew back and forth across the highest mountains in the world and brought supplies into China. Of course, many of these planes never got to the other side of the mountain. Quite a few hundred of them disappeared entirely, and their pilots were never heard of again.

"Headquarters for this huge army operation was in Calcutta in a place called Hastings Mill. Before the war it had actually manufactured jute, which India exported all over the world. Taken over by the Americans, it was remodeled with offices and luxurious quarters for top army brass. It became a transient way station for soldiers being assigned to bases in the Assam Valley or into China. Among other things, Hastings Mill offered an Officers' Club equal to any night club in America, with daily floor shows and the longest bar in the world."

Sylvie paused and then, satisfied that he had their attention, continued. "Now, in those days, long before most Chinese people had been converted to Stalinism, China had its own paper currency which Americans obligingly engraved for them in Philadelphia and shipped to China in huge metal containers. But as you well know, even today paper money, when you print too much of it, has a way of becoming devalued. You need more and more of it to buy the things you need. Finally, when the people realize that the government is playing around with them, inflation goes from bad to worse. Pretty soon, although the leaders originally promised that you could swap the paper currency for gold, a law is passed that you no longer can.

"Today we have stopped pretending. Everyone knows that paper money may not be worth the paper it's printed on. But whether in a democracy or a dictatorship, there's no choice: control of the money supply is in the hands of the leaders. So it's put up and shut up. In those days, long ago, that I am telling you about, people still believed in fairy tales, and our financial leaders usually tried to maintain an aura of honesty. In the case of China it quickly became necessary to underwrite the country's financial credibility—especially so because we needed Chinese soldiers to fight the Japanese.

"So, back in Washington, D.C., the Pentagon convinced the Treasury Department that we'd better back the Chinese national currency with gold, or else! How much gold was shipped to China probably no one will ever know. But our hero, Colonel Gamble, arrived in Calcutta sometime in 1943 with twenty wooden boxes tightly nailed and strapped. These boxes were destined for China, and each of them contained twenty gold ingots, or bullion as some people call it. You've probably never seen a gold ingot. They're not very bulky, but gold is very, very heavy. They weighed 27½ pounds each. In those days the value of gold was $35 an ounce. Each ingot weighed 450 troy ounces, so each ingot was worth $15,755."

Sylvie smiled, happy to note that he now had their rapt attention. "To fully understand this story you must understand that in those happier economic days you could buy a fifth of Chivas Regal for about three dollars. Gasoline was twenty cents a gallon, a package of cigarettes was about twelve cents. Not realizing that they were encouraging the manpower of America to smoke themselves to death, the army gave cigarettes to soldiers with their rations." With that, Sylvie lighted a cigarette. "Give or take a few dollars, Colonel Gamble's ingots (and I use the possessive advisedly) were worth about $6.5 million.

"Colonel Gamble had no love for the Chinese, or for the Indians, for that matter. To him they were simply 'chinks' or 'wogs,' and what inflation was doing to the Chinese national currency and the war effort was really of no concern to him. But being a finance officer, he did have a high regard for money. The shipment of gold from America was loaded onto two six-by-six army trucks and taken to a motor pool on an airstrip near Calcutta, run by the Army Air Force and called, of all things, Dum Dum. There, while Colonel Gamble waited for his orders to be cut to take the twenty boxes to Chengkung, an army base on the China side of the Himalayas, the boxes were put in charge of a Master Sergeant Broke." Sylvie laughed. "His first name was Gofer. Sergeant Broke was dimly aware that the boxes contained gold ingots, but he was sure that no one would try to run away with them since each of the boxes weighed about 500 pounds. So he didn't have any sleepless nights over them. Not until later, that is. In the passing days, Broke wasn't aware that Colonel Gamble, by some devious means that occur only in fairy tales, had discovered that Captain Blue (his first name was True) and his copilot, Lieutenant Poorman, were assigned to fly Colonel Gamble and his ingots across the Hump, as the Himalayas were called, to Chengkung.

"Sharing a few drinks together in the Officers' Club, Gamble, Blue, and Poorman became very friendly. They discussed the hazards of flying the Himalayas in planes with only two propellers and the sad fact, not generally publicized, that quite a few pilots had lost their lives when their planes went down in the three-mile-high mountains. Both Blue and Poorman had been in the CBI for several years, and they were happy that soon after this flight they were going to be rotated back to good old Uncle Sugar.

"'Speaking of Sugar,' Colonel Gamble joked with them, 'it sure would be nice if after the war we all had a few gold ingots tucked away. It would make this waste of our financially productive years much more tolerable.'

"Feeling quite exhilarated from the Indian gin they were drinking straight with a dash of bitters, Blue and Poorman got Colonel Gamble's message loud and clear. 'Instead of flying the Hump with that shipment, we could fly south,' Poorman suggested, quite sure that he was only playing a game. 'With that kind of mazuma, we could live like rajahs.'

"But living in India for the rest of his life—even if he had his own elephants and a harem—was not Colonel Gamble's idea of the good life. Anyway, Captain Blue had a better idea. Of course it was only an idea, mind you, inspired by the good fellowship of their coming flight together, and the gin which they were washing down with dozens of shrimps, served by Muslim waiters who watched, wondering why they didn't drop dead from eating the 'uneatable.'

"'What if our plane developed engine trouble and all three of us had to parachute out?' Blue wondered aloud. 'Even if a search were made for the plane, we could make sure it was never found by the simple process of checking it out with a different longitude and latitude than where we actually would land. We could have been driven off course by a storm.'

"Poorman carried the story a little bit further. 'Many pilots have crashed and have managed to walk out,' he said. 'It takes them about a month to get back and the natives usually help them.' He pointed to the American flag stitched on their leather flying jackets and the message written on the reverse in various tribal dialects. 'It says a reward of salt will be given for helping an American flyer to get back to his base. With a little bit of luck,' Poorman laughed, still thinking he was plotting a Hollywood movie, 'after the war we could meet right here in Calcutta, arrange a safari, or whatever you call it in India, and drive a couple of trucks into the Himalayas, pick up the loot, and split it fifty-fifty.'

"'Actually, there's a better way,' Colonel Gamble told them, and it was obvious that he had figured it out in advance. 'Why should we take a chance on never finding the gold again? It would be much simpler if the plane crashed and there was no gold on it at all, but the gold was right here in Calcutta. It would certainly be preferable if after the war we didn't have to go plowing around the Himalayas searching for El Dorado.'

"That plan, of course, involved our Sergeant Broke. To make a long story short—and easier sounding than it was in reality—Gamble, Blue, and Poorman stopped pretending. The next day they shared a few snorts with Sergeant Broke, who grasped the idea immediately and was agreeable to a four-way split. That night they drove the two six-by-six trucks out in the country, where Sergeant Broke had already located an abandoned pile of bricks. Carefully unfastening the boxes, they loaded the gold into barracks bags and repacked the boxes with their less valuable cargo all nicely cushioned with good Indian earth and drove back to Dum Dum, where, after an exhausting day, they all had a good night's sleep.

"Two days later, following Colonel Gamble's orders, and with the help of several enlisted men, they drove the trucks out to the runway where the C-47 was waiting. In the meantime, Colonel Gamble advised Sergeant Broke that he, Blue, and Poorman would be back in Calcutta just as soon as possible. In the meantime, Sergeant Broke had an important job to do. Colonel Gamble had bought a house for $3,600. Actually, it would be called a villa today. Built of stone, it was located in an affluent British section of Calcutta. Sergeant Broke's job, which wasn't easy but, as Colonel Gamble pointed out, was a lot easier than walking out of a jungle from the top of a mountain, was to bury the 400 ingots in the floor of the living room. Then one bright day when this war was over, the four of them would have a reunion in Calcutta and dig it up. From that day on they would enjoy life off the top of the hog.

"Blue and Poorman had revved up the engine and were about to take off in the C-47 when, to Colonel Gamble's horror, two army nurses ran up to the plane, waving their orders. They had been dispatched to Chengkung on this very plane. Colonel Gamble stared at them in total shock. 'No way!' he shouted angrily. It was one thing for the three of them to abandon ship in the middle of the Himalayas but something else again to explain to two young ladies their reason for doing this."

"What happened to the gold?" Peachy, who had been listening open-mouthed, interrupted Sylvie.

"Have patience, I'm coming to that," he said. "You fail to understand what complete consternation these women caused. Blue and Poorman turned off the engines. Gamble spent the next two hours trying to get the nurses' orders changed to another flight. He almost convinced a chicken colonel, who took the problem up with a one-star general. But the general's reaction was that, although it was a secret shipment, neither the gold nor the secrecy of the shipment endangered the two young women, who didn't have to know what was in the boxes anyway.

"Waving forlornly to them as they took off, Sergeant Broke wondered if Gamble would try to convince the ladies to jump with them and thus be obligated to split the loot six ways instead of four, or, worse, would arrive in Chengkung with six boxes of bricks and have to explain where the gold went. But Broke himself had no choice. For the next week, every moment that he could take off from the base, he worked like a maniac and finally got nearly eleven thousand pounds of gold into the living room of Gamble's villa and buried under the floor, which he carefully recemented and covered with a cheap Oriental rug.

"Expecting any day that Gamble might confess and implicate him, Broke spent a miserable week. He pictured himself handcuffed and flown back to Leavenworth, where he would spend the rest of his life. But the week passed and then another and then another and finally a month, and nothing happened. A few weeks before Hiroshima was blown off the face of the earth, Broke learned, after discreet inquiries to a friend of his who worked in the aircraft operations office at Dum Dum, that in fact the C-47 had crashed. Gamble, Poorman, Blue, and the two nurses were presumed dead. No mention was made that the plane was carrying gold ingots. Broke suspected that this was a secret still being maintained at the very top level of army brass. Then, about a month later, his friend told Broke that the Colonel Gamble he had inquired about and a nurse named Anne Winship had stumbled into a supply base—Shamshenagrar—far up in the Assam Valley. Nearly dead from starvation, Winship told the base commander that they had all survived the crash but Lieutenant Poorman had broken his leg. Slowly inching down a hazardous, snow-covered mountain, Gamble and Blue had started fighting over whether they should abandon Poorman. They weren't too happy either that Poorman was being comforted by Millie Loser, the other nurse, who had been snuggling with him all night to keep them both warm. Then, one day when it became apparent they could no longer carry Poorman and survive themselves, Gamble trudged off. Captain Blue pointed his .45 at him and threatened to kill him. At which point Gamble charged into Blue, who was standing on the edge of a precipice, and pushed him over—but not before the gun went off, killing Millie. According to Anne, Gamble told her that it was survival of the fittest."

Sylvie shrugged. "Poor Broke. For many years he never knew whether Gamble had told Anne the truth about the gold, but he finally discovered, long after the war was over, that Gamble was confined in a veterans' mental hospital in the States and that he constantly raved about some mythical gold that was ready for the picking up in the Himalayas. Broke also located Anne Winship. She believed Gamble's story and was ready to go with Broke on an expedition into the Himalayas to see if they could find the gold, but by that time Broke had other fish to fry and he finally convinced her that Gamble was really off his rocker."

Sylvie got up and poured himself another drink.

Roje laughed. "That's the best World War II story I've ever heard. Someone should write it into one of those thrillers."

"Help yourself," Sylvie grinned at him. "People like that kind of shit better than some of the stuff you write."

"Are you Sergeant Broke?" Peachy demanded, scowling at him.

Sylvie shrugged. "I told you that it's a fairy tale. But if you wish, it might come true."

"If that gold is still available," Roje mused, "its current market price is about $90 million."

"You said *you*," Emily said. "Who do you mean by 'you'?"

"Roje and Matt," Sylvie said evenly. "You and Peachy can participate, or, if you prefer, you can stand on the sidelines and cheer them on."

Roje shook his head. "Sorry, Sylvie, I'm not interested in a trip to Calcutta."

"The gold is much closer than that," Sylvie said.

"I'm sure the FBI is probably well aware of it," Matt said. "If not, why hasn't Sergeant Broke already sold it?"

"For many years Broke was sure that Gamble would crack up and tell the truth and someone would believe him. A few years ago Gamble died. Then, Broke took a little trip to India. The villa was occupied by an Indian family who had never heard of Gamble. The cheap Oriental rug that he had bought was still on the floor, and it appeared that his cement job had not been tampered with. Crossing his fingers, he took a chance and bought the house for 70,000 rupees, or about $20,000. It took him about a month and a sacrifice of three of the ingots, worth at the time close to a million dollars. An Indian banker took them, no questions asked, for half the market price, which was then $600 an ounce." Sylvie grinned. "It wasn't easy, but three months later the gold was reburied, in another villa, on a small island in the Caribbean."

"What island?" Peachy demanded.

"All in good time," Sylvie said. "First we should be in overall agreement."

"I fail to see what all this has to do with Roje and me," Matt said impatiently. "Let's drop this Sergeant Broke charade. I assume that you also are Broke." Matt couldn't help grinning at the play on words. "Why haven't you got rid of the gold? I'm sure that you could sell it, even at half-price, and enjoy your ill-gotten gains all by yourself."

"Up until now, I haven't really needed that kind of money. Not that I felt guilty about it," Sylvie said coolly. "Keep in mind that Broke didn't steal the gold. He simply became an inadvertent caretaker. In any event, because of my other activities, which I assure you are not criminal but some people think are morally reprehensible, I decided to let well enough alone. Getting the gold safely to the Caribbean, a couple of years ago, nearly gave me an ulcer. Then there was the problem of what to do next. But recently an interesting solution occurred to me. Right at the moment, I need about ten million dollars to underwrite a new franchise company I am planning to launch. I agree with you; the gold can probably be sold at about one half the current market price, but I think a really interested party could do even better. What if it could be traded for about 45 million? All I want is 10 million. My problem is that I need to have that 10 million properly laundered. It must be apparent to you that I can't suddenly appear with $10 million without tempting the Internal Revenue Service to ask how I got it," Sylvie chuckled. "On the other hand, a wealthy Godwin could lend it to me."

Matt grimaced. "Why does everyone talk about money to the *poor* Godwin? Call up my father. If you make sure that Ike gets the First Parish Church cheap, he might really loan you $10 million, especially if you offer him collateral like that."

"No thanks," Sylvie smiled. "Ike Godwin may be temporarily friendly with me, but he's not very happy about Silly Willy's. If all of us work together on this, you'll have more than enough money to buy your First Parish Church. And you could make your old man happy, too. You could build Controlled Power Corporation headquarters right across the street from the church, where the Saven-Haven Building is located. Lennie Cashman, who owns the building, told me that he would be glad to sell it, if the price is right, and move the store to a new location in Adamsport."

"Why do you persist in the notion that I want to buy this church?" Matt demanded.

"Until I heard your sermon, I wasn't too sure," Sylvie said, "but now I think that I'm on the right track. Personally, I think you're crazy. I'm sure that you will have a hard time convincing anyone that Sylvanus Williams is God—let alone all the other nuts out there in the world. But if you are going to persist, you're going to need your own church, and you will need God's only real power on this earth—money, and lots of it."

"That's the Devil's power," Peachy scowled at her father. Up until now Peachy didn't really believe in the Devil, but listening to her father's temptation of Matt, she was nervous that Matt might be seduced by him. Peachy was sure that any deal with Sylvie would carry more penalties than Faust's pact with Mephistopheles. "You seem to forget that Matt is proposing a completely new moral structure for Americans," she said. "Building a new church on stolen money is the kind of sick morality that he's preaching against."

"There's one thing I don't understand," Emily intervened. "It would seem to me, Sylvie, whether you're the Devil tempting a Godwin or not, Roje and Matt are in no better position than you are to launder your money. They'd be investigated, too."

Emily hadn't told Roje, but she had actually spent a delightful afternoon in this very house in bed with this man, and now she was seeing him in a very different light. Sylvie was obviously dangerous and a man of greater subtleties than she had realized.

"You have to understand, Emily," he said in a reassuring tone, "ministers with legitimate churches are not required to publicize specific donors. Let's assume from the standpoint of the world out there that Matt has touched a common chord with a few million Americans, and they send him their hard-earned money in bits and pieces." Sylvie laughed. "Like a lot of other evangelists, it wouldn't take him long to accumulate $45 million or so—and I'm in no hurry for my ten; he could feed it to me gradually."

"I don't see why you need me," Roje said.

"For moral reinforcement. Someone has to convince Matt that doing good, even if a lot of people don't agree with his viewpoint of good, has many different perspectives. Money itself and how it is used changes one's beliefs about good and evil." Sylvie laughed. "But I must admit, if I were in either of your shoes and someone made me this offer, I'd think that I was entitled to a small piece of the action. So I wouldn't be unhappy if you would each slice off a million or two for your personal use. I'm sure you could roll the money over into your own private accounts."

Roje shook his head. "It's a long time since I read the Gospels, but this seems to me like the temptations of Jesus that Matthew wrote about. What did Jesus tell the Devil when the Devil challenged him to turn the stones into bread?"

"I'm not Jesus, and I won't give Jesus' answer." Matt was grinning, but it was obvious that he was intrigued. "In some cases bread may come first. But I'm not interested in being nailed to a cross, either."

Peachy was suddenly afraid of the faraway look in his eyes. "My father may not be the Devil," she said, "but, to use a Yiddish expression, Sylvie's obviously a gonif—a thief." She leaned over Matt and massaged his neck lovingly. "I think we should forget this fairy tale. Come on, Matt, I have to go home to Saul."

Sylvie stood up. "Think it over, Matt. And keep one thing in mind. Gonifs make the world go around. Anyone in America who has a million dollars or more in all probability is, or has been, a thief. America would never have come into being or continued to exist without thievery. Peachy simply doesn't understand the many dimensions of morality. Maybe none of the Godwins ever made a fast deal, but when it came to making money, the Vanderbilts, Rockefellers, Goulds, Fisks, and Carnegies had their own standards of morality. Many wealthy Bostonians can trace their family fortunes to the slave trade. Whether God is up there in heaven or just simple folks like us, God knows the truth. If you are one of the owners of the American Banana Plantation, you or your ancestors got control of it by financial skullduggery."

Sylvie shrugged. "Why is Sergeant Broke's gold worth ten times more than when it was expropriated? Simply because our political leaders found a new way to cover their sins: printing money instead of working for it."

Matt laughed. "Thievery as such doesn't bother me. Man as God is in a never ending process of dealing with his own imperfections. Man as God never stops trying. But obviously man as God would be lonesome without the Devil." He shook his head. "You're an interesting man, Sylvie, but I'm not too sure I'd be happy trying to build a new moral world on your *comme ci, comme ca* moralities. What do you think, Roje?"

Roje tossed his palms in the air. "I think we've been listening to a Grimm's fairy tale. If you remember, the Brothers Grimm always got rid of the white knights and saints; the world is filled with dragons and evil monsters who don't hesitate to eat the good guys alive."

Surprised to discover that Sylvie was a far more devious person than she had realized and wondering why, although he had revealed many intimate things about himself to her, he had never told her about India or gold, Emily said, "Before we all leave, I'd like to know on what island in the Caribbean did the famous Sergeant Broke rebury his gold?"

Sylvie patted her arm reassuringly. "Before I tell you, I think we need a consensus. Is this a fairy tale or isn't it? Are you being tempted by the Devil or aren't you? Do you really believe in your First Church of Modern Moralities, Matt? I'm sure that a lot of Americans would think that your idea of a more moral world isn't much better than mine."

15

Two warring days later, spent trying to decide whether Sylvanus Williams's gold was a fairy tale and, if it weren't, whether he should personally get involved with him and Robert Lovejoy and, if he did, why he felt compelled to "take on" the whole world when he couldn't even convince his family that his motives were pure and healthy, Matt ate breakfast with his sons, served by Mrs. Goodale.

Irene was still in bed or avoiding him in some other part of the house. Eating through a mountain of cereal, bacon and eggs, and toast, both Ink and Able seemed happily oblivious to the tension and eruptions of vocal anger between him and their mother.

"I think your mother and I need a little breathing space," Matt told them. "I'm going to sleep on the boat for a few nights." He knew that Irene would stay away from the *Odyssey*, their fifty-foot sailing yacht docked at the Adamsport Marina. Irene sailed occasionally with him and the boys, but she preferred golf and the companionship of her female friends at the country club. Getting no response from the boys, Matt wondered whether they realized what was happening on another level in their family.

"I guess you know that Grandpa Ike is very angry with me and that I'm no longer working at the shipyard," he said. "And I guess it's pretty obvious that your mother and I can't seem to discuss our problems without screaming and yelling at each other, and your mother is always sobbing because she thinks that I don't love all of you."

"Are you really going to be a minister?" Able asked, his mouth full of eggs. "Grandpa was pretty angry, but I like hearing you preach and giving everyone hell. I don't know what the yelling is all about."

Ink looked at his younger brother scornfully. "Grandpa Ike doesn't want him to preach, dummy. Preachers don't make any money. We'll all be poor." He stared at his father. "Are you going to let Gramp kick you out of Controlled Power, too?"

Matt shrugged. "He can't do it alone. He has to get the approval of a lot of other men who help run the company. That's probably why he's flying back to Los Angeles today. But you don't have to worry. You won't be poor. Controlled Power and the shipyards will be here waiting for you and Able when you're old enough to take over and run them."

"Do you like Gillian better than Grandma Sarah?" Able asked.

"Sarah was my mother." Matt smiled, and gave him a hug. "I really don't know Jill too well, but I guess she's a very nice lady." He knew that Irene and Father Timothy had waited for Jill in Irene's car. To their surprise, when Jill joined them after the sermon, she had been enthusiastic. "I don't think that he's putting down Catholics," she told Father Tim. "I think Matt's saying that we should explore other moral options that might work better than some we have sworn allegiance to."

"Mom says that Jill defended you," Ink said. "That made Gramp very angry with her and they had their first fight. Is Jill in love with you?"

"Not like that." Matt decided that now was not the time to explore the many aspects of loving with the boys, but he was amused that a twelve-year-old and a fifteen-year-old boy could spout adult insanities. "You can still love people and disagree with them. I'm sure that Jill loves Gramp." Matt hadn't talked with Jill alone since her arrival in Adamsport. But according to Irene, during a blustery Sunday luncheon at the Big House, after the sermon, while he had been listening to Sylvie's fairy tale, Jill had told Ike that he really should love his son.

"She told your father that she didn't think you were out to get him, that you're a very idealistic man—a minister of love," Irene had said sarcastically.

Now, Ink repeated her words. "Are you really a minister of love? Sunday on television you said that everybody should love everybody. So why couldn't Jill love you and Gramp, too?"

Matt suspected that he was being hoisted by his own petard.

"You're right, Ink. I love Jill and I love Gramp and I love your mother, too. But from now on, you're going to learn that most people are afraid to love. You have to dare to be like a chameleon. Loving is daring to take on another person's coloring, and trying to be that person and see the world the way he or she does." He grinned at Ink. "And don't you forget it with your new girl friend, Susan. Loving her doesn't mean jumping into bed and popping your cork. You have plenty of time for that. Love her like one of King Arthur's knights and protect her from the dragons."

He looked at his watch. "You guys have got to get going. The bus for the Academy will be going by in ten minutes. If you need me, you can reach me on the boat telephone. But please don't tell anyone the number. You can also tell your mother that I may take a man named Lovejoy sailing with me, and you can tell her that she won't be driven crazy by the telephone any longer. I've had all calls to our home phone transferred to an answering service."

"Are you going to live on the boat forever?"

"No. You know that it's going to be hauled for the winter in a few weeks. But don't worry, we'll get some sailing in together first."

Moving to the boat was the path of least resistance. Irene had made it clear that if he was determined to return to the ministry and seek fame with such insanities as he had proposed Sunday, then they should separate. Ike had agreed with her and told her flatly that Matt, not she, should move out of the carriage house. She and the boys were Godwins. Matt was a traitor to the family.

Bill Walsh, publisher of the *Adamsport Chronicle*, telephoned Ike after the sermon. Walsh had located Admiral Jonathan Nichols to get his reaction to Matt's ideas about deployment ships, and Nichols had responded: "Such stupidities coming from the mouth of a Godwin could jeopardize negotiations for future naval contracts with the Godwin Shipyard."

Walsh had repeated the conversation to George Gallagher, who telephoned Ike in a state of panic. "If the shipyard ever closes down, Adamsport will become a financially depressed area," he told Ike.

Ike was much more concerned that the story would filter back to the *Wall Street Journal*, which would be happy to make front page news of Matthew Godwin's strange behavior. Ike telephoned Matt the next day and told him bluntly: "Keep the hell away from the yards. I told Walsh that from now on Henderson is in charge, and he damned well better cool Admiral Nichols down. As for you, you struck out, son." Ike slammed the phone down.

Not only was Matt persona non grata in his own home, but the story in the *Chronicle* and his picture splashed all over the front page made it impossible to wander casually around Adamsport or stop to talk with Peachy at the church. After Sylvie's fairy tale and his offer, Peachy, who was obviously quite shaken, had driven him back to the church, where his car was parked. "No wonder my mother left Sylvie," she told Matt with tears in her eyes. "Sergeant Broke—that's one for the books. Sergeant Thief would be a better name, and his real name is probably Colonel Gamble."

"Why Gamble?" Matt asked.

"Daddy wasn't a sergeant in India during World War II; he was a major, a finance officer stationed in Calcutta. I'll bet this so-called Colonel Gamble never flew the Hump with the phony gold, either."

"What does that mean?"

"That Sergeant Broke took the colonel's place and uniform temporarily. Daddy is not the type that would leave millions of dollars with a sergeant he had known only a few days." Peachy gave him a quick kiss good-bye. "Please, I beg you, don't get involved with him, Matt. They wouldn't give me wifely visiting privileges at Walpole Prison."

Monday, when he talked with Peachy again on the telephone, she told him that the place was a madhouse, and she wasn't too happy that he was transferring his phone calls to the church, even via an answering service that he would pay for himself. "It may get Irene off your back," she said, "but if John Codman finds out—and he's been in and out of here preparing for the board meeting tomorrow—he isn't going to be happy. He's quite sure that you're the kind of UU minister that most of the members wish would move to California and join the rest of the crazy UU's."

Even during their short conversation, Matt could tell that Peachy was fending off various women who were asking if Matt Godwin was coming to church today. She left the phone dangling so that he could hear one woman saying, "I never heard such language in a sermon in my entire life. But he speaks like such an angel."

Laughing, Peachy finally picked up the phone. "That was Mabel Thatcher. She's sixty-five and she loves you. She just wrote out a check for fifty dollars to save the church. There's a half-dozen others who would be happy to turn over their pensions and Social Security to subsidize the church—but only if you're the minister and promise to go to bed with them occasionally. Don't let it go to your head," Peachy warned him. "My estimate is that more than half the members are cheering for your father. They think that you are a dangerous radical who has picked up 'commie' ideas at Harvard and that you are oversexed."

After talking with Peachy, Matt telephoned Roje. "I think the time has come for us to get better acquainted," he said. "There are only a few people left in the world who still believe in fairy tales."

Matt invited him to spend the afternoon sailing in Adamsport Bay and was happy to discover, when Roje arrived at the marina, that Roje was an enthusiastic sailor. "We have one thing in common," Roje told Matt as he took the helm. "From what I've heard about your wife, she and Emily agree that dry land is preferable to challenging the wind and water, or getting wet and becoming seasick as you zigzag to nowhere at great expense."

"I try to convince Irene that it isn't where you go," Matt laughed, "it's where you are. Out here you give the God-You a chance to breathe. But Irene doesn't listen to me."

Roje guided the boat into the Adamsport River, where a southeasterly headwind made it impossible to sail until they were in open ocean. Jesting, Matt told Roje that he was tempted to motor in close to the weighs of the Godwin Shipyards and tack back and forth in the lee of an LNG tanker still under construction. Shedding his clothes, he'd yell through a battery-powered speaker and tell Ike to come out and join them. But Roje dissuaded him. "I've had one encounter with Judge Gravman already," he laughed. "I'm sure your old man would call the harbor police. With Ike Godwin on his side, Gravman would commit me for observation." He noted a little apprehensively that Matt was standing midships and hoisting the mainsail stark naked. Matt told him to relax and take off his bathing suit.

"Thanks, I'll wait until we get out of the traffic," Roje said. "Two naked men sailing a boat in the Adamsport River would corrupt public morality more than a man and a woman. We're just the kind of trump card that your father needs. The police would be sure that they had arrested a gay novelist and a gay minister."

Matt laughed. "Irene would probably be happier if I were a homo rather than a seducer of women. Have you ever been attracted to men?"

"Nope. Never!" Roje grinned. "I usually find most men, and male pursuits, endlessly boring. Snuggling with a woman is much more intriguing."

Matt watched the mainsail flopping gently in the headwind. "What about Sylvanus Williams?" he asked, getting to the point of their meeting.

Roje grimaced. He wondered if Peachy had told Matt about their sex-making interlude. He couldn't believe that Matt, too, hadn't succumbed to Peachy's affectionate and spontaneous offering of herself to men she liked.

"You might as well know the truth," he said. "I think that inadvertently I may be more intimately involved with Sylvie than you ever will be." He wanted to say "both with my wife and Sylvie's daughter," but he refrained. Knowing that self-disclosure often invites self-disclosure, he decided to be partially honest. "Not personally, you understand. But my wife is. Emily goes to bed with him."

Matt stared at him, astonished. "How do you know that?"

"She hasn't actually told me yet, but I can tell the way she responds to him and champions him to me. Emily insists that Sylvie is really a laughing person—which I often am not—and that, despite rumors, he's really a nice guy."

Trying to absorb this revelation, Matt shook his head. "You and your wife seem to be practicing what I'm preaching. You obviously know what you write about."

"Only up to a certain point," Roje grinned. "My characters all exist in some future era, or on another planet where boys and girls from childhood are taught to enjoy their differences and not repress their sexual drives. Like you, I believe in the perfectability of man, but unlike you, I don't believe it can be accomplished tomorrow."

"Do you have an extramarital friend, too?"

"Not at the moment. But I don't object to Emily's enjoyment of Sylvie. It transforms her. Emily and I never discuss sexual details of our extracurricular friendships, or who's better than whom in the sack. We're both well aware that we've melded many parts of our diverse personalities, but we also know that, for the most part, when it comes to recapturing romance in an otherwise monogamous life, you are often handicapped by honesty."

"By honesty?"

"Sure. You can usually be more honest with a new friend than an old one who has long since rejected certain aspects of your personality or your particular fantasies or never liked them in the first place. This makes the romantic illusion between old friends very difficult to maintain. On the other hand, romance is a form of escapism that broadens your horizons and should be experienced frequently in a monogamous marriage. At the moment Emily hasn't actually confirmed to me that she's enjoying sex with, or is in love with, Sylvie, and I suspect that Sunday afternoon was the first time she had heard his fairy tale. She obviously was just as startled by it as the rest of us."

Matt shook his head in wonder. "I really am happy to get acquainted with you. Next time you talk with Irene at the club, do me a favor—see if you can seduce her."

They had just reached open ocean, and Roje turned the boat on a westerly starboard tack. Matt released the roller jenny, unfurled it and winched it, and Roje stripped off his bathing suit. They yelped in glee as the boat leaped forward, heeling and cutting the waves while the sun beat down on their naked bodies.

"Your wife is a very attractive woman, but Emily tells me that she's a devout Catholic," Roje said, picking up Matt's thought. He refrained from asking why a UU had married a Catholic. Obviously Matt had not converted her. "Unfortunately, she ignores me at the club. On the other hand, she may detest me sufficiently for me to catch her off guard," he chuckled. "It's even conceivable that I might strike the right chord with her religiously. The truth is that I find Catholic ritual and mysticism more fascinating than your UU pragmatism, or your secular concern with moralities."

He guessed that would challenge Matt and it did.

"You missed the point," Matt said. "Sex worship is the worship of the ultimate mystery."

For the next hour, as they sailed past other yachts, whose occupants were startled to see two laughing, naked men waving blithely at them, Matt tried to convince Roje that his sermon on modern moralities and the blending of church and state with a common objective was only an outline of the new religion he was proposing. He told Roje that when they got back to the marina he'd give him the first draft of a working scenario for a church that didn't depend on cannibalism—eating bread and drinking wine—to achieve unity with the divine.

"I want to do what the architects of the Gothic cathedrals did—create a twenty-first-century environment for a church that functions for man and woman subjectively and objectively. Functionally, the First Parish Church now belongs to another era. I'd like to tear down the dilapidated Parish Hall and erect a seven-story, all-glass building in its place. This could be butted up against the present sanctuary to provide a stage and dressing room on the first floor entering into the sanctuary. Then within the sanctuary itself, a total remodeling, with modern stage lighting, projection and sound equipment which would be designed to create a total involvement between the minister, the choir, and various parishioners who would take part in the services." Matt laughed. "To tell you the truth, I got so intrigued with the concept that I turned my sketches over to Drew and Liscomb, a Boston architectural firm. They're doing some preliminary drawings and cost estimates for me."

"So all your protest to Sylvie really was a red herring," Roje said. "You really do plan to buy the church. Are you going to finance it yourself, or are you going along with Sylvie and find out how his fairy tale ends?"

"Apart from his relationship with your wife, why don't you trust Sylvie?" Matt asked, parrying Roje's question.

"Because I don't understand why he has waited so long. If he actually has gold, free and clear of the fuzz, why does he want to send you and me to repatriate it? I can understand why he can't personally negotiate the sale of the gold, but so far as I can discover, he doesn't even want to come along and help dig it up. Why?"

Matt shrugged. "Damned if I know. I suppose because he's in too much legal trouble with his other ventures. Anyway, I'm not depending on Sylvie's gold. I have another potential resource. My sister Sally mailed me a copy of a letter that my mother wrote to Ike when she was on her deathbed. The poor old lady didn't trust Ike sufficiently, so she laboriously wrote it out in duplicate and mailed the copy to Sally. She told Sally to wait six months and see what Ike did about it." Matt frowned into the waves breaking over the bow.

"Did about what?"

"About $2 million of her money that she specifically left to the Unitarian Church. Sally mailed me her letter. I got it yesterday." Matt couldn't camouflage the anger in his voice. "It's not 45 million, but it would get the ball rolling."

"So, you've decided not to play Dungeon, Fairies, and Dragons?"

"I'm not sure yet, but I gather that you're not interested."

"Under the multiple circumstances, no. I told you that I'm not a risk taker," Roje said. "Anyway, how do I know that Sylvie hasn't concocted an elaborate plot? He may want to send me to a Caribbean El Dorado to get rid of me. He may want Emily more than he wants his damned gold." Roje chuckled. "I told you that writing about multiple relationships—or preaching about them—is much easier than doing it. Even if we are God."

16

When Matt telephoned Peachy from the boat on Wednesday, he could hear her sob of relief. "I thought you were angry with me for being so abrupt yesterday," she said. "I thought maybe you had decided to reform and leave me holding the bag. I was just about to telephone your wife and brazen it out with her, but no one is answering your home phone."

"Irene has probably moved up to the Big House with Becky," Matt told her. "Ike has gone to California to see if he can get the CPC directors to change their minds and fire me. I need to talk with you before I see your crazy father again. You know where the Adamsport Marina is. You can be down here in ten minutes. We'll have lunch together."

"I can't. I'm supposed to stay in the church until four o'clock. There are at least three or four people in here every hour—mostly looking for you, trying to find out where you're hiding."

"Hang a big note on the church door. Print it in big letters. Say: 'It's all my fault. Six months ago I seduced Matt Godwin. If it hadn't been for me, he never would have preached such terrible things. The reason that I'm not here this afternoon is that I'm trying to get him to retract everything he said. I'm going to tell him to stop pretending that he's a preacher when he's really only a half-ass businessman.' Sign it 'Peachy Stein, your future minister.'"

"You are crazy!"

"If you don't come here right away and help reinforce me, I might really throw in the sponge," Matt laughed. "I haven't heard what they decided at the board meeting last night. You'd better be nice to me. Who knows, one day soon I might become your minister, in which case I would hire you as chief cook and bottle washer and my favorite assistant."

Peachy knew when she walked out of the church door that she wasn't just going to have lunch with Matt. At the marina, a weather-beaten workman pointed to a tall mast at the far end of one of the docks. "That's the *Odyssey*," he told her, when she asked where the Godwin boat was kept. "It's worth a quarter of a million dollars. Did you hear young Godwin Sunday? Guess his old man would be happy if he'd take off in it like Ulysses and leave Penelope knitting at home."

Peachy was sure that he was casting her in the role of Circe, but she thanked him anyway. A few minutes later, threading her way through the piers, she saw Matt, wearing only bikini trunks, waving at her from the cockpit of the boat. It was the first time that Peachy had been exposed to the Godwin wealth. She gasped her surprise as he led her below into the cabin, which could seat eight people comfortably. "My God, it's nice to be rich," she told him as she bounced on one of the two sofas and her eyes took in a complete galley with a stove, a refrigerator, and a well-stocked bar.

Swinging her in his arms, kissing her mouth, eyes, and nose, Matt was jubilant. "I'm glad you came," he said. "I took your friend Roje sailing yesterday. He's a nice guy, but he's not huggable like you are. After three days alone, God Yang was getting restless. He needs to complete himself with the Goddess Yin." Matt's fingers had found the zipper at the back of her neck, and her dress quickly dropped to the floor, followed by her bra and panties. Her hand caressed his face and ruffled his hair as he continued his laughing, kissing exploration of her body.

"What did you and Roje talk about?" Peachy was shivering despite the warmth of the cabin. If Roje had told Matt that they had made love last week, Matt didn't seem to be angry with her. She was enjoying the reverent touch of his fingers and the hunger of his mouth, but she knew that she must be honest with him about Roje.

"Oh God, Matt, I hope that you and Roje decided to stay far away from my father and all that gold nonsense."

"Right now," Matt whispered into her stomach, "I'm going to escape myself and the world. I'm going to disappear into your body."

Sobbing happily, unable to focus him through her tear-filled eyes, Peachy slid down beside him on the sofa and released his penis from the tight elastic of his bikini shorts. "Oh I do love you, Matt, and I love your dreamy ideas about a saner kind of sexual world. But you and I aren't living in it now."

"What do you mean?"

"What about Irene and your children?"

"What about Saul and yours?" Matt grinned at her and led her forward to bunks in the prow of the boat.

Lying in his arms Peachy gazed at him, her eyes round and doubtful. "You really don't know very much about me. You think that

I'm a feminist. Maybe I am, but I know something that most feminists never discover. Women who dare to love men on their own terms quickly discover that they have superior rights." She cupped his face in her hands and kissed his lips tenderly. "And vice versa, of course." She stared at him and decided that she must be honest. "There's something you should know about me. I'm a pushover for a certain kind of man. I'm not really promiscuous, but men like you and Robert Lovejoy are an aphrodisiac for me. Years ago, when I read Roje's first novel, I fell in love with him. I guess he didn't tell you yesterday. Did he?"

One hand cupping her vulva, his mouth gently sucking her nipples, Matt mumbled, "Tell me what?"

"Poor man, he really didn't know what was happening to him."

"You mean Roje?"

"I seduced him last week. I made love to him near his swimming pool."

Matt was suddenly leaning on his elbow, looking at her quizzically. "Seems as if you are trying to change the ministry more than I am."

"What do you mean?"

"Long before you went to divinity school you told me that you wanted to be a psychologist. Therapists often go to bed with their clients. Male ministers have a history of bedding with their female parishioners. Why not vice versa?"

"You really are shocked, aren't you?" Staring at Matt with wide open eyes and a loving expression on her face, Peachy tried to hold back her tears. "Now you know why I have resisted you for the past six months. I'm really not the nice little housewife intent on becoming a minister that you thought I was. I haven't intellectualized your modern moralities. I've lived them." Her eyes were coffee-brown saucers. "My life has been considerably more fucked up than yours. My mother divorced Sylvie when I was in college. Twenty years ago, before she moved to Newton, she was a member of the First Parish Church. She knew your mother, Sarah. After college I didn't know what I wanted to do. Part of the time I lived with Sylvie, part with my mother, Anna. Sylvie subsidized me and I traveled all over the world." Peachy sighed. "Did I tell you that Saul isn't the father of my kids?"

Kissing her breasts as he listened, Matt raised his head and grinned at her. "I knew that you were married before."

"Before Saul, there was Mike. Michael Walsh. We were both students at Tufts. Four years out of college, back in Adamsport, I had also met Moses Fletcher. He was pastor of the church then. I don't know where you were in those days, but your mother was always in the church. I think she was in love with Moses. Was she?"

"Could be," Matt said, remembering how devastated his mother had been ten years ago when Moses died. "But Sarah would have confined her attentions to an affectionate sisterly kiss. I'm sure that she was sexually inhibited." Matt shrugged. "Ten years ago I was my father's fair-haired boy. I had stopped going to church except on Easter and Christmas."

"Maybe you really didn't know your mother," Peachy said. "Maybe she wasn't faithful to your father. Moses Fletcher was quite a temptation. The only reason that I didn't try to seduce him was that I was involved with Michael. But Moses had convinced me that the ministry might offer an interesting future for a woman like me—better than being a psychologist. So there I was in the second year of divinity school, knowing I couldn't be a priest, but screwing with an Irishman. Mike was studying for a law degree. My heavenly career was quickly terminated. Practically over his father's dead body—Bill Walsh, as you know, owns the *Adamsport Chronicle*—Mike and I were married *post facto*. I was much too sexy for his puritanical, frum, Irish family. And I quickly proved how bad I was by getting caught in bed with a professor by the professor's wife. I was already three months pregnant, a second time by Michael, but he was convinced that David was Moses Fletcher's son."

Peachy sighed. "Obviously I have bad blood. My father owned two porno movie theaters and a couple of dirty bookstores—he was the Jewish Mafia all by himself. Mike and I were divorced. Sylvie met Saul in one of those Sunday brunch clubs where unmarried men with their tongues hanging out look for single women. Saul's wife had died of cancer. I wasn't exactly single, since I had two kids, but Saul's children had left the nest long ago. Saul didn't like Sylvie very much and, in truth, Sylvie's sexy, half-Jewish daughter scared him to death—and still does." While she was talking, Peachy was gently swaying Matt's engorged penis. "Am I driving you crazy? Will you only make love once a week when you're fifty-five? Do you think I'm an easy fuck? Mike does. He keeps calling me up even though he's married again."

Laughing, Matt spread her legs and thoroughly laved her vulva with his tongue. Then he left her hanging. "To answer your questions in order: no, no, no. What about Michael, do you still go to bed with him?"

"God no! I've learned a lot about myself in the past ten years. I'm not really promiscuous; I never want a man just for his prick. But when I fall in love with a man's brains, I become totally addicted to him."

"But brains or not, you love Saul."

Peachy nodded. "I make Saul very insecure. Not just because I'm twenty years younger than him. He wasn't too happy last spring when I decided to go back to Tufts and after ten years get my divinity degree, but he agrees that I should be able to support myself. Saul is a very nice guy. He's not a laughing man like you are, and he's rarely just silly and spontaneous, but he's probably more reliable than you." She laughed. "He's the kind of person your father should have had for a son."

"For that you get your ass whacked." Matt rolled her over and gave her behind a good smack, after which he kissed it. "I can assure you, you're not an easy fuck. But you sure are a talkative one. All this adds up to the fact that you've made love to a half-dozen men in your thirty-eight years of life, and you think that you're better able to cope with your sins than I am."

"If you're actually counting, it's eight men, and that includes you and Roje, which will make four since Saul. Of course, Saul doesn't know. But you have to understand I don't feel guilty about it. And I have a feeling, despite your wild sermonizing, good sir, that you have never been unfaithful to Irene."

"And you think this could lead to trouble."

Peachy nodded sadly. "I don't want you to stop now, but I'm afraid that we shouldn't try to make this a way of life. One or both of us might soon prefer each other to our own spouses."

"That's a chance we'll have to take," Matt grinned. "Let's say that I'm a slow starter. But I've never felt guilty about my attraction to certain women. Nor would I be angry with Irene if she found another man. Father Tim is the kind of man she needs. Once you join hands with a spouse's lover, it makes it possible to play ring around the rosie."

Peachy laughed. "After which you all fall down. How many other women can you fit in your life?"

Matt was kneeling between Peachy's legs. Merrily lifting them and spreading them over his shoulders, he kissed open her labia, and circled her clitoris with his tongue. "We'll all fall down," she murmured happily. "Oh honey, please, please come inside me." She had passed beyond words. Her thinking brain was floating free and no longer constraining her body. She clasped him with her legs and dug her heels into his buttocks. "Oh God . . . dear God, please make this last forever." Slowly riding the razor's edge, she balanced on the edge of momentary oblivion and then gave up with a wild shriek.

After a few moments she shyly opened her eyes. Then she joined him in a rollicking explosion of laughter. "But you didn't answer me," she finally gasped.

Rolling her on top of him without separating and still laughing, he said, "If they're all like you, not many. If you are asking whether I'm involved with any other woman at the moment, the answer is no." But as he said it a memory of Jill's face absorbing his sermon flickered across his mind. Peachy had a compulsion to merge herself with men with brains. He was deeply hooked on women who admired him . . . no matter who they belonged to.

"Do you want me to be faithful to you?" Peachy was nibbling his cheek.

"That's too constraining. Just love me," he said. Still big inside her, he snuggled his face in her neck. "Maybe I'll never come out. You'll own my prick forever."

"That's great. I'll bet I can still function, too. Do you want me to tell you about the board meeting?"

"Lord, no. Not yet. Float with me into Nirvana."

"Like this?"

He could feel her vaginal muscles milking his penis. "Yes," he sighed. "This really is the resurrection and the life."

An hour later, wondering if she could summon the strength to break the lovely euphoria of their flesh merger, not wanting to face reality but compelled to after another wild ride on their private roller coaster, Peachy whispered to Matt, "I've got to go."

"You can't. Not yet."

"Silly, I mean I've got to pee. Where?"

Laughing, Matt pointed to the door he had closed on their triangular bed. "In the head. Open the door and turn left." Slipping to the floor behind her, both hands on her rump, he told her, "I'll come and help you."

"I don't need any help. Just a place to squat." Giggling, she opened the door. Then her laughter turned to screaming shock. She was staring into her father's grinning face. "Oh, my God!" she yelled. "What the hell are you doing here?"

Slumped on a sofa, he waved her dress at her. "I might ask you the same question, my darling daughter."

Matt strode naked into the living area, not bothering to pull on his bathing trunks. He stared belligerently at Sylvie. "Who told you I was here?"

"Lovejoy's wife," Sylvie laughed. "Emily was reluctant at first. She isn't very happy with me, either. Your wife told her you were living on your boat. Emily warned me not to expect to see Irene at the come-as-you-are party that I've been planning for Lovejoy." He coolly watched Peachy pulling on her panties and fastening her bra. "I haven't seen you bare-assed since you were six and your mother told me I couldn't give you a bath any more." He grinned happily at her. "You're really built, sweetie. If you decide you don't want to be a minister, you could make a lot more money on the strip circuit."

"Cut out the crap," Peachy told him. "What do you want? How long have you been here?"

"Long enough to know you haven't been playing tiddlywinks. But I really didn't come here to see you, or hear your ecstatic sighs." He grinned at Matt. "Just for the record, at the other end of this marina, down with the hoi polloi, I keep an Egg Harbor powerboat to entertain my lady friends. But I'm more discreet than you are, and I always lock my hatch. You really should be more careful. Both of your cars are in the parking lot, practically side by side. Jed Sellers told me if I was looking for my daughter she was visiting with Matt Godwin. Who's screwing whom is everybody's business in this marina."

Suddenly realizing that Irene could have arrived unexpectedly, too, and well aware that if he decided to get involved with Sylvie, the fact that he and his daughter were lovers would complicate their future relationship, Matt sank onto the sofa opposite him. "So what the hell do you want?" he asked.

"Has Peachy told you about the board meeting last night? I set it up for you."

"I haven't told him, yet," Peachy grinned sheepishly at Matt. "We had other problems to discuss. I don't think he's going to be too happy about it."

"He damned well should be," Sylvie snorted. "Henderson Inch was there, but I pulled the plug on him. John Codman introduced him and told us that he had invited Henderson so that Controlled Power could present its offer for the building. I told Henderson that the board had the cart before the horse. If we listened to CPC's offer then and there, they'd be at a disadvantage. After all the publicity, a large Boston realty firm is interested, too. They want to build a condominium over the sanctuary of the church and around it. Then they'd rent the heated sanctuary to the UU's. The members could have their cake and eat it." Sylvie laughed. "Codman was trying to wrap it up for your old man. To make a long story short, Henderson never got to present his offer. I convinced the board to call a meeting of all the members next Monday. First they must find out whether a majority will agree to sell the building or prefer to struggle along the way they are. If the vote is to sell, then there would be one more meeting of the members, a week later, to hear the bids. And there would be a prior agreement to auction the building off to the highest bidder exclusive of furnishings and any detachable property. The parsonage could be included in the deal or not. I also dropped the hint that there might be another bidder." Sylvie smiled triumphantly at Matt. "That gives us two weeks."

"The board also voted on whether to search for a new minister," Peachy said, holding Matt's hand and playing with his fingers. "Or whether to offer you the job. I'm sorry to tell you it was ten to five against you. They're scared to death of you."

"The board is not all the members," Sylvie said. "My guess is that the liberals outnumber the conservative creeps. Not by much—and that doesn't mean that those who want to sell are enthusiastic about you, Matt. But the whole problem is academic. When you own the joint, you can charge admission. If no one shows up, you can afford to preach to an empty church."

"I keep telling you that I'm not interested in owning a church," Matt said gloomily.

"You don't have to own it, personally. You can set up a foundation to spread Godwin's word. With a multi-million-dollar endowment, you'd have a pretty loud voice. Roje and Peachy could run the foundation, following your advice. All we need is some Arab sheik to endow it." Sylvie chuckled. "Ninety-five million dollars' worth of gold at half-price should be a considerable incentive."

"Matt doesn't know any Arab sheiks." Peachy looked at Matt hopefully. "Do you?"

Matt shook his head. But, as a matter of fact, he once did know the son of a sheik, Amir Faisal Saud. Amir's father was a Saudi Arabian oil billionaire. Long ago, when they were at Harvard Business together, Amir had liked Matt. "Goddy, the Protestant Allah," he called him. Matt had often helped him with his term papers. But Matt had lost contact with Amir and most of his classmates. He hadn't seen or heard from him for more than twelve years.

"Let's be honest, Sylvie," Matt said. He was suddenly intrigued with Sylvie's idea of a foundation. Such an arrangement might make it possible for him to function in two worlds. "Peachy is afraid that you'll corrupt my morals." He leaned over and kissed her cheek. "She's probably right, but she doesn't realize that right now I'm pretty far out on a limb. I can't go crying to my Daddy for financial help."

"And you shouldn't go crying to mine," Peachy said coldly. "Not until he tells you the whole sordid story. Not until he admits that he's Colonel Gamble and that the FBI is hot on his trail. Not until he tells you that you may be the patsy if you try to maneuver with stolen gold."

Ignoring her, using two hands, Sylvie lifted an attaché case that he had been holding between his legs onto his lap. He snapped open the lock. Inside, in a neat row, lay three gold ingots. "It ain't Christmas, yet," he grinned, "but just in case you might be the Messiah, here's a gift from the Magi. At current prices these bars are worth over three quarters of a million dollars. I'm giving them to you, Matt. No strings attached. Your father won't bid that much for the church. Buy your temple and preach your gospel. The rest of the 395 bars can stay on Grand Cayman until hell freezes over."

"So that's where the gold is," Matt said. "Are you really Colonel Gamble?"

"What the hell difference does it make?" Sylvie asked angrily. "We both know that it's stolen money. If you give it back to Uncle Sam, he'll quickly piss it away at places like the Godwin Shipyard, building naval deployment vessels or nuclear cruisers or some such crap. It's the government's morality against yours. So a few people died stealing the gold. I didn't personally kill them. The Vatican is filled with treasures that didn't come from clean hands or pure hearts. The cathedrals all over Europe didn't get built without plenty of corruption. You told everyone last Sunday all they had to do was make the sign of the cross. You can do it when you get the gold and sanctify it. As for the FBI, if they're still looking for the gold, I can assure you they think it's in the Himalayas, not on Grand Cayman Island."

17

Deeply shocked that Matt had gone public in Adamsport with his sacrilegious sexual ideas, angry that he had exposed their marital dissent to everyone in the city by living on their boat, fearful that he might tell people that she had driven him out of his home, but feeling sure that he couldn't abide the crowded quarters of the boat for very long, Irene kept thinking each day that she'd find him casually poking around the house. Laughing at her worries, as usual, he'd be trying to have sex with her standing up, sitting down, bending over, lying on the floor, or more calmly after she relented in bed. Actually, she wanted to make love as much as he did—but on her terms. Finally, after a week, she telephoned him early Monday morning. And she was trembling, wondering if the rumor she had heard from Jane Motley that Peachy Stein had been seen sunbathing on the deck of the boat was true.

When Matt finally answered the boat phone, without any preliminaries she demanded: "I just want to know one thing. Are you planning to divorce me?"

"I don't believe in divorce. Anyway, I love you." Matt couldn't tell her that she had just caught him in time. In less than two hours he would be on a plane to New York to talk with Amir Faisal Saud. He couldn't tell her either that if Sylvie weren't lying and the gold actually existed and by some miracle Amir followed through and bought it, then her days of trial and tribulation with him were probably just beginning.

"That's the problem," she said. "You love everybody. Are you sleeping with that minister friend of yours?"

Matt laughed. "So far as I know, she sleeps with her husband."

"You know damned well what I mean."

"You mean am I fucking with her?" A vision of Peachy speared by his penis and bouncing on his stomach flashed across his mind. "I have never fucked any woman, including you."

"I know that she's been seeing you on the boat."

"Who told you?"

"Jane Motley. In case you don't remember, quite a few of our friends own powerboats at the marina."

"We have a sailboat," Matt said. "It's called the *Odyssey*. It doesn't go very fast, but if you prefer power, it has a very nice diesel engine." Crossing his fingers, he asked her if she'd like to go sailing. "Or you could just come down here and we could spend the day making love."

"You really have gone crazy," she said, responding as he had anticipated. "I just want you to know that this is your home, too. I'm sure we can coexist somehow under the same roof."

"I hate to sleep alone."

"So do I, goddamn you," Irene sobbed. "But I'm not sleeping with you after you've screwed with her."

"I can't figure out why you want me to come home."

"Because I love you—or I did before you decided to go in for sex worship."

"Do you love Father Timothy?"

"That's ridiculous. Of course not. Not that way."

Matt laughed. "Poor man. I watched him while I was preaching. I thought he was going to take you in his arms and comfort you. You should practice on him. If he discovered the joys of loving a woman as God instead of a Holy Spirit, he might help me with my Church of Modern Morality."

Irene scowled into the telephone. "Ink and Able miss you."

"I miss them," Matt said and then, risking her acceptance but being pretty sure of her reaction, he teased her. "Tell you what. Repeat after me: 'Oh honey, honey, I need you. I need all of your magnificent prick inside me. If you come right now I'll be waiting naked. I'll jump into your arms and smother you with kisses!'"

"Don't hold your breath waiting," Irene replied coldly. "I'm not a member of your adoring harem. Good-bye." She hung up.

Driving to the airport, Matt wondered if one day he might prove to Irene that in private, alone with him, she could let down her hair and be a lascivious, lusting, loving woman without compromising her public self.

He hadn't seen Peachy since Wednesday. When he telephoned her at the church she told him that she loved him, but she had children, a husband, and, since there was no other minister available, a sermon to write. "Are you coming to hear me Sunday?" she asked. He told her that he couldn't. Not until he had decided what to do. Until the church was sold or not, he didn't want to get into a probing discussion with church members. He tried, but he couldn't persuade Peachy to deliver her sermon privately to him while sitting naked penetrated by God.

If, after eight sexless days and nights, Irene had responded with a sense of humor, he might have even gone home. If she weren't so judgmental, he might have even taken her to New York with him and told her the whole story of Sylvie's gold and Amir's potential interest in it. It wasn't sexual release that he needed. Having a loving orgasm was only a partial response to his driving need to share himself with another person. He needed someone to talk to, someone to whom he dared reveal all his conflicting drives and emotional needs. Someone who would dare listen to his wild ideas and would challenge his mental meanderings, not with anger, but with laughter. Someone who would realize that only in a loving verbal objectivization of his thoughts could he find his own answers, or modify them to her reality. The pronoun was right. Like Roje, Matt had never been a man's kind of man. Sarah had feminized him. He never traveled with the boys. Through college and divinity school and even business school he had been a loner, too shy with women and not competitive enough for men. Peachy had guessed the truth. Before he met Irene, he had known only one other woman. They had had a one-year romance, with very little sex, and it had ended sorrowfully for him when she found a quarterback on the football team who fit her image of a male better than a philosopher and a poet who believed then that some of the atoms of Keats and Shelley had been resurrected in the body of Isaac Matthew Godwin.

He was obviously a late bloomer. Although he had been sexually faithful to Irene, he had never thought of himself as monogamous, and, strangely, marriage had released him. Not that he lusted after all women; but he was no longer shy with them, and he had discovered that with some women his genuine interest in females and joy in conversing with them made them unafraid to reveal their parallel needs for male mental companionship. Many married women were lonely. They had discovered to their sorrow that their spouses might still enjoy their vaginas but were often bored with what went on in their minds.

Peachy was the first woman with whom he had thrown caution to the wind. Long before they had actually made love, they had discovered that they could bounce their doubts and fears off each other in their incessant search for answers, a kind of reaching toward the most ineffable goals that not only exceeded their grasp but probably exceeded their abilities. When they finally made love he knew that she was still testing him and challenging him. Were his modern moralities just words he spouted on the wind? Could he really love her and Irene, too? Obviously, she was asking if he could share her love with Roje and Saul. Could he? Or deep down was he like his father, a patriarchally possessive male? And, a more dangerous question, to what extent was his search for modern moralities the product of a marriage in which his wife would not or could not provide the catalyst he needed?

Thinking about it as he parked his Mercedes in the airport garage, Matt grinned. Maybe he needed a harem. Long ago, when they were at Harvard, Amir Faisal mentioned that his father had four wives. Had Amir followed in his father's footsteps? After wrestling for nearly a week with the devil that Sylvie had offered, Matt decided that he would try to locate Amir. Many wealthy Arabs commuted regularly from Saudi Arabia. If he could find him and talk with him on an "as if" basis, it might tip the scale. Amir might not be interested in a gold transaction himself, but he might know who might be. Matt knew that if he could whitewash—or, to use Sylvie's words, "launder"—half the value of Sylvie's gold, it could give him the leverage he needed to take off on a new career. In one sense, it was no more immoral than Ike failing to carry out Sarah's deathbed wishes.

It was now or never. "Never" meant that he'd probably spend another thirty years playing Ike's empire building game for no purposes that made any sense to him. "Now" meant believing in himself enough to risk failure. Men and women were God, of that he had no doubt; but their willingness to play the deity role varied. Most of them felt no compulsion to lead the way "beyond freedom and dignity" to a world where most men and women could live more fulfilling lives. If they did, very few of them would dare to play footsies with the devil aspect of God to achieve that goal.

It had been surprising that after so many years Amir remembered him. Matt had traced him through the Saudi Arabian embassy to a cooperative apartment in New York City. Amir owned it and evidently stayed in New York or in his mansion in Beverly Hills when he was in America.

"Goddy!" Amir marveled over the phone yesterday when Matt had finally been cleared through to him by a woman who sounded like an efficient secretary. "I'm so happy to know that you're alive. Of course I haven't forgotten you. You were the minister whose father owned a shipyard. Now the shipyard is owned by Controlled Power Corporation. I understand that your father is a very clever conglomerator. My family has been diversifying into American projects. Do you want to sell me something?" Amir laughed. "We have enough tankers. I don't think we need a shipyard."

"I do want to sell you something," Matt told him. "It comes in small packages weighing about twenty-seven pounds each. Think about more than 300 such packages. The packages don't earn any interest, but many people trust them better than dollars."

Amir immediately understood, and chuckled. "Has Goddy become a smuggler? Three hundred is a lot of packages. Are they, as you say in America, 'hot?'"

"No, I don't think so. You can consider it buried treasure that everyone has forgotten. I'm simply acting as a broker. The finder doesn't want to share with Uncle Sam."

"It's a very volatile treasure, my friend. A few years ago it would have been worth twice as much as it is today."

"I know that, but the owner will offer a substantial discount over the current market prices. Say 25 percent? You can keep it for appreciation or turn it over for a fast ten million or more."

"Forty percent discount would sound more interesting. Where is it?"

"On a Caribbean island."

"Can you bring samples?"

"Yes."

"Good." Then to Matt's surprise, Amir told him that he was free next week. "But you would have to understand. Before any transaction could be completed, we might have to bore holes in your packages— even saw them in half—to make sure there are no worms inside. Does your island have an airport? Perhaps we can fly there. Tuesday or Wednesday would be good for me. We can take a look at your packages while we renew old friendships."

"I don't believe that there are any direct flights from New York."

"It doesn't matter. I have a Grumman jet and a pilot too. But I can fly it myself in an emergency. Can you meet me here tomorrow for luncheon at one o'clock?"

Standing in line to board the nine o'clock shuttle to New York, Matt knew that he was allowing plenty of time for his luncheon appointment with Amir. He had made a reservation at the Sheraton, assuming that if Amir was interested they would fly to Grand Cayman Wednesday, weather permitting. Still trying to absorb the completely out-of-character adventure he was embarked on and then not believing his eyes—wondering if he were seeing a look-alike—he saw Gillian enter the departure area. Staring despairingly at the long line, she was obviously wondering if she were too late and would have to wait for a second flight.

"Jill! Jill Godwin!" he yelled and waved at her, drawing the attention of several hundred people.

Laughing, she ran to him. "What good luck! Are you really going to New York, too?" Her eyes caught the irritated glances of passengers standing in line behind Matt. "Maybe I should go to the end of the line?"

"No way." Matt bussed her cheek and, shifting the weight of the heavy attaché case he was carrying, pushed her in line ahead of himself. "For better or for worse, you're a Godwin." His eyes were searching the area. "Where's Ike?"

"He's still in California. I'm alone. Hendy drove me to the airport."

"I can't believe that Ike would let you wander around loose. You might meet a Rockefeller who has more charm and money." Matt's tone was teasing. For a moment he was about to tell her that he could introduce her to a Saudi Arabian billionaire. Then he noticed that Jill's eyes had suddenly flooded with tears.

"Hah, the truth comes out at last," she said bitterly. "Well, damn it, you're right. I did marry your father for his money. You shouldn't resent that, Matt Godwin; the way you're going, you're not going to get any of it anyway."

Grinning, Matt took her arm and pushed her along in the line that was now moving toward the waiting plane. "We might just as well sit together, and share a taxi into the city," he said. "I was sure that if we ever got to talk with each other alone, we might find some ground for communication. When Irene walked out on me last Sunday, I thought I might catch up with you at the social hour, but there was too much confusion."

"Irene and Father Timothy waited in Irene's car for me," Jill said. "They couldn't stand listening to you anymore. But when I arrived, they couldn't wait to hear how you wrapped it all up." Jill dabbed at a tear trickling down her cheek. "You really do believe that I'm a gold digger, don't you?"

Amused, Matt gestured to two seats on one side of the cabin. She slipped in ahead of him while Matt, wondering what she would think if she could see the gold ingots inside the attaché case, managed to juggle it under the seat in front of him.

Jill watched him. "It looks quite heavy. Are you leaving Adamsport permanently?"

"No. I expect to be back by Saturday. What about yourself?"

"I'm just going to New York for a few days. I talked with Ike last night. He won't be back until the first of next week." Jill sighed. "I'm not sure I should have ever got mixed up with the Godwin family. I guess you heard, I made the mistake of defending you and telling Ike that some of the things you said in your sermon made sense. But some of them, like Man is God, *don't*. But Ike never sees gray. You're a bad guy in his book. Right at the moment he isn't too happy with me, either. Ike doesn't appreciate a bed companion who disagrees with him. So I decided not to fly to California with him. That left me with your wife and Becky . . ." Jill paused and stared at him. "Quite honestly, I'm not used to sharing personal problems with other women. I've always been too busy working for a living." She laughed. "So, it was either go to New York or play golf with Irene or listen to secondhand rumors about whether God was sleeping with one of his loving angels called Peachy."

Matt laughed. "I think you and I should have a long talk. What are you going to do in New York?"

"Some shopping. And a friend of mine is opening in a new play that I want to see." Jill grinned. "Don't worry, the friend is female. Also my agent wants to talk with me about a new play. It's a subject which should amuse you. It's based on a book by Altina Waller, *Reverend Beecher and Mrs. Tilton*. Are you sure that you're not a reincarnation of Beecher? He reminds me of you. Abraham Lincoln called him the most influential man in America when he was preaching against slavery. But fame is fleeting, as you will probably discover. One hundred and fifty years later there are very few people who have ever heard of Beecher or Elizabeth Tilton."

"I have." Matt was beaming. "And I'm sure that Ike has, because Sarah was in love with Beecher even though he was long dead. Take my advice. Don't play the part of Mrs. Tilton. Ike wouldn't be very happy watching you on stage being seduced by old Henry Ward Beecher."

"You mean because it's too close to home? And because Beecher preached a Gospel of Love?"

"Not only that. He practiced what he preached—he went to bed with his parishioners."

"Don't you? Irene thinks that you're a sex maniac."

"Have dinner with me tonight," Matt said, finally evoking a thought that had been nibbling in his brain. "We'll talk about Beecher. He had the congregation I'd like to have. In his heyday some three thousand of them arrived on Sunday morning to hear him preach. The Brooklyn Bridge wasn't even built, but people were so enthusiastic about him they arrived from Manhattan by ferry boat to hear him. I'll meet you around six. Where are you staying?"

"Sorry," Jill was smiling but she shook her head decisively. "I may have defended you, but I'm not a true believer in your modern moralities. Poor Henry Beecher got mixed up with two women and he got tried for adultery. Preaching that sex makes the world go around will get you hung—and not by the neck."

"I didn't ask you to go to bed with me." Matt grinned at her. "But if you remember much about Beecher, he preached that certain people have 'affinities' for each other. We can find out if we have over a bottle of wine in some quiet little restaurant."

Jill shivered, feeling his magnetism, as she looked at him speculatively for a moment. She wondered how the younger Godwin might compare with his father as a lover.

"If Ike knew that I was sitting this close to you, my life would be in danger," she said lightly. "I'm your mother, remember? Let's change the subject. Are you going to resign as president of CPC?"

Matt shrugged, "I assume that I have been fired already."

"You should understand CPC politics better than that. That's why Ike flew back to Los Angeles. He may bluster and shout at you, but he's sure that a man named Gus Belshin, who is a director and controls at least a 20 percent block of stock, is out to get him." Jill suddenly wondered if she were revealing things to Matt that Ike wouldn't want him to know, but she plunged on. "You see, if Ike reveals that you and he are not entirely in accord, or the directors feel that there's an incipient family feud, Belshin may try to get enough proxies to sabotage him."

"That will take some doing. Ike controls 35 percent of the shares."

"But Gus will try to play you against your father from the middle. He'll take the preacher rather than the senile old man—and he's already intimating that your father is getting senile. I can assure you that it isn't true. Ike might die of a heart attack if you don't stop bugging him, but his brain," Jill grinned at Matt, "and all the rest of him, is in good running order."

Matt guessed that Jill was reflecting conversation that she had had with Ike. "I doubt if Ike is running scared. If I don't take up the ministry, I'd better find another job."

"You still don't understand. Gus is not in favor of a CPC relocation in Adamsport. But now Ike is afraid that if you're president you may help Gus put a spoke in your father's wheel and then, after Gus has got rid of Ike, he'll take care of you later."

"Well, Gus is wrong. I'm not against the relocation of CPC in Adamsport. It just so happens that I have different plans for the First Parish Church than Ike has."

Jill shrugged. "You've made that clear enough. Why have you moved out on Irene? You really don't have to live on your boat to have another woman. Irene may not like what you're doing, but divorce is a worse alternative for her. Are the UU's really going to sell the church to CPC? What response have you got to your sermon?" Jill noted that Matt wasn't responding to her questions. For a moment he seemed far away. "I'm really not being nosey, but since you're not talking to your family, someone has to act as the ombudsman."

Matt laughed. "I'm talking to my family, but they're not talking to me. Since you seem to know everything else, you must know that Irene doesn't want me near her. After the sermon, although our phone is unlisted, the number got around and it never stopped ringing. Some of the callers were not too friendly and she was frightened." Matt didn't tell Jill that Irene was furious with him and Peachy and had threatened to call Peachy's husband and tell him to lock her up or put a chastity belt on her. "Irene is sure that I've opened the gate of Hell." Matt stared at Jill's long fingers on the armrest between them. The only ring she wore was Ike's wedding ring on her left hand.

"What are you going to do when CPC buys the church?" Jill said.

With his foot on the attaché case, Matt wondered again what Jill would think if he opened it and showed her the contents. Even he wasn't sure whether he was trying to build a Church of Modern Moralities on immoral foundations. "I really don't need the First Parish Church," he said. "I'm sure that somewhere there's a congregation that would have me. But I am happy about one thing. Since the sermon, more than five hundred contributions have been received to save the church. Of course, they only average about five dollars each."

"The trouble with singing in the wilderness," Jill said, "is that no one will ever hear you."

Matt looked over her shoulder out the window of the plane. "We'll be landing in a few minutes. Have you changed your mind about having dinner with me?"

Jill shook her head. "I'm not like you. I never play with fire."

But when they got in a taxi together at La Guardia, she had to tell the taxi driver that she was staying at the Plaza. "I'll drop you off first," Matt said, and Jill realized that it wasn't going to be easy to convince him that she couldn't have dinner with him.

"The reason I came to New York," Matt was saying, "is to meet a very wealthy Saudi Arabian sheik. He owns a cooperative apartment uptown. Who knows? I may convince him to create a Modern Moralities Foundation. Would you like to meet him? He could buy Controlled Power Corporation and not even miss the money."

"Don't tell me that you are going to try to get an Arab to buy you your own Temple of Love?" Jill giggled. "Your father should be proud of you. Islam needs you more than Christianity. You can tell the rich Arabs that it's all right to have several wives, but not to forget the ladies. They should have the same sexual privileges as the men." She suddenly took Matt's hand and looked at him seriously. "Why don't you forget it all and go back to business? Allah knows that men and women aren't God."

"If you'll have dinner with me tonight, maybe I can prove to you that Allah is wrong," Matt said. The taxi driver was pulling up in front of the Plaza. "I'll meet you in the Oak Room at six. Who knows, maybe you can save me from myself."

As he got out of the cab, Jill shook her head and stared at him. Her eyes were pools, deep enough to drown in. "I must be crazier than you are. All right."

18

After his luncheon with Amir Faisal Saud, which extended until four, Matt returned to his hotel, showered, and then took a taxi to the Plaza. Walking into the Oak Room at quarter of six, he told the headwaiter his name. Chuckling inwardly, he said, "My wife, Jill Godwin, is meeting me here. She may be here already."

The waiter shook his head. "To my knowledge Mrs. Godwin is not here yet. But we have a nice table overlooking Central Park. I'll make sure she finds you."

In a secluded corner of the lounge Matt ordered a scotch on the rocks and relaxed for the first time since he had left Jill that morning.

He needed to reconnoiter and reassess his meeting with Amir. During his twelve years as manager of the shipyards he had negotiated many times with Arabic nationals, but he was never sure whether their smiling, agreeable responses were a cover for devious thinking.

Nefwazi, a heavy-built bull of a man, with a vicious-looking scar on his right cheek, who was evidently Amir's bodyguard, met him at the elevator of Amir's penthouse condominium. He ushered Matt into a glassed-in living room that overlooked Manhattan all the way to the Statue of Liberty. Unlike Nefwazi, who was carefully dressed in a Brooks Brothers suit, Amir, dark-skinned, wearing a heavy mustache, and even leaner than he had been during his Harvard years, was sprawled on a sofa, wearing an open shirt and lounging pants. He looked as if he might have just got out of bed with the pretty young American woman whom he introduced as Kitty. Kitty greeted Matt with the cool sophistication of a lady accustomed to bantering with wealthy men.

"I am pleased to meet you," Kitty smiled. "Amir has told me a little bit about your college days together, and I would love to stay for your reunion. But since Amir doesn't like me to hang around when he's talking business, I'll excuse myself to go shopping." She looked at Amir questioningly. "Do you want me to ask Lisa to come with us tomorrow?"

Amir smiled at Matt. "It will be up to Matt. I don't even know if we're going anywhere. I'm only here for a very short visit this time," he explained to Matt. "And I expect to be returning to Jidda Sunday. I told Kitty that if she wished—and if we actually take a little Caribbean holiday—that she could come along." He laughed. "As I remember, at Business School you were married. If you are still married, your wife can accompany us; or if you prefer, Kitty will ask Lisa. She's very pretty, and I'm sure she would provide a pleasant change of scenery for you."

Matt shook his head. Too many people were becoming aware of this treasure hunt. But he tried to be nonchalant. "As a matter of fact," he replied, "I have a lady friend who might be persuaded to join us." Matt couldn't help smiling at the thought. He knew he was having a late summer night's dream. For a moment he saw himself and Jill, his stepmother, walking arm in arm, naked, on a moon-drenched Caribbean beach. Somehow he had explained to Amir who Jill was, and why she was there, and why she was helping him to acquire the fortune with which he would finally subdue his father and make Ike love everybody, too.

After Kitty left, Amir assured him that she would know nothing about any transactions they might engage in. But Nefwazi would. Sitting on a semi-open terrace, they were served a fruit salad and sliced chicken by a turbaned male servant. Amir told Matt, while Nefwazi stared at him with an impassive this-is-my-master-I-would-die-for-him expression on his face, "I trust Nefwazi, not just for sentimental reasons, but by the simple process of making him a partner in any of my nefarious activities." Amir grinned. "Thus his neck is on the chopping block along with mine."

"That makes sense," Matt said, feeling uneasy that, like it or not, dealing with Amir wasn't going to be an entirely private transaction. "How am I protected?"

"Honor among thieves," Nefwazi said coolly. "In addition, Amir needs me on this project for several other reasons. I can pilot his airplane, and I know how to verify the gold content of your ingots, if they actually exist."

Matt pointed to his attaché case and told Nefwazi to open it. Nefwazi carefully lifted out each bar of gold and inspected it with a happy leer on his face.

"There's a half-million-dollar down payment on the final transaction," Matt said. "Unless I've been listening to a fairy tale, somewhere in the Caribbean, buried in the cellar of a private home owned by my client, there are 392 identical so-called good delivery bars just like that one."

"They seem to be the right weight," Nefwazi said, handing one to Amir and pointing to the seal of the United States molded in the bar. "That number below it may be the U.S. Assay Office refining number," he told him and he was obviously impressed.

Censoring Sylvie's story as he went along, Matt told them that during World War II his client had heard of a shipment of gold, intended for China, which had been diverted, and, although the Finance Department of the Army and the U.S. Treasury officials believed that it had disappeared in a plane crash in the Himalayas, had actually remained in Calcutta for nearly forty years. "Two years ago my client carefully repackaged the ingots in twenty-five-hundred-pound containers and consigned them to a duty-free island in the Caribbean which even today is not too well known to most tourists."

"Before you tell us the name of the island," Amir said, "I am very curious as to why a man of your wealth would get involved with a man of such low moral character as this client of yours—and what you propose to do with your share of the money."

"I suppose I could ask you the same question," Matt said, smiling. "But first let me assure you that I am only the son of Ike Godwin; I am not my father. My access to big sums of money is severely limited."

Amir laughed. "That reason makes us friends. As the spendthrift son of a very conservative sheik whose assets I'm sure exceed ten billion dollars, I have a very difficult time living in the manner to which I'm accustomed."

Matt pulled a copy of the *Adamsport Chronicle* out of his attaché case and handed it to Amir, who read the headlines aloud: "'*Matthew*

Godwin, Manager of the Godwin Shipyards, Offers New Moral Vision for America. Sunday in a lengthy sermon delivered at the First Parish Unitarian Universalist Church, Matthew Godwin not only challenged his father Isaac Godwin's policies in seeking Navy deployment ship contracts, but also criticized Moral Majority and Christian and Jewish leaders for advocating what he describes as 'outdated biblical moralities.'"

"You can read it later," Matt said. "I plan to donate my share of the proceeds from our venture to a non-profit Foundation for Modern Moralities. Obviously, I can't do it directly, but if things work out, you might be able to do it for me. It would give you and your family some very interesting publicity in the United States. Even Allah might be pleased that you would be helping change American morality."

"Don't count on it," Amir replied, smiling. "I'm not at all sure that it's the kind of publicity my father would appreciate, and unless you are going to introduce Islamic morality into the United States, I don't think Allah would be too happy about it."

Matt spent the rest of the afternoon trying to explain to a bewildered Amir why a rich man's son would jeopardize his fortunes and his position in the world trying to enlighten the masses.

"There will always be the rich and the poor," Amir told him. "The rich should be very happy that the poor have their Son of God and saints and their Meccas and their Allahs. You don't seem to realize that the masses need both God and the devil to keep them in line and help them behave. What you do with your money is up to you, but you can't escape reality. A rich man's morals are a poor man's poison. Only rich Muslims can afford four wives. Only rich Americans can afford a mistress."

"Are you married?" Matt asked.

Amir nodded. "But my two wives know their place, and they are aware that like you I straddle two worlds." He smiled. "There's never enough money for that. Allah has decided that I accompany you on your search for El Dorado. We can leave for your Caribbean island tomorrow at ten in the morning from Kennedy. Where is the island, and after we get there, how do we find your client's treasure?"

"I have specific directions when we get to the island," Matt said cautiously. "The gold is in a villa about eight miles from the airport. The island is Grand Cayman. It's about five hundred miles south of Miami—not far from Cuba."

Amir beamed at Nefwazi and said, "Hah! I was right. That was my guess." He shook hands with Matt. "We are your enthusiastic partners in this venture. Your client had good sense. My family has several banking connections on Grand Cayman. If we are in agreement, we could make the financial arrangement in Euro dollars very quickly. I'll make reservations for us at the Grand Cayman Inn for tomorrow night."

Now, waiting for Jill, it occurred to Matt that he hadn't asked Amir to make a prior agreement on the price he would pay for the gold. Once again he realized that he was not in the driver's seat. Amir could offer him a take it or leave it deal, and Nefwazi could back it with a knife to his throat. But that was silly. The very fact that Amir was inviting Kitty along—she was obviously an expensive mistress—precluded James Bond-Goldfinger-style insanities. Wondering if he dared to ask Jill to come with him on a short vacation and how she would react if he did, he finished his scotch and looked up in surprise at her smiling face.

"I've been standing here for at least a minute," she laughed. "I hated to interrupt you. You seemed to be having a happy daydream." She squeezed into the cushioned seat beside him. "You must have had a good day."

Matt grinned at her and helped her slide out of her coat. "So far so good," he said, wordlessly admiring her black suit dress with a frilly white blouse that framed her long neck. She had changed her clothes for dinner, but she was wearing only a faint touch of eyeshadow, no lipstick, and her clear, creamy cheeks had only a faint blush of makeup. "How was your day?" he asked, noticing that she was carrying what looked like a manuscript in a binder.

"Very amusing." She flipped the typewritten pages. "This is the first draft of a new play, *Reverend Beecher and Mrs. Tilton*. I never gave it much thought before, but obviously ministers, like doctors, are father figures for their female parishioners." She chuckled. "Obviously many women, including myself, get hooked on father figures. They feel safer with them than dashing younger men who are more promiscuous and will tumble into the sack with any available female. But before I tell you about Beecher and the play, tell me what you've been doing. Then I'll decide whether I can save you from yourself or should refer you to a psychiatrist." She nodded at the waiter hovering over them. "I'll have a martini," she said. Matt ordered a second scotch. "I hope that you're not hungry," she told him. "I had a late lunch." She curved into her seat so she could watch his face. After the waiter had set their drinks in front of them, she said, "All right. I'm listening."

"Tomorrow morning you and I are flying to Grand Cayman Island," Matt said. "Our companions will be a sheik, his bodyguard, and a high-priced call girl named Kitty."

Laughing, Jill was equal to such silliness. "It's too early in the season for the Caribbean. Ask me next February. I'm sure by that time Ike would enjoy a vacation, and you could bring Irene along and we'd all have a lot of fun." Over her martini glass her eyes met his in a long, silent exchange that seemed to Matt to express thoughts she would never put into words.

"Actually, I'd prefer to spend the next few days with you right here in the city," he said. "At least I don't have to go until tomorrow." He grinned at her provocatively. "Don't you hate to sleep alone in hotel rooms? I do. We could spend the night together here or at my hotel."

Jill was not flustered. She continued to engulf him with her eyes. "Poor you. You sound sexually deprived. But if you are in such a spending mood, why not call up this high-priced call girl?"

Matt shook his head. "She belongs to Amir, but he offered me her friend, Lisa."

"Good. That settles your problem. And in case you've forgotten, I belong to your father. I just talked with him in Los Angeles. You really are giving him a bad time."

"Did you tell him that you knew that I was going to ask you to sleep with me tonight?"

"I'm not hearing you," Jill said coolly. "So far as I'm concerned, you are the prodigal son. As I told you on the plane, Ike is temporarily stuck with you. Gus Belshin is convinced that you deserve your chance to . . ." Jill fell silent.

"To what?"

"To fuck up," she grinned and finished her martini. Matt nodded to the waiter to bring her another one.

"I may be on the verge of doing just that," Matt said, and he had a dangerous compulsion to share the golden fairy tale with her and get her reaction. Was it simply a reflection of his suckling need for a loving woman who of course must adore him too, no matter what? Other than Peachy Stein, and Lovejoy, who had told him that he was sure there must be a fly in the ointment somewhere, he had really no one to weigh the pros and cons with of this insane adventure. And now Amir had left him with a gnawing worry about his motives. But why Jill? If she knew, she would have to tell Ike, and that was all the ammunition Ike needed to shoot down his crazy son.

Nibbling on some tiny knishes that the waiter had brought, Matt said, "Actually, if you did agree to fly to Grand Cayman with me tomorrow, for my own protection I'd have to seduce you."

"For your protection?" Jill raised her eyebrows. "What about mine?" She knew that she should have closed the subject or at least expressed contempt that he would admit such ideas to his father's wife. She really wasn't sure whether Matt was just teasing her, but she was finding it increasingly difficult not to respond to the hypnotic feeling that he was actually touching her body and caressing her, although quite a few inches still separated them.

"I don't know what you're worried about," she said, quite aware that her second drink was making her feel giddy. "If your father knew that I was having a rendezvous with you in New York, calmly listening to you tell me that you want to go to bed with me, and I didn't slap your face or walk out of here in total shock and disgust, I'm sure that he'd divorce me the next day. So you may be quite sure, no matter what you tell me, I would never admit to Ike that I knew you so well for such confidences—sexual or otherwise."

Matt looked at his watch. "It's only six-thirty. Since you're not hungry for food or sex and tonight I really need to run the whole business by some sympathetic ear, I'll tell you the reason I'm here—but not why. I'm not really sure why. Perhaps I'm trying to play both ends against the middle."

Enjoying her almost loving concentration, Matt told her in detail about Sylvie's golden jackpot, his meeting with Amir Faisal Saud today, and his projected flight to Grand Cayman tomorrow. Occasionally Jill shook her head in wonder, but her changing expressions, including a brief scowl when the waiter placed a third martini in front of her, indicated that her interest was balanced by fear and disapproval.

"So, in a nutshell, that's it," he concluded. "You really should fly to Grand Cayman with us tomorrow. Even if El Dorado doesn't actually exist, we'd have a pleasant little vacation."

Jill shook her head vehemently. "And you're not flying there either, Matt Godwin. Have you gone crazy? Do you realize what could happen to you? I should call your father right now, or, better still, the police, and have you locked up for safe keeping. Please, Matt, I beg you, forget the whole sleazy business. The FBI could be patiently waiting for you, or someone, to arrive and lead them to that gold. If it's such a sure thing, why didn't your friend Lovejoy come with you? And your so-called friend Sylvie must think that you are still wet behind the ears. And he's right. Why did he pick you to sell the gold? And don't believe all that nonsense about laundering money. He could have found plenty of shady gold dealers, Arabic or not, and kept all the money for himself. The trouble is that he's afraid that somebody else may be after it. You're the patsy."

Tears were trickling down her cheeks, and she knew that she was slurring her words, and it was not entirely logical for her to be so concerned, but she had an overwhelming feeling that Matt was on a disaster course. Saving him from himself would really be saving the entire Godwin family from what could end in a family tragedy.

"I don't see how you can even be sure of your so-called friend Amir," she shivered. "The way you described Nefwazi, I have a feeling that he is the kind of person who would be happy to slip a knife in your back if Amir told him to. You don't seem to realize that you are in a free-for-all. It's worse than finders-keepers. It's dead man out. Once you show Amir where the gold is, he can kiss you good-bye and take it all."

Listening to her without comment, a tiny smile flickering on his lips, Matt said, "I've considered all the possibilities. But the truth is that I'm not sure that this isn't a dream. I'd really hate to wake up before I find out how it all comes out."

"I'll tell you." Jill was getting a little angry with him. "Your whole life—including the First Parish Church and your modern moralities—is a daydream. When you wake up you'll be holding your severed head in your hands, and I don't want to be Salome and dance with it on a platter before your father." She suddenly wondered if Matt was trying to get her drunk. Although he had finished at least three scotches, he seemed to be more sober than she was. But he seemed oblivious of the waiter, who, without asking, was happily running up the check and was now placing a fourth martini in front of her. She ate a few knishes, hoping that they would absorb the alcohol.

"Like Martin Luther King, I have a dream," Matt said, "about a new kind of church and a new approach to religion. You know I don't plan to use the money personally. Unless you think that creating a new kind of church and a new religion is a balm to my ego. My plan is to use quite a few of these millions, if we negotiate this, to rebuild the First Parish Church and make it the flagship of hundreds of sister churches throughout America which will function as a new kind of self-supporting community club for their members. Without being sure that it will ever come to pass, before I left I turned over some of my ideas to Roje Lovejoy, and I told him that I was having drawings made of the church. I didn't tell him that if I continue to function as president of CPC, there's no reason why Ike's dream of CPC headquarters in Adamsport can't be realized too. Across the street from the church is a jerry-built bargain store building and behind that an outmoded courthouse. I'm sure that we could pick up both structures for less than the cost of the church." He laughed, "Especially if I decide to bid Ike up on the church."

Jill guessed that Matt was trying to prove to her that a basically immoral act could, by some magic, be transformed into a moral one when the proper reasoning was applied. But now she was in no condition to argue philosophy with him. "I enjoyed your sermon," she told him, "but you really do talk out of both sides of your mouth at once." She was trying to focus his face, and she was only dimly aware that under the table he had slipped his fingers into hers. "Why don't you be honest with me? You really don't believe that man is God, do you? That's ridiculous! Is your friend Sylvie God? Is your father God? And those Arab friends of yours, who are obviously eager to make a fast buck, are they God?" She unclasped her hand from his and tried to stare at him disdainfully. "And what about you—trying to seduce your stepmother. Are you God? Some God!"

"You are assuming that God is good," Matt replied calmly. "But if you simply accept that God is all there is—everything, every animal, every bird, every fish, every atom, every animate thing, all culminating in man and woman, who are the only beings able to correlate their actions and their memories—then God must encompass evil as we understand it as well as good."

He cupped Jill's hand again and she didn't pull away. "God as man and woman certainly should be able to define ultimate evils and try to prevent them. God as a man or woman who murders another man or woman, or engages in war, is obviously enacting the ultimate evil. Beyond that I'm not sure what the other evils are, but as I tried to point out in my sermon, most of what we believe to be evil is based on a morality of time and place. Thus I believe that man and woman, as God, must constantly refine and define their moralities with the ultimate objective of producing the greatest good for the greatest number." Matt grinned at Jill's wide-eyed incomprehension. "I'm really asking you to help me. You could become a moral stemwinder. A Church of Modern Moralities should never be static; it should be continuously searching for ultimate moral beliefs."

"You obviously don't think stealing money is immoral." Jill was about to add, "or having sex with any woman who meets your fancy," but she censored herself.

"I didn't steal the gold originally," Matt protested. "Who are its rightful owners? The people of the United States? If it were recovered by the FBI, it would be put in the cellars of the Federal Reserve Bank of New York, and it would do the average American no good personally. I plan to use it for the good of the people. You must realize that there are situations where the morality of stealing is relative. Stealing food or medicine for survival, for example."

Jill suddenly slumped against him. "My God, Matt, how can you talk so sensibly?" She giggled. "I'm sorry, but the truth is that I'm tipsy. I'm not even sure that I can walk out of here."

Helping her to her feet, Matt draped her coat over her shoulders. Grinning, he paid the waiter and engineered her through the crowded lounge. "Where are you taking me?" she demanded. "I'm not hungry. I just want to lie down."

"Where's your room key?"

"In my pocketbook. Just get me to the elevator, I'll be all right." But, leaning against him for support, she didn't object when he got off at her floor. In the empty hallway, she kicked off her shoes, and while he retrieved them she disappeared around the corner singing, "How high can a little bird fly—is there a ceiling to the sky? If there's a ceiling—I am feeling higher than a little bird can fly," after which she collapsed on the rug in a laughing heap. She pointed to a door. "My room, a suite," she gasped. "The fruits of gold digging." Her eyes closed, she curled in a ball on the floor. "Never mind, I'll sleep here. I can live without it."

Matt extricated the key from her hand, opened the door, and

turned on the lights. Ignoring her protests, he picked her up and carried her through the sitting room into the bedroom and propped her gently on the bed. Sitting beside her, he snapped on a bedside light and kissed her closed eyes. When that evoked no response, he kissed her lips. She stared at him with a bleary grin. "Thanks. That was nice. How in hell did I ever get mixed up with the damned Godwins? I should have my head examined."

"Are you all right? Are you going to be sick?"

"I'm fine. Just pooped from listening to you and worrying about you. Good-bye. I need to sleep." She closed her eyes and then opened them with a frightened expression. "Promise me. Don't go to the Cayman Islands with those Arabs." She closed her eyes again.

Matt shook her gently. "You'd better wake up," he said. "You're in my power."

But she only kept repeating, "Goo-bye, Mattie sweetheart, goo-bye, see you in Adamsport."

"I didn't expect to sleep with a corpse," he said, thinking that would bring her to her feet. But there was no response. She didn't react either when he unhooked her skirt and took it off, and she was a limp doll with her legs, thighs, and behind flopping against his hands as he extricated her from her panty hose.

Finally naked, she continued to sleep blissfully, totally oblivious to his hands caressing her breasts and ruffling her pubic hair. He stood beside the bed and stripped. Grinning, he noted the time. It was only eight-fifteen. He pulled the covers from under her, slid in beside her, and rolled her gently toward him. When he kissed her she opened her eyes and looked at him blankly.

"All right, Matt Godwin," she sighed, and a tear trickled down her cheek. "You got your way. So prove you are God. Be a gentleman. Don't fuck me!"

19

The next morning, half in a trance, half-asleep, an angelic expression on her face, Jill gave up protesting, momentarily, and let Matt lead her through the lobby of the Plaza to a taxi waiting near the fountain. Inside the cab she slumped in one corner. Stretching her legs across Matt's knees, she closed her eyes and prayed that the taxicab driver wasn't trying to drive and watch Matt in the rear view mirror. His fingers, under her skirt, were erotically tugging one pubic hair at a time. This was ridiculous. After nearly continuous loving, tasting, touching, and blissful merger, interspersed with catnaps, and then commencing again, how could she still be sexually responsive to this crazy man?

"Please, honey," eyes closed, she murmured her ecstasy. "You're making me glide again—and I want to . . . forever. But I'm so pooped I can scarcely talk." Then, suddenly frightened, she stared at him. "Why am I here? I don't remember agreeing that I'd go on this madcap trip with you. Let me out." Trying to assess the passing traffic and get her bearings, she put her feet on the floor of the cab determinedly. "Matt, please tell the driver to pull over. I'll catch a taxi back to the hotel." A little grin flickered around her mouth. "I flew enough last night to get to the Caribbean and back. I'm going to stay in bed all day and recover."

Matt leaned over and kissed her cheek. "You can sleep on the plane." He swept her legs back over his knees. "Don't worry," he said softly. "I'm as happily exhausted as you are. I still can't believe it. Last night when I carried you to bed you had disappeared into a never-never land. I held you in my arms for two hours. You were breathing so heavily that I was afraid that you were about to take your last breath. I kept kissing you from head to foot. I played doctor with you so long that I know every intimate part of you better than you do yourself."

He grinned at her. "Including a mole on the upper inside of your left buttock. Through it all you were a corpse. I was beginning to think that I was a necrophiliac. Then, *mirabile dictu,* you suddenly woke up. Bright and perky you stared at me. You seemed amazed that I was there. 'Where did you come from?' you demanded, 'Outer Centurian? I'm sure that I've met you somewhere in outer space.' Then you moaned, 'Oh my God, no! Go home to your Godwins! This can't be!' After which you kissed me passionately. For the next hour, when you weren't snuggling me against your breasts like a worried mother bear, you were a joyous, insatiable tigress biting and eating me and adoring me as enthusiastically as a kitten playing and purring over catnip."

"Don't confuse the play with the reality." Jill was embarrassed by his intimate recall. "I'm an actress, you know. Often I can't tell truth from fiction. Sometimes I don't even know who 'me' is or whether I'm a character that I may be playing."

Matt's finger was tracing her labia. "If last night wasn't the real you, I'll settle for the actress." He smiled at her. "What's the real you really like?"

"Like right now," she sighed. "Matt, I'm worried about the driver. He obviously knows what you are doing. And I'm panic-stricken about Ike."

"You mean that you feel guilty?"

Jill shook her head. "I don't think so. Not yet, anyway. But I'd kill myself if Ike ever found out. And I'm really worried that I let you get me so sexed up. I'll surely burn in hell."

That was the truth, and it made her nervous to try and think subjectively—especially since she was sure that any guilt she might have felt would never lessen her bodily and mental compulsions toward Ike's son. Was it a hormonal attraction for Godwin males? Thank God there were only two of them. But she had never surrendered with Ike, or any man, as she had last night with Matt. For the first time in her life she had dared to become a true daughter of Lilith. A lascivious temptress, she had let herself go and made love as if she were a symphony of sex incarnated. With a lover who seemed programmed to her moods, she glided from quiet dance movements to never ending crescendos, in a surrender so complete that for moments at a time she no longer existed. Never in her first two marriages nor in the last year with Ike had she been so thoroughly absorbed by a man, or in turn had tried to blend a man's flesh into her very being.

Why had she let it happen? When she awoke from her alcoholic trance and realized that even though Matt's eyes were closed his hand was gently cupping her vulva, she was momentarily shocked. But her guilt dissipated in her sudden protective need to embrace this vulnerable, daisy-picking giant. When he slowly opened his eyes and smiled at her, she couldn't help herself; she rolled on top of him, kissing him fervently. But at the same time she tried to tell him that he must go—get dressed, leave now before it was too late. But it was already too late. She could feel his penis pressing hard against her belly, and before she could pull away, his hands were on her buttocks. Then he eased himself slowly into her and the hard fullness of him was as necessary to her as breathing. Sobbing her fear and joy, she undulated on his penis, her body moving in slow waves. Then, too quickly, past the point of no return, her current and his undercurrent merged. Screaming, laughing, sobbing, they broke into the sunlight of their passion.

Stretched out flat on top of him, his hands still gently massaging her back, she whispered, "So now you've had your revenge. Are you happy?"

"Revenge? What do you mean?"

"You've screwed your father's wife."

Matt slapped her behind stingingly. "Is that what you believe? In my book that *would be* immoral. Loving you isn't a weapon. It isn't something I would ever use against you or Ike or Irene. This is our secret, our joyous affirmation that you and I, as God, are totally loving creatures and would never use our love for each other or any person to hurt them."

"You really are a dreamer," she sighed and kissed his eyes and nose. "You're so far out of the reality of this real world that you're really dangerous. Oh God, I wish that I had never met you. Don't you understand? I love your father. Not passionately, but with admiration and respect. He's been really good for me, and I for him. Alone with me is one place where Ike dares to drop his guard. He makes love to me as if I'm some kind of saint. I must be a very bad woman. How can I love your father and love you, too?" Her mouth was soft and trembly on his lips. "You're the stranger across the crowded room—and I never believed in such silliness. But that first night we met at Becky's, I knew you were silently trying to cast a spell on me. I'm really afraid of you. Maybe you can love and run away. Maybe I can't."

She was straddling Matt's stomach, bending over him so he could kiss her breasts, and his suckling was arousing her again.

"As soon as this gold caper is finished," he said, "I'm going back to Adamsport, and . . ." He paused, unable to visualize the future and his new relationship with Jill.

"And you'll go on trying to be Christ, the savior." Jill shook her head, but she couldn't help chuckling. "Oh, to hell with it. *Carpe diem.*" She swung around, opening her moist vulva to his lips. Taking his penis in her hand, she told him it was a tower of Babel. It talked to her in many tongues, all of which were saying one thing: "Take me in your mouth and suckle me, and restoreth my soul!" Which she did.

Around eleven o'clock she suddenly told Matt that she was starving. She dialed room service, ordered four sliced chicken sandwiches and two bottles of champagne to be left outside the door as soon as possible, and then she smiled primly at him. "I'm registered here alone, remember? Anyway, I don't want to dress for dinner. And I don't want any bellboy to interrupt us. I want to shower and then eat you and my sandwich naked."

In the shower they soaped each other from head to foot, kissing their newly washed genital areas reverently and passionately. After which Matt discovered that the champagne had been delivered. He toasted her with the first glass and then poured a libation on her breasts and vulva, then she dunked his penis in her glass and lapped it off. With a half a chicken sandwich in one hand, she decided that he simply must hear a few lines from the new play, *Reverend Beecher and Mrs. Tilton.*

Standing naked on the bed—her stage—and giggling, she became a star of a Broadway opening.

"I'm going to read you just one tiny scene between Henry Beecher and Elizabeth Tilton," she said. "In this scene Beecher is on his knees wooing Elizabeth. She's married to Theodore, but he's out of town. Beecher says, 'I never knew how to worship, Elizabeth my dear, until I knew how to love.' 'Oh Henry,' she responds, 'I have been in profound wonder and hushed solemnity at the great mystery of our soul loving to which you have awakened me in the past year. Am I your soul mate?'"

Jill grinned at him. "Henry is now on the couch beside Elizabeth, slowly undoing the buttons on her blouse: 'Oh Henry . . . Henry, my husband, Teddy, believes in love, but not in sexual love. Could Christ love sexually and still be pure and noble? he asked me, and he replied, Nay, this fact would have so completely humanized him in the eyes of all the world that he could never have been regarded as God!'"

Jill giggled. "But this reply doesn't slow Beecher down at all. It really entices him. He kisses the top of Elizabeth's breasts and says: 'God has appointed woman for the refinement of the race. Anyway, my dear Elizabeth, the ties of blood do not always represent the highest human relationship. Jesus knew that there are affinities far higher and wider than those constituted by the earthly necessities of family life. The truth is that an affinity like ours is the way to Godliness. It's the cornerstone of my preaching, and my message for all the world.'

"'A Gospel of Love?' Elizabeth asks.

"'Of course, my dear.' Beecher kisses her on the mouth, and she responds so passionately that she's frightened. But he reassures her: 'Confusion and doubt is a transitional stage common to all sensitive natures like yours, sweet Elizabeth. It's an inevitable stage in one's moral evolution. Eventually one's higher nature triumphs. When that occurs, you are released from the arbitrary constraints of social institutions and traditions.'"

Back in his arms, Jill told him that he must read the entire play. The author had tried to tell the story of Henry Ward Beecher and Mrs. Tilton mostly in their own words, which were fully recorded in Beecher's sermons and during his famous trial for adultery. "If you played Beecher and I played Mrs. Tilton," she told him, "the play would be an instant hit!"

But Matt's quick laughing response, "Ike no like," had momentarily brought her back to reality. Now, remembering the sexually abandoned woman that she had been last night, she was convinced that it was the stuff that dreams were made of. In a few moments, when they got to Kennedy Airport, she'd kiss Matt good-bye and take a taxi back to the Plaza. Although Matt had persuaded her to toss another dress and a change of underwear into her smaller suitcase, she had wisely not checked out of the hotel. If Ike should try to telephone her from California, he'd simply get no answer. If he left a message she could call him eventually or even say she hadn't got it. She could legitimately be anywhere in the city. She had the freedom to be gone. But she most certainly wasn't going to the Caribbean.

Expecting to arrive in the airport circle at Kennedy, she was surprised when the taxi left them off instead at a side field, the Operations Office of Butler Aircraft. "We're flying in a private plane," Matt said as he guided her out of the taxi, "not Pan American." Protesting that she should have returned in the taxi that they came in and looking hopelessly around for another one, she let Matt lead her into the building. Before she could escape he was introducing her to a handsome, swarthy man with a thick, unruly mass of very black hair.

"Amir, this is my friend, Jill Marlowe." Matt winked at her. Although they had not conferred, Matt had sense enough not to reveal their true relationship. "For the record, I have no secrets from Jill. She knows where we are going and why."

"I just told Matt that I came to say bon voyage. I really can't go with you," Jill responded, smiling at Amir. "It sounds like an old-fashioned thriller instead of reality, but I hope you have a successful trip."

Amir nodded a little curtly. "Nefwazi and Kitty are waiting on board," he told Matt. "I made reservations at the Grand Cayman Inn, but I'm afraid that your client may be on his own trip."

"What do you mean?"

"I told you yesterday that my family has banking connections on Grand Cayman. Last night, I called a friend of mine on the island and told him that I might arrive with a friend who was speculating in gold. He thought that was a very intriguing coincidence. It seems that a couple of weeks ago, a Hindu named Ramachanda, who dresses like a Sikh, arrived from Miami in a decrepit three-masted cargo ship complete with a crew. My friend discovered that the boat had been bought in Key West. Ramachanda has talked informally with several bankers on the island. He's been dropping hints that he might be able to offer an exceptional price on an undetermined amount of gold ingots." Amir's eyebrows were curved in a questioning parenthesis of doubt. "It occurred to me that your client may be playing both ends against the middle."

"I don't think so," Matt murmured, trying to cover his confusion and doubt. Matt was sure that Sylvie, if he thought the situation warranted it, was capable of double-dealing, but Sylvie needed him and trusted him, not only because he was a Godwin, but because he could deliver "snow white dollars." Whether he'd be satisfied with ten million, if Matt turned his gold into four times that amount, was another question. At the moment Matt Godwin offered the safest way for Sylvie to put his fingers in his own pie.

"Why don't you telephone your client?" Amir suggested. "Or, if you prefer, you can give me the address of your client's villa. Nefwazi and I will fly down and check things out for you. I'm sure that you realize that ill-gotten gains imply certain risks. On the other hand, if someone else is searching for El Dorado, perhaps we can discourage them in a pleasant but forceful way."

"Where's the phone?" Matt asked. "I'll call my client. You can be sure if someone else is there first, Jill and I will check out."

Following Matt toward a telephone and out of Amir's hearing, Jill exploded: "For God's sake, Matt Godwin, I wouldn't trust that man to empty my garbage. Let him and his friends go by themselves. He gives me the creeps."

"Amir's all right," Matt said. "I'd trust him with Sylvie's gold but not with you. Didn't you notice the way he was inhaling you? Not that I blame him, but one half of his brain was in bed screwing with you. Anyway, I'll try to reach Sylvie and find out what this is all about."

"I don't care what Sylvie tells you, I'm not going with you," Jill said emphatically. "I want to live a few years longer, and not in Amir Saud's harem."

The telephone operator tried Sylvie's home, but there was no answer. She finally located him in his office at Silly Willy's. Matt quickly brought him up to date on his dealings with Amir. "There's something weird going on. Who in hell is a guy named Ramachanda?" Matt demanded. "Give it to me straight, Sylvie. Is he a friend of yours?"

There was a momentary silence, then Sylvie replied, "Look, Matt, why in hell would I share the wealth with some damned Indian? I was just trying to think who in hell he could be. I told you the truth. Two years ago, when I finally got the gold on a freighter out of Calcutta and then transferred it to a smaller boat a few hundred miles off Grand Cayman, the gold was still sealed in the original wooden boxes. Twenty of them. They arrived okay, unopened. They were consigned to Colonel Robert Gamble and listed as ancient Indian carvings and statuary. It could be that someone in the Indian bank I dealt with was tailing me. But I doubt it. If so, why has he waited so long? Anyway, I don't want you to think I'm putting your head on the chopping block. I'll catch a plane right away and meet you there tomorrow."

"No. Never mind," Matt said. "I'll handle it—or not, if it looks too dangerous. I don't want to take a chance that someone may be following you. We're staying at the Grand Cayman Inn. If I need you, I'll call you tomorrow night."

"You're really not going to go?" Jill demanded when he hung up. "It's very stupid. Let Sylvie and your Arab friends work it out together."

"You forget, I'm in too deep to quit now. Do you think I'm going back to Adamsport and beg Ike for a job? I'd rather steal his wife and become a Caribbean beach bum."

"Not with me, you won't," Jill said. "I enjoy civilization too much."

"I've changed my mind," Matt replied, becoming serious. "I don't think you should come. Go back to the hotel. Amir told me that he has to be back in New York by Saturday. If I'm not snuggled in bed with you at the Plaza Saturday night, send my obituary notice to the *New York Times*." He kissed her cheek. "Last night was heaven, sweet lady. In heaven or here, I'll always have an affinity for you."

With Jill tagging after him, he walked back to where Amir was waiting. "My client has no idea who this Ramachanda is. I trust him. If you're game, I think my client has prior rights, though, of course, we can't bring in the law to prove it."

Amir grinned approvingly. "What about your Jill? Is she coming along to fetch a pail of water?"

Matt shook his head, but Jill pointed grimly at her suitcase. "I'm coming! I haven't any tropical clothes, but my friend obviously needs a keeper—even if she's naked."

20

Driving to Logan Airport with Sylvie in his Mercedes, Emily was wondering aloud why she had agreed to fly to Grand Cayman with him. "This is really quite crazy. I'm sure that Roje isn't very happy with me. But sometimes he is such a stick in the mud. He could have come along with us. Whether he likes it or not, we're all kind of involved with Matt Godwin." She stared at Sylvie nervously. "How are you ever going to find him on the island?"

Sylvie patted her knees affectionately. "Calm down, Emmy. Roje is probably happy to get rid of you for a day or two. He needs some space. I should have told one of the girls from the club to give him a ring. If he took Milly to the Adamsport Country Club, she'd start some tongues wagging." Sylvie laughed briefly and then became serious again. "When Matt telephoned me, he said they had reservations at the Grand Cayman Inn. I'll send him a telegram from the airport. With a little luck and good connections in Miami, we should be there by six."

Less than two hours ago, Emily had been eating breakfast with Roje. When the bell chime played its *Eroica* greeting, she opened the front door and gasped. Sylvie had never come to the house before. She had planned to meet him later at the club, ostensibly to play golf, but she knew that more likely they would have lunch somewhere. One thing was sure: if she ended up in bed with him in his house, she was going to make it clear how disconcerted she had been to hear his gold story for the first time with Roje and Matt and Peachy. They had certainly been intimate enough in the past two months for him to have trusted her and told her privately what was truth and what was fiction.

She had made it clear to Sylvie that although she had enjoyed four different lovers at different periods in her long marriage to Roje, and even though Roje was often living in another world of writing that she didn't share with him, nevertheless—for good or bad—Roje came first in her life. And he always would. In addition, she couldn't understand why Sylvie was interested in her. Now in her sixties, she really didn't feel that she was physically attractive to men any more. She was at least five pounds overweight. Sylvie could have his pick of the young strippers at his club, and probably did. But Sylvie assured her that he never mixed his sexual life and business. A woman of his own generation was more enjoyable in bed than a young flit-brain who might have a better shape but could only wiggle her ass when some hot young rock star was singing to her while she "took it off."

Emily hadn't seen Sylvie for ten days. Not since the Sunday he had told them all, without any advance warning to her, his incredible golden fairy tale. Today would have been the fourth time she would have bedded with him, and although she had let herself be swept into this gold chase with him, she still was none too pleased that Sylvie apparently was an even more devious man that she had suspected. She hadn't told Roje the extent of her surrender to Sylvie. She was sure that Roje didn't like him very much. Besides, she would have felt much more confident if Roje, for the first time in their long and relatively happy marriage, hadn't given up extracurricular romantic pursuits—or at least seemed to have. Nearly two years had passed since Jeanne Stanley had decided that her occasional afternoons with Roje were jeopardizing her marital bed. She told Roje that she was afraid that if her husband, Richard, ever discovered that she was sharing her affections with him once a week, Richard, in one of his rages, might murder her. Since then Roje had seemed to be content with the more placid but somewhat predictable joys of monogamous marriage.

Before she could ask Sylvie what he was doing on her doorstep so early in the morning, he had given her a quick hug and said, "The Great Gold Salvage Conspiracy is in trouble. Where's Roje? I want to talk with him."

Roje had shown no particular surprise at seeing Sylvie. Without getting up from the table, where he had been sipping coffee while meditating on a scene that he was about to spend the morning writing, he gestured for him to sit down.

"I'm sorry to burst in on you," Sylvie said, while Emily poured coffee for him, "but we've got to move fast. Matt Godwin is on his way to Grand Cayman, and I'm afraid he may be walking into a somewhat sticky situation."

Roje nodded and told Sylvie that Matt had telephoned him yesterday and asked if he'd like to come along with him to New York and meet an Arab sheik. "He didn't tell me that he was flying to Grand Cayman," Roje said, and stared at Sylvie quizzically. "So that's where your treasure is hidden. Matt must have convinced his friend to fly down and take a look."

"Matt telephoned me less than an hour ago," Sylvie said. "I don't know whether it's simply a coincidence or not, but someone else on the island is offering a deal on gold bullion."

"Maybe it's a sting operation. The FBI is trying to smoke you out."

"Impossible. But it makes me nervous." Sylvie grimaced. He didn't tell Roje that he had been trying to reach his villa on the island for the past two days to tell Fernando and Maria, his caretakers, that Matt was arriving. But there had been no answer. It didn't mean anything in particular. While he had always kept the phone active, Fernando and Maria, who knew nothing about the gold buried under the living room floor, didn't live in the villa regularly. They had their own home on another part of the island.

"Anyway, I think that I should fly down and look things over. I'm hoping that both of you will come along with me." Sylvie grinned at Emily. "I made reservations for three to Miami. Grand Cayman is a beautiful spot. You both need a change of scenery. The plane leaves at eleven-thirty. I know it's short notice, but we'll be back by Sunday—with Matt, I hope. Monday, we auction the church to the highest bidder."

"I just told you. I refused to go to New York with Matt," Roje said coldly.

"But that was to New York. This is for some fun in the sun."

"It doesn't sound like fun to me. I told Matt that he was playing out of his league. It sounds to me as if someone has got to your gold before you did."

"Not necessarily. Grand Cayman is an offshore banking center. The banks there are just as private in their dealings with their customers as their Swiss counterparts. There's plenty of illegal gold smuggling going on in the world."

Emily had been jubilant. "Why can't we go, Roje?" she demanded. "We haven't been anywhere since last February. You've got to stop being a recluse. At our age we should relax and enjoy life."

"It doesn't sound relaxing to me." Roje had been obdurate. "You know damned well that I'm three months overdue on my novel. The contract specified final manuscript delivery in June. The publishers aren't very happy with me, anyway. If I keep coming up with excuses, they could cancel the contract."

"That's just the point and you keep missing it," Sylvie said. "If things work out, you can tell your publisher to shove it. You'll have a new career, and be a damned sight richer than you are now."

"I don't want a new career. And I wouldn't enjoy you as a cell mate at Walpole prison. But I am happy that you're not letting Godwin stick his neck out all by himself." Then, seeing the disappointment on Emily's face and curious to see their reaction, he said, "Why don't you take Emily with you? She's more intrigued with your fairy tale than I have ever been."

Actually, after Peachy's broad hint that Sylvie and Emily were enjoying a little romantic interlude together, Roje was convinced that the only reason the Lovejoys had been invited to share in Sylvie's great gold conspiracy was to weave the webs of their lives a little tighter.

Sylvie grinned at Emily, but she shook her head sadly. "I couldn't go without you, Roje."

"Why not? Sylvie knows that I'm not the jealous type. Go ahead. Have fun. If Sylvie's fairy tale comes true, you can support me on our share."

Emily knew that Roje's tone had been more than a little sarcastic, but she hugged him. "If you really don't mind, I'd like to go," she said.

Now, sitting beside Sylvie on an Eastern Airlines jet to Miami, where they would transfer to Jamaican Airlines, for the first time Emily tackled Sylvie head-on. "I don't know why I'm doing this. I'm risking my marriage, you know," she told him. "And I'm certainly not trying to find another marriage partner at this late stage in my life. I want the truth. I have shared more of me with you than you have with me. I want to know who the real Sylvanus Williams is, including the various roles he may have played—such as Colonel Gamble."

21

A few minutes after they had reached their flying altitude, Amir left Nefwazi at the controls and joined Jill, Kitty, and Matt sitting in the cabin informally in a semi-circle, drinking coffee and eating croissants that Kitty had brought along.

"Our arrival time at Grand Cayman should be approximately four-thirty," Amir told them as he joined the group. "Whatever happens now is in the hands of Allah. *Mutab*, 'it is written,' as the prophet tells us, and no one can change that."

"Abou Ben Adhem did," Jill challenged him with a little grin. "Wasn't he an Arab?" Having decided "to come along for the ride," as she put it to Amir, she was now curious to know what motivated him. She couldn't ask Kitty because, walking out to the plane, he had told her that although Kitty was his American wife, he never discussed business with her.

"Abou Ben Adhem," Amir smiled, "is a fantasy of one of your English poets. When the angel asked the names of those who loved the Lord, Ben Adhem's name wasn't there."

"But he loved his fellow men," Kitty said.

"He was a dreamer, just like Goddy." Amir was enjoying the

exchange. "Your God might forgive Ben Adhem, but not Allah. Allah comes first."

Matt laughed, knowing that Amir was teasing him.

"Kitty and I read your sermon last night," Amir said. "We wish you luck. 'May your tribe increase'—but I doubt it! God, or Allah, might make an exception for Ben Adhem, but Allah would never be happy in a democratic heaven. If everyone was sure that he was God, they'd all be calling their lawyers and suing each other. Allah knows there is only one place on the throne. But you do have something in common with the Arabs, Goddy. You want us to worship sex." Amir smiled beguilingly at Jill. "The Arabs can't get enough of it, either!"

"That's not quite true," Kitty scowled at him. It was obvious that in certain areas she wasn't afraid to challenge him. "The Arab male worships sex, but the Arab female must worship one particular male—the man she marries. And, praise Allah, that first night when she hops into bed with him, she'd better be a virgin. And forever afterwards she can never screw around with another man again, even if her God and master divorces her."

"What happens if she's not a virgin?" Matt asked.

"Her father will kill her," Amir said coolly. "She has violated her family's honor. If she should get involved with another man after she is married, her father or brothers are still obligated to kill her." Amir laughed. "I don't know about you, Jill, but if Kitty were an Arab woman, she'd be dead by now."

"What about her lover?" Jill demanded, happy that Amir didn't know the truth about her and Matt.

"Her husband must kill the lover, of course," Amir said. "But it is not the husband who is disgraced by his wife's infidelity; it's her family. Her father or brothers must protect the family honor. That's why your sermon fascinated me, Goddy. If you preached it in an Arabic country, you would be denounced. You are obviously a very dangerous radical. On the other hand," Amir shrugged, "the way the world is going, with the Arabs being corrupted by their contact with what we consider a very sick Western morality, some of which you are obviously preaching against, a few Islamic leaders might still listen to you." Amir laughed boisterously. "But not for long. They'd have to cut your balls off for their own protection."

"You do have a problem," Matt said. "Your countrymen are still living in the Middle Ages. Honor—*sharaf*, I think the word is—motivates your behavior. In America we no longer give a damn about honor."

"*Sharaf* is male honor," Amir replied. "We're much cooler about our *sharaf* than Christians. We believe that bravery, courage, honesty, hospitality, even being caught in a nonsexual, immoral situation such as the escapade we are now engaged in—how one behaves in this situation—is written in the stars. There's nothing we can do about it. But we don't let deviations from this kind of honor keep us awake at night."

"But *sharaf* is not female honor." As she spoke, Kitty was bending Amir's stubby, well-manicured fingers. She was smiling at him affectionately, but she gave the impression that she wouldn't hesitate to bend his fingers against the joints if she were crossed. "I'm an American, so for me it doesn't apply. But an Arab girl has her *ird*, female honor. Before marriage it is almost synonymous with virginity. If she loses it, her whole family is disgraced. Her father or brothers will have to kill her. But they make sure that doesn't happen. They de-sex her when she's about ten years old, or try to. While her mother or father spreads her thighs, a *daya*, a local female witch doctor or a male doctor with equivalent credentials, slices off her clitoris with a sharp razor. In the Sudan they go all out. They trim her labia, too, and then they sew it partially up so no man's penis can get into her vagina until she's married, and then the threads are cut."

Amir shrugged. "Kitty reads too much. That's a dying custom."

"Not according to Nawal El Saudawi. She's an Egyptian M.D.," Kitty explained, "one of the few Arabic women who dares tell it like it is. In a book she wrote just a few years ago, she insists that close to 60 percent of Arabic women still get a clitordectomy very early in life."

Amir grinned. "Sometimes educated women are what you call 'a pain in the neck.' Kitty has a master's degree in anthropology. I met her on a 'dig' in my country. But she has given up exploring for her ancestors for more lucrative digging."

Kitty laughed. "There have been some sacrifices. For being absolutely faithful to Amir—ready to be at my master's service when he arrives in the United States and willing to live without him, often for months at a time—I own an expensive condominium, and I have a non-reportable income that would be hard to duplicate even if I were as famous as the Leakeys."

"Kitty is a realist," Amir said. "What about you, Jill?"

Jill sighed, and smiled tentatively at Matt. "Without going into details, although I have been a successful actress, at the moment I depend on a lord and master, too."

"Aha!" Amir smirked at Matt. "The truth will out. Our sermonizer does not practice what he preaches." Matt didn't dispute him, so he continued: "We have something in common, Goddy. We're blessed. We have women who are not challenging their ordained role in the world. American women like that are not easy to find. Most of them want to be men. They're screwing up your society. Look at what has happened to the United States. You've created a world where the women have to work to keep their families intact. A hundred years ago, American men were much more like the Arab men. They supported their wives. In return, their wives respected them—even adored them—took care of their homes, raised the children and made it possible for their men to attend to their religious duties. By contrast with Arabic countries, your women have taken more jobs away from your men than the Japanese have. You have a divorce rate that's 50 percent of the marriage rate. Millions of your children are born out of wedlock or are being brought up by women with no male input . . . And I don't mean a penis. In Saudia Arabia we control our social moralities by protecting a woman's honor. It's really no worse than the cracks in your own foundations. Sexual freedom without responsibility, the way you have it in America, spells the end of a civilization. America cannot survive."

He chuckled. "Maybe your Moral Majority makes more sense than you do. In any event, your golden daydream intrigues me. I agree with you, both America and Islamic countries need new moralities. We both need to create new societies that are twenty-first-century oriented—societies where the average person knows where he or she is going and what the purposes of life are. We've got to define individual lives and give them a larger perspective. We've got to convince people that our varying nations are not in conflict but are all directed toward one goal." Amir paused, lost in thought for a moment. "Until we got involved with the West and your insatiable demand for oil, Islam was successful. We had a family-oriented structure that worked. It would still work if we weren't conned by your global village philosophy. I know we can't go back. I admire your daydreams, Goddy. The problem is, they aren't realistic."

"Are you married?" Jill finally dared to ask the question that had been plaguing her.

Amir smiled. "I love women. I have two wives," he said. "And I have Kitty. If Matt would let you go, I can make room for you. I know you find this shocking, but if I were a wealthy American, like Matt, I would have a wife and girl friend too. Only not so happily, in all probability. As it is, my wives know each other, and actually, they are very much like sisters. I won't inquire whether you know Matt's wife, but the chances are, even if you do, you are not friends. The prophet Mahomet had fourteen wives. Like him, I am proud of my sexual necessities. Your prophet Jesus was a sexless man, and I fear that he was ashamed of human loving."

"Don't your wives ever complain that you don't give them enough loving?" Jill asked with an impish grin. "Even if they do, from what Kitty has told us, I guess that it wouldn't do them much good."

"Arabs are more realistic. The Islamic world is a man's world." Amir shrugged. "I'm not saying that it's the best of all possible worlds, but neither is your world of equal rights. Our women not only have family security but polygamy, which, although it seems to horrify you, for many women is preferable to no man at all. I read that you have at least ten million women in America who have no male companions. Although an Arab male may not obey the Koran and love all his wives equally, he is required to protect them."

"Amir is skipping over the real problem," Kitty said. "Like it or not, as Matt has pointed out in his sermon, the same attitude motivates American males. When you mention the word *woman* to an Arab, he immediately thinks of *fitna*, or seductiveness. Arab women themselves know that they can drive a man crazy. They are dangerous to men. Men cannot resist them. There's an ancient Arab saying: 'Whenever a man and woman meet together, the third person present is always Satan.' The prophets anticipated Freud by hundreds of years; they were positive that civilization was the result of repression. Without restraints men and women would never stop fucking. Mahomet solved the problem. He told his people: 'I have been preferred to Adam in two ways. Adam's wife incited him to disobedience, whereas my wives helped me to obey. Adam's Satan was a heretic, whereas mine was a Muslim, inviting me always to do good.'"

Kitty laughed. "So the Arabs, who believe that passion is the most compelling aspect of human nature, have confined it to marriage. They really are not far from Catholic theology. Making marriage a sacrament provides social restraints. The big difference in the West is that they don't burn heretics at the stake any more. In Islam they do."

Amir invited Jill to the cockpit so that he could relieve Nefwazi, and he promised to show her how to fly the plane. Before he left he said, "Ibn Abbas, a famous Inman, Allah's blessing be upon him, sums it up: 'He who enters a woman is lost in the twilight . . . If the male organ rises up it can be an overwhelming catastrophe. Once provoked it cannot be resisted by either reason or religion. For this organ is more powerful than all the instruments used by Satan against man.'"

Later, after a lunch of lamb and rice (which Nefwazi heated up in a microwave oven) and wine for their guests, Matt kept searching with Amir for the basic differences between Islam and the West. "It's in the verb itself," Amir told him. "*Aslama*, from which the word *Islam* is derived, means 'to submit, surrender oneself wholly and give oneself in total commitment' to the will of God. The faithful Arab knows that the universe is on a predetermined course. Allah not only guides the world at large but also plans the fate of each man and woman individually."

Listening to them with closed eyes, memories of her fiery lovemaking with Matt filtering without sequence through her mind, Jill gave a little prayer that Allah might make an exception for her and Matt. In their case—although she couldn't figure out why he should—

she prayed that he would refrain from being vindictive or vengeful.

Jill was surprised that during the flight neither Amir nor Nefwazi brought up the subject of gold or why they were all going to Grand Cayman. While Nefwazi, who spent most of his time flying the plane, was still a mystery, Amir was not so scary as she had thought. She would still hesitate to cross him, but she could see how Kitty would enjoy his bright mind. "He may be a patriarch," she managed to whisper to Matt, "but he likes women who challenge him."

At 4:50 P.M. they landed at Owen Roberts Airport in Grand Cayman, and a half-hour later they arrived at the Grand Cayman Inn in a rented Chevrolet, which Matt handed over to the doorman. Jill and Matt followed Amir, Nefwazi, and Kitty into the busy lobby. Lagging a little behind Matt, Jill was wondering how he was going to register them. She noticed a deeply tanned man across the lobby who was staring quizzically at Matt. Then his face suddenly lighted up in recognition. To her horror, he was smiling and walking toward them.

"My God! Is that man a friend of yours?" Jill managed to ask before he was in hearing distance. "Just pray that he doesn't know Ike."

"Matt Godwin!" The stranger thrust out his hand. "I'm Dave Crispin. You remember, Crispin, Fowler and Milburn." Matt knew him all right. Crispin was one of the lawyers representing Gus Belshin during the takeover of Infinity Corporation. "What brings you to Grand Cayman?" Crispin glanced inquisitively at Jill. "Business or pleasure?"

"A few days in the sun," Matt responded uneasily, hoping that Crispin wouldn't mention Gus Belshin's name. He knew that Jill had probably met Gus. But knowing that he had no choice, he gambled, and introduced Jill. "This is my wife, Irene," he said.

For a moment there was a puzzled expression on Crispin's face, but it quickly vanished. "We just arrived," Matt said, gesturing toward Amir at the registration desk, "with some friends from Saudi Arabia. Are you staying here?"

Crispin shook his head. "My wife and I are at the Galleon Bay. We decided to dine here tonight and take in the floor show." He pointed to one of the hotel shops. "Alice is busy spending our money. If you have some free time, give us a ring, Matt. Maybe we can do some scuba diving together."

Gently pushing Jill toward the registration desk, Matt noted that she was trembling. "Who is he?" she demanded.

"Just a lawyer. He was involved in one of CPC's acquisitions."

"Does he know your father?"

Matt nodded. "But don't worry. He's never met Irene."

"Irene—Jesus! That tops everything." Jill shuddered. "He kept staring at me. He knows damned well that I'm not your wife."

Matt grinned. "So, you're my girl friend. Don't worry, he'll never meet Irene." Matt decided not to alarm Jill and tell her that Crispin worked for Gus Belshin, or probe Jill to discover whether there was any chance that she might have met Gus in California when she married Ike. It seemed unlikely, and right now Jill was jittery enough.

While he was registering as Mr. and Mrs. Matthew Godwin, the clerk handed him a telegram, and Matt opened it so Jill could read it too. Any worries about Crispin vanished. "Make no connection until I contact you sometime this evening before nine o'clock." The telegram was signed "Colonel Gamble."

"Is Sylvie here?" Jill asked.

"Damned if I know. He may be planning to telephone me from Adamsport."

A bellboy stood by patiently with their bags. Amir, who had been waiting with Kitty, nodded at the clock. "It's only quarter to six. After we've 'rested,' say about eight-thirty, we can meet in the dining room. Before we get down to more practical matters, perhaps we can pursue our philosophic discussion. I'd like to explore your ideas about sex worship, which intrigues me."

Smiling, Jill demurred. "I'm really pooped."

During six hours of confinement with Amir, Kitty, and Nefwazi, Jill had been unable to voice her fears and uneasiness as she tried to absorb their very different philosophy of life. Now, all she wanted was to be alone with Matt and try to convince him that he was playing out of his league.

Matt's folly—really a by-product of having a father like Ike—was not only that he needed to prove himself on his own terms but that at the same time he needed accolades, no matter what the source, but preferably from a woman who would give him the encouragement and love and enthusiasm that Ike had denied him. Matt didn't seem to realize that he was involved with Amir and Nefwazi in a fatalistic, no-choice kind of way. Win, lose, or draw, it didn't matter to them. Amir had made it clear . . . Allah willed their fate. If circumstances forced them to write Matt or her out of this adventure—dead or alive—it was simply *quismet*. There could be no complaints. Not even a last-minute Christian prayer, "God save me," but rather grim acceptance: "*Allah Keerem*, Allah is bountiful . . . no matter what."

Matt temporized with Amir but didn't mention Sylvie's telegram. "We'll ring your room around eight," he told Kitty and Amir. "Let's wait and see if we're hungry enough to get dressed."

When the bellboy finally left their room Jill followed Matt onto the balcony. Unable to enjoy the remote beauty of the cool red sun splashing the sky with a Surrealist painter's palette as it slowly disappeared on the limitless Caribbean horizon, she flung herself into Matt's arms. "I know that it's beautiful. If we were alone, I'd walk the whole Seven Mile beach with you tonight and make love with you naked in the warm ocean. But right now I can't think straight."

Her eyes were awash with tears. "Oh God, why did I ever get involved in this mess? I'm not only scared to death of Nefwazi and Amir, but I'm feeling terribly guilty about Ike. What if that man Crispin sees Ike and describes your wife to him? Irene's hair is black; mine is a mixture of gray. I have brown eyes and Irene has blue eyes. Please, Matt, I beg you—tomorrow let me fly back to New York. While you were renting the car, I checked, and there are three or four flights a day to Miami. I can connect from there. You can stay here and play James Bond with your friends. You don't need me."

Matt sighed and slipped the zipper on the back of her dress. "I do need you," he said. "You give me a loving kind of mental-sexual interaction that Irene isn't capable of. I love you and I love Irene, too, for the kind of woman that she is. I know damned well that loving more than one woman is against all the possessive patriarchal moralities cooked up by Christian theologians, but I don't feel guilty about it."

He eased the dress over her shoulders and it fell to the floor. "Maybe you should go home. But I think that you and I are very much alike. We can really love more than one person, and we can, momentarily at least, really become the other person and surrender completely to him or her. Neither Ike nor Irene can. But they can experience as much of each of us as they wish. What more can they ask?" He picked her up and put her gently down on the bed. He knew that he wasn't being completely honest. It was one thing to challenge the world, but to have involved his father's wife in this insanity was wrong, and he knew it. Immoral. Man as God did not have carte blanche to try and re-create another person in his image. He kissed Jill and lay down beside her. "I suppose I'm using immoral means to achieve moral ends," he mused aloud. "Even worse, I have to face the truth. Do I only want Sylvie's gold so that I can force my moralities on others? That's Nietzsche-Hitler-style insanity. Maybe I'm just playing God and not *being* God."

Jill couldn't help herself. Suddenly she was laughing and kissing him. "You're my God. I love you. Stop blaming yourself. I'm not a child. Maybe I'm weak-brained, but I'm sure of one thing. I'm a patsy for a man like you who can still lie here and philosophize about God and morality when he's in danger of getting his balls shot off. I'm scared. I love you. I know I can't stop you, but I really am going to leave tomorrow." She sighed. "I'd still like to know what your plans are."

Matt scowled. "Right now I'm waiting for Sylvie. Is he going to telephone me from Boston, or is he going to arrive here? Why did he hesitate when I told him about Ramachanda? I don't think he lied to me, but it really looks as if this Indian, whoever he is, has already found Sylvie's gold. I showed you the letter Sylvie gave me to deliver to Fernando and Maria. They're caretakers for the villa and have a room there. This island isn't very big; Rum Point is probably only a few miles from here. Sylvie told me there's a crowbar and shovel in the garage. After we get rid of Fernando and Maria, all we have to do is dig up the floor in the living room." Matt stared silently at the ceiling. "My plan was to drive out to the villa with Amir and Nefwazi after breakfast."

"Then what?"

"If the gold is actually there, and someone else hasn't dug it up, that's it. I'll turn it over to Amir. If there is honor among thieves, it's because, in this case, Allah decreed it. If not—to hell with it."

Listening to the intermittent caress of the waves on the sand a few floors below them and the faraway rhythms of steel drums being pounded in a calypso beat, Jill arched her thigh over Matt's hip. He slid between her legs. Eyes closed, his head on her shoulder, they were joined. Time had stopped. She gently feathered her fingers through the hair of this child-man whose face was nuzzling her breasts. The faint pulse of his penis, deep inside her, matched the timelessness of the moment. The disappearing rays of the sun created dancing shadows on their bodies, and they were floating together in the warm darkness. This was heaven.

Then the telephone rang. Jill jumped away from Matt as if an actual presence was in the room. "Oh damn, damn, who's that?" she demanded.

"Either Amir or Sylvie." Matt looked at his watch. "It's quarter past eight. Amir and Kitty are probably anxious to join the world again. I'm sure that he's not the kind of man who would prefer to disappear forever into a loving woman's body."

Jill noticed a sudden doubtful tone in Matt's voice as he said "Yes?" into the phone.

"Yes. Yes, I am he." Matt's face had a troubled, cautious expression. "How did you know I was here? Did you telephone Amir Saud? I really think that's too late. Why not tomorrow?" Matt listened for another minute and then said, "All right, within the hour." He hung up.

"Who was that?" Jill asked, with an ominous feeling in her stomach.

"Kalki Ramachanda. He's the guy Amir told us about this morning. He said he heard that I'd be arriving today and that I might be interested in buying precious metals. He insists that we must talk tonight. He said that he has another potential customer. It's nearly eight-thirty. Where the hell is Sylvie?" He stared glumly at Jill. "There's something rotten in Denmark. The address he gave me is the same as Sylvie's villa on Rum Point."

"It looks as if Ramachanda got to your friend's gold before you did." Jill felt almost relieved. "You sure as hell can't buy it from him."

"It's not his gold. It's Sylvie's. At least, I thought it was."

"Why tonight?" Jill wanted to remind Matt that it really wasn't Sylvie's gold either, but she refrained.

"He said he has another buyer. If he hadn't discovered, evidently through some friend of Amir's, that I might be interested, he would have already completed the transaction."

"What does he expect from you?"

Matt shrugged. "I told you, he thinks I'm a buyer. He thinks I might pay more than his current offer." He picked up the phone.

"Who are you calling?"

"Sylvie in Adamsport. I want to find out what his telegram is all about." Matt was wondering if Sylvie was somehow double dealing, but he didn't reveal his thoughts to Jill.

Ten minutes later, unable to locate Sylvie either at home or at the club, Matt dialed Amir's room. Jill listened nervously while Matt explained Ramachanda's phone call. Finally he told Amir, "Okay, I'll tell Jill to meet Kitty at the bar in a half an hour." He hung up. "They were just getting ready to telephone us. You can wait with Kitty in the lounge. Amir and Nefwazi are going to meet me in the lobby immediately. We'll take a look at Ramachanda's gold."

Terrified, Jill jumped off the bed and grabbed his arm. "Matt, don't be stupid! What about Sylvie's telegram? It says make *no* connection until he contacts you. Why didn't you tell Amir about the telegram?"

Matt looked at his watch again. "I may have to, but I want to give Sylvie time to call."

"If this Ramachanda has the gold, I think you should quit. What can you do about it?"

"Amir thinks that we might persuade him to share the wealth."

"Are you going to hold a gun to his head?" Jill demanded sarcastically. "You really are a new breed of minister. A few minutes ago you told me that you were afraid you may have been shoving your moralities down my throat. Now you're going to have a showdown at the O.K. Corral. The trouble is that I don't know who the bad guys really are!"

Matt smiled, trying to conceal his own misgivings. "Stop worrying, I'm not an old-time gunslinger." He didn't want to tell her that a frightening thought had occurred to him: What if Sylvie had decided to fly to Grand Cayman? What if he had gone to the villa and discovered Ramachanda in possession of his gold? "I simply agree with

Amir," he said. "We have as much right to Sylvie's gold as this character does."

"Some right." Jill snapped on her bra and slipped her dress over her head. "If this is just going to be a friendly discussion between bad boys who really wouldn't hurt each other, then I'm coming with you. I'm not spending the evening with Kitty. She doesn't have the faintest idea what's going on."

Matt tried to dissuade her, but Jill followed him down to the lobby insisting that her only excuse for being there in the first place, and for ending up in bed with him, was to save him from himself. "I want to make sure that you get back to Adamsport. Then you can continue to be a thorn in your Daddy's flesh. But not in your new mummy's!"

22

Amir and Nefwazi were waiting. To Matt's amazement, Amir thought Jill might prove an asset. "Ramachanda probably knows that you are with a woman. Before we appear on the scene, you and Jill can have a nice discussion with him. You can discover if the gold is still in the house. If it is, we can drive back here and decide how badly we want it." Amir shrugged. "After we've sized up the situation, we can decide if we can negotiate with him—and at what cost."

"But Matt can't afford to buy gold," Jill said.

"He can make an offer," Amir replied smoothly. "Whatever price may be necessary to complete the transaction. Obviously it can't be concluded until the banks open tomorrow. That will give us the time we need."

"Where will you be while this is happening?" Matt asked.

"In a situation like this, you need us as back-up," Nefwazi said. He opened his coat and revealed a gun in a shoulder holster. "Amir and I will wait outside. We'll give you a half-hour."

"If you don't reappear," Amir smiled grimly, "we obviously can't call the police. You can use my gun, if you wish, but it would probably be better if you went in unarmed."

Matt kissed Jill's cheek. "I don't want you to come with us," he said.

She shook her head adamantly. "Maybe Allah has decided that we deserve to die together. Momentarily, at least, I've hitched my wagon to your star."

Ten minutes later, Amir was driving the Chevrolet along a lonely unpaved road close to the ocean. A three-quarter moon sprinkled the rippling water with glittery pearls. They passed several walled-in villas, monitored by disdainful, black palm tree sentinels. Then they drove by a lonely one surrounded by a six-foot pink stucco wall almost hidden behind a grove of palm trees. A lighted Moorish lantern hung over a closed wooden door. Amir stopped a few hundred yards beyond the entrance. "I think this is the place we're looking for," he said.

He turned off the car lights. "It's nine-thirty. We'll give you forty-five minutes. You should try to make this man feel at ease. Make sure that he trusts you. He obviously knows that I am here, so you can tell him that I am the source of your Euro dollars." Amir chuckled grimly. "If the gold is still there, we won't need your help. We'll come back ourselves. I'm sure that Nefwazi can pick up a few recruits to help us convince Ramachanda that half a loaf is better than none."

Amir's suave tone made Jill shudder. She was positive that Amir had no intentions of sharing the prize with Ramachanda, and he confirmed it with a double entendre. "You must be aware, Matt, that this man is using a pseudonym. Kalki is the Hindu goddess of death. Ramachanda is an avatar of Vishnu. Little wonder we Muslims can't tolerate these ridiculous Hindus. There is only one God, Allah. No matter what, Allah will prevail."

Amir and Nefwazi waited in the shadows of a bougainvillaea while Matt backed the car up to the entrance. Jill was sure that if you wanted to murder someone, this lonely road, a few miles from the only city on the island, was an ideal place. Dumped overboard from a dinghy, with a few pounds of sand to anchor their bodies, they would disappear forever—food for the fishes in the vast Caribbean Sea.

Softly whistling "Strangers in the Night," Matt pulled the bell plunger at the left of the Gothic door that provided the only entrance in the six-foot-high wall. Far off they could hear the tinkle of the bell. Minutes passed. Jill clung to Matt's arm and whispered, "Jesus! I'm scared silly. Let's run like hell and forget the whole business."

As she said it the door opened on squeaky, rusty hinges. A heavy-built, dark-skinned man, gun in one hand, flashlight in the other, stared at them grimly. He motioned them back on to the road next to the Chevrolet where he quickly examined the car, obviously trying to discover if they were alone.

He stared searchingly at Jill. "Mem-sahib? We did not expect you."

"She's my wife," Matt said quickly. "Are you Ramachanda?"

The man shook his head negatively. He gestured them back through the door and pointed at the wall and told them to lean against it face forward. "I must search you for weapons." He quickly patted their bodies, and Matt was startled to see a huge diamond ring flickering on the man's left hand. He was certain that he had seen it before. Then he remembered. It was just like Sylvie's!

Satisfied that they had no weapons, their churlish guide pointed the beam of the flashlight on a tiled walk. "Go first," he said and pointed toward the house a few hundred feet ahead of them.

"We're in trouble," Matt whispered to Jill. "I think that bastard is wearing Sylvie's ring." There was no doubt in Matt's mind that this was Sylvie's villa. In his pocket were snapshots that Sylvie had given him of the patio and the kidney-shaped swimming pool that they were now passing. A tall, very dark Indian wearing a Sikh-style headdress greeted them from the verandah. Behind him stood another sinister-looking man, naked to the waist, with a protuberant belly, wearing billowy pants and sneakers. Gun in hand, he watched them impassively. The patio was dimly lighted. Mosquitoes snapped angrily against the lanterns and buzzed around their heads.

"Good evening, I am Ramachanda." The tall Indian in the headdress stared coldly at them. His voice reflected training in English schools. "I didn't expect that you would bring a woman with you, Mr. Godwin. I'm sorry if our welcome appears hostile, but my friends, Yama and Kubera, are well aware of the delicacy of this business."

Matt glanced nervously at his watch. He wanted to ask Ramachanda point-blank what he was doing in Sylvie's villa. Where was Sylvie? Did Ramachanda know that he was Sylvie's emissary? Matt knew that their only hope was to spar for time and pray that Amir and Nefwazi would rescue them if necessary.

"My wife is my financial partner," he said. "We didn't come to Grand Cayman on business. You obviously know that we are traveling with Sheik Amir Faisal Saud. We've had a long flight and we're very tired, so I think that we should come to the point as quickly as possible. Who told you that I might be interested in buying gold?"

"A banker friend of your Sheik Saud told me that he was in the market and that you might be the go-between."

"Do you have the gold here?" Matt asked. "Keep in mind that we are not interested in any transaction where the police would be breathing down our necks."

Ramachanda smiled at Jill, who was desperately waving her hands around her face. "Mrs. Godwin is being attacked by mosquitoes. Come inside and we'll cover the main points as quickly as possible."

Following him into a Spanish-tiled living room with an open raftered ceiling, Matt quickly surveyed the area. A large Oriental rug covered the floor in the center of the room. It was impossible to tell if anyone had been digging under it. And it was just as impossible to ask any questions that might alert Ramachanda and let him know that Matt knew more about the villa than he should. A frightening thought crossed Matt's mind. If Sylvie had flown to Grand Cayman and arrived before them, was he being held prisoner right here in the villa? Where were Sylvie's caretakers, Fernando and Maria?

Ramachanda gestured toward wicker chairs. As they sat down,

Matt noticed a gold ingot on the end table beside him. "That's a sample," Ramachanda said. "You may inspect it if you wish."

Matt picked up the bar and turned it over. Trembling from fear as much as from the weight of the gold, he saw that the markings were similar to those on the ingots that Sylvie had given him. "Where did you get it?" Matt tried not to see the frightened expression on Jill's face.

"I'm sorry, Mr. Godwin, that's a question I cannot answer. But I can assure you that, present company excepted, very few people are aware of this treasure. I can also assure you that the bars were refined many, many years ago. They have been purposely left untouched to make sure that there could be no police interest in them."

"What are your clients willing to pay?" Matt demanded, wanting to make sure that he didn't underbid. "How many ingots have you got?"

"Three hundred and eighty-five similar bars are available. I prefer to have you make an offer first."

"What if it's not good enough?" Matt was well aware that his offer better be, or he and Jill might live to tell the story.

"This is not a transaction in which one haggles," Ramachanda said coolly. "The bars all weigh 400 troy ounces each; altogether roughly 150,000 troy ounces. Gold has been selling for around $400 an ounce. That's $60 million. If you can handle a transaction to a Calcutta bank in Euro dollars, it's yours for $40 million."

Seeking a possible escape route, Matt nodded. "Of course, you understand that I'd want the ingots delivered to a place on Grand Cayman to be determined." He looked at his watch; he still had twenty-five minutes before Amir and Nefwazi would arrive. But what could *they* do? Perhaps it would be better if they didn't appear at all. But first, he had to know whether the gold was here, and where Sylvie was.

"I'll telephone you tomorrow morning," he said, trying to sound casual. "I'm sure that we can arrange the transaction. This is a nice home. Do you own it?"

Ramachanda shook his head. "We rented it. We wanted a convenient spot to negotiate." He smiled at Jill, who had listened to the conversation with astonishment at Matt's apparent coolness. "In the meantime, if you are leaving, I'm sure that you won't mind if Mrs. Godwin stays here tonight as our house guest."

"What the hell for?" Matt demanded, as Jill shook her head in dismay.

Ramachanda shrugged. "Gold creates strange bedfellows. I must admit that your wife is pleasingly plump, Mr. Godwin, but this is not for sex. It's for our protection. Mrs. Godwin would simply be our temporary hostage. Her presence would assure us that unwanted people do not interfere in this transaction before it is completed."

"That's impossible!" Matt said. He knew that he was running out of time. Only Amir and Nefwazi could save them. "If necessary, we'll both stay here, but I'd like to see this gold. Where is it?"

"If Mrs. Godwin will wait here, I will be happy to show it to you." Ramachanda smiled unctuously at Jill. "Yama will keep her company."

"No thanks, I'm coming with you." Jill stood up, determined not to be left alone.

"I was simply trying to save you from mosquitoes, Mrs. Godwin." Ramachanda led them toward the patio. Behind them, Kubera had picked up the ingot and was following. "If you will both come with me." Ramachanda, holding the flashlight, led them on a dark path that passed the swimming pool. They were walking toward a stucco garage at the back of the house. It suddenly occurred to Matt that the garage faced onto a different road from the one they had arrived on. Should the necessity arise, Ramachanda had a fast exit route in a different direction.

Yama opened a side door and snapped on a light. A closed van with no side or back windows was facing outward toward the large doors. It was a two-car garage, and in the other space a tarpaulin had been tossed over a mound of something. For a moment Matt wondered if it might be the gold. He noticed around the edge of the garage several shovels and garden tools, which Sylvie had said would be available to dig up the living room floor.

To his surprise Ramachanda was opening the front door of the van. "If you will climb in front, Mr. Godwin, with your wife, Yama and Kubera can get in the back. We'll take you to the gold."

Matt looked at him astonished. "You mean it isn't here?" he demanded.

"What makes you think it should be here?" Ramachanda asked suspiciously.

Matt shrugged. "It just seemed logical."

"The gold is on my cargo schooner in George Town Harbor. We have a dinghy at the pier. We can be there in fifteen minutes."

"For Christ's sake," Matt yelled, suddenly wondering if Ramachanda might be planning to hold both of them as hostages on his schooner, "let's cut out the crap. If you want to sell the gold, I'll buy it tomorrow morning, not tonight!" He grabbed Jill's arm and tried to edge her toward the door they had just come in, but Kubera and Yama, with guns in their hands, moved in menacingly.

"It is you who should cut out the crap," Ramachanda said icily, suddenly pointing a gun at them. "It's become obvious to me that you know a great deal more about this gold than you are admitting. I assume that you knew Colonel Gamble."

"I sure as hell do," Matt said, alarmed by Ramachanda's past tense. "Where is Sylvie?"

For a moment Ramachanda seemed bewildered by the name. Then he walked over to the middle of the garage and flung back the tarpaulin. "Perhaps this is your friend Sylvie."

Jill screamed. Stretched on the garage floor, Sylvie lay motionless on his back, his eyes wide open, staring straight up. Beside him a woman lay on her side, her hands and feet tied, her dress disheveled around her hips. Panty hose covered her limp lower body.

Aghast, unable to believe that Sylvie was dead, Matt kneeled on the floor beside him and the woman. He turned the woman over. "It's Emily Lovejoy," he muttered, shaking her but getting no response.

Jill sobbed hysterically. "Oh, dear God, why did she come here?" She struck out at Ramachanda. "You bastard, you murdered them!"

"It was kill or be killed." Ramachanda coolly backed away from her, pointing his gun at her head. "Your friend was a little shocked to find me here. As for the woman, she isn't dead; we drugged her to calm her down. It's against my religion to interfere with Shiva's plans, unless, of course, circumstances give us no choice. It's obvious, Mr. Godwin, that you and your wife know too much about Colonel Gamble's treasure." Ramachanda nodded grimly at Yama and Kubera. "We can no longer postpone our sea voyage. I'm afraid that we all must leave here together."

Thrusting his gun in his belt, Yama grabbed Jill by her hair. Twisting a fistful in his hand, he dragged her screaming to her knees. She tried to stand up but he flung her on her back. Her dress slid up to her hips as Yama dragged her by her hands toward the van. Her buttocks scraped across the cement floor. Grinning lasciviously at her partially naked body, Kubera tried to catch her flaying legs and pick her up. He slapped her face with a stinging blow. "Shut up, memsahib, or your God will no longer hear you."

Eyes glazed, beyond fear, like a wild animal with his back to the wall, Matt growled his anger as he moved to rescue Jill.

"Don't interfere or I'll kill you." Ramachanda's fingers were flexing on the trigger of his gun. "I am a Hindu. I detest killing any living thing. If you will come with us to the ship, we'll work it out from there."

The memory of a flat-back shovel leaning against the wall of the garage flicked across Matt's brain. He grabbed it. Jill was fighting back. Momentarily she had managed to kick herself free from Kubera, but now his fingers were clutching the V-neck of her dress. Yama was still trying to hold her by her armpits and somehow obey Ramachanda's order to "Tie her up and throw her in the van."

Then Jill's dress ripped off in Kubera's hand. Losing his balance, he fell back on the floor. Oblivious to Ramachanda, Matt swung the shovel wide. It smacked against Kubera's chest and caught Ramachanda's hand as he fired. The bullet hit the shovel with a nasty ping. Then another shot whizzed by his head. The garage was plunged into darkness. Matt felt a stab of pain in his left shoulder, and he knew that he had been hit. Just before the lights went out, he saw Jill struggling to get to her feet. Yama was clutching her torn bra.

"Jill—run! Get the hell out of here!" Matt screamed. He could feel blood trickling down his arm.

Naked and barefoot, Jill ran across the gravel onto the eerily moonlighted lawn, gasping, her breasts flapping against her ribs. Her heart was trying to beat its way out of her chest. Was she going to drop dead? Her foot caught the jagged edge of an underground water sprinkler. Screaming, she fell on the wet grass. Her leg was painfully twisted under her. Panting, knowing her only hope of escape was to find Amir, she crawled on hands and knees. Ignoring the excruciating pain in her leg, she staggered to her feet. The rays of a flashlight found her. "Get down, Mrs. Godwin, for Allah's sake!" She recognized Nefwazi's gutteral voice, then the roar of an automobile engine. A volley of shots whizzed by her and she felt a sharp, searing pain in her thigh. Then she realized that she was standing on cement. She was tottering on the edge of the swimming pool. "Damn it, they got away!" she heard Amir shout. "They've got Matt in that van!"

Clutching her thigh, feeling warm blood, Jill knew she was going to faint. She fell face forward, hitting the water with a loud smack of her flat-out naked body. I'm drowning, she thought as she sank to the bottom. A line from a poem by Rimbaud flashed through her mind: "J'ai seul la clef cette parade, de cette sauvage parade." Oh no, God! No! Not just me!

23

Hours later? A day later? Groaning, his head throbbing, Matt slowly opened his eyes. He stared into the beady eye of a slimy wet rat a few inches from his nose. Was he dreaming? Despite a yell of primeval terror and a wild swipe in the direction of the repulsive animal, the ugly thing simply gave him a distasteful glance and waddled away. Was he having a nightmare? Was he dead? Had he come to life in some kind of Hieryonymus Bosch purgatory whose existence he had always sneered at?

Jill! My God, where was Jill? He remembered telling her to run. Then, in the total blackness of the garage, a flashlight had picked him out. "Get him," someone shouted. "There he is!" Words were followed by an excruciating thud on the back of his head. He had slumped to his knees as an explosion of light filled his brain. As his consciousness dimmed he heard Ramachanda giving orders. "Throw all of them in the van and let's get out of here. If there are no bodies, there'll be no questions."

From then until now his heart had evidently been beating, but his brain had stopped recording. Feeling with his hands around him, Matt realized that he was lying on piles of damp burlap. High above, fifteen feet or more overhead, he could see a round glimmer of daylight. It was a porthole. He could see the vague outline of the ribs of a ship. A dull throb of an engine was vibrating his body. He suddenly realized that he was naked. The bastards had stripped him and taken his billfold. What did it matter? He was only carrying a few hundred dollars. The odor of engine oil, salt water, and sea-rotted wood filled his nostrils and made him retch. Amir had mentioned that Ramachanda had arrived in Grand Cayman on a schooner. This must be it.

Ramachanda had mentioned that Sylvie's gold had been loaded aboard. That was last night, or was it even longer? How long had he been unconscious? The light through the porthole meant that it was daytime. He and Jill had arrived at the villa around nine-thirty. A half-hour later the top blew off. Had he been lying here eight hours, or even longer? Where was Jill? Had Amir and Nefwazi rescued her? Matt crawled to his knees and felt a sharp pain in his left arm. His muscle had been covered with a crude bandage. Underneath it felt swollen and tender. He must have been hit by a bullet ricocheting in the cement-block garage. He vaguely remembered Ramachanda leaning over him with a hypodermic needle in his hand. Had they drugged him? My God, Emily? Emily Lovejoy! Where was she? Ramachanda said she wasn't dead, that she had been drugged. And Sylvie? He could still see Sylvie's rigid face. Sylvie was dead. Was Emily dead too? Numbed by the pounding in his head, he moaned both from the throbbing in his arm and the knowledge that he was responsible. If he had refused Sylvie's insane offer, none of them would be here. He slumped back on the burlap, and his hand touched flesh.

"Jill!" He yelled his fright. Groping in the dark, he moved his fingers over a naked body. He felt the curve of buttocks and the softness of a female breast. The woman was lying in a fetal position. He pulled her over, and, in a ray of light that was now wobbling deep into the ship as it yawed back and forth, he glimpsed her face. It was Emily Lovejoy. She stared at him. She didn't recognize his face in the shadow.

"Please don't hurt me," she moaned. "Kill me—but please don't hurt me."

He patted her cheek. "It's me, Matt Godwin." Emily continued to stare hopelessly at him. "Do you hear me? You understand? What have they done to you, Emily? Is Sylvie really dead?"

Sobbing hysterically, she leaned against his chest. "Oh Matt, Matt! It was awful. They got there first. They told Sylvie they would cut him in, but Sylvie wouldn't listen to them. He didn't trust them." Emily's hand touched her breast and she traced the outline of her body. "I'm naked! Why am I naked? What are they going to do with me?"

"I don't know. I think they drugged us," Matt said, but he really did know. Emily and he were a noose that Ramachanda didn't need around his neck. "I still don't understand why they murdered Sylvie."

For a moment Emily couldn't answer. Matt held his arms around her. Between uncontrollable sobs shaking her entire body, she gasped, "One of them—Ramachanda—kept telling Sylvie it was against his religion to take any life. He told us that we both could leave, that there was no gold. He had already sold it to someone in Cuba. But he promised when the transaction was completed that Sylvie would get his share. Sylvie told him that he wasn't sharing his gold with any god-damn mooching Indian. Then Sylvie pulled his gun, but he never got to use it. There was a shot and Sylvie slumped to the floor. Oh Matt, why wouldn't he listen to me? Sylvie didn't need that gold. He's a millionaire already."

"I guess I'm to blame," Matt said, but he could shed no tears for Sylvie. "If I hadn't been trying to solve problems the easy way, Sylvie probably would have left the gold buried in his villa. None of us would be here."

And what about Jill? Poor Jill. Had Amir and Nefwazi rescued her? Was she alive? If she were, Matt knew he had risked her life and her marriage. He no longer cared what happened to him. He was sadly aware that he couldn't pray for any of them. Pray to whom? To God? To Allah? Rather pray to man—and accept the consequences. Grasping for gold, really grasping for power, dragging Jill into this mess, and indirectly Emily and Sylvie, he had renounced himself as God. When man or woman fails to act as God, they betray themselves as God. When that happens sane religious thinking should condone self-destruction. A kind of hari-kari, not for betrayal of some indefinable human honor, but for one's failure to act as God, thereby failing all men and women as God. But Matt was sure that he wasn't going to be put to that test. Ramachanda was going to resolve the bitter problem for him, and for Emily, too. The only reason they were alive, at this moment, had nothing to do with Ramachanda's religious beliefs. Bodies left in Sylvie's villa were evidence. If there were no evidence, no one would ever know that a king's ransom, formerly buried on Grand Cayman, had been stolen by one thief from another. Now there was nothing to alert the island police. Even if Jill had survived, Matt was sure that Amir wouldn't risk himself any further. This was a rainbow-chasing game that a billionaire, non-Christian unbeliever didn't have to play.

Trying to soothe Emily, he heard a rumble above them. A hatchway was opened, and a shaft of brilliant sunlight penetrated the darkness. Like suppliants awaiting a message from heaven they stared into the cloudless sky. "Bring them all up. Let's get this over with." Matt recognized Ramachanda's voice. For a moment daylight was obscured as two men clambered down the companionway. They pulled him and Emily to their feet.

"They've come to life," one of them yelled, and Matt recognized Yama. He shoved Matt ahead of him up the steep wooden access to the deck. Behind him Matt heard Emily scream as the other man, evidently Kubera, carried her up the companionway over his shoulder and dropped her on the wooden deck.

For a moment the world turned black while Matt's retinas painfully adjusted to the searing bright sunlight. When he opened his eyes he realized that he was standing beneath a boom swinging in a small arc several feet above his head. In all directions there was only glaring, blue-green sea stretching to the horizon. Three very ugly dark-skinned men had gathered around them. Grinning, they stared lasciviously at Emily's naked body. Blinded by the sunlight, she could scarcely see them. Her face was dirt-streaked and tear-stained. Her white hair was damp and limp, molding her skull. Lying on her back trembling, she moaned unintelligibly. Her black pubic hairs contrasted with the fragile beauty of her untanned, creamy white flesh. It flashed across Matt's mind that Emily Lovejoy, despite her age, was a physically attractive woman. The native crew evidently thought so, too. Chattering in Spanish, they began pawing her body and squeezing her breasts as she tried to curl up in self-defense.

"Leave her alone." Ramachanda appeared, waving the revolver angrily at them. "Go below and get the other one." He smiled coldly at Matt. "I'm sorry about this, Reverend Godwin, but the time has come when we must part company. I was a little surprised to discover from your billfold that you are leading a dual life. If I remember your Gospels correctly, Jesus would not approve. 'Provide neither gold nor silver in your money belts,' he told his disciples."

"Where's my wife?" Matt was trying to keep his balance as the ship plunged up and down in the rolling sea.

Ramachanda shrugged. "I do not know. She may be dead. When your friends started shooting we did not wait to find out."

Kubera emerged, backing out of the hatch, followed by Yama. Between them they were carrying a man's naked body. His head was hanging down below his shoulders at an impossible angle. They dropped the lifeless body with a thud on the deck. Emily, who had been vaguely watching them, screamed: "Sylvie! Sylvie! Oh God—dear God why did this have to happen?" She crawled over to him, hesitated before touching him, then gently closed his empty, dead eyes.

"I regret your friend's death," Ramachanda said coolly. "Taking any life is repugnant to me, but there is a point where morality gives way to reality. *Samsara*—the ceaseless flow of life of which your friend is now a part—goes on. Unfortunately for all of us, our *karmas* become intertwined. Many years ago Colonel Gamble gave me a gold ingot. How could I not suspect that there were many more where that came from?"

Matt noticed that the crew had begun lowering a lifeboat to the deck level. "What are you going to do with us?" he demanded.

"Realistically, I should put a bullet through your heads. Or I could have you thrown overboard—food for the sharks." There was not a flicker of emotion on Ramachanda's face. "The essence of you, your *atman*, will survive. All of us here will be born again and have to suffer through this again. Before my life became entangled with Colonel Gamble, I was a very religious man. I was almost ready to give up worldly possessions and try to achieve Brahma in this life. But seeking eternal salvation is not easy."

Matt stared at him hopelessly. It was apparent that he and Emily were in the hands of a man who would not feel guilty over their inevitable death—only the means. "If you're so religious, why don't you give us some clothes and put us ashore?" he demanded.

Ramachanda shook his head. "I'm sorry, but this is the way it has to be. Naked as you are, along with your dead friend, after a few days identification of your bodies will be difficult." He gestured toward the lifeboat. "Put Colonel Gamble's body in the bow," he told Yama and Kubera. "Reverend Godwin and the lady can get in the middle and rear seats. There are the oars. I am not happy about this, but as you can see I am not personally going to take your lives." He made a sweeping gesture of the horizon. "Cuba is about 300 miles in that direction. Honduras is over there. If it is your fate to live, you will live."

Yama dragged Emily toward the boat and shoved her onto the stern seat. Huddled over, her head on her knees, she was shuddering despite the heat.

"Give us something to cover ourselves with," Matt pleaded as Yama forced him into the boat. "We'll burn to a crisp out there. Give us some water." He knew that they could drift in this rolling cauldron for days and never be sighted by another boat.

The crew had swung the lifeboat on its stanchions, ready to lower it. "For God's sake, if you really are a religious man, give us some food and water."

As the boat was lowered into the sea, Ramachanda smiled benignly at them. "There's a salt water conversion kit under the seat. As for food, if you don't throw Colonel Gamble overboard, you can eat him before he rots." He laughed grimly. "I'm sorry, Reverend Godwin, but remember the commands of your god, Jesus. He told his disciples: 'Whoever causes one to sin, it would be better for him if a millstone were hung around his neck, and he were drowned in the depths of the sea.'"

The boat hit the water, and Emily slid onto the floor. Crouching between Matt's knees as the schooner slowly pulled away, leaving them bobbing on the ocean, she was nearly in shock. "We're going to die, Matt, aren't we?" She stared dazedly at him as he stroked her head. "How can you still believe that man is God?"

24

Four days after Emily had gone to Grand Cayman with Sylvie, Roje was beginning to get a little restless. Although he didn't pay much attention to her during the day when he was writing, he missed her presence in the house. If she weren't there, he knew that soon she would return from shopping or playing golf and she'd be regaling him with stories and local gossip. He usually scowled at her and appeared bored. She never worried whether she was interrupting a train of thought, but he had to admit that she did jar him out of his never-never land and his involvement with characters who could never walk off the typewritten page and hug him.

Late Saturday afternoon, when the telephone finally rang for the first time that day, he was sure that it was she. But a strange, agitated voice greeted him. "Mr. Lovejoy? You don't know me, but I know that you're a good friend of Matthew Godwin. Has he telephoned you?"

Roje was sure that the caller was not Matt's wife, Irene. Irene would have identified herself. "The last time I saw Matt, we went sailing together," he said cautiously. "Who are you?"

There was a long pause, and Roje thought he could hear the woman sobbing. "I'm Gillian Godwin. Jill. Ike Godwin's wife. I'm very worried about Matt. He told you that he was flying to Grand Cayman, didn't he?"

"He didn't tell me personally." Roje was wondering why Jill Godwin, actually Matt's stepmother, was worrying about him rather than Matt's wife or his father. "But it occurred to me that Emily might meet him there." Roje wondered if the Godwin family had somehow heard about Matt's search for the golden fleece. He had to be careful how he responded.

Jill was now definitely crying. "Please forgive me, Mr. Lovejoy. If

I could leave the house, I'd have tried to meet you personally, but I broke my leg, and I have a nasty flesh wound on my thigh. At the moment, I'm kind of a prisoner here."

"Were you in an auto accident?" Roje asked. "Where's here? Perhaps I can come and see you."

"Oh God, no! You can't come here. I'm at the Big House on the Godwin estate. I may not be able to talk to you very long. If you hear the phone being picked up, or I should hang up suddenly, please don't call back. I'll phone you later."

Again there was a long pause as Jill tried to get control of herself. "Last Tuesday, when I was walking back to my hotel from the theater on Forty-fourth Street in New York City, I was mugged, nearly raped, and shot by a man on Forty-ninth Street." Jill's voice was choked with tears. "Oh, God—Mr. Lovejoy, I really have to trust you. That's the story I told Ike and Irene, but it's a lie. Tuesday I was on Grand Cayman with Matt Godwin."

"You must have met my wife Emily?" Momentarily Roje was elated. "She flew there with Sylvie to meet Matt." He was only dimly aware that Ike Godwin's wife being with Matt, some two thousand miles away from Adamsport, was strange, to say the least.

"Oh dear, I don't know what to tell you." Jill was sobbing. "I think I saw your wife. Whether she was alive or not, I don't know. The man with her was dead. There was a terrible shoot-out. I don't know whether Matt is alive. That's why I'm calling you."

Roje stared into the phone, not believing what he was hearing. "Are you telling me that Sylvie Williams is dead?" he shouted. "For Christ's sake . . . my wife was with him!"

"I'm really not sure about your wife, Mr. Lovejoy, or Sylvie Williams. Before the lights went out, I saw a man called Colonel Gamble. He was dead on the garage floor. Matt recognized your wife lying beside him. Ramachanda told him that she wasn't dead."

"Who the hell is Ramachanda?" Roje asked.

"I'm sorry, I can't talk to you any longer. Someone is coming. Please, for God's sake, don't call me back. If Matt telephones you, tell him to call Irene or his father and then I'll know he's all right."

"Wait a minute. Hold on! How did you get back to Adamsport?" Roje demanded.

"A friend of Matt's, Amir Saud, flew me to a hospital in Miami."

The phone went dead. Bewildered, Roje stared at it in dismay. There was only one person he could talk to—Peachy Stein. But if he telephoned her, she couldn't answer questions, not with Saul and her children listening. And what could he tell her? That her father was dead? That Emily might be dead? Ridiculous. Sylvie wasn't the type to engage in a gunfight. If someone else had got to his gold first, Sylvie would have backed off, especially with Matt and Emily along . . . and

Jill Godwin! How in hell did she get involved in this crazy business? Was Matt sleeping with her?

During a worried, sleepless night, missing Emily sleeping beside him, Roje decided that if this insanity were ever resolved, the time had come for him and Emily to stop adventuring into other people's lives and beds. Personally, he was going to stay clear of all religion and particularly UU's. He was tempted to storm up to the Godwin estate and insist on talking with Jill. But if he couldn't talk with her privately, he would put her and Matt on the spot. He was sure that neither Ike nor Irene were aware that Matt and Jill had been in Grand Cayman together. Why in hell had Matt involved his father's wife in his mad quest for Sylvie's gold? Roje was enthusiastic about most of Matt's modern moralities, but this was a little too incestuous for him.

Alone in his king-size bed, his eyes filled with tears, Roje couldn't pray, but he hoped that Jill's story was a figment of her imagination. He wished that Emily was lying beside him right now, telling him: "Oh, Roje, it was silly fun with Sylvie, but I need you and I love you most." Damn. How could he live without Emily?

By morning he had decided to fly to Grand Cayman and see if he could locate Sylvie's villa and find out what really had happened. But then it occurred to him that Peachy might have heard directly from Matt. He had no choice. He had to go to church today.

Peachy had telephoned him once after their meeting at Sylvie's house and had invited him to hear her preach. She told him that even though she had finished her internship under the Reverend Littlejohn, she wasn't yet fully qualified by UU Headquarters. Nevertheless, the board of governors of the church had decided she could be the temporary minister until they could find a replacement for Reverend Littlejohn.

Roje was sure that Peachy's joyous gift of love wasn't something he should get accustomed to. The memory of her moving erotically on top of him, her breasts swaying, her behind in gentle oscillation, had been fired into his brain cells. Like an etching on a Greek vase, it was a gift of joy, a memory that shouldn't be eradicated by an inevitable second-time rejection. Her spring had touched his winter for a moment, and that was that.

A few minutes before the services started, Roje walked in the front door of the First Parish Church. An organist was playing. Twenty or more people were seated in the pews, but many more were congregated in the rear of the sanctuary, eagerly discussing some juicy bit of church gossip. Their heads were shaking in rhythm to the whispered buzz of their words. Roje noticed that several of them were reading the front page of the *Boston Globe*.

John Codman, who was evidently one of the greeters this morning, recognized him. "Have you seen the *Globe*?" he asked. "Everyone is wondering whether the Matthew Godwin is *our* Matthew Godwin."

Before Roje could answer, an elderly woman (Ada Bass, whom Roje didn't know) looked at him soulfully. "Poor Matthew. His sermon was a little crazy, but I really liked it. It looks as if he's fallen in with bad company. I hope that he's still alive."

Realizing that Roje was bewildered, Codman handed him the front page of the newspaper. Before he could glance at it, Peachy, in her ministerial robes, ready to conduct the service, entered the sanctuary. Dorothy Belcher, returning from ushering the Hancocks to their pew, smiled warily at him and asked him where he would like to sit. Since he had no preference, she led him to a center pew.

"It's a mystery to me," she said in her prim, Puritan manner. "Why is Matthew Godwin in the Caribbean, especially on a nice Indian summer day like this? The temperature is supposed to reach ninety degrees." She handed him a program."Ms. Stein's sermon this morning is 'Sin and Salvation.' It's an appropriate subject, don't you think?" Her voice was edged with sarcasm.

Alone in the pew, Roje flipped over the newspaper. The organist had stopped playing, and Peachy was leading the congregation in the Call to Worship and hymn #20, "God is My Strong Salvation." It was followed by a unison affirmation. Standing with the congregation, Roje tried to read the headlines on the seat beside him even before he sat down.

ADAMSPORT MAN AND WOMAN ACCUSED OF ESPIONAGE BEING HELD IN CUSTODY BY CUBAN OFFICIALS

According to an official communique received from the Fidel Castro Government yesterday, a Cuban naval vessel picked up a man and woman adrift in a lifeboat a hundred miles off southern Cuba. The man and woman were completely naked and evidently had not eaten for three days. They were both suffering from overexposure to the sun and elements. Brought to a Havana hospital, the man is being treated for an infected gunshot wound and is presumed on the danger list.

Probed by Cuban police, the man identified himself as Matthew Godwin, a citizen of the United States, from Adamsport, Massachusetts. His female companion was not identified. He told Cubans that they had been kidnapped on Grand Cayman by persons unknown, for possible ransom. Whether the ransom was paid, or why they were cast into the sea in a lifeboat, is not known. Cuban officials are trying to link them with a mystery cargo schooner which blew up in Cuban waters last Wednesday. One of two Indians who were rescued from the schooner, a man named Ramachanda, who was in a state of shock, said that the ship might have been carrying gold bullion to

Honduras, but he later denied it. Cuban officials stated that whether there was actually gold on board will probably never be known. The ship sank near the Cayman Trench, one of the deepest spots in the Caribbean, with soundings in excess of 24,000 feet.

Isaac Godwin, President of Controlled Power Corporation, who is planning to relocate the corporation headquarters in Adamsport next year, told Globe reporters that he had no idea of the whereabouts of his son and that his son is no longer associated with the corporation. Two weeks ago, Matthew Godwin preached an inflammatory sermon at the First Parish Unitarian Universalist Church in Adamsport, calling for a new modern approach to morality. It was rebroadcast last Sunday morning on a national television network.

Shaken, unable to absorb the story, Roje kept reading it over and over again. He was sure that the unidentified woman was Emily. Since there was no mention of Sylvie, Jill must have been right. Sylvie was dead. Roje couldn't concentrate on Peachy, who was now reading from the *Book of Common Prayer*, evidently trying to distinguish between salvation from man-made sins and divine deliverance from natural forms of evil, such as floods and tornadoes, over which man has no control. She glanced in his direction several times but showed no special recognition.

As is the custom in UU churches, before the offertory Peachy walked down the center aisle and gave her words of welcome to the members and guests and invited them to the social hour after the services.

"I'm sure that all of you are as surprised and shocked as I was by the story in the *Boston Globe* this morning," she said. "Matthew Godwin is a member of this church and has been a very good friend to me. I telephoned his wife, Irene, just a few minutes ago. She is quite distraught. She had no idea that Matt was in the Caribbean. But she pointed out to me that Matt's position with the shipyard entails worldwide commitments. She denied Isaac Godwin's statement to the *Globe* that Matt is no longer associated with the corporation. Wherever he may be, we hope that Matt Godwin survives this terrible ordeal."

During her sermon Peachy carefully stressed that all major religions had evolved various paths to salvation. But most UU's couldn't believe, as Jesus evidently did, that the Devil, as God's adversary, tempted men and women to commit evil. "Jesus told his disciples," Peachy preached, "that when 'the time is fulfilled, and the kingdom of God is at hand,' that they must repent. But repentance is too late. Evil between men and women, acting as God toward each other, eliminates the need for repentance."

Knowing that he would have to endure the social hour and endless gossipy undercutting of Matt Godwin before he could talk with Peachy, Roje dallied and tried to be the last in line to shake hands

180 THE IMMORAL REVEREND

with the minister. A whiskered man ahead of him introduced himself with a heavy Scottish accent: "My name is Frank Burns. You're the writer, aren't you? I read one of your books. Pretty silly stuff, but I guess a lot of people read you. You may be a UU at heart. I guess you've heard the news. Tomorrow night the members are going to sell the church to the highest bidder. Too bad you're not a member, you could come and hear the fun. Ike Godwin is going to tear the church down. Good luck to him. We may have to hold services at the Holiday Inn, but at least we'll have enough money to afford a male minister."

Roje grinned at him. "I enjoy women. They're closer to God than men. If you don't like Peachy's sermon, just looking at her should give you a little lift."

Burns laughed. "Aye, lad, and you know where. That's why she ain't gonna last. The ladies don't like their men to get that kind of lift."

Finally, at the door of the Parish Hall, Roje was alone in the sanctuary with Peachy for a second. "I have to talk with you," he said, and was surprised to see that she was smiling affectionately at him. "The woman with Matt must be Emily. Did you hear from Sylvie?"

"Oh God," Peachy sighed, "don't tell me that Sylvie is mixed up in this." She squeezed his hand. "Slip into the minister's office. It's the first door on the right. Close the door. After the coffee hour, I'll be with you."

An hour later, as Roje's impatience was mounting, Peachy opened the door. "It wasn't easy," she said, shedding her robe. "All of them are either clacking their tongues over Matt Godwin or worrying about tomorrow. Some of them think we've made a mistake; we shouldn't have voted to sell the church. If they change their minds, what will Matt do with his damned gold then?" She touched Roje's hand. "I've missed you," she said with a teasing, provocative expression dancing in her eyes. "After my enthusiastic welcome in your back yard, I was positive that you would be a devoted UU by now."

Roje wanted to hold her face in his hands and kiss her wildly, but he resisted. She listened to him, shaking her head in disbelief when he told her that Emily and Sylvie had flown to Grand Cayman to help Matt. Omitting her afternoon with Matt on his boat and their confrontation with Sylvie, she told him that she hadn't seen her father since the members' meeting last week.

"I guess I should have telephoned you," Roje said. "But much as I like you, I'm not sure I want to be a UU."

"Be who you are," she answered. "I love you anyway. I jogged by your house a couple of times, but I didn't dare disturb you again. Why did you let Emily go with Sylvie? You must have a lot of confidence in your wife. I begged Matt not to get involved, but he insisted that it was like drawing to an inside flush. He had to see if he could do it.

Damn, damn! Why do I fall in love with men like you and Matt? And since I do, why do they have to be married to someone else?"

Peachy sighed. "I think Irene knows more than she told me. She wasn't very friendly; she thinks that I'm the other woman in Matt's life." Then Peachy remembered the news story. "There was another woman with him in the lifeboat. What makes you think it was Emily? Matt can't resist *any* loving woman."

Roje told her about Jill's telephone call. Tears in her eyes, Peachy listened unbelievingly. Without going into details, she said, "I talked with Matt a week ago. How did he ever get Ike Godwin's wife involved with him in this gold insanity? If Matt isn't dead, he'd better watch out—Ike Godwin will murder both of them." She took Roje's hand. "I've locked the doors. A few members have keys, but they won't be around on a nice day like this. I think we should discuss this lying down."

Roje couldn't help smiling. If there were going to be a rejection, it would be his, not Peachy's. But immoral or not, he didn't have that kind of strength. "Where?" He laughed as she led him into the Parish Hall. "If we're going to make love on top of the Adamses' tombs, let's try John Quincy's wife, Louisa. She was sexier than Abigail."

"It's too damp down there." Peachy pointed to the stage. "There's an Oriental rug on the floor. We could borrow some cushions from the pews."

Roje had a sudden vision of the Belchers or the Hancocks arriving in the middle of things. He shook his head. "It's too wide open. Why not come back to my house?" Roje couldn't actually believe that he and Peachy were going to make love again.

"I'd like to, but I have to be home by two. Saul is waiting. We only have an hour." Peachy laughed. "I've got an idea. What about the belfry? There's a landing halfway up near the clock. We can lock the door from the inside. On a day like today it will be nice and warm."

Roje tried to shake the guilty feeling that right now he should be at the airport trying to get on a flight to Miami or Grand Cayman. Instead, here he was enjoying the lovely piece of cake that Peachy was offering him once again. He should be fasting with his heart filled with remorse. But he couldn't believe that Emily was dead, and if she were, hadn't she made her own choice? Anyway, the long days of missing her and of loneliness were still ahead.

Carrying pew cushions Roje told himself aloud, "Roje, you are not a hot-rock, twenty-year-old stud any more. You're too old for this kind of silliness."

"You're not that old, for God's sake," Peachy grinned back at him as she led the way up rickety wooden stairs. She was wearing a drindl skirt. He could catch a glimpse of her lilting behind just ahead of him, pantyless, teasing him along. "I was just thinking," she sighed, "we may be the last people to ever climb this belfry. By tomorrow night, Ike Godwin will own this steeple. If Matt is wrong and there really is a God out there somewhere, I don't think he blames Matt. Whatever else happens in this crazy world, God can't be unhappy when a man and woman make love to each other."

She dropped the two cushions she was carrying, took his two, and snugged them together until they made a reasonably comfortable mattress. Forty feet in the air, they were surrounded by granite walls. Thirty feet above them, a wooden ladder led to the cupola and a gold-leafed dome which was supported by eight wooden Doric columns. Cynosure of the city, the four-faced clock that no longer kept very good time and the bell that no longer rang had once been the timekeeper and alarm system for the citizens of Adamsport.

"Matt gave me some sketches for the church," Peachy said. "He was hoping to build a seven-story glass building where the present Parish Hall is. He wanted to create a new kind of church club that would really attract the younger generation. He was going to keep the belfry just as it is, and get the bell ringing once again." She shed her clothes in three swift movements. Grinning, she lay down and pointed to a rough wooden bannister. "Hang your clothes and your heart on a hickory limb. Later, we'll climb the ladder and take a look at the city on a sleepy Sunday afternoon."

Naked, he kneeled on the cushions beside her and gently kissed her lips and breasts and belly. "You're a very beautiful woman," he told her. "And I'm a very lucky old man."

She giggled happily at the size of his penis. She held it and grazed her lips around it. "Not bad for an old crock," she laughed."Oh, Roje, I wish that you could see your face. You look so bewildered—like a little boy seeing his first birthday cake. Or maybe you're the cake! And you most certainly have one big candle. Don't worry, I won't blow it out. Not too soon! If I do, I promise I'll light it up again—once more, at least. Come inside me."

And Roje did. Now there was an easy familiarity with each other's bodies that dissipated their egos and set them momentarily free. Breathing erotically in his ear, Peachy said, "This is rapture. It should be a daily counterpoint to reality." She kissed him, and when it was no longer possible to stay balanced on the edge of eternity, they climaxed together in laughter. Then she kissed him reverently and held his penis tenderly. "You're a part of my forever," she said. "But I haven't forgotten Emily or Saul or Matt. I love them, too. And I know you love Emily. And I don't want Sylvie to be dead." There were tears in her eyes. "He cared for me in his fashion." She leaned on her elbow and stared at Roje. "Jesus! If my father is dead, I'm his only heir. It will be a hell of a note if I inherit Silly Willy's." Like a child she kissed Roje's face with a lot of little kisses. "What about Jill Godwin? I don't think I ever saw her. Is she pretty?"

"You've got me." Roje eased her on top of him. She happily squeezed his rejuvenated penis between her legs. Roje knew that losing himself in Peachy's big dreamy brown eyes could become as addictive as merging with her body was. "But you are right about one thing," he said. "If Matt has been sleeping with his father's new wife, he'll never convince Ike that incest is moral."

"Jill's not Matt's mother. But what if Matt has been sleeping with Emily?"

Roje shrugged. "Emily likes Matt. But I'm afraid they weren't enjoying themselves in that lifeboat."

"Men and women often make love when they are threatened or near death," Peachy persisted in her thought. "If Emily really were in that lifeboat, and they were comforting each other, would that bother you?"

"How could I deny Emily love when I don't deny myself?" Roje stopped nibbling Peachy's nipple. "This is natural, but is it moral? What about Saul?"

Wide-eyed, Peachy stared at him. "If Saul is deprived, it's his own fault." She rolled over on her back and gazed at the patch of blue sky high above them. "Let's pretend that you're the king and I'm the queen." She chuckled. "Before we make love once more, let's climb to the top and look over our kingdom. Let's see how our dominions are doing on this warm Sunday afternoon." To Roje's astonishment, like a happy child she bounced to her feet and started up the ladder.

"Come on!" she called down to him, and her eyes were dancing with excitement. "You told Judge Gravman that you were going to walk around the Prudential Tower bare-ass. You don't have to wait. You can walk around the First Parish bell tower. I won't tell anyone."

Above him Roje could hear the ladder creaking. There was nothing to do but follow her. The rough wood of the ladder's cross-steps cut into his feet. From the cupola high above him, she peered down. Her beautifully molded breasts caught flashes of sunlight. "Come on, for heaven's sake," she bubbled. "You'll probably never get any closer to heaven. You don't have to worry. All you have to do is stoop a little. The balustrade up here is high enough. No one can see your balls."

Halfway up, Roje had the first warning. Just below him the side rails of the thirty-foot ladder cracked beneath his weight. Somehow he scrambled up the last rung and sprawled on the floor of the cupola just as the ancient ladder broke loose and collapsed on the landing thirty feet below them with a sickening thud.

Dumbfounded, they stared down into the cool, dark interior of the steeple. There was absolutely no way that they could get back down. To jump would mean a broken leg or, worse, crashing into the clock mechanism.

"What do we do now?" Peachy's voice was a shocked whisper. "We're trapped in the belfry."

Roje could see the grim face of Judge Gravman staring coldly at him and pronouncing a life sentence. "We're sunk," he said gloomily.

"You're sunk," Peachy groaned. "I'm dead! I've just committed ministerial suicide. I can see the headlines now: FEMALE MINISTER TRIES TO FLY TO HEAVEN WITH HER PARAMOUR."

"There's got to be some way out of this." Roje was leaning over the balustrade. Heedless that he could be seen from the street nearly two hundred feet below them, he noticed that they were only thirty feet above the slate roof of the church. But there was no niche in the granite wall of the steeple that he could cling to to negotiate that distance.

"There's no salvation from sin," Peachy said with tears in her eyes. "I guess Jesus was right. All we can do is repent."

Roje crouched down. "There's a couple of people walking by on the sidewalk. Good thing they didn't look up. If I could get to the roof of the church, I might slide down the column of the door that goes into the Parish Hall." He leaned over the side and the afternoon sun warmed his behind. "The problem is that it's almost as far down to the roof as to the landing inside the belfry."

"It wouldn't work," Peachy said sadly. "Even if you got down, you couldn't get back in the church. The doors are locked from the inside, and my key is on my desk. I'm sorry. It's really my fault. What will Emily say?"

Roje shrugged. "That her kooky old sex-pot got what he deserved. I just hope that she's alive to say it. What's Saul going to say?"

"Just what the Board of Examiners of the UU are going to say: Good-bye!" Peachy tried to smile through her tears. "Saul hasn't been too happy with me, anyway."

"So what do we do now, yell for help?"

"What time is it?"

Roje grinned. "My wristwatch is in my pants pocket, down there."

"If you hold my legs," Peachy said, "maybe I can lean out and see what the steeple clock says."

Her behind in the air, ignoring the fact that Roje was absent-mindedly patting it affectionately, Peachy peered over the balustrade. "I think it's about three o'clock. Eventually, Saul will come looking for me," she said as Roje pulled her back in.

Roje drummed the bell with his fingers. "There's not a soul down there right now. Adamsport is really deserted on Sunday afternoon." He was totally at a loss as to what they could do. "It's nice and warm now," he said, "but keep in mind, Indian summer or not, that this is October. Pretty soon it's going to get cold."

"If we freeze to death, that will solve everything." Peachy looked like the poor little kitten who lost her mittens. "Everyone will be sure that God was pissed off at us." She edged around the eroded cast-iron bell toward Roje. The sun had made the metal quite warm. Heedless of the rust, she leaned back against it and held her arms out to Roje. "Oh sweetie, don't look so bewildered. Since there's no help for it, come make love to me. Screw me to a fare thee well. Make us both disappear."

This time Robert J. Lovejoy not only made local evening and national network television, but he and Peachy also appeared in the *Adamsport Chronicle*, properly airbrushed, of course, just as they were being rescued from the First Parish belfry by the Adamsport Fire Department. "BATS IN THE BELFRY?" the headline read. "You won't get to heaven in an old Ford car," an enterprising reporter wrote,

> but some people try to get there in their birthday suits. Yesterday, after services at the First Parish Church, the minister, Peachy Stein, and a local novelist, Robert J. (for Jesus) Lovejoy, were celebrating God naked together in the church. For some reason, as yet unknown, they climbed the steeple, and then the ladder broke, making access back to the sanctuary impossible. Late Sunday afternoon, trying to draw attention to their dilemma from someone in the deserted square, Lovejoy climbed out on the balustrade. Clinging to the wooden columns, he yelled at passing automobiles, whose occupants may have read his books but scarcely expected to see him waving naked at them several hundred feet above the ground.
>
> Toward evening, as the sun slowly disappeared from the sky, he was finally spotted by a local resident who thought that either the church was on fire or some former believer, rejected by God, was about to splatter himself on the street. This good citizen, who prefers not to be identified, turned in a fire alarm, unaware that Lovejoy had a naked companion in the belfry. As luck would have it, just about this time, Bill Gates, a television cameraman who works for Adamsport Cable Television, was returning with his assistant from a Knights of Columbus picnic. Alerted by his police radio, Gates arrived just as the hook and ladder equipment pulled up in front of the church.
>
> By this time several hundred people had gathered to watch the excitement. Firemen pried open the church doors, but, not taking any chances, they also raised the boom on the fire truck's hydraulic lifter. One of the firemen, Jack Donato, in the aerial platform, with arms outstretched—all duly recorded by Bill Gates, which should entitle him to some kind of television cameraman's award—yelled at Lovejoy, 'For God's sake don't jump!'
>
> Then, to Jack's everlasting surprise and the endless amazement of Adamsport residents, instead of Lovejoy getting into the cherry picker, a naked woman appeared on the railing and stepped gracefully

into the fireman's arms. In the meantime, the firemen who had entered the church via the door and had arrived in the cupola with a ladder to replace the broken one, appeared behind Lovejoy and his companion and were grinning enthusiastically at the provocative sight. By this time the square was filled with people, and Lovejoy was quickly identified from his previous appearance in the Adamsport Chronicle. Many of them were cheering, 'Lovejoy . . . Lovejoy . . . Attaboy Lovejoy!' and yelling, 'What were you doing? Looking for a naked angel?' They were even more enthusiastic about Peachy Stein, with some of them singing, 'Peachy-weachy, queen of them all!' Others insisted that Ms. Stein had probably planned the whole thing as an advertising stunt for Silly Willy's, her father's strip club.

25

Saturday, a few hours after Jill telephoned Roje, Ike Godwin received a telephone call from Senator Williams. The State Department had informed Williams that a man who identified himself as Matthew Godwin of Adamsport, Massachusetts, and an unidentified woman had been found naked adrift in a lifeboat by a Cuban naval patrol. Was the man Ike Godwin's son, Williams demanded, or someone with a similar name?

Jill had been hiding out in the music room, listening to a Mozart concerto and trying unsuccessfully to keep her thoughts off Matt. What would she do if Matt were dead? Could she stay married to Ike, knowing that she had lied to him? And what if Ike discovered the truth that she had been with Matt on Grand Cayman? She had come back to Adamsport in a moment of desperation, but now she wished she hadn't. After making love with Matt, could she ever respond to Ike without thinking about his son?

She heard Ike's growl of anger into the phone, "If he is my son, I don't know what he was doing in Grand Cayman, or why he was kidnapped. If he's in Cuba, it's not because I sent him there—nor did he go to Grand Cayman in any official capacity for Controlled Power Corporation or for me personally."

After telling Irene and Becky to make sure that the children were not listening, Ike immediately called a family conference to discuss Matt's latest insanity. Neither Henderson nor Becky had any clues to Matt's wanderings. Irene said that Matt had telephoned her, but she thought that he was still sleeping aboard the *Odyssey*.

"That was just last Monday," she said. "Matt was his usual quippish self. He even told me that he might come home, if I told him that I really adored him." Irene's eyes filled with tears as she remembered Matt's actual proposal to her. Who was the woman? Had Matt run away with that sexy little minister at the First Parish Church—Peachy Stein—who adored him and thought he was the Second Coming of Jesus himself?

She voiced the thought and Becky tried to calm her. "We're not even sure that it is Matt. If we don't hear from Matt by Monday, I think Hendy should fly to Havana. I'm sure Senator Williams could arrange that."

To find out if Peachy Stein was involved and to check her whereabouts, Becky telephoned John Codman. John had talked with Peachy yesterday, and as far as he knew she would be preaching tomorrow at the First Parish Church.

Ike reluctantly told Hendy to make arrangements to fly to Havana. "But not until Tuesday. I need you Monday night. I'll be there with you, but I want you to handle the actual bidding on the church." Ike slumped back in his chair and for a moment looked like an old and betrayed King Lear. "I wouldn't be surprised if Matt was playing footsies with some of those damned communist revolutionaries in Cuba or Honduras. He'll do anything to discredit the Godwin name."

Irene tried to placate him. "Deep down Matt really loves you, Ike. I think he was quite shocked when you told him that he was finished at the shipyard." Irene was sobbing now. "I don't care who the woman is, I'm just praying that he's all right."

Jill listened silently. Her leg was in a cast, supported by a footstool. She wanted to blurt out that if Ike hadn't been so involved with his own need for power and the need to perpetuate a family image, generation after generation, he might have discovered that his only son had genius in other directions. Or if Irene had loved him enough and had encouraged him to be something in the world other than a reflection of his father, Matt would probably have had a very happy life as a small-town preacher. She remembered Matt, snuggled against her neck, telling her about the Adams family and how much Sarah had admired old John Adams and Abigail. But after several generations the Adams family had slowly "descended from glory"; after Charles Francis Adams, none of the sons came close to the achievements of their fathers.

Frightened by the thoughts churning in her mind, Jill tried to hold back her own tears. She was drowning in the memories of her few hours with Matt. He really is a loving man, she thought, and she almost said the words aloud. She wanted to defend Matt to Becky and Ike, and she wanted to tell them that when Ike let down his guard, as he often did with her, he was a loving man, too. At least he and Matt had that in common. Their love of her, and she of them, might even be a kind of genetic compulsion. She wondered what would be happening now if Amir and Nefwazi hadn't pulled her out of that swimming pool and pumped the water out of her. They had actually saved her life. Amir told her that she had been lucky. If she hadn't collapsed into the pool after being shot in her thigh, she might well have been killed in the exchange of shots with Ramachanda and his crew. Right now Ike could be waiting for her body to arrive at the airport, hating both her and Matt for their betrayal of him.

Amir and Nefwazi had carried her back to the rented Chevrolet, ignoring her frantic protests that they must save Matt. "We'll find him later," Amir told her, and they drove her to a hospital on Grand Cayman, where a black doctor stitched up the wound in her thigh and put her broken leg in a cast. Desperate, not wanting to leave Grand Cayman without Matt, she finally confessed to Amir that she was really married to Matt's father. To her surprise, Amir burst into laughter. He had more in common with Matt than he realized, he told her. As a young man he had often been tempted to seduce one of his father's younger wives. "If I had, I wouldn't be here to tell about it, and neither would she. It's a good thing that you're not an Arab lady." But Amir had agreed with her: What a seventy-year-old man didn't know, whether he was a sheik or a corporate conglomerator, wouldn't hurt him. Leaving Nefwazi to search for Matt, at one o'clock in the morning, he flew Jill to Miami. There, with the help of reservation people and stewardesses, despite her broken leg, she had finally gotten back to her room in the Plaza in New York, late Wednesday night.

If it hadn't been for Amir, she wouldn't be here right now, trading on the lie she had told Ike and wondering if she had been wrong. To save her marriage she had abandoned her lover. Did she have a choice? She had lied to save Irene, too. Her lover's wife was sitting there in front of her right now, submerged in her own fears and worries.

If Amir and Nefwazi hadn't arrived in time, instead of one naked woman in that lifeboat—the unknown woman must be Emily Lovejoy—there would have been two women. Right now, she could be at death's door in Havana, or she could be dead. Was there any sense to all this? Less than a year ago she had never heard of the Godwins. Less than a week ago, if some fortune teller had told her that less than a month after marrying the father, she'd go to bed with the son, she would have told her that she was insane. Amir would have said that it was preordained by Allah, but no, she had done it herself. She wasn't sorry she had made love with Matt. It was the most complete surrender of herself she had ever made to a man. But even if they managed to get back to Adamsport without this tragedy hanging over their heads, she would never have gone to bed with him again.

She had married Ike, and she loved him, too—not with the same abandonment of herself as she experienced with Matt, but warmly, as a good friend. He was so solicitous of her welfare that it brought tears of guilt to her eyes.

"I thank God that you weren't murdered by that sex maniac," he had told her, and she had a difficult time dissuading him from calling the New York City police or hiring a special investigator to make sure that they found the rapist.

"Why didn't you telephone me Tuesday in Los Angeles?" he kept asking. "You shouldn't have tried to carry on by yourself. I'd have flown to New York immediately." He insisted that with her broken leg she should have a bed of her own in one of the guest rooms. Since Thursday afternoon when he had met her at the airport, kissing her gently, he had treated her more like a daughter than a new wife. "I love you, Jill," he told her. "You've made it possible for me to survive the terrible disappointment I have had with Matt."

How could she tell him that she loved him but she almost hated him when he was at war with his son? Instead of complaining about the lack of sex, he didn't pressure her. He patted her cast affectionately and said, "In a few weeks your leg will be as good as new, and then we'll make up for lost time."

Jill wasn't at all sure of that. If Matt came back to Adamsport, she knew she must cool her relationship with him by putting distance between them. Ike might not like it, but she would accept the offer to play Mrs. Tilton in that new play. They could rent an apartment in New York, and he could fly down for weekends. The truth was that she really didn't trust herself to be in the same room with Matt Godwin. She had a magnetic compulsion toward him that could destroy the polarities of all their lives.

Sunday evening, during supper, plagued with her guilt and the continuing family discussion and tearing of hair over Matt, the black sheep son, brother, and husband, Jill was only partially aware that the housekeeper had whispered to Irene that she was wanted on the telephone. By the time Irene returned, they had finished eating and the children had been dismissed from the table.

"God, I'm glad the kids aren't here," she said. "You'll never believe it. Doris Tilburg just called me. She couldn't stop laughing. It's all over Adamsport. I don't know what to tell the boys. They are sure to ask what they were doing."

"Who was doing what?" Becky demanded.

"Robert Lovejoy and that female minister, Peachy Stein—the one Matt is so enamored with. They were trapped in the belfry of the church. They were both naked—without a stitch of clothing on. The Fire Department rescued them." She scowled. "Matt used to tell me that we should get acquainted with the Lovejoys. I play golf with Emily Lovejoy once or twice a month and she's quite pleasant, but her husband is a little sick in the head. He must be a frustrated sex maniac. Poor Emily."

"What about Peachy? Isn't she married?" Becky asked.

Irene shrugged. "Her husband is Jewish," she said, as if he might have different moral standards from a Christian.

To their surprise, Ike thought it was funny. "I always told Sarah that most of the UU's were former hippies. None of them give a damn whom they go to bed with. The conservative ones like John Codman, the Belchers, and the Hancocks will be damned glad that they agreed to sell the church."

"You may be right," Hendy said. "If the majority of them—the sane ones—should rejoin the Congregational Church, and if they toss in the money we're going to give them for their church, the Adamsport Congregational Church would have a new lease on life."

Driving to the shipyard Monday morning—Hendy never objected to chauffeuring the old man—Ike confirmed that if they hadn't got a fix on Matt by tonight, Hendy should make a fast trip to Cuba. Last night he had tried to make an overseas phone call to Havana, but it had never been completed. "If it really is Matt," Ike told him, "I want to avoid any unfortunate surprises. Matt has given CPC enough nasty publicity with his sermon. If the directors ever hear it, it will cause a total rumble-grumble."

Ike was careful not to reveal to Hendy how shocked and aggravated he was by Matt's behavior. How could his only son—a boy and a man he had really loved—treat him like this? As it had many times, the thought crossed his mind that Matt might not really be his son. He acted more like Moses Fletcher, who, Sarah had once admitted, she loved almost as much as she loved him. When he expressed his worry to Sarah, she had stared at him with shocked tears in her eyes. "That's the most terrible thing you have ever said to me," she said, but she didn't really deny it.

From an early age, even before Matt went to Harvard, the boy always persisted in taking the opposite point of view from his father. Whether it was an argument over who among the candidates should be elected president, or whether Mao Tse-tung's China should have been recognized long before Richard Nixon got around to it, or whether Ho Chi Minh made more sense in Vietnam than Lyndon Johnson—from politics to religion, from capitalism to communism, they had never agreed on anything. But Matt often presented his case so convincingly that he occasionally had Ike wavering; and Ike had to admit there were times he enjoyed his son's quick-thinking mind, especially during the past few years when Matt seemed to have outgrown his love affair with UU's and religion and had concentrated on new contracts for the shipyard.

But now Ike knew he had to face reality. Matt was on a real God-binge this time. He had made a mistake in insisting that Matt be elected president of CPC. Of course he planned to continue as chairman and chief executive officer, at least for a few years. Even Gus Belshin admitted that marriage obviously agreed with Ike: he was acting like a young stallion in the fields with a pretty mare. But Gus implied that at seventy-two Ike should spend more time with his young wife, that he no longer had the energy to fend off other potential wild stallions and also take care of the myriad problems of CPC.

Ike didn't like to admit it, but he knew the time had come for the transfer of power to a younger president, a man who was more on the cutting edge of everyday problems, a man who was thoroughly at home in this rapidly changing, computer-oriented world. A man who was a leader in his own right. With Henderson to back him up in accounting and computer communications, Matt had been the ideal choice. Hendy, alone, was still a possibility, but Hendy was too bland. In a crisis he would weave back and forth. He didn't have the cool nerve needed to challenge Gus or most of the other directors. Hendy wasn't a hard-bitten glad-hander who could love you one minute when you were doing your job and dump you the next if you were blocking the ever moving traffic in a multi-billion-dollar company.

Ike knew that Gus wanted the president's job. He had fought a desperate rough-and-tumble fight to prevent the CPC takeover of Infinity Corporation nearly two years ago. But once his company was in the CPC stable he had continued to run it as profitably as ever. Gus was a man who could make fast decisions and see them through, but Ike didn't trust the bastard. He was sure that Belshin, who had a wife and two kids in their late teens, was probably sleeping with Sally. (Sally admitted that Gus had visited her studio in Big Sur.) The son of a bitch had gone out of his way to get acquainted with Sally, obviously determined to move into the family one way or the other. Ike hadn't made an issue out of it because the real problem, more than any other, was that Belshin was a Jew. The president of Dupont might have been a Jew, and a few other companies on the top of the heap might have Jews running them, but as far as Ike was concerned, God and the Godwins were Christians. Ike would tell anyone that he wasn't prejudiced. He had many Jewish friends. But he wasn't having a Jew run his company.

Ike knew that Belshin and his wife were recently separated, and he was willing to bet that even though Belshin didn't really give a damn about Sally, he would marry her anyway. Sally didn't know anything about the company, but if all else failed, Gus would try to assert that he had finally become a Godwin by injection—the injection of his prick into Sally. That was the kind of Jewish humor that Belshin indulged in that totally irritated Ike. Ike was sure of one thing: once the headquarters of CPC were right here in Adamsport, whoever the president might be, Ike would be able to keep a watchful eye on him.

Thinking of the Devil, the Devil telephoned him at the office. "I waited until noon," Gus's voice sounded like the rat-a-tat-tat of a machine gun being fired. "It's only quarter of nine out here. But I'm not going to stew about it any longer, Ike. When you were out here last week, I disagreed with you. I thought since we had elected Matt president, we should play along with him. I thought it might give us some good publicity if we had a president who was caring enough about people to be a part-time minister. But yesterday, I caught his sermon on early morning television. I hope to hell that most people were watching Oral Roberts instead. If all that crap he preached about not building deployment ships wasn't the straw to break the camel's back, then yesterday, the story about Matt being picked up naked and half-dead from a lifeboat in Cuban waters with some dame really spilled the marbles. If that wasn't enough, I was watching the late news on television last night, and what do I see but some naked nuts who were caught bare-ass in the belfry of that church you're trying to buy. I'm sure that you are aware that CPC was identified as the corporate villain. According to the newscaster, we're about to build our headquarters over the bones of two former presidents of the United States."

"It's a tempest in a teapot," Ike responded. "Don't let it worry you, Gus. I warned you about Matt. I told you that I kicked him out of the shipyard. We've got two months before January and before Matt was supposed to take office. I won't move up to chairman until we find the right man."

"That's not all," Gus said, silently cussing the old bastard for not admitting that he was the only possible "right man." "This is symptomatic of other, deeper Godwin problems. Neither you nor Matt are in touch with reality. I have the third-quarter report on Gigabit Corporation. That's one of your babies, Ike. They were supposed to come out with a bubble memory system that would have a 10-gigabit potential. In five years it would do away with disc drives. Three years later all they've got is a 45-million-dollar loss. That's going to cut our dividends to hell. I told you a year ago we should bite the bullet and take our loss."

"Gigabit is going to be the best investment we ever made." Ike was deliberately trying not to blast away at Gus. "It will give us a nice loss carry-back. Keep in mind, I put CPC together when you were still shitting in your diapers. I know when to cut my losses. As for Matt, whatever he does will have no effect on the company. Within the next year to eighteen months we'll be operating out of our new headquarters here in Adamsport. As a matter of fact, Gus, I think we've got the new president of CPC right here. I'm grooming him. He'll be ready to take over in January."

"Who?" Gus demanded.

"Henderson Inch." Ike smiled grimly into the phone at the long silence.

When Gus snapped back, his voice was controlled, but harsh and determined. "Don't fuck around with me, Ike. I own a big slice of this pie. There comes a time when a man like you who founds a company should roll down his sleeves and go out and play with the daisies. Henderson Inch is an Ivy League do-nothing. He doesn't know whether to shit or get off the pot." Gus chuckled. "At your age you're a little constipated yourself. Most of the board agrees with me; they think your crazy whim to relocate the company in Adamsport is an old man's idea. You don't want to play in the traffic any more. Well, I don't give a shit whether they *give* you that goddamned church. We should either make our permanent headquarters out here or relocate in Chicago. Think it over—and get ready to back off, Ike. If you don't, you may discover that right now you've been talking to the next chairman and chief executive officer of CPC. If you work with me, you can die with your boots on. Otherwise, I'll go to the stockholders. There's enough proxies out there to put you out on your ass."

"It will be your ass if you try it," Ike snarled at him. "Don't get any fancy ideas of buying a page in the *Wall Street Journal* and washing our dirty linen in public. If you do, I'll cream you. All that you'll accomplish is to lower the value of your CPC stock. If CPC ends up in a takeover, you can count on it, you'll go bye-bye, too. And don't challenge *me*. I've got a hundred million bucks or so without the company stock. I'll be around long after you're on the unemployment line."

"You don't scare me, Ike," Gus said coldly. "I'll give you a few days to think it over. While you're thinking, maybe you can tell me what your wife was doing on Grand Cayman Island with Matt last Tuesday. Have she and Matt gone into business together—selling gold to Cuba?"

Ike could feel hot blood flushing his face. "What in hell are you talking about?"

Belshin laughed. "If you don't know, maybe you should ask her. One of my lawyers, Dave Crispin, just got back from Grand Cayman. He recognized Gillian when she walked into the lobby of the Grand Cayman Inn with Matt. Dave saw her in a couple of plays on Broadway, and a few weeks after she married you, her picture was in the *Hollywood Reporter*. 'Jill Marlowe, One-Time Broadway Actress, Goes After the Big Buck' were the headlines. Matt introduced her to Dave as Irene, his wife. Maybe it was Irene. I've never met her." From the dead silence, Gus knew that he had struck pay dirt. "Maybe Irene and Jill are look-alikes, Ike. Or maybe Matt's got some new kind of free-love thing going. It fits in with his sex-worship crap."

26

Late Monday afternoon, driving back to Adamsport from Logan Airport with Peachy sitting beside him, after a surprise luncheon meeting with Amir Saud, Roje couldn't help laughing. "God—Allah—must be smiling on his naked angels," he told her. "If I don't wake up and find that I am dreaming, tomorrow I'm going to call my publisher and tell him that I am going to stop writing fiction. For the first time in my life I'm living a story I couldn't plot. Like Coleridge, when he wrote *Kubla Khan*, I think I must have been smoking hash."

"Your stories are easier to live with," Peachy said morosely. "Whoever is writing this scenario is making it a little too scary for me." She looked at the dashboard clock. "Two hours from now we have to be at the meeting of the church members. In the meantime, I have to get up the nerve to call Mrs. Phalon, the woman next door, and see if she'll sit with David and Cheryl. Honestly, Roje, I hate to walk into the Parish Hall tonight. You've got to save my life. Tell everybody it was your fault. You dared me to take off my clothes, and I did."

Peachy told him that this morning Cheryl had questioned her before she went to school. "Did Roje really make you take your clothes off, Mom?"

Hugging her, Peachy told her, "Not really, honey. I guess for a moment I thought I was a bell and I should be ringing." To divert her, Peachy had sung the song a few times and danced around the living room with her.

"Daddy Saul didn't think you were a bell," David reminded her. "He must have been pretty mad. He didn't come home last night."

There was no denying that. Saul had arrived in front of the First Parish Church just as she stepped out of the aerial platform onto the sidewalk, followed by Roje. Ignoring the wildly cheering crowd, Saul wrenched himself out of her arms and said grimly, "You're a disgrace. You may be able to explain this to your children, but you'll never explain it to me."

"I can't explain it to anyone who is afraid of loving," she told him quietly. "I do love you, Saul."

"I'm sorry," he said bitterly. "I don't understand this naked, bare-your-ass-to-everyone kind of love."

Saul left her standing there, and walked angrily through the suddenly chastened crowd, who realized that a domestic drama was being played out before their eyes. After recovering her clothes and picking up her children, Peachy drove home and waited through the long evening without calling Roje. But Saul didn't come home and he didn't telephone.

Now, Roje was grinning at her in the rear-view mirror. "I'll be happy to tell everyone that it was my fault. After all, I do have the reputation of being a flasher. But you can't escape tonight. Two hours ago, you and I stuck our collective necks out with Amir Saud. You may never become an accredited UU minister, but you sure as hell are Vice President of the Foundation for Modern Moralities."

"Even if Amir had told me that I was Allah's girl friend," Peachy said, "I really haven't got the sheer nerve to walk into the Parish Hall tonight and try to outbid Ike Godwin for the church."

"You don't have to try. You and I *will* outbid him." Roje shrugged. "God Almighty—or Allah, if you prefer—it's really all your fault. If it hadn't been for you, I'd never have jumped into this frying pan. A few weeks ago, before you seduced me and tried to convince me that I was a UU, I was a peaceable citizen. Hiding out in Adamsport, I could write inflammatory novels, and no one read them anyway, and no one knew whether I was alive, or cared less. Now we're going to take on the Moral Majority and all the conservative, law-abiding citizens in the United States—not to mention half the population of Adamsport, who will be burning us in effigy or throwing bricks through our windows."

Peachy squeezed his arm. "I love you, and don't forget $75,000 annual salary is a lot of money."

"So is your $40,000." Roje drove silently for a moment, trying to recapitulate the last twenty-four hours. At least he didn't have to worry about Emily or her reaction to his naked belfry caper. She had called him from Key West early this morning. Between tears and laughter, she managed to say, "Thank God—and thank Matt Godwin, too! I'm back in America. I'll never leave again. I'll have nightmares about it the rest of my life." She was sobbing. "Oh Roje, I hope you forgive me. Sylvie is dead. It was so awful. I don't want to think about it. They forced Matt and me into a lifeboat with Sylvie's dead body. There were sharks everywhere. Matt had to push him overboard. We were three days without food. Our skin burned to blisters during the day and at night we froze. Then the Cubans found us and that was even worse. We don't know what happened to Sylvie's gold, but a day later they found that awful man, Ramachanda, who shot Sylvie. He had already sold the gold to the Cubans—only there was no gold. Now they're sure Matt knows where it is."

Emily told Roje that after an endless interrogation—even though she was half-dead—she had finally been released, with the approval of Cuban government officials, and had been picked up in Key West by a

Cuban refugee group. She would be home tomorrow. She confirmed that Matt was very sick. He had been hit by a bullet and the wound was infected. "Even if he gets better, they are never going to let him go till they find out where the gold is," Emily said. "They never stopped questioning us. We were both very sick and throwing up when we tried to eat, but they left us naked in a cement cell. They finally took us to a hospital. Matt had a high fever. I think they were afraid he was going to die. Then yesterday they told me I was free to leave. All they gave me was a dress that fits like a sack."

Emily was calling from a motel room. If Roje would wire her money, she'd buy some clothes and be on a flight from Miami by tomorrow afternoon. The last time she had seen Matt, he whispered in her ear that a friend of his, a Saudi Arabian sheik, had contacted Fidel Castro, or someone high up in the government. The man had convinced the Cubans that Emily Lovejoy was not involved. "Poor Matt, he was so sick, but he kept trying to tell me that a man named Amir Saud would be contacting you and to please do whatever he asked. But please don't, Roje," Emily begged him, and now she was crying hysterically. "If it has anything to do with Sylvie's gold, please don't get involved."

Before she hung up, her sobs had turned to giggles. "Oh, Roje, you are a nut," she said. "But I love you. I forgot to tell you that I saw you on television this morning with Peachy Stein. Poor Peachy. I know she thinks you are the greatest writer in America, but why did you make her take her clothes off? She'll never live it down. I don't know about you, Roje, but from now on I think we better thank God we're alive and be a good little husband and wife together."

A few moments after Emily called, Peachy was standing at the front door. She had already taken David and Cheryl to school. Saul had finally telephoned and told her that he couldn't take it any longer. It wasn't just her amorality. Peachy jumping into bed with any man who titillated her brain was only the tip of a larger problem. Ever since she had decided to become a UU minister, it had become increasingly apparent that they were traveling on different ships. "I'm not Orthodox," Saul told her. "God may be Jewish . . . or even Christian, but God is not Robert Lovejoy, or Matt Godwin—even if you think so."

"Saul told me that I could have the house," Peachy said, "but it's his. He owned it before me. I'll find an apartment." She was sobbing in Roje's arms, whispering, "I can't help it if I'm a loving person," when the telephone rang. A woman's voice asked if he were Robert J. Lovejoy. Roje grinned into the phone. "Sometimes I'm not sure who I am," he said, "but I guess so."

"You have a call from Sheik Amir Faisal Saud," the woman said. Roje felt a nervous rumble in his stomach as he waited. Was this the sheik whom Emily had mentioned?

"Mr. Lovejoy," a cultured male voice said, "I'm telephoning you at the request of Matthew Godwin. I'm here in Boston in the office of Nate Billings, President of the First Merchants Bank of Boston. I flew in from Grand Cayman last night. We're in the process of drafting the necessary papers to create a non-profit Foundation for Modern Moralities. Matthew indicated to me that you were aware of this project and that you and Ms. Peachy Stein would assume the office of president and vice president. The salary would be nominal, $75,000 and $40,000 respectively. There would be no restrictions on any other interests that you may be pursuing. I'm flying home to Jidda tomorrow afternoon. Nate has promised that he can have all the legal papers ready by three o'clock this afternoon. In the meantime, if you can locate Ms. Stein, we can have lunch at the Meridian Hotel. We'll meet Nate later on my Lear jet, which is now at Butler Aviation. After you sign the papers, I'll be on my way."

Astounded, unable to assimilate the words he was hearing, Roje could only respond, "What about Matt Godwin, where is he?"

"He's still in the hands of the Cuban authorities," Amir said. "They think he's mixed up in a gold smuggling deal. I'm sure they'll cool down in a few days and begin to think more rationally. In the meantime, my contact in Havana tells me that they have released your wife. I assume that by now she must be back in the United States and telephoned you."

Roje acknowledged that he had heard from Emily, and Amir Saud continued: "It's my plan, assuming that you and Ms. Stein are agreeable, to endow the Foundation with $45 million. The bank will act as the depository and oversee the Foundation's expenditures to make sure that they are in keeping with the purposes of the Foundation, which Matthew Godwin can modify or enlarge when and if he returns."

"When and if?" Roje asked. "For God's sake, is he that ill?"

"I understand that he has an e-coli infection from a gunshot wound." Amir sounded cautious. "Can you contact Ms. Stein? I'd prefer to talk with you over lunch."

Feeling that he had no choice, unable to resist Peachy's wild enthusiasm, Roje drove to the Meridian Hotel. "Don't you understand?" Peachy hugged him. "Matt has done it! He must have got Sylvie's gold and sold it to the Arabs." Then Peachy remembered her father. "Poor Sylvie. He may do some good in the world after all. It sounds as if Matt got his hands on enough money to buy the church."

"You mean the Foundation will have enough money," Roje said.

"And we're the Foundation!" Peachy hugged him again.

At Julien's, a restaurant in the hotel, the headwaiter led them to Amir's table. Roje noticed that the entire staff was deferentially, smilingly alert. An oil billionaire was having lunch with them. Amir shook hands with Lovejoy and introduced him to Nefwazi. He smiled appreciatively at Peachy. "So this is Matt's minister. He really does have an eye for beautiful women," Amir grinned, "and they for him, it seems. I trust that Jill Godwin has returned safely to Adamsport?"

Roje told him that Jill was very worried about Matt.

"As I told you, I haven't seen Matthew personally," Amir said, "but my contact in Havana assured me that he is now getting excellent medical attention. Unfortunately, I was telephoning from Grand Cayman, so my conversation with my contact was very circumspect. Details of our friendship could not be discussed." Amir smiled conspiratorily. "That is also the reason I wanted to talk with you here and not at the First Merchants Bank. Nate Billings is quite puzzled by my motivations."

"Your motivations are obviously quite charitable," Nefwazi said. "You have created this Foundation because of your deep friendship with Matthew Godwin and your belief that his ideas might help give Americans a new moral perspective on themselves as well as the world."

"Exactly," Amir beamed at Nefwazi. "As for myself, I wish to maintain a very low profile. I understood from Matthew that you and Ms. Stein are familiar with the plans for his church in Adamsport. And for the spreading of a new gospel according to Matthew." Amir grinned at his little joke. "I'm assuming that, if necessary, you could carry on yourselves. But if for any reason you and Ms. Stein should decide that you are not in accord with the basic purposes of the Foundation, which the bank's lawyers are now excerpting from the sermon that Matthew delivered several weeks ago, then you can advise Nate Billings that you wish to withdraw. I'm sure the Foundation will not lack for leadership."

"You seem to be assuming that Matt Godwin may die," Roje said in alarm. He was feeling a little like Tevye in *Fiddler on the Roof*. He wanted to look up and talk to God and ask his advice.

"Only Allah knows," Amir replied. "Whatever happens, including your involvement in this Foundation, is already written." He bowed his head. "*Allah Kareem.*"

Sipping expensive white wine with the luncheon, feeling as if she were dining with two characters out of the *Arabian Nights*, Peachy wanted to make sure that the Foundation could use some of the money to buy the church. She told Amir that tonight the church would be sold to the highest bidder."

Amir smiled. "I haven't seen your church, but I hope that you won't have to bid $45 million for it."

"I gather you were able to sell Sylvie's gold," Roje said, trying to ferret out exactly what had happened, "and this is basically the reason for your generosity."

Shaking his head, Nefwazi picked up the ball. "After we rescued Mrs. Godwin and Amir flew her to Miami, I rented a helicopter and went searching for a certain schooner on which we were sure Matthew was being held a prisoner. We were totally unaware that your wife was mixed up in this, Mr. Lovejoy. I located the ship the next morning. It looked as if it were headed in the direction of Havana. Based on the speed it was making, I figured that we could overtake it with a high speed powerboat. Finding such a boat and getting it properly equipped with necessary weapons on an island where various strange commodities are exchanged under the guise of the police was fairly easy. When Amir returned from Miami we hired three natives and took off. We finally overtook the schooner on Wednesday afternoon. When we signaled to them that we wanted to board, they opened fire on us with a depth gun and machine guns. A few minutes later there was an explosion somewhere midship and a fire broke out. A rather scurvy crew piled into a lifeboat. We let them go, but not before discovering from one of them that they had cast Matthew and your wife adrift early that morning." Nefwazi shrugged. "We regretted later that we didn't sink the lifeboat with them in it. We searched for two days for Matthew and your wife, but we couldn't find them. It's a very big, lonely ocean out there." Nefwazi smiled. "But evidently their time had not yet come."

"According to the newspapers, the schooner sank." Roje raised his eyebrows at Amir. "It makes your generosity somewhat baffling."

Amir shrugged. "As Nefwazi just told you, Mr. Lovejoy, I have created the Foundation because I admire Matthew Godwin. I'm not personally a billionaire yet. On the other hand, when my revered and aged father dies, I will have access to several billions. So the search for your friend's gold was an interesting adventure. Whatever the source of funds, it would be best to consider this endowment a gift from Allah."

"Do you know what happened to my father?" Peachy changed the subject.

Amir looked puzzled. "I know nothing about your father."

"Presumably, my father owns a villa on Grand Cayman." Peachy wanted to say, "which was filled with gold, and which is really the reason that you are being so damned generous."

"Matthew had a friend . . ." Amir's piercing black eyes were trying to probe Peachy's brain. "A Colonel Gamble. Was he your father?"

"His real name was Sylvanus Williams. Emily told Roje that he was dead."

"I'm afraid that may be true. Before we cast those Indians adrift, Nefwazi questioned one of them—a man named Ramachanda—rather forcibly, I'm afraid. Ramachanda admitted that there was a third person in the lifeboat with Matt and Mrs. Lovejoy but that he was dead. Amir patted Peachy's hand sympathetically. "At least we've closed the circle of doubt."

Amir let a respectful silence follow. The waiter bustled around the table, removing plates and bringing in the next course. Finally Amir said to Peachy, "Your father's villa on Grand Cayman is a valuable piece of property. I have several good friends who live on Grand Cayman and I find the climate agreeable. If you'd consider selling it, I'd be happy to pay you $500,000 for it."

"That's about twice what it's worth," Nefwazi said.

"A half-million dollars?" Peachy was astonished. "But I don't own it."

"Who does? Do you have brothers or sisters? Is your mother alive?"

"I guess I'm his only heir. My mother hated him. But how do I prove he's dead—and what if he isn't?"

Amir smiled. That was no problem. He'd have Nate Billings draft an informal, tentative sales agreement, and give her $100,000 immediately against the final price when the estate was settled and her father's death legally established.

A half-hour later they met Nate Billings, who arrived with a bank lawyer, aboard Amir's jet, and they signed several piles of papers which they only half read. Billings agreed to handle the sale of Sylvie's villa, but was somewhat doubtful. "Not about the reality of your money," he assured Amir, "but the whole damned business—the Foundation, and why you would want to pay this young lady for a villa that she might not even own." Then, receiving a cool look from Amir, he laughed. "Mine not to reason why," he said. He gave Roje and Peachy his business card. "Should the need arise, I'll be happy to confirm your new resources."

When Roje dropped Peachy off at home so that she could arrange a sitter for David and Cheryl, she waved Amir's check at him. "I feel like Scheherazade," she said. "I'll pick you up at seven in my car. Maybe I should buy the First Parish Church myself." She bussed his cheek. "I'd still like to know if they got poor Sylvie's gold."

Roje shook his head. "If they did, why didn't they take the money and run? And why does Amir want the villa on Grand Cayman?"

27

Driving to the First Parish Church with Irene Godwin next to him in the front seat of his Cadillac, Henderson Inch felt as if he had just staggered off the floor after a slugfest boxing match. Years ago when he married Becky, he had been dimly aware that he had not only got a Godwin for a wife but had married a whole damned family. A family, he learned gradually, that required a tongue-swallowing statesman to deal with. But he never suspected that he would be in the front line of a battle over a church that he had never attended, or that he would be going to this meeting without Ike to guide him. Sitting silently beside him, lost in her own thoughts, Irene finally broke the silence.

"We're Ike Godwin's patsies, aren't we?" she asked. "You were afraid to say no, and so was I."

"It was the worst hour I've ever spent in my life. Ike didn't say a thing about it all the way home from the yard. Then he lowered the boom. I thought sure that he was going to drop dead."

Fifteen minutes ago, lying on the sofa while Becky propped him up with pillows and told him that, like it or not, she was telephoning Dr. Adler, Ike was still not subdued. "Stop worrying about me," he said. "I'm not going to let that woman—or my son—kill me." He smiled grimly at Hendy. "Obviously I can't go tonight, but I want you to be at that meeting, and you too, Irene," he told her as she hovered in the background. "I want you to go with Hendy. I want a Godwin there to show that this family is united and in agreement to fight my son."

Irene knew that Becky had to stay with Ike. She wanted to tell him that Hendy was a Godwin as much as she was, but she didn't contest him. A Godwin carried the family name. Henderson was an Inch and so was Becky. Before they left, Hendy asked Ike if he should stay firm on the $450,000 offer for the church.

"Don't take any chances," Ike muttered. His usually rosy complexion was still gray. "We don't want to lose to that realty firm by a few thousand dollars. Play it by ear, Hendy. Use your own judgment, but don't come away empty-handed."

Hendy's own judgment was that there were plenty of other potential sites in Adamsport on which CPC could build a new headquarters, including one right across the street which had been offered to Ike by the owner, but he knew enough not to provoke the "old gent" further.

Even before Ike confronted Jill, Hendy had warned him that he was much too overwrought to deal with the members of the First Parish Church tonight. He offered to telephone John Codman and postpone the meeting until next week. But Ike was adamant. "I'm not letting any johnny-come-lately like Gus Belshin tell me how to run my company." Ike had reviewed most of his conversation with Belshin as Hendy drove home from the yard, but he hadn't said a word about Jill and Matt—not until he walked in the front door. Becky and Jill were waiting for them with a pitcher of martinis.

Ike brusquely refused a drink. "You smug little bitch," he snarled at Jill. "If I were ten years younger I'd drag you out of that chair and beat the shit out of you. So you were nearly raped in New York City, were you? You goddamned liar! The real 'rapist' was Matt Godwin. Is your leg really broken, or is it just an excuse to keep you out of bed with me? Did my son rape you in Grand Cayman—you filthy whore— or did you just lie down and spread your legs for him?"

Totally surprised, Jill didn't have time to wonder how Ike had found out or just how much he really knew, but she knew it was useless to try to pile lies upon lies. Tears in her eyes, she couldn't help thinking this was a more tragic scene than any she had ever played in the theater. "I'm sorry, Ike," she sobbed. "I shouldn't have lied to you. I should never have come back here."

"You thought you'd get away with it, didn't you? You rotten whore! You and Matt thought I'd never find out." Ike grabbed the neck of Jill's sweater and pulled her off the sofa. Tottering, she managed to balance herself on one leg while he held her. "That slimy son of mine convinced you, didn't he? Together you'd screw Daddy Warbucks. If you didn't kill him outright, you'd make him insane with jealousy." Ike smashed his free hand across her face, and let go of her.

She collapsed on the floor moaning. "Please, Ike, I'm responsible. Don't blame Matt. Do anything you like to me. It's not Matt's fault. He loves you, Ike. I know you'll never understand, but I love you, too."

"Love me?" Ike was infuriated. Afraid that he was going to try to kill Jill, Hendy tried to restrain him. "I'd rather have hate than that kind of love. I want to know the truth. How many times have you fucked with Matt?"

Becky gasped. She was as shocked as her father, but she had never heard him use such a word. To her surprise and Hendy's, Irene knelt on the floor beside Jill, trying to help straighten out her legs. She gently stroked the welt across Jill's cheek and tried to soothe her.

Jill smiled gratefully at her through her tears. "Matt loves you too, Irene. Don't hate him," she sobbed. "We didn't fuck. We made love. Matt doesn't try to possess a woman or have her exclusive love. Being with him was a kind of surrender, a joyful recognition that for a moment at least, you and he are God." Her fingers clutching the rug, she cried pathetically. "Truly, Irene, loving me, Matt does not love you less."

"I don't want to listen to such shit," Ike said contemptuously. "I don't love you, Jill, but I'm sorry that I hit you." His face suddenly blanched and he sat down heavily in the nearest chair. "I don't feel well." Ike's voice was a feeble whisper. He patted his pocket. "My pills. Get me one!"

"What are they?" Hendy asked in alarm as Becky fished in Ike's pocket, quickly found a pill dispenser, and put a pill on his tongue. Hushed, they stared at Ike, wondering if he was having a heart attack.

"It's nitroglycerin," Becky said. "Dad's had angina pains for several years, but he didn't want anyone to know."

"Who told you?" Ike asked glumly.

"Dr. Adler, at Mother's funeral." She patted Ike's hand. "He told me that you'd live to be a hundred, but you had to stop blowing your top. You've got to ease up. Right now, I'm going to telephone him and you're going to lie down."

"Like hell," Ike grunted as the pill took effect and quieted his fibrillating heart. "I'll lie down an hour, but then I'm going to that meeting." He stared at Jill, still weeping on the floor. "I don't give a damn if I relocate the company in Adamsport anymore," he told Hendy grimly, "but I'm going to buy that church. The UU's have been in my craw for thirty years. Once I own it I'll have the wrecker turn it into a pile of rubble. I'll leave it there—a monument to my two wives who never really gave a damn about me and a son who thinks love is a merry-go-round and doesn't care whose mare he jumps on."

With Irene's help, Jill had slowly balanced on one leg and found her crutch. "Where are you going?" he demanded as she tried to leave the living room.

"I think I'd better leave. I'll go to a motel."

"Good. Get the hell out of my life." His voice cracking, tears in his eyes, he stared up at her and said, "I loved you once, Jill. I still love you. But I can't look at you without thinking of you with Matt. I'm not sharing my woman."

Sick at heart and not at all sure of her own emotions, but somehow feeling empathy toward Jill, Irene begged her not to try to leave town. "I don't think Ike can ever forgive you," she told Jill, "but he does need you." Irene suggested that she could stay in the carriage house with her. "Please stay at least until Matt comes back." She looked at Jill sadly. "I don't think I can live with him any longer, but I'm not blaming you. Maybe some day you'll tell me what Matt was really doing on Grand Cayman. And I understand what you mean by sexual surrender . . . It happened once or twice with Matt and me."

She looked so pitiful that Jill wanted to hug her.

"Will the Adamses Give Way to the Godwins?" That was the way the *Adamsport Chronicle* headlined the sale of the First Parish Church.

When Roje and Peachy entered the Parish Hall they were greeted with a buzz of conversation, laughter, and surreptitious glances. Although she had many friends in the congregation, no one rushed up to greet the minister. The Belchers were sitting near the front door checking a membership list against arrivals. One section of the floor was already filled with more than a hundred interested spectators sitting in folding chairs. Roje recognized George Gallagher, the mayor, and various members of the city council. Bill Walsh, publisher of the

Chronicle, stared at Peachy disgustedly, probably gloating that he had saved his son Michael from this promiscuous woman. Several men with cameras were wandering around. Bill Gates, a portable television camera slung on his shoulder, waved happily at Roje and Peachy.

"We've set up two sections," Horace Belcher said, acknowledging Peachy and Roje with a cold expression on his face. "One is for interested spectators and one for the members of the church. I'm sure that you understand," he said, calling her Ms. Stein instead of Peachy, "although you're a member of this church, as minister of the church you are not eligible to vote tonight."

"I didn't expect to vote," Peachy responded. She tried to stare Belcher down and wondered if he were trying to atomize her on the spot. "The voting was over ten days ago. I assume that the purpose of this meeting is to sell the church to the highest bidder."

Frowning at her, Dorothy replied for her husband. "The bylaws of the church make it possible for the members to consider unannounced new business if 80 percent of the members are present. So many questions have been raised during the past week that the executive committee decided if enough members do show up, we will reconfirm the decision to sell the building." Her lips were pursed in a hard line. "Quite frankly, Peachy, you may not wish to be here tonight. A motion will be made not only to relieve you of your ministerial duties but to ask for your resignation as a member of this church."

Noticing the tears flooding Peachy's eyes, Roje took her arm. "We didn't come here to vote," he said crisply. "Ms. Stein and I prefer to sit with the bidders." He guided Peachy to a row of still empty chairs in the back of the hall that were available for the general public. "Get a grip on yourself," he whispered. "Tomorrow you'll own the damned church. You can tell them all to go to hell."

Too late Roje discovered that he was sitting directly behind Irene Godwin. She turned and nodded coldly at him. "You're becoming quite famous, Mr. Lovejoy," she said frigidly. "How is Emily? I haven't seen her at the club for some time." Without saying it, they were both wondering why the other had come to this meeting. Roje was well aware that Irene believed that Emily was probably ashamed to be seen with him at the club. Poor Emily, she'd have to tell her golfing friends that she wasn't a bit shocked to have a husband who cavorted naked in the First Parish Church with a woman nearly half his age.

To satisfy his curiosity, Roje asked Irene if she had any further news about Matt, other than what had already appeared in the newspapers. He realized that Irene had problems of her own. The world was well aware that her husband had had a fling in a lifeboat with an unidentified naked lady. Roje was pretty sure that Irene didn't know yet that the woman was Emily, and he was sure that Emily wouldn't be standing in line to tell her.

"No," Irene said curtly. "Matt seems to be on his own trip lately. Henderson may fly to Havana tomorrow to find out what happened to him. Tonight he's representing Isaac in the bidding for the church."

Standing behind a lectern that had been set up on the stage, John Codman noted the time. It was 7:32 P.M. The Parish Hall was filled to capacity. He rapped his gavel for attention. "The meeting will come to order," he said. "I'm happy to see that so many people in Adamsport are finally interested in the fate of the First Parish Church. If we had this many in attendance on Sundays, none of us would probably be here tonight."

"Wait until next Sunday," someone yelled. "Everyone will be here to see if Peachy is going to preach her sermon in her birthday suit."

Codman rapped his gavel angrily. "I will not tolerate comments from the floor that are not previously acknowledged by me," he said. "What happened here last Sunday may seem amusing to some of you, but I want to remind you that this is a church of God. There is a cross over the altar." He glared defiantly at the audience. "Dorothy Belcher informs me that we have 117 members present. That means 21 are missing. Since we have close to 90 percent of our membership here in the Parish Hall, we are in a position to consider any business, old or new, without an advance notice being given."

He ignored several waving hands and continued: "During the past week we have had numerous requests to reconfirm our previous vote to sell the church. The previous vote was ninety for, twenty-five against. Twenty-three didn't attend that meeting. Before I request a motion to reconfirm the sale to the highest bidder, I think we should hear from Wilson Truman of the National Park Service. Mr. Truman believes that because John Quincy Adams personally paid the original builders of this church to create space for his father John's and his mother Abigail's tombs under the front portico of this church, and because this building has been designated a National Historic Landmark, that we are not legally in a position to sell the building."

Immediately the chair was besieged for recognition. Codman acknowledged various members who declared angrily that the present members actually owned the Parish Hall and the sanctuary and could do what they damned well pleased about selling it.

"Historic landmark, my eye," Ada Bass said. "The Adams family may own the tombs, but they don't own the church. There are no Adamses who are members. But there is a Bass." She shook her cane at Codman. "The United States Government has never given a cent to this church. We, the members, with our donations and pledges—our own hard-earned money—have kept the roof over our heads."

Ada was enthusiastically cheered, but they finally quieted down to listen to Truman's short speech. He insisted that the historical landmark designation and the acceptance of the building by the Congress of the United States and the National Park Service, even though no money had been forthcoming and probably never would be, made it impossible for the members to destroy the building and permit an apartment or office building to be erected on the site.

A motion was made to reconfirm the sale of the building. Codman pointed out that the agreement to sell to the highest bidder carried with it a prior agreement that proper housing for the Adamses' tombs would be provided by the winning bidder, regardless of what form the ultimate new building might take. The vote was eighty to sell, thirty-seven against.

"Even if the missing twenty-one members were present they could not add enough nay votes to constitute a majority," Codman pointed out. "Does anyone have any old or new business to come before the members?"

"Mr. Chairman, I do." Henry Hancock stood up and surveyed the members. "I'm aware that Ms. Stein—I'm sorry, but I can't call her Reverend Stein—is here tonight. She is accompanied by a certain Mr. Lovejoy, who in the past month or so has become quite notorious in this city and has now made a laughingstock of this church. I don't know what excuse Ms. Stein may be offering for her conduct in this church last Sunday afternoon. I'm sure that no legitimate excuse is possible. Even if it were, I would not be interested in hearing it. Ms. Stein is a disgrace to the Unitarian Universalist ministry. For the honor of this church, and the prestige of our religion nationally, I make a motion that Ms. Stein be terminated immediately as the minister of the Adamsport Unitarian and Universalist Church—wherever it may hold its services in the future—and that the UU headquarters disqualify her as a minister for any UU church. I also make a motion that Ms. Stein be asked to resign as a member of this church."

"Second the motions!" someone yelled.

"We have to have one motion at a time, and I'm afraid that the first motion will have to be modified," Codman said. "This body cannot vote for UU headquarters."

Within a minute the motion was rephrased. Roje heard Peachy suppress a little sob. He could feel her arm trembling against his. Codman called for discussion of the motion. Once again Ada Bass stood up: "Since we were all young once and probably did things we shouldn't have done, and since Peachy is here in the Parish Hall, I think we should give her a chance to tell us what really happened."

Roje shook his head vehemently at Peachy, trying to convince her not to stick her neck out. But she stood up. "Some people climb the Himalayas," she said quietly and her heart was fluttering. "Sunday afternoon, I was so happy, so in love with love, knowing that sin and salvation come from within and there's no one out there to help you, that I wanted to feel at one with whatever makes the earth turn. I took off my clothes and climbed the rickety old ladder that leads to the cupola. I wanted to share the joy of the whole world, which is greater than all its sorrows, with someone. The unseen fingers of the warm Indian summer air were caressing my body, making love to me. Roje—Robert Lovejoy—was there, and I teased him to shed his clothes and come up with me and see Adamsport drowsily sleeping in what was sure to be the last breath of summer. He did and the ladder broke." She paused. "People who are careless shouldn't climb mountains. They often die before they reach the top."

There was a scatter of applause, but many members were shaking their heads disgustedly. There was no further discussion, and Codman called for a vote. A hand count determined that sixty-five members wanted Peachy's resignation both as a minister and as a member of the church; fifty-two voted against the motion.

To Roje's surprise, the cantankerous old Scotsman, Fred Burns, stood up. "This vote is invalid," he said. "There was no warrant issued on this meeting, or on this problem. The twenty-one members who did not come tonight might have appeared if they knew this was going to be on the agenda. If fourteen of them had voted for Ms. Stein, she'd have a majority."

"Old Fred must want to join Peachy in the belfry," Jim Esposito, one of the young members, said to enthusiastic applause. "If my wife wouldn't object, I'd be happy to climb to the top with Peachy."

Codman rapped his gavel angrily, and ignored him. "We now come to the purpose of this meeting. To my knowledge we have two bidders here tonight: Henderson Inch, who has advised me that he is representing Isaac Godwin and Controlled Power Corporation, and Harold Hough, who is here from the Boston realty firm of Cabot and Hough. Both bidders have provided drawings of their concepts for the new structures to be erected on this site. These have been available in the Parish Hall for study during the past ten days. Each of the bidders have offered different approaches to protect the Adamses' tombs, but essentially both offer a small chapel within the grounds which would be incorporated as part of the new structure. At our last meeting we established the floor on the bidding at $400,000. If there are no further questions, we will proceed . . ."

"Mr. Chairman," Roje stood up. Codman and the audience gaped at him in surprise. "Ms. Stein and I, representing the Foundation for Modern Moralities, are also planning to bid for this building, the sanctuary and the parsonage. We will not bid on the communion silver, or any furnishings of this church or other buildings. I simply want to make sure that we are all bidding on the same properties." Roje grinned at Henderson Inch, who had turned around and was staring at him with his mouth slightly ajar.

"This is quite a surprise, Mr. Lovejoy," Codman said. "Naturally, you are welcome to bid, but I'm sure that all our members would like to be assured of your financial creditability. Since you have presented no drawings for your proposal or for the care of the Adamses' tombs, we're concerned about this also."

"Unlike the other bidders, the Foundation does not plan to destroy this church," Roje said. "Our plans include a complete modernization of the interior of the sanctuary. We plan to rejuvenate the belfry with a gilded dome and a new bell, and we will expand the crowded space now occupied by the Adamses' tombs so that most of the space under the sanctuary now used by the Sunday School and the kitchen area will be devoted to the Adamses' memorabilia and the history of Adamsport. In addition, within the remodeled sanctuary we will offer scheduled films for residents and tourists, dramatizing the history of this area and the creation of our nation."

Roje paused for dramatic effect, well aware that he had captured the attention of the entire audience. "We also plan to tear down this antiquated Parish Hall. In its place we will erect a seven-story modern glass building which will be butted against the church just as the present building now is. This new building, with approximately 7,000 square feet per floor, will give the church dining and recreation areas; video areas and a library; day care facilities; and a modern dance, drama, and music center which will provide programs for the church."

A wave of excited conversation rolled through the Parish Hall. Several cameramen flashed Roje's picture as he was speaking, and Bill Gates had video-taped the entire speech. Once again Codman rapped for attention. He acknowledged Henderson Inch.

"I know that you are fairly well off, Mr. Lovejoy," Henderson said sarcastically, "but you are obviously talking in the millions of dollars. So that I'm sure that we aren't playing games, I think the members of this church have a right to know the source of funds for this pie-in-the-sky proposal."

Roje held a business card out to him. "Anticipating this question, I asked the president of the First Merchants Bank, Nathan Billings, to give me his home phone number. Mr. Billings assured me this afternoon that he'll be home tonight. You're welcome to call him and confirm the financial credentials of the Foundation and the fact that Ms. Stein and I represent it."

Henderson refused the card, but Horace Belcher popped out of the members' section. "I'll telephone him," he said crisply, snatched the card out of Roje's hand, and disappeared into the minister's office.

"We're sorry to question your financial credibility, Mr. Lovejoy," Codman said, "but in view of your behavior in other areas, and the fact that in some ways you seem to be trying to actually live your so-called Modern Moralities, you must be aware that your offer to bid is not only incredible but also quite shocking to us. I presume that you are indirectly representing Matthew Godwin. You must be aware that most of us sitting in this room were quite appalled by Matt's sermon and his new approach to morality, which I personally think is rather sick."

Roje smiled coolly. He wasn't sure, but he hoped that he was responding with the same aplomb as a character in his novel would have. "As the only officers of the Foundation, Ms. Stein and I are fully responsible for our decisions. We're happy to tell you that the legal purposes of the Foundation permit us to advocate and pursue a new approach to morality such as Matthew Godwin outlined in his sermon. When Matt returns, we hope that he may function as an advisor to the Foundation. In the meantime, John, I can assure you that we're authorized to proceed without him."

Horace Belcher returned, mounted to the stage, and had a brief whispered conversation with Codman. A little bewildered, Codman scowled at Roje. "It would seem that you have more than sufficient resources to buy this church. In deference to Ike Godwin's age, and his wife Sarah's long-time association with this church, we'll let Mr. Inch, representing Isaac Godwin, start off the bidding."

Henderson stood up. "In view of the fact that the parsonage is included in the bid, although Controlled Power has no use for it and will sell it later, we raise our initial offer from $450,000 to $550,000."

Harold Hough stood up. "Representing Cabot and Hough, I bid $575,000."

Roje nudged Peachy and she stood up. "The Foundation bids $625,000." She stared defiantly at Henderson Inch.

Henderson was suddenly whispering in Irene Godwin's ear. "It's more than it's worth," he told her nervously, "but I don't want to face Ike if we come home without it." He asked her if she thought Matt was providing the money for the Foundation. Irene could only answer, "Matt may have enough money to buy the church, but not to rebuild it."

"CPC bids $650,000," Henderson said. He was well aware that by now all the members were listening with rapt attention. With that kind of money they could not only build a new church but also have enough left over to keep it running indefinitely.

"Cabot and Hough bids $675,000," Harold Hough said.

Roje stood up. "Before the bidding continues, I'd like to inform the members and everyone present tonight that we are in a somewhat different position from the other bidders. As you now are aware, we plan to continue to operate as a church. Hopefully, we will still be affiliated with all UU churches but with a new identity: The First Church of Modern Moralities. Within eighteen months we expect to be functioning as a new style, annual membership church club. There will be no pledges and no collection on Sundays. Dues will be scaled to the income of a particular member or family. We expect to attract a thousand members. This will be a pilot church with totally new approaches. We expect that the members' dues and voluntary contributions from various organizations and individuals will make it possible for us to completely cover all operating expenses."

Roje paused. He hoped that he was expressing Matt's daydreams as well as possible. "I'm making a point of this because we hope that after the church is sold the present members won't embark on a hasty rebuilding program. We would welcome them as members of the new church, and we hope that they may decide to merge with the new church as a body." Roje couldn't help smiling. "If they vote to donate the full purchase price of this building, as well as their income from funds provided by bequests, to the Foundation for Modern Moralities, all present members and their families would automatically become lifetime, paid-up members of the new church." Roje paused to let his message sink in. "Despite some discontent among the members at the present time, we think that there's a good possibility that this may happen. In any event, the Foundation bids $750,000."

There were no further bids.

Roje hugged Peachy triumphantly. "Naked or clothed, you won't have to stop preaching. I hope we're in agreement." He shook his head, still trying to absorb his own commitment. "You'd better be—look what you've done to me!"

28

Matt's first encounter with Torvo Vigilar occurred a few days after he and Emily, still naked but covered with unwashed Cuban navy blankets, were ushered with no apologies into a cockroach-infested cell. Snickering, their jailors pointed to a musty, urine-stained mattress on a cement floor and a grimy chamber pot.

A little delirious, running a high temperature from the infection in his shoulder wound, Matt crawled on to the mattress, and when the guards were gone he whispered to Emily, "If they start to question you, tell them you were visiting a friend, Sylvanus Williams, on Grand Cayman."

They were still oily from a fish that Matt had swooped out of the water the second day. After they had chewed it, raw and bloody, they had smeared the oil over their burning flesh. Sobbing and moaning "Poor Sylvie," Emily cradled Matt's hot face against her sunburnt breasts. "Tell them Sylvie invited us for a little vacation," Matt moaned. "Don't tell them about the gold. Just tell them that when we arrived we found that someone had broken into his villa and murdered him. The murderers were afraid that we'd go to the police, so they kidnapped us and set us adrift." Muttering unintelligibly, Matt relapsed into semiconsciousness.

Dazed, only half-alive herself, Emily had covered them with the blanket. Matt vaguely remembered her shivering in the damp cell and her body feeling cool against his fever-wracked body. "Please, please, Matt!" she had pleaded. "Don't die. Don't leave me here. I'm so afraid. If they hurt me, I won't be able to be brave. I'll tell them the whole story."

Matt didn't see Emily again until January, three months later, when he finally got back to Adamsport. Although he had been nearly unconscious when two men carried him out of the cell on a stretcher, he remembered Emily hugging him. Tears were streaming down her face. Heedless that she was naked or that the guards kept feeling any part of her that was handy, she kept begging him: "Matt, don't die. Matt, you've got to live. I love you. Roje loves you. Please don't give up. I'm praying for you."

Matt had grinned feebly at her. "Just pray that these people would rather play at being God than play at being the Devil."

Two days later, responding to whatever medicine they were injecting into him, he slowly became aware that he was in a hospital ward. Cast-iron beds lined up against both walls were filled with moaning patients. The odor of ether and alcohol, mingled with the smell of vomit and death, made him feel nauseated. When he finally opened his eyes, his brain suddenly alerted to a new smell of stale tobacco, he was staring into the florid face of a man wearing a black moustache.

"I'm Torvo Vigilar." The man was chewing an unlighted cigar only a few inches from Matt's nose. "I see that like Jesus himself the Reverend has returned from the grave."

"Where's Emily?" Matt asked weakly.

"Your lady friend, if she really is your lady friend," Vigilar smiled coldly at Matt, "is in the women's detention ward. She's very—how do you say it—incoherent. She keeps insisting that a man named Ramachanda murdered her lover. Fortunately, we picked up this Ramachanda person floating at sea in another dinghy. He tells us a different story. He insists the lady's lover tried to murder him."

Gradually, Matt discovered from Vigilar that the day after the Cuban patrol boat had rescued him and Emily, they had found Ramachanda and two other men floating in a lifeboat. Ramachanda insisted that the Reverend Godwin had been negotiating with him to buy 400 gold ingots. The Reverend and a friend of his named Colonel Gamble refused to pay Ramachanda's price and threatened to kill him and take the gold anyway. Ramachanda had no choice, he told Vigilar;

he shanghaied the Reverend and the colonel's girl friend to save his own life.

"Your Hindu friend claims he didn't murder Colonel Gamble and he doesn't know any Sylvanus Williams," Vigilar said. "He wanted me to tell you that you should be thankful that he's not a murderer, which is proved by the fact that you and the unknown lady have survived."

Vigilar grinned at Matt, waiting for his response, but Matt was absorbed with his own thoughts. He wondered if Amir and Nefwazi had caught up with Ramachanda and set him adrift in the ocean. Had Amir found Sylvie's gold? Where was the schooner? Matt remembered that Sylvie had told him that he had used three ingots to finance the transfer of the gold from India. Sylvie had never gone into details, but he had mentioned a banker in Calcutta whom he had dealt with many years ago. Was that Ramachanda? Maybe Ramachanda had brought one of the ingots with him to Grand Cayman—the one he had shown Matt. Maybe Ramachanda had never found the rest of the gold and had been searching for it when he and Jill had arrived.

"No body has been found," Vigilar was saying, "so we don't have a problem with murder. We tried to calm Senora Lovejoy, but she's afraid that we're going to torture her. She keeps mumbling about somebody named Roje and saying, 'Roje, please forgive me.' I gather that Roje is her husband," Vigilar said sarcastically.

In the following days, as Vigilar kept questioning him, it became apparent that he must be a high ranking officer in the Cuban secret police. He told Matt that Ramachanda's schooner had been found drifting in the Caribbean. It had been scuttled and much of the superstructure burned. Ramachanda insisted that the gold had been aboard the schooner and must have been removed by the pirates who had attacked the ship and set them adrift. But Vigilar never brought Matt and Ramachanda face to face.

A few days later, Vigilar, shaking his head in disgust, told Matt: "Whatever your sexual involvements with the lady may be, I am convinced that she doesn't know very much. I am releasing her to Key West tomorrow." Then, to Matt's surprise, Vigilar waved at a nurse and said, "Bring in Senor Mohammed Husayn." He grinned at Matt. "Maybe he can shed a little light on your activities."

Husayn, wearing an Arab headdress tied with an agal but otherwise dressed in a conventional business suit, looked like a foreign diplomat. He greeted Matt with an impassive expression. "Your friend Sheik Amir Saud read of your strange adventure in the *New York Times*. He telephoned me from New York. He's concerned about your health. He wanted you to know that he hopes to be in Boston soon to confer with your associates. He wanted me to tell you that he will do his best to facilitate your religious projects."

"Your sheik wouldn't be involved in a little gold smuggling, would he?" Vigilar demanded.

"Sheik Amir Faisal Saud is a billionaire," Husayn replied disdainfully. "I'm sure he has all the gold he needs. He instructed me to tell you that this man is not only a good friend of his, but he is also a minister of God and Allah. Sheik Saud prays that you will release Reverend Godwin very soon and see that he gets home to the United States."

But neither Husayn nor Henderson Inch, who arrived a few days later, could get Matt released. "We've informed your friends," Vigilar told him, "that there is a problem of Cuban security. For all we know, Reverend Godwin, this entire business may be a cover for espionage. We have rescued five people in two different dinghies in the middle of the ocean, and we have found the hull of a scuttled schooner with nothing aboard. There is also another problem. It seems that our bankers had made arrangements with Ramachanda to purchase a quantity of gold whose market value exceeds $100 million. But Ramachanda claims that the gold was stolen by pirates. If that is true, who were these unknown parties who attacked his schooner and set it on fire?" Vigilar frowned at Matt. "Obviously, our leaders are very interested in the gold. It would improve our trade balances. Perhaps you can tell us who has it now?"

Matt shook his head and continued to insist that he knew nothing about the gold or who had it. With Vigilar listening at Matt's bedside, Henderson confirmed that Matt was in truth Isaac Matthew Godwin from Adamsport, Massachusetts. "Beyond that," Henderson said, scowling at Vigilar, "we know nothing about Matthew Godwin's activities or what he was doing on Grand Cayman. And for the record, whatever insanity he may be involved in has nothing to do with Controlled Power Corporation."

Unable to contain his anger, Hendy finally spoke directly to Matt. "You're a very bad actor, Matt. I don't feel sorry for you. You've disgraced your father, your wife, and your children. When Ike discovered that you and Jill had been screwing around, he had a heart attack. You spout all this shit about being God—why in hell couldn't you keep your filthy hands off your father's wife? Or is that all part of your modern moralities?"

"Jill? Who is she?" Vigilar, bewildered, interrupted Hendy. "The lady told me that her name was Emily."

"Jill is another person," Matt said wearily. "You're right, Hendy. Chasing a daydream, I stopped being God. I just want you to know that it's not Jill's fault. I seduced her." Matt wanted to ask Hendy a hundred questions about Jill, but he knew that this would send Vigilar searching in other directions. "Is she all right?"

"No thanks to you." Hendy glanced at Vigilar and evidently made a quick decision not to go into full details. "Her leg is broken. When the cast comes off she's moving to New York. At the moment she's living in the carriage house with Irene. Why in hell Irene didn't kick her out is beyond me." Hendy handed Matt an envelope. "We're doing our best to try to get you released. Here's a thousand dollars. That will get you home, but don't expect a warm welcome. Irene may forgive you, but Ike never will. He wouldn't listen to his doctors and take it easy. He's gone back to California. You can expect that the directors of CPC will revoke your appointment as president. Ike never wants to see you again."

Seven weeks later, three days before Christmas, Vigilar gave up and told Matt that he was free to leave. "There's no reason to keep you any longer," he told Matt gloomily. "Your friend Ramachanda, and the two other Indians that we rescued, escaped two days ago. We recaptured two of them. They were trying to get to Key West, but there was a bad storm and we think that Ramachanda may have drowned. We found an overturned rowboat."

Vigilar drove him to the airport. "I hate to leave things in the air," he said. "Maybe some day you'll write me a letter and tell exactly what did happen. And just for the record, bring me up to date on your love life." He laughed. "I was a Catholic and now I am a Communist, but I never managed to keep three women happy at the same time."

Part Three

They maintain that God is essentially in every creature and that there is as much of God in one creature, as in another, though he does not manifest himself so much in one as another . . . They say there is no other God but what is in them, and also in the whole Creation and that man ought to pray and seek to no other God but what was in them . . . They say that man cannot either know God, or believe in God, or pray to God, but it is God in man that knoweth himself, believes in himself, and prayeth to himself.

John Holland, *The Smoke of Bottomlesse Pit*, London 1651, as quoted in *The World of the Ranters* by A. L. Morton

29

Jill was sure of one thing; the forge may have been hot and glowing in Grand Cayman, but the die was finally cast in Beverly Hills. For weeks she didn't know when, if ever, Matt might be released from the Cuban jail. Ike refused to make any further effort to get him released. "He can rot there for all I care," he told Becky. "If he dies, tell them to send his corpse to Jill." Whatever happened, he wasn't going to make it easy for them. "Jill can divorce me, but I'm not going to divorce her."

His anger sustaining him, Ike returned to California, where, he told Hendy, he had more important things to worry about. A special meeting of the board of directors of CPC had to be called. In a little over a month, unless he put a stop to it, Matthew Godwin, even in absentia, would become president of Controlled Power Corporation. With tears in his eyes he had hugged Irene before he left and told her that he was sorry for her. "I know you still love my damned fool son," he said. "We both have the same problem. We need to hate more and love less."

Before she left for New York, with her leg still in the cast, Jill thanked Irene and assured her that she had nothing to fear, nor had Becky, that she didn't want any of Ike's money, and, although she really cared for him, she would "never see Matt again." For the next two months she spent her days becoming Reverend Beecher's darling Mrs. Tilton and her lonely nights wondering how she could survive the rest of her life without the man who played God and told her that she was God, too.

Then, a week before Christmas, just a few days before the play was to open, Irene telephoned her. She was sobbing. "Ike collapsed in Gus Belshin's office today. He has had a stroke. Dr. Chandler doesn't know if he'll recover; right now it's touch and go. He's lost control of his vocal chords and he can't use his right hand. Betsy and I are flying out tonight. I thought you should know. You're still his wife."

Jill told the director of the play no more rehearsals. But she promised to be back from California in time for opening night.

Thinking about it later, Jill was sure that if some dramatist could re-create those four days in Ike's condominium in Beverly Hills, he'd most certainly hold theater audiences spellbound and probably get an award. Basically only one stage setting was needed: Ike Godwin's exquisite penthouse living room overlooking Los Angeles and in the distance the Pacific Ocean. A dream environment right out of *Town and Country* magazine. The characters: Matthew Godwin, leaner but still handsome and charismatic, and four women—Irene, his wife; Jill, his lover; Becky, his older sister; and Sally, his younger sister. Two other women in Matt's life, Peachy and Emily, were missing, but their entire involvement with him was known.

Jill arrived at the airport at 7:00 P.M. and took a taxi to Beverly Hills. Irene and Becky were still at Ike's bedside, but Sally had returned to the condominium to wait for her. She greeted Jill wearing only panties and a bra. All the rooftop windows were open. "The air conditioning isn't working in your million-dollar home," she told Jill. "You'd better strip down and get out of your New York clothes. You, Matt, and I are the only Godwins who dare to be naked with each other," she laughed. "I mean mentally as well as physically."

Jill tried to correct her. "This is Ike's home, not mine."

Sally shrugged. "You're still his wife, and for better or worse I like you. I hope we can be friends." She laughed. "We'd better be, we're the bad guys." Then she explained that the Pacific Coast highway had been closed for two months, cut off by severe earthquake damage, so she had moved to Santa Barbara and was sleeping with Gus Belshin. "Ike knew that I was the other woman," she said, "but he didn't know that Gus's wife had left him and I had moved in. It's not quite so bad as you sleeping with my brother, but it's a close second. Anyway, Gus is sweating out six months before his divorce is final. He wants to marry me, but now I'm not sure that I should have gotten involved with him. He's responsible for Ike's stroke. Yesterday he told Ike that he didn't give a damn whether Matt screwed you or not. If Ike refused to vote for him as president of CPC, then so far as he was concerned, Matt could have the job and would probably run the job better than a senile, cuckolded old man. He told Ike that he should know when to call it quits and now was the time to cash in his chips." Sally smiled ruefully. "A few minutes later, Ike damned near did."

Listening to her, Jill had been remembering the few happy months that she had lived with Ike in this condominium and his delight when she had tumbled with him on the white sofas and made love to him on the pale blue rugs. Beyond the window walls was a patio and a swimming pool. Many nights she and Ike had swum together and made love under the skies.

Then to Jill's shock Sally told her that Matt had been released from Cuba and right now was en route from Miami to Los Angeles. He should be arriving within the next two hours. Fearing from what she had heard about the sanitary conditions of Cuban jails that Matt might still be ill, overwhelmed with memories of herself lost in the warmth of Matt's body and his boyish joy in the delights of her flesh, Jill panicked.

"Oh, my God, Sally," she sobbed. "This is insane. It was going to be hard enough facing Irene alone. How can I face them together? I won't have to tell Irene; she'll know that I still love Matt. I haven't spent a waking hour in the past few months without thinking about him and wanting to be with him. Please God, why did you ever let me get involved with two Godwins? One should have been enough."

Even before Sally told her that Matt was arriving, she had been thinking that she had better find a hotel room. She knew there were three guest rooms and the master bedroom where she had slept with Ike, but there would be five of them. Who would sleep with whom? It was bad enough to have been trapped with a broken leg in the carriage house with Irene for a couple of weeks. Although Irene had never accused her of seducing her husband, Jill had felt guilty and ashamed to be dependent on her. Now she wished that she hadn't come. A few miles away, Ike was at death's door. Directly or not, she and Matt were responsible. If she hadn't gone to Grand Cayman with him, Matt might be dead, and she would still be living with Ike, who would have been alive and still healthy. How could Matt and she talk sensibly to each other in front of Irene, or Sally and Becky? How could she tell him how much she had worried about him during the past three months, or how much she loved him?

She tried to tell Sally some of the thoughts galloping through her mind, but Sally wouldn't listen.

"Unless he specifically asks for you, I don't think Dr. Chandler wants you to see Ike. Becky and Irene told him all about you, and of course they believe you're responsible. But don't let it worry you. You may have contributed a few fibrillations, but Ike had a stroke, yelling at Gus and telling him that neither his goddamned son nor Gus was going to run CPC. Gus is a bastard. He didn't mince words with Ike. He told Ike: 'Matt screwed your wife, so you might as well give him a chance to screw CPC.'" Sally put her hand on Jill's arm. "You can see that Matt needs you. Outside of me, you're the only one he can talk to."

"I still don't understand," Jill told her with tears in her eyes. "I know Gus Belshin must have found out that Matt and I were together in Grand Cayman and he told Ike. But I thought Belshin hated Matt as much as Ike does."

Sally shrugged. "It's really a power play between Gus and Ike. Ike would murder Gus if he thought he could get away with it, then he could do what he wants to do—elect Henderson Inch president."

"So what happens now?" Jill asked. She didn't want to say "if Ike dies," but Sally said it for her.

"My bet is that Ike isn't going to die. He's a tough old cookie. Ten days from now, even if he can't get to the directors' meeting and stop Matt from taking office, he can give Hendy or Irene a proxy to vote his stock. But he can't be sure of winning. If the directors agree with Gus, the only thing Ike can do is to go back to the stockholders. There's 65 million shares outstanding, so that will take some time."

Sally pointed at Jill's overnight bag. "Since you lived here last, you have priority. The master bedroom is yours. If you want, I'll sleep with you." She grinned. "That will keep you out of bed with Matt, at least temporarily. It's too damned hot for sex anyway. Why don't you take off that hot winter velveteen and cool off."

Jill admitted that she had left a lot of her California clothes there four months ago. "When I married Ike I thought we would be coming back and forth," she said sadly. "At least until the new CPC headquarters was built."

Sally watched her poke around in the master bedroom, where she found a string bikini but decided it was too sexy. She finally found a flowered beach coat in the closet and put it on.

Sally nodded approvingly. "Daddy must have flipped when he first saw you in your birthday suit." She laughed at Jill's embarrassment. "And Matt, too! The Godwin males have good taste in female bodies. I suppose you've heard that Matt has another female admirer in Adamsport. A minister—Peachy Stein. Gus told me that she and a lascivious old man, Robert Lovejoy, were caught naked together in the belfry of Sarah's church—and now they've bought the church and are spending several million dollars remodeling it. Irene doesn't know where they got the money, but she is sure that Matt is involved. Following Matt's famous sermon, nearly a year ago, they're going to change the name to the First Church of Modern Moralities." Sally chuckled. "Becky is having a fit. She and all the stuffy UU's and Congregationalists in Adamsport are horrified."

Irene and Becky arrived about two hours later. Irene greeted Jill coolly, but Becky was crying and immediately vented her anger. "I really don't know why you came, Gillian, or why Matt is coming here either. Dr. Chandler says that Ike is going to live, but he may never speak fluently again, and it will be several months before he has control over his right arm and leg. Chandler told us that even if Ike asks for you, you are *not* to see him."

Becky sobbed, unable to continue for a moment. Jill tried to put an arm around her, but she pulled away vehemently. "I don't want your sympathy," she said angrily. "Neither does Ike. When he left Adamsport he told me that you are still in the will, so no matter what you have done to him, you'll get your share. I told him that it was obvious that you and Matt hoped that he would die."

With tears streaming down her cheeks, Jill said, "I don't want Ike's money. I married him because I really liked him. It wasn't a dreamy first love, but we did enjoy each other's companionship." Jill knew that if she could somehow abjectly apologize for being unfaithful with Matt—even blame Matt for seducing her—she might have elicited Becky's sympathy. But she couldn't apologize for loving him. She didn't want to own Becky's brother, Irene's husband, Ike's son. She just wanted to love him.

"You and Matt and Sally, all three of you are sick and disgusting," Becky said grimly. "None of you believe that loving someone means being faithful to him. God damn you, Gillian! How could you do such a thing?"

Without waiting for an answer, Becky stomped out of the living room saying, "If you want the master bedroom you can have it, if you can live with the memory that you and Daddy screwed in there. Irene and I will sleep in one of the guest rooms."

In the uneasy silence that followed, Irene said softly, "Becky really loves her father. Too bad she wasn't the boy." She turned to Sally. "Speaking of Matt, has the prodigal son arrived yet?"

She had scarcely spoken the words when Matt telephoned from the lobby to get clearance into the penthouse elevator. "You're the one Matt really wants to see," Irene said to Jill with tears in her eyes. She started to follow Becky toward the guest rooms. But noticing Jill's contrite expression and the reciprocal tears, she said, "I'm not really in the mood to greet my wandering Ulysses tonight. Maybe we can all talk more sensibly tomorrow."

Behind the wet bar in the living room, Sally opened a bottle of gin and poured a pitcher of martinis. "I don't know about you, my friend," she said, grinning at Jill, "but I think I need to get drunk."

30

When Matt stepped out of the private elevator and saw them, he yelled "Hi sweetie!" at Sally and swooped Jill in his arms. Embarrassed for a second, Jill tried to pull away, but then she was sobbing, holding him tightly. Cupping her face in his hands, he kissed her mouth and her eyes and nose fervently, and then, sweeping open the clasp on her beach coat, he kissed her breasts, kneeled on the rug, and quickly examined her stomach and behind. He noted the bullet scar on her thigh and snuggled for a moment against her pubic hair.

"Thank God. You are all in one piece," he said and smiled at Sally, who was watching him admiringly.

"I thought you were God," Sally teased him.

"I am," Matt said. "We all are. But sometimes we commit the only mortal sin. We forget to act like God." He pulled Jill down on the sofa beside him. "I hope you can forgive me. I love you."

Taking one of the martinis that Sally offered them, he explained that not until yesterday, when he arrived in Miami and telephoned both Henderson and Roje, had he finally learned what had happened to Jill. He smiled ruefully at her. "Amir says that you can't change your kismet, that Allah has it all written down. But more realistically, Amir was acting as God and I was the sinner."

"If you really believe this 'you and I are God' crap," Sally said, "how in hell can anyone be a sinner? I was taught that God was good. If God is good, he couldn't stay that way very long and know evil."

"That's the philosophic argument," Matt replied. "But man as God really knows enough about ends and means to avoid means that will bring grief and even death to others." He hugged Jill as she was blushingly trying to refasten her beach coat and escape from his ecstatic appreciation of her, even while Sally watched.

"It looks as if ends and means coincided for you," Jill said. "You must have gotten Sylvie's gold. Irene told Sally that your friends Roje and Peachy have bought the First Parish Church and started to remodel it."

"Who the hell is Sylvie?" Sally demanded. "Does he own a gold mine?"

Matt bussed Sally's cheek as she settled on the arm of the sofa. "I'll tell you all about it later. Even Roje isn't sure whether we are working with Sylvie's gold or Amir's oil money. Right now there are more important things. How's Ike? Where's Irene and Becky?"

Sally had begun bringing Matt up to date when Irene and Becky surprised them. They sauntered back into the living room, Irene wearing a transparent, pale blue shortie nightgown that revealed her full breasts, Becky more sedately attired in a housecoat. Matt tried to embrace Irene, but she pulled away from him. "You look awful," she said grimly. "Did they starve you?"

Matt grinned a little feebly at her. "No, but they damned near scared me to death. I missed you and the kids—are they all right?"

"Ink and Able never stop talking about you. They wondered whether the Russians in Cuba were torturing you or brainwashing you like they do in those spy movies. How bad was it really? Do you still think that all men are God?"

Matt shrugged. "Let's say that it was a learning experience. They didn't torture me. I spent most of my time making friends with cockroaches, learning to speak Spanish, and wondering why our politicians couldn't let the Cubans have their revolution. I have no doubts that each of us are God, but individually we haven't learned to live our lives as loving Gods." He smiled affectionately at Jill. "Mostly I worried about you. I'm not ashamed, nor do I feel guilty about loving you. In many ways I may be your alter ego, but I am sorry that I persuaded you to fly to Grand Cayman."

"You should be," Irene said angrily. "You nearly got her and Emily Lovejoy murdered. Honestly, Matt, I worry about you. You're so determined to play God, you don't care who gets trampled on."

Feeling totally embarrassed, Jill said, "It's getting late. I think we should let you and Irene talk. You can have the master bedroom."

"Sorry, I am not sleeping with him," Irene said emphatically. But the tears in her eyes and her bewildered expression belied her words. "If you have any explanations or apologies we can hear them together. By birth or accident we are all Godwins. Our marriage isn't private any more." Irene noticed the pitcher of martinis that Sally had refilled. She poured herself one. "Maybe getting drunk is the only way to survive this."

Sally agreed with her. "I'll be the bartender. Let's tie one on while Matt tells us about Sylvie's gold and his sex life and how he expects to get away with it—the gold and three women. Or is it four women, Matt?"

"I think that Sally's a little drunk already," Becky said primly, but she accepted the martini that Sally poured for her. "But you're right. I want to hear what Oedipus has to say. If he isn't too tired, maybe he can tell us why he can't resist his father's wives."

Matt laughed and assured her that he wasn't too tired. He had slept on the plane. "And for the record, I loved Sarah, but I never had a sexual thought about her. On the other hand, if you expect me to entertain four half-naked women in a million-dollar penthouse with no air conditioning, I hope you won't mind if I get into something cooler."

They watched him shed his jacket and unzip his trousers. Irene scowled. "Matt never could resist showing his balls and prick to everyone—especially women."

Stripped down to his jockey shorts, Matt laughed. "If I seem to be saluting you through my underwear, you only have yourselves to blame. You are all beautiful women and, to use a biblical euphemism, I haven't known a woman since October."

Jill blushed, knowing that all of them were well aware that she was the October woman. "That's not what Emily Lovejoy told me," Irene said and was happy to see Jill's startled expression.

Sitting on his haunches in the middle of a white velour couch, Matt sipped his martini. "This is a very powerful drink. While I still can, let's take things in sequence. First, there was my search for El

Dorado. Jill knows the story and probably understands my motivations better than anyone else. Not that she ever agreed with me, but rather, she listened and withheld judgment." He smiled at Irene. "I love you, but maybe listening to each other is not possible in marriage. And maybe it's mostly my fault. Up until now I've tried to make you into something that you're not. You wanted a replay of Ike, which I couldn't give you."

"Obviously your friend Peachy understands you better," Irene said bitterly and brushed the tears from her eyes.

"Peachy knew about her father's gold, but she didn't know that I had gone in search of it with Jill," Matt shrugged. "Peachy is a love bug. She'll bombard her lover with incessant questions, but if she's not satisfied with his answers, it really doesn't matter to her. She'll love him anyway." He laughed. "Peachy's not monogamous. She's learned that a really loving woman must be very careful. Most men are hogamous."

Then, to Becky's and Irene's shock and Sally's fascination, he told them in detail about Sylvie's gold, and how he had involved Jill and Amir Saud in his quest for a free ride. "Don't ask me why I did it. Don't tell me that my sudden desire to change the world and return to the ministry is some kind of midlife crisis. I don't think it is. The truth is, I wasn't having any fun building LNG tankers. In another lifetime, I might have decided to be a pirate. I've always been a rebel. But up until the past year I've been the kind of person who daydreamed his rebellions. In real life I always took the path of least resistance. It was easier to give in to Ike than to fight him. It was easier to live according to his and Sarah's sexual mores than to defy them. It was easier to act like the upright citizen who Irene thought she had married than to be true to my own beliefs."

Rambling on, Matt was aware that all four women were listening to him attentively. They were fascinated, in spite of themselves, with a man who dared to openly verbalize the kind of sexual creature that he really was. "The only sexually honest president we've ever had was Jimmy Carter," he told them with a grin. "Jimmy admitted that he lusted after women besides Rosalyn. Becky, when you were sixteen and I was fourteen, I lusted after you. Sally was only twelve, but actually she was sexier than you were. You were Miss Prim-dim. You locked all the doors behind you." He chuckled. "It's not too late, Becky. At forty-five you seem to be in pretty good shape. Why don't you take off that housecoat and let me admire your bare ass for the first time?"

Becky stared at him coldly. "You're getting drunk," she said. "It's obvious, Matt, that you still haven't grown up. Sex and loving mean a lot more than drooling over naked female bodies."

"I've never drooled over any woman," Matt said. "But I was

blessed with happy, erotic genes that keep urging me to merge with the flesh of a woman. Eons ago, I was probably a hairy ape. My nose told me when females were present and in heat. In those days I was instantly erect and ready to penetrate them to perpetuate the species. A million years later, I am a man. My nose is no longer so useful, but my eyes tell me that women developed breasts and behinds whose sole purpose is not to feed their children or sit on but, rather, to lure the male into copulating with them. I'm sure that women are just as happily lustful as men, but unfortunately tribal leaders, who call themselves priests, made them afraid to admit it."

"I wasn't afraid," Sally said, enjoying the confessional. "I lusted after you, Matt. But I was second choice. Never mind, I finally seduced you."

"You mean that you actually went to bed with him?" Becky asked, quite shocked.

Sally grinned affectionately at Matt. "It took a long time. We played doctor for about a year. That was long before he met Irene. I told Matt that I was on the pill. I was afraid of boys, but I really wanted to do it. Neither of us had ever done it before, and we were both scared, but I remember Matt was almost worshipful. I loved him. I still do. Maybe that's why I haven't been in any hurry to get married. Except for Gus Belshin, when he's in a gentle mood, I haven't found anyone like you."

"Maybe you're the reason Gus gave Ike a stroke," Irene said.

"That's a terrible thing to say," Sally flared. "Ike gave himself a stroke. Gus Belshin wants Matt to be president of CPC."

"You're so naive," Irene said. "Ike told me that Matt is only a pawn that Gus is playing in the game. Ike may be checkmated; but even if Matt becomes president of CPC, Gus is very sure that he will hang himself." She stared at Matt sourly. "Hanging yourself seems to be a specialty of yours."

Matt laughed. "Not this time. Eventually, if Gus plays ball, he can take over as president. I'll move up to chairman and chief executive officer. If Ike is nice, we'll make him honorary chairman. But first I have to resolve my personal life. I love three women, not including my sister whom I will probably never bed again." He grinned at Becky. "And I love you, too. Even though I have no sexual desire for you."

"I count four women," Sally said. "What about this Emily Lovejoy?"

"I guess I love her too. But living with and loving Irene the longest, I've learned one valuable thing. Trying to play Pygmalion and creating a Galatea who adores only you is one of the problems of modern marriage. At forty-three I haven't stopped learning about love. I love the women I love, not because they are reflections of me, but because they are very much their own persons."

Listening and discovering new depths of Matt Godwin that she had been vaguely aware of but unable to verbalize, Jill was surprised to discover that none of them could stay angry with Matt very long. Occasionally, as he continued to expose himself as a totally woman-oriented man, they told him that he was "idiotic" or a "dirty old man," but they all sensed that he was revealing aspects of their own amorphous sexuality that they had long denied.

"We've been brainwashed by religious sexual moralities that tell us that our basic lovely genital stirrings, and our genetic compulsion to physically love each other and adore each other as God, are evil," Matt told them. "As a result, we have created premarital and postmarital environments where men are the predators and ejaculating into a female is a short-lived pyrrhic victory. Joyous sexual loving is a mutual mind and body surrender that can be learned. Unfortunately, many men and women are preconditioned by their parents and religious leaders. Instead of surrendering to each other as Gods, the men become mechanized penetrators and women coexist with them by becoming accommodators."

Matt grinned at Irene, but she shook her head unsympathetically. "You're preaching again, Matt," she said coolly.

He laughed. "I can't help myself. But it is quite possible that women who are accommodators could learn how to attune themselves more closely with a male and become a participator." Matt noticed that Jill, sitting opposite him on a sofa and giving him a shadowy view of her thighs, was embarrassed.

"You're not dealing with reality," she said softly. "You're married to Irene."

Matt finished his third martini. "Despite your conviction that you may be listening to a sex maniac," he said, "the reality is that in the past fifteen years I really have been a sexual 'have not.' I've been inside Irene's vagina about fifteen hundred hours, inside Peachy's about two hours, and Jill's about twenty hours. The second reality is that with Emily I discovered that in the face of death, a man and woman may try to escape the thought of dying by sexual loving. But that only added one or two hours to my sexual lifetime total. Now, on a more normal basis, allotting two hours a day for sexual merger would add up to seven hundred twenty-eight hours a year. Assuming that the age of seventeen would be the normal starting time for human sex-making, I should by this time have clocked in about eighteen thousand hours of happy sexual merger." He grinned at them. "It's obvious that I have a lot of catching up to do."

Sally was choking with laughter. "Two hours every single *day?*" she asked.

Matt shrugged. "Most people spend two hours commuting to work. They spend eight hours working and eight hours sleeping.

What for? We'd all be less neurotic if we loved each other two hours a day."

"It would be boring," Becky said disgustedly.

"Not with three different women," Matt laughed.

"What about the women?" Becky demanded. She was vascillating between disgust and fascination. "If they were your women they would have to take turns every three days. You really are a sexist male."

"Not really, Becky. For example, your life might be much more adventurous if you had a lover in addition to Hendy. Maybe I am oversexed, but I'm sure that there are many women who need to blend themselves with a man several hours a day. It doesn't have to be the same man each day. A loving sexual interlude can be a more satisfactory escape from the cares of the world than any other means man has devised."

Jill's eyes flooded with tears. She wanted to tell Matt that most of her life she had been an accommodator, but with him for the first time she had discovered the joys of complete sexual surrender. And she wondered how Irene could listen to Matt so coolly. Weren't Irene's breasts and vagina telling her something different? Weren't they telling her to stop being judgmental and reach out and hug him? If she had been Irene she would have taken Matt's hand and said, "If you love me, I don't care who else you may love. Come to bed. Preach to me when you are inside me."

Instead, Jill said to Matt, "I guess none of us are dealing with reality. If I'd known that you'd be here tonight, I'd have stayed in a hotel."

"You feel guilty about us?"

Jill shook her head. "No. But Ike—the world—expects us to be guilty. I really shouldn't have come. Even if Ike forgave me, I'd worry about Irene." She smiled at Irene sadly. "The problem is that I love you, too. But I'm sure that we couldn't ever function together."

"Why can't you and Irene both go to bed with Matt?" Sally suggested.

Jill shrugged. "That's not very realistic, either."

"It's getting pretty late," Sally said, and she hugged Matt. "One of us—or all of us—should relieve the poor man. Remember, he hasn't had a woman for three months." She laughed. "Poor Matt, that's another 180 hours down the drain."

"Jill can have the pleasure," Irene said. Then, surprising herself and everybody else, she walked over to Matt, kissed his cheek, and said, "I know that mostly I've only been an accommodator with you. But I did love you."

31

Jill knew that she should never have come back to Adamsport. Sleeping with Matt at least twice a month, during his frequent visits to New York City, and sharing his plans and his excitement at the re-creation of the First Parish Church should have been enough. She was fascinated by his continuous maneuvers to realign Controlled Power Corporation. He was convinced that, despite his self-conceived dual mission as a radical minister and a corporation executive, he could align a majority of CPC stockholders behind him and win a proxy battle with Gus Belshin.

The truth was that she was happily obsessed with Matt Godwin. Not just sexually, but with his total involvement with his cause and his commitment to remake the world in what she laughingly called "his own image and likeness." She told him that at least he had a one-person adoring audience. It was like sitting in a darkened theater and becoming totally engrossed with the action on the stage. She was cheering for her hero, and even though he was a tough blend of idealism and pragmatism, she worried whether he was tempting even stronger gods to destroy him. Act One had been on Grand Cayman. Somehow they had survived, but in Act Two, with the curtain rising right now, they were sailing directly into the whirlpool. Jill was afraid that at the end of Act Three the Devil would be waiting for them at the entrance to Hell.

She could have gone on the road with *The Reverend Beecher and Mrs. Tilton,* but after a year on Broadway the history of the Reverend Beecher became much less fascinating than the very real problems of Reverend Godwin.

Matt had asked her to take charge of dramatic programs at the First Church and the production of films exploring fertility worship and all aspects of men's and women's need to understand the mystery of life and transcend themselves. So, she had finally relented and had come back to Adamsport.

Irene was living in the Big House and hadn't slept with Matt for more than a year. Still, there was no question in Jill's mind that moving into the carriage house with Matt three months ago, a few hundred yards down the road, while still married to Ike, who never wanted to see her again, was stretching civilized moralities to the breaking point. She respected Irene's belief that she shouldn't try to visit the Big House, where Ike was slowly recovering from the stroke he had had nearly eighteen months ago.

She occasionally talked with Irene on the telephone and even had lunch with her at the Adamsport Country Club several times. Although it was obvious that she was sleeping with Matt, Jill tried to convince Irene that Matt loved her, too.

"Each of us—you, Peachy, and I—relate to Matt differently," she told Irene over lunch. "If you're not interested in the Foundation or the church, with your background in business you could really help him with the problems that he is encountering with Controlled Power. What he's doing in that area is beyond Peachy and me. Believe me, Irene, when the First Church opens in April he's going to need all three of us, and Ike and Roje, too."

But Irene was adamant. She wouldn't admit it in words, but she still loved Matt in her own way. "Ike, Becky, Hendy, all my friends," she told Jill, "even Father Tim, think that I am being too damned soft and easy. I should get tough with Matt and lay it on the line to him. I actually did when I found out how involved he was with Peachy, and that you had actually gone with him to Grand Cayman. But you know Matt. He never said that he was sorry. He kept telling me that he loved me, and told me to remember Eleanor Roosevelt. She didn't divorce Franklin when he had another woman. But I told him to remember one of his favorite preachers, Paul Tillich. His wife, Hannah, wrote a book about him. 'He broke our marriage into small pieces by his relentless assault on so many women,' she wrote. If I divorce you, I told Matt, you'll never see Ink and Able again. No court will give visitation rights to a father who is a flagrant polygamist. I think Matt always envied the Arab billionaires with their multiple wives.

"I should hate him, and you and Peachy, but I don't," Irene said sadly. "Instead, I've let Ink and Able spend the weekends with you in the carriage house, and I know damned well that they are having more fun and laughter and maybe even more caring love than they get up at the Big House with me and Ike and Becky and Hendy. I have such mixed feelings about it. I know that you're not having a sexual orgy, but I worry about what the boys may be thinking. I'm not like you, Jill. I don't relate to Matt's need to change the world. It's suicidal.

"Poor Ike, even he's confused. Because of you he detests Matt, but not quite enough to go along with Belshin. Ike knows that he's too old to run the company, but he wants a Godwin in control."

Secretly, Irene believed that Ike was happy that Matt had overridden Gus. The thirty-story CPC headquarters building was nearly ready for occupancy. Many times during the past year she had driven Ike downtown so that he could watch the gradual emergence of his dream. He wasn't very happy with the new seven-story glass parish building, or the new translucent dome on the First Church, but he did admit that the CPC building had been attractively linked with the church by landscaped walks, green lawns, fountains, and trees on the former Washington Boulevard. He knew that Matt had convinced the city council to deed a section of the roadway to the corporation in exchange for a five-tiered underground garage that would serve the entire city. But he wasn't at all happy that the new Adams Mall and the garage gave the impression that the church and Controlled Power were somehow interconnected.

"If you could see Ike, you'd feel sorry for him, Jill," Irene said. "He looks fine, his mind is just as sharp as ever, but he is still aphasiac. When he speaks his mouth is distorted, and it's hard to understand his words." Irene admitted that Ike was a long way from any kind of sane discussion with Jill, but she was often on his mind. "He wants to hate you," she told Jill, "but he can't. So he hates Matt."

Matt didn't have to tell Jill or Peachy that Mike Wilder and the staff of his nationally famous television program "Showdown" were planning to do a full hour program on the First Church and the Foundation. Irene did. Wilder traced Ike to the Big House and tried unsuccessfully to convince Irene that he should interview Ike. Gus Belshin had told Wilder that Ike had returned to Adamsport many months ago and was living with Becky and Irene and that he could now talk well enough to keep CPC's stockholders in a turmoil. Irene guessed that Belshin wasn't adverse to using Mike Wilder to see if he could smoke out the old man and resolve the problem of who was going to be at the helm of Controlled Power.

Irene informed Wilder angrily on the telephone that Ike Godwin wouldn't talk to reporters under any circumstances and he would most certainly not appear on "Showdown." Then, she immediately telephoned Jill and warned her: "I thought you and Peachy should know that the top is about to blow off of my husband's harem." She couldn't conceal her bitterness. "Mike Wilder is fascinated by the gossip. He's sure that you and Peachy share the immoral Reverend's bed. I have a feeling that's going to be the title of his show: 'The Immoral Reverend.' I told him that he couldn't talk with Ike, so he tried to set up a television interview with me—or, better still, all three of us. I told him to go to hell." Irene laughed, but not happily, Jill thought. "Then he asked me point-blank if I still sleep with Matt, and if I approve of you and Peachy, and if not, why I haven't divorced Matt."

Jill was a little shocked, but Matt was elated. "Publicity, good or bad, we need it," he told her and Peachy. "It would cost millions to get the kind of exposure that Mike Wilder can give us. It will help us make the Foundation and the church a force in national life."

Jill hadn't asked Irene how Wilder could know so damned much about their private lives. It was obvious. Last week Belshin, heading up a protesting stockholders' committee, had taken a full-page advertisement in the *Wall Street Journal* trying to discredit Matt. In addition to calling for a government investigation of the source of funds for the Foundation and the First Church of Modern Moralities, Belshin had told the reporters that Jill Godwin, Isaac's wife, after a year on the Broadway stage, had returned to Adamsport and joined Matthew Godwin's "Sex Worship Love Cult" along with the notorious Mary Peachy, the former Peachy Stein. On top of that, several hundred other women, all hypnotized by Godwin and in his sexual control, had arrived in Adamsport. They called themselves Feminists For Modern Moralities, and were encamped in the city to await the opening of the church.

Belshin's advertisement, paid for by a Stockholders' Committee to Save Controlled Power Corporation, suggested that Matt Godwin was planning to take over the city of Adamsport and turn it into Sex City, U.S.A., and that Modern Moralities would be subsidized from the earnings of CPC. He compared Matt Godwin with Reverend Jim Jones, whose followers had committed mass suicide after Jones had brainwashed them. The advertisement concluded with the scare threat that Matthew Godwin was wasting company resources and was now in the process of spending $100 million to build a new headquarters in Adamsport, Massachusetts. In addition to CPC, the new building would house the First Foundation, a radical organization that was determined to destroy America's Judeo-Christian heritage.

Jill called Irene back later that day. "I really think you should come to dinner with us tonight," she said. "Belshin is crazy, but Mike Wilder is even more dangerous. Peachy and I agree on one thing; it's pretty weird—we're living in the carriage house with your husband and you're living a few hundred yards away taking care of his father."

Crossing her fingers, Jill tried to interject a little humor into their multiple relationship. "You're still the queen-pin in Matthew's heaven," she said. "Peachy and I are the God-King's concubines. I honestly believe that a *ménage à quatre* might be more joyous for us than for the God-King himself." Jill laughed. "God needs all the angels he can get."

"No thanks," Irene answered grimly. "There aren't enough bedrooms in the carriage house to accommodate all of us." She was more than a little shocked by the idea, but she couldn't help laughing. "Believe me, I'm not sleeping four in a bed—not even with God—especially in my own bed!"

"Neither Peachy nor I have ever slept with Matt in your bedroom. We've each taken over one of your guest rooms. Please come home," Jill pleaded. "It's your house. If you don't like us, we'll move out."

Ink and Able didn't seem to be at all bothered by their father's "girl friends." They told Irene that Jill and Peachy were a lot of fun and that Peachy wasn't at all bashful. "She's pretty," Ink said. "I like to watch her bare-ass. It's better than looking at *Playboy*."

The boys stayed overnight twice a week, usually on Fridays and Saturdays. They reported to Irene that Dad slept in the master bedroom alone. Irene assumed that when the boys were in bed, or were asleep, Matt joined Jill or Peachy or both of them in the guest rooms. What their housekeeper, Mrs. Goodale, who slept in the maid's quarters, thought about all this wasn't known.

Jill again confirmed their sleeping arrangements to Irene. "But you know Matt. Right now he is planning to turn your garage into a huge bedroom with sliding glass doors. It will overlook the swimming pool and gardens. It will be big enough to hold two king-sized beds and then some. Matt told me to tell you that if you come home you can have the master bedroom. He'll sleep in the new bedroom with any lady or ladies who wish to join him."

"I get the picture," Irene replied sarcastically. She wondered how Matt could be so damned confident that she wasn't going to divorce him. "When the King of Siam rings his bell, all his ladies will come running to the new playroom and jump into bed naked with him." She sighed, struggling to erase a picture of her, Jill, and Peachy naked and falling all over her egotistical husband. "Maybe if I were drunk I might do it—but I'd have to be pretty damned drunk."

Strangely, since Jill had returned to Adamsport and admitted to her with tears streaming down her cheeks that she loved Matt "and all the damned Godwins," Irene had felt a warm empathy with her. Now she said, "I told you more than a year ago, before your play opened in New York, that I wasn't angry with you. I never agreed with Ike or Becky; I know that you're not an evil woman or that you'd go after any man, come hell or high water. But I really think that you are kidding yourself, Jill. I think that you are just as monogamous as I am. You are only putting up with Matt because he has got you hypnotized." Irene laughed bitterly. "And don't tell me that he can't hypnotize people. He did it to me for years."

Although Irene continued to maintain contact with Jill, she refused to socialize with all three of them. She told Jill to tell Matt that Mike Wilder had asked her if she agreed with her husband. "Do I think that every man or woman is God? I told Wilder I am damned sure that Matt isn't God, but I love him anyway." Irene paused. "Even if I refuse to sleep with him and to share him—but just for the record, I didn't tell Wilder that."

"Don't let Mike Wilder frighten you," Jill said. "I knew him very well six years ago. He was running after fame then, and he was no saint. No man is, and that includes Matt and your Father Timothy."

Jill tossed in Father Timothy's name to see if Irene would react, and to change the subject. She really didn't want to explore her own feelings about monogamy and a lifetime of fidelity to one man. Maybe, if by some miracle, she had met Matthew Godwin at the same age as Irene did, and had never been married to two other men nor had experienced sex with a half-dozen others—including Mike Wilder—

she would have been a one-man woman. But that was another lifetime ago, and her first husband wasn't Matthew Godwin. Somehow Matt had catalyzed all the vagrant meanderings of her brain and made her aware that she really wasn't like Irene. She didn't need to possess a man to love him. Her never ending affinity and need for Matt Godwin was a kind of mutual admiration society. They shared each other's volatile, driving curiosity and need for reassurance as much as they shared a need for each other's body. The joining of their flesh was solace for their questioning minds, and even better, from the first day, they had become caring friends who would laugh at their necessity to play God and be applauded for it.

Before *The Reverend Beecher* had finally closed on Broadway, she told Matt that it was really her last fling on the stage. Matt's Folly, as she called it, excited her more. She knew that when he was in Adamsport, between frequent trips to various Controlled Power subsidiaries, he had lived "almost alone" in the carriage house. "Becky refuses to let me talk with Ike," he had told her, "but I worry about the old buzzard and miss him. She told me that even if Ike asked to see me, she'd refuse. 'This time you'd kill your father for sure,' she said." Finally overcoming her own objections, Jill had spent a weekend with him in the carriage house. When she questioned what he meant by "almost alone," he had grinned at her, a little embarrassed. "I told you a year ago in California, I love three women. When Saul Stein divorced Peachy, she moved out of his house. She had nowhere to go except to the parsonage, but that was becoming overcrowded with the offices of the Foundation. I told her that there was plenty of room here and that she might as well move in. Then we could discuss modern moralities in bed just as well as out. Irene knows that she has stayed here. I'm sure Mrs. Goodale, the housekeeper, tells her what's going on."

Matt had leaned on his elbow and stared into Jill's tear-streaked face. "You're angry with me?" he said.

"You bet I am! Why in hell are you inviting me to live with you?" Jill had demanded. "You must be trying to imitate your friend Amir. If not, why don't you divorce Irene and marry Peachy?" Over her protest, Matt's answer had been an enthusiastic, erotic kissing of her from head to toe. "Because I don't believe in divorce," he said. "I love you. I told you that in California. But if Irene divorces me, I'll be happy to marry you." He grinned at her. "Of course, not until Ike divorces you or you divorce him."

Jill shrugged. "I don't think I should divorce Ike until he is back on his feet. What about Peachy?"

"Peachy doesn't want to get married again," Matt laughed. "Anyway, just so long as it isn't legal, they can't put me in jail for polygamy." He tried to kiss the scowl from her face. "Since the Foundation is questioning other out-dated moralities, I see no reason why marriage must be a lonely corral with only one mare."

Jill slapped his bare behind. "Damn you. You are an egotist. I'm not at all sure that you'd support equal rights for me, Irene, and Peachy." She sighed. "But there's not much I can do about it. At the moment I'm very partial to one stallion." She couldn't help herself; she knew that when the play closed she'd come back to Adamsport. "I never thought I'd be content to share a man," she said, grinning at him. "But going to bed with a *God*-win is another matter."

32

By early April, two weeks before the First Church of Modern Moralities opened its doors, Roje and Peachy and Jill, with occasional advice from Matt, had accumulated a staff of thirty-two people, all crammed into the former parsonage, which had temporarily been converted into offices for the Foundation. In addition, they had generated so much national publicity for the church that hotel rooms as far away as Boston were hard to come by.

The *Adamsport Chronicle* estimated that at least two hundred non-residents had already arrived in Adamsport. They were not only picketing the church but were also circulating throughout the city passing out religious tracts and copies of the angry diatribe against Matthew Godwin that Gus Belshin had run as a full-page advertisement in the *Wall Street Journal.* One group called S.U.S., Save Us from Sodom, was trying to organize all Adamsport residents in a nightly candlelight demonstration against the church and against Matt Godwin's Modern Moralities.

The night before, a hundred or more people had milled around the new Adams Mall between the First Church and the CPC headquarters. A contingent from Feminists for Modern Moralities, who were camping at Morton Park for the summer in former army barracks, taunted some of the purse-lipped women carrying Jesus Saves banners. "You're medieval Bible thumpers!" they yelled at them. "Jesus didn't like women. He told all the guys to forsake their wives and mothers and follow him."

In reply, an angry male Bible student forgot his religious heritage and yelled: "You are all feminist ball breakers!" After which five women carrying "Matthew Godwin Loves You" signs jumped on him and stripped off his trousers and fondled his genitals. "We're God," they shouted jubilantly at the police who lugged them away. "We don't break anybody's balls. We love them all."

Roje wouldn't admit it to Emily, but during the past year his involvement in remodeling the church, building the new parish building, and creating the church's unique underground recreation area had ended, temporarily or maybe forever, his solitary and lonely occupation of writing novels. He told Emily and Peachy that sailing against the wind in reality was much more exciting than writing about it on paper. It was impossible to have any sexual rapport with a typewriter. He admitted to Peachy that he probably hadn't become the kind of UU she might have expected, but neither was she. She, too, was relishing the conflict created by the former First Parish UU's who were not in agreement with them.

A group of the dissenters, headed up by Dorothy Belcher, were waging an unremitting campaign against the follies of sex worship. But Roje wasn't worried. When Dorothy tackled him, he told her that this was a great moment in history, the beginning of a new Protestant Reformation. Roje told anyone who would listen to him: "We're challenging people out of their apathy. We're giving them a religion that they can believe in and get involved with."

Emily was not so optimistic, but she agreed that managing the Foundation for Modern Moralities was more inflammatory than being caught bare-ass on the top of the Prudential Tower. She might have added "and more challenging." This career switch wasn't the only change in Roje's life. He now had an occasional extra bed companion to share his day-to-day problems with. Surprisingly, Emily wasn't jealous of Peachy. In fact, she told him it was all right with her if he slept with Peachy a few times a month. She admitted with tears in her eyes that Peachy had a way of smiling and speaking with laughing brown eyes that reminded her of Sylvie. "I loved your father," she told Peachy, "but I never stopped loving Roje."

Peachy assured her that she wasn't trying to steal Roje from her. "He loves you very much," she told Emily. "I'm the occasional frosting on his cake."

But Roje wasn't at all happy about Mike Wilder or Matt's calm acceptance of the publicity that the First Church would get if Wilder featured the church on "Showdown." He told Matt that Wilder would not hesitate to tilt the truth for dramatic impact. Fabricating along the way or not, Wilder went after the "bad guys" like a surgeon with a scalpel, determined to cut out the disease whether the surgery killed the patient or not. In Roje's opinion, on "Showdown" you were judged guilty before you appeared on the show. Wilder gave you a chance to prove your innocence—if you could.

Wilder wasn't the only one interested in Matt Godwin's First Church. At least fifty representatives of national magazines and news services had asked for preferred seating on opening night. And nobody knew how many religious and evangelical organizations had sent protesters.

Trying to keep tabs on Wilder, Roje discovered that he had made reservations at the Sheraton Tara more than a month ago, but now, two days before the opening of the church, he still hadn't arrived in Adamsport.

Roje was trying to bring Matt to reality. "I'm afraid of Wilder," Roje said. "He can cut and edit his interviews and give his own voice-over interpretations of what we're doing. I'm sure he'll try to scare hell out of some seventy-five million Americans who watch him."

"Maybe he'll frighten seventy million of them," Matt laughed, "but that will still leave us quite a few million who are the real movers in this country. You'd better read Mitchell's *Who We Are: The Values and Lifestyles of Americans*. We're not aiming at the Survivors, only the Sustainers, the Belongers, the Emulators, or even the achievers. But you can count on it; in the next few years we'll intrigue the I-am-Me, the Experimental, the Societally Conscious, and the Integrated people. We're going to create a new kind of UU network—a hundred or more First Churches, with at least five million members, all probing for new Unitarian Universalist directions. When that happens, we'll run the country."

Roje got nervous when Matt played the Jesus role. "You may be counting chickens that will never hatch," he said. "I've heard rumors that UU headquarters is very wary of you. We've picked up about sixty members of the former First Church, but the other half of the congregation, including the Belchers and Hancocks, are gung ho to build a new church. They are never going to offer the First Parish's million-dollar assets to the Foundation."

Matt tried to reassure him. "I'm not a messiah; I'm a dreamer. So are you. That's why you wrote all those utopian novels. The members of the First Parish Church will come around. The church isn't even open yet, but take a look at your membership list. Both Fred Burns and Ada Bass have joined, and each of them paid a $750 membership fee. They never gave that much to the First Parish Church. John Codman told me that the sexual-spiritual side of the church is hard for him to swallow, but he is very interested in some of the approaches to new moralities.

"As for Mike Wilder, you can stop worrying about him. Whether we cooperate or not, he'll go ahead." Matt smiled and patted Roje's arm affectionately. "If you can't stop them, Roje, first you join them and then you convert them. A month ago, when Wilder telephoned me, I told him that I'd be happy to have him interview me, but only after he showed me the rest of the show exactly the way it will be televised. He has to clear all interviews with me so that I can correct any false impressions that he might have given in them."

"It's not only Wilder," Roje said in exasperation. "To coin a phrase, 'the Empire is building up against you.' I hope you read the *Adamsport Chronicle* last night. You can pray that Mike Wilder doesn't. One of the reporters talked with George Gallagher about you and the First Church and the hysteria that we are presumably creating in the city."

Matt hadn't seen it, so Roje read it to him: "'Matt Godwin is laying the groundwork for a religious civil war here in Adamsport, which may ultimately involve the whole country. The First Amendment to the Constitution may guarantee the right to establish a religion and to freely exercise it, but there are limits to the kind of religious beliefs that the state can tolerate. No sane church permits young and old people to play together naked on church property, or offers the kind of sex education to its members' children that Godwin has proposed. Matt Godwin is going to make the former First Parish Church a greater blot on Adamsport than Silly Willy's.'"

Roje sighed. He hadn't planned it that way, but during the past eighteen months, while the church was under construction, he had become a believer, a cautious St. Paul to Matt's Jesus.

Actually, Matt looked more and more like an Old Testament prophet. Maintaining a grueling schedule, he had divided his time between touring CPC's nationwide subsidiaries, talking with major CPC stockholders, and planning with Roje, Jill, Peachy, and a growing staff the directions and goals of the First Church. They all agreed that he should become the spokesman of the Foundation. As a result, Matt hadn't put on the weight he had lost in the Cuban prison. His high-cheekboned face was not quite emaciated, but he had acquired an ascetic look, accentuated by his hard, angular jaw and a burning expression in his eyes. Jill hadn't made up her mind whether Matt looked more like Juan Orozoco's painting of Quetzacoatl or John Stewart Curry's rendition of John Brown.

Jill and Peachy knew that "Showdown" was the most popular Sunday night television show in America, and like Roje, they were afraid that Wilder would try to undercut the First Church. "He'll do his best to try to convince the public that you're a con man," Jill told Matt. "He'll look for your Achilles' heel—and it will be Peachy and me and our sex lives."

She was sure that Wilder would try to interview her and Peachy. Matt told her that it was their decision one way or the other. "If you do, tell him that I love you both—and Irene, too."

Peachy agreed with Jill. "If we said that on television, we'd receive a million hate letters in a week. American women only want men who love one woman at a time."

Discussing it with Matt before bed, Jill and Peachy wondered if he and Roje might have been wiser not to light the bonfire in advance. "The church isn't even open," Peachy said. "Only a few of us know what the services will be like, and yet you have half the city at war with us already."

"Not half," Matt grinned. "Only a few hundred Christians who are making mountains out of mole hills."

Jill reminded Matt that she knew Mike Wilder better than they did. "He's dangerous," she said. "I told Roje that Mike's an egotistical maniac. He's not like you, Matt." Grinning, she gave him a swift kiss on his cheek. "But you do have something in common. There are nice egos and nasty ones. Mike believes that he's God, too, but unfortunately, he doesn't think anyone else is."

Peachy worried that Mike would revel in the sexual aspects of the First Church and do his best to shock Bible-thumping Christians—especially if he discovered that Jill and she not only lived in the carriage house but also took turns sleeping with Matt (and occasionally, in a silly mood, they all made love to God together).

How could they explain to Wilder—and to a shocked television audience—that with or without a legal ceremony, they were married to Matt in a marriage that could easily embrace Irene, too, if she wished. Matt told them to look up the definition of marriage in Webster's. "You'll find that it's a state of being married to a person *or persons* of the opposite sex, as husband or wife. Note the plural." He grinned at Jill, who was listening with raised eyebrows. "Webster further defines marriage as 'the institution where men and women are joined in social and legal dependence. Marriage is of two types, monogamous and polygamous.'"

Matt laughed. "In the past twenty years, Americans have accepted the social idea of monogamous cohabitation, but they've overlooked the legal side. Millions of couples live together without legal permission. Polygamous cohabitation with responsibility and commitment can be just as valid as monogamy. Particularly for older people who have tried monogamy and not found it playful enough or very adventurous."

In a quiet moment together, when Jill had just come back to Adamsport, Peachy had probed her feelings about marriage. She told Jill: "I know that you love Matt. I do, too. At thirty-nine, with two children, I don't want to start searching for another man. I'm too damned critical and hard to please. I don't want to join the disillusioned, screw-around-aimlessly singles, hoping that by some miracle I may finally find one more 'one and only.' It's taken most of my life, but I've found two men whom I'm really happy with mentally and sexually." She hugged Jill and said, "I love you because you listen to me like an older sister. I need you to snuggle against for reassurance, but I'm not bisexual. Can the three of us live together for a while and see what happens?"

Jill couldn't help herself. Unsophisticated, open, ingenuous people could reach into her brain and bring tears to her eyes. She hugged

Peachy. "You're no stranger to me, honey," she told her. "For the past year, even when we've been in bed making love, Matt has talked about you constantly." She had noticed Peachy's frown and quickly added, "Not sexual details. He makes no comparisons. For all I know, you may be just an accommodator."

Laughing, Jill explained what an accommodator meant, and Peachy, blushing a little, told her that with her the reverse was true, especially with men like Matt or Roje.

Peachy assured Jill that Matt had never discussed their love-making with her either. "Matt loves you because you argue with him—disagree with him—but you can understand his necessities."

"He loves *you*," Jill replied, "because he admires your overflowing affection and your joyous see-no-evil, hear-no-evil approach to life. I realize that I've come to a point in my life where I need a family of loving friends, too. I'm still married to Ike, but only in name. I have two children, but I don't want to live with them or get involved in their lives. They're happy that I'm an actress, but frankly, my love life horrifies them."

Together they tried to analyze Matt, and they agreed that he was more highly sexed and female-oriented than most men. "He has a compulsive need for erotic merger with a woman, but he's not promiscuous," was Jill's assessment. Peachy concurred with a slight modification: "He needs women who challenge him mentally. Men can't do that for Matt because they can't offer him a compensating sexual surrender." Peachy smiled reminiscently. "Thus he conquers a woman without conquering her."

"I think that between us—and I include Irene," Jill said, "because she's really a loving person, too—that we can keep Matt confined and happily romping in a corral with his three mares." Jill hoped that Irene might eventually meander into the stable, but Peachy wasn't so confident.

Peachy asked her about Ike. "Matt told me that his father doesn't really hate you and he'll never divorce you. Would you still go to bed with him?"

"Oh God, I don't know. One day I think I might, and then the next I'm sure I couldn't. Anyway, I'm sure Ike wouldn't want me now. He's a very possessive man." Jill sighed. "You love Roje, and he's twenty-seven years older than you are. You're fortunate that Emily accepts you."

"Yes, I think I'm almost like a kid sister to her," Peachy said. "I love Emily, too."

"If Ike would accept me as a friend and lover," Jill told her, "I wouldn't reject him. But under the circumstances, I doubt if there'll ever be a three-way Godwin merger."

33

At dinner, a few hours before they all drove to church for the opening night, Roje asked whether Irene was really coming with Father Tim. "She told Emily that she might."

Jill shrugged and said, "I'm not sure, but evidently Father Tim is intrigued by Matt."

"And he's intrigued with Irene," Matt interjected, "though he won't admit it. Jill told her we'd reserve a couple of seats for them—and for Becky and Hendy, but I'm sure they won't come."

Roje had ribboned off ten seats in the second tier, and he said that he would watch for them. "Emily and I want to watch the proceedings from the sanctuary as objectively as possible. Father Tim and Irene can sit with us and Peachy's kids. Do you think Irene will bring your boys?"

Matt shook his head. "Ink and Able have been eating dinner with us three or four times a week, so they know what's going on. But otherwise Irene is in charge of their moral lives."

Roje told him that Mike Wilder had telephoned from California this afternoon. "He's trying to set up an interview with Gus Belshin. A couple of his people will be in the audience. He expects to be here himself in two weeks. He wanted to talk to you about Cuba, but I told him you weren't available. Believe me, Matt, whether he proves it or not, he's going to insinuate that the modern moralities that we live with and don't talk about may be more shocking than those we do."

"Necessity is the mother of invention," Matt said and patted Roje's shoulder. "We can confess our sins later. Anyway, relax. It's too late to worry about Sylvie's gold. In an hour and a half the First Church will be a reality."

They arrived at the Parish Hall at 6:30. By 7:00 P.M., a half-hour before services began, the church was rapidly filling with more than a thousand people, buzzing with excitement.

Outside the church, in the Adams Mall, on tree-lined walkways between the church and the new CPC headquarters, five hundred or more people were protesting. Some carried lighted candles, others waved "Jesus Saves" placards, and many had angry, hand-lettered signs: "Cast Out This Sodom and Gomorrah"; "Sex Worship is Sick Worship"; "God's Church is not a Sex Club"; "Matt Godwin is a Bigamist—ask Irene"; "Lovejoy is a Dirty Old Flasher"; "Keep Out, Pornographers Own This Church"; "UU's and Humanists are Destroying America"; "The First Church is The First Godless Church"; "In the War Between the Godwins, God Will Win."

But other than urging the few hundred people who were still trying to get into the church not to let Adamsport become Sex City,

U.S.A., the demonstrators did not act militant. Police on foot and parked in nearby cars kept a watchful eye and subdued a few raucous kids who weren't quite sure which side they were on but ran screaming through the crowd to see what they could stir up.

Backstage, in one of the dressing rooms on the first floor of the new seven-story glass-faced parish building built flush against the back wall of the sanctuary, Peachy and Jill watched the arrivals. Their shoulder-height one-way see-through observation post was invisible from the sanctuary. It had been built into a thirty- by fifty-foot-long movie screen behind a twenty-two-foot deep back stage that now flanked the entire back wall of the church and replaced the former pulpit area.

The ushers had arrived earlier, men and women wearing a new gold version of the Flaming Chalice. The emblem overlaid a two-tone, blue Yang and Yin symbol and was inscribed with a white U on either side of the S divided oval. All of the ushers had been working and playing in the recreational areas of the remodeled church during the past month. Most of the fifty-two former members of the First Parish Church who had become members of the First Church had also spent long hours in the church in preparation for the month-long open house.

But the majority of arrivals were staring in astonishment at the interior. None of them had ever seen a church like this. The balconies and pews of the church had been removed. Now there were ten circular tiers of seats, slightly inclined and built in a huge horseshoe around a center stage. Each tier could accommodate at least one hundred people, and, as ushers were explaining, the first circle of seats was reserved for older and physically handicapped people. Folding armrests, which provided normal theater spacing, could be pushed back if needed and provide closer seating for several hundred additional people. Mystical light filtered in through the original stained-glass windows. Above the awed faces of the congregation, the plaster dome inscribed with lotus blossoms had been replaced by a clear glass dome that offered a breath-taking view of the evening sky. As would become apparent later, during the services, the clear dome could be transformed into a curved opaque screen and anything could be projected onto it, from a reproduction of a Michelangelo ceiling to a symphony of color, from a voyage into outer space to a perfect facsimile of the former lotus blossomed dome.

The "Ode to Joy" choral movement of Beethoven's Ninth Symphony filled the sanctuary. The music was not overpowering, but the acoustics of the building provided a body-embracing sound that merged brain and heartbeat into the music. But Peachy and Jill could see from the expressions on their faces that most of the arrivals were only dimly conscious of what they were hearing. Everyone seated or walking into the church was staring at an ever changing scene being projected from a booth high above the former front balcony of the church onto the movie screen on the back wall of the sanctuary.

"Look at them!" Laughing, Peachy nudged Jill. "Some of them are really shocked. Look at Dorothy Belcher. She can't believe her eyes."

Jill shook her head. "I told Matt that he might get away with this in New York City, but not here in Massachusetts. I just hope that our opening night isn't our closing night."

They both knew that Matt was still in his office with George Gallagher. Gallagher had warned him that the moralities of the First Church were not the moralities of the majority of the voters in Adamsport. Nudity in the church, live or projected on the screen, was in defiance of all Judeo-Christian teachings.

Many of the people in the sanctuary were watching the screen numbly, unable to believe their eyes. Others with glazed expressions of disgust were whispering angrily to each other. On the huge screen men and women were playing together naked. White, black, Asian, spanning all age groups—children, fathers, mothers, grandfathers, and grandmothers—they were in back yards, on beaches, in forest streams, on lake shores. Cutting into the long shots, the camera closed in on their faces and bobbing breasts, behinds, and genitals. They were admiring each other, hugging each other, with expressions of joy and wonder at each other's playfulness. Fast-moving distant scenes became intimate camera shots with old and young kissing and embracing. Occasionally the camera revealed a loving flesh and mind surrender and a bodily merger.

Most of the people in the sanctuary, whatever their age, were watching for the first time in their lives naked human beings expressing their deep, caring, sexual need for each other.

Jill noticed several people leaving the church in shocked anger fifteen minutes before the services were to start. Although Peachy seemed outwardly calm and kept telling her, "We knew we weren't going to please all of the people all of the time," Jill knew that she was nervous too. They were both awaiting their time on stage tensely, vacillating between enthusiasm and fear that things might not go as smoothly as Matt predicted. Then they both saw Irene and Father Timothy at the far end of the sanctuary. The ushers had recognized them and were bringing them to seats next to Emily and Roje.

"I really didn't think that Irene would come," Peachy said as they watched them walking toward the seats that Roje had ribboned off. She grinned at Jill. "Father Tim is playing with fire. The cardinal certainly won't approve of the First Church."

Jill was surprised too. Father Tim had corraled Matt in the church last week, and Matt had taken him on a tour of the building and tried to convince him that with few exceptions, such as abortion and birth control, they might not be so far apart in the search for new moralities as Father Tim might think.

"For example, sacramentalizing sex," Matt had told him, "is really more realistic today than sacramentalizing monogamous marriage. With a 50 percent divorce rate, and millions of people living together out of wedlock, and millions of kids conceived premaritally and extramaritally, we've got to extol sex-making and make it an act of joyous worship of each other as God. Thus, we can counteract and challenge the sexual devaluation that has become endemic in secular life."

Surprisingly, Father Tim, who was at least ten years older than Matt, partially agreed with him. "Some Catholics have a system of belief called probabilism," he told Matt. "Daniel Maguire, a Catholic professor of moral theology, points out that 'probabilism was based upon the insight that a doubtful obligation may not be imposed as though it were certain. Where there is doubt there is freedom.' This is precisely the situation among Catholics today regarding abortion."

With a twinkle in his eye, Father Tim had also told him that legalizing prostitution was not such a modern morality after all. Both St. Augustine and St. Thomas Aquinas, although they felt prostitution was morally repugnant, believed that it should be legalized for the greater good of society.

But Father Tim could not accept Matt's belief that men or women could make lasting commitments, sexually or otherwise, to more than one person of the other sex.

Teasing him, Matt had asked Father Tim if he loved Irene, and Father Tim had responded: "Of course I do, but not in a sexual way."

"I can't believe that," Matt had grinned at him. "Irene is an attractive woman. She obviously enjoys you as a golfer and as a man friend as well as a priest. Haven't you ever felt the need to touch her, to put your arms around her? Haven't you ever wanted to make love to her or any woman?"

Matt had told Jill and Peachy that Tim's answer was equivocal. "Tim implied that he resisted such compulsions, for God's sake, as well as for Irene's and mine. He's sure that Irene, like any good Catholic, would be horrified with herself if she broke her marriage vows with him or any man."

Father Tim had told Matt that he really couldn't understand him and his multiple sex relationships. "Irene loves you. She's your wife. And she even admires Jill and Peachy, but I'm sure she can't accept a polygamous household. She's also afraid that you are much too idealistic. She's sure that the pope, and even the cardinal, will ignore you, but men like Mike Wilder will try to burn you at the stake."

"Tell Irene that I love her, too," Matt had responded. "Tell her that I still have plenty of time to share with her in bed and out. Tell her that I am happy that she loves you, too. As for Mike Wilder, tell her not to worry. I am sure the First Church will survive him."

Knowing that Jill and Peachy were probably watching them through the one-way window above the back stage, Roje waved in their direction and gestured quickly toward Father Tim and Irene. From the expression on their faces, Jill knew that they were absorbing with some shock the naked action on the screen. Roje greeted them cordially and introduced them to Peachy's children, David and Cheryl. He thought that Emily was gushing a little too enthusiastically as she bussed both Irene and Father Tim on their cheeks. Father Tim, with white hair accentuating his deeply tanned face, was, in Roje's opinion, too athletic to be a priest. Even Emily admitted in private that she found it difficult to call him Father. The patriarchal name negated his obvious sex appeal.

Irene reluctantly sat down next to Roje. She had continued to play golf with Emily and evidently forgave her for her involvement with Matt, but whenever she met Roje she had been cool and remote. Now, she seemed a little more friendly, but her words revealed an underlying sarcasm. "I hear that you are practically a member of Matt's communal family," she said, trying to ignore the image of men and women playing naked together on the screen above them.

Roje smiled. He wasn't sure how much Emily had told her about Peachy, if she knew that Peachy had convinced Emily that she didn't want Roje "for her own," but did enjoy going to bed with him two or three times a month. He knew Irene was fishing, so he offered her some bait. "We commune mentally," he grinned at her. "But Emily and I still live together at Happy Shores. As you probably know, we have dinner once a week in your carriage house with Peachy and Jill and the children. We all wish that you would join us."

Irene scowled at him. "I'm not interested in Matt's saturnalias."

Roje guessed that Ink and Able had probably told her that last summer they had all swum together naked in the carriage house swimming pool. He laughed. "I can assure you that, while we approve of group nudity, the First Church would label saturnalias and group sex immoral—a product of sexual repression that devalues the miracle of one-to-one surrender."

"You sound like Matt," Irene said. "He obviously has brainwashed you."

"He hasn't brainwashed *me*," Emily intervened. She had picked up part of their conversation while Father Timothy was watching the sanctuary screen with a bemused expression on his face. "I love your husband," she said, "but he's too intense for me. I couldn't live with him day in and day out."

"It's easy," Irene said, laughing, but without humor. "All you have to do is to agree to share the lord and master with his female disciples.

Matt has forgotten that there are still laws against adultery on the books of Massachusetts." She pointed to the screen, where now a man was gently kissing a naked woman with a dreamy expression on her face. "There are also laws against showing pornography to minors."

"What you are watching is not pornography," Roje said with a smile. "But I'm afraid that our mayor, George Gallagher, agrees with you. He's on the warpath. He corraled Matt an hour ago in Matt's office in the parish building." Roje looked at his watch. It was 7:20. "I reserved one of those empty seats for him, but it doesn't look as if he's coming."

34

Actually, Roje hoped that Gallagher had decided not to come. He'd had enough of him yesterday. Bessie Summers, a First Church member working for the Foundation, brought Gallagher to Lovejoy's office in the former First Parish Church parsonage. Each of the ten rooms in the brick house was overflowing with people. Bessie led him to Roje's office in the converted garage. "I told him that Matt Godwin was really putting Adamsport on the map," Bessie said, and Gallagher, obviously distraught, had responded: "The only reason I am here is to get Adamsport *off* the map."

Roje had apologized for the confusion. "I expected by this time that we would have moved into our new location in the CPC building. The Foundation has rented one floor, but, as you probably know, everything is at a standstill concerning the building. If Matt doesn't win the proxy battle, the new directors may decide to sell the building." Roje laughed. "The way things are going, the Foundation might just decide to buy it. We could convert it into a College for the Study of Modern Moralities. If Jerry Falwell, Oral Roberts, and Billy Graham can have a college, why can't Matt Godwin?"

Gallagher stared at Roje sourly. "Not in Adamsport, I pray."

"Your prayers may not be answered," Roje smiled. "We've got thirty-two people on the Foundation payroll already. About half of them—illustrators, filmmakers, sound and lighting engineers, and a playwright working with Jill Godwin—are creating background material to enhance the programs of the First Church, and to create changing spiritual environments for our religious services. In the area of social concerns we have lawyers, teachers, and social scientists who are forming a Committee of Modern Moralities to refine and define the Foundation's position on everything from the right to life to nuclear warfare, prison reforms, and new approaches to delegislating old moralities that have been written into laws but no longer serve the needs of the people."

Roje had been well aware that he was propagandizing and that Gallagher didn't come to extol the church. But having a captive audience, he rattled on. "Of course, the Foundation does not administer the church," he said. "Mary Peachy is in over-all charge of that. We now employ two additional ministers, and Peachy and Matt give their services free. We also have a paid director of the choir, a religious education director, a recreation director, a dance and ballet instructor, and a supervised day care center which will open in the fall for members only." Roje grinned at Gallagher's lack of interest. "I hope you are coming Thursday to our opening services."

"I'm a good Catholic," Gallagher said angrily. "And you can cut out the commercials. You know damned well why I am here. The city council is close to the boiling point. They think you're going to turn the First Parish Church into a sexual side show. Even before it opens you've attracted sexual crazies from all over the country."

"We're exalting human sexuality," Roje said. "We're not degrading it. You'd better come and see for yourself, George. Jill Godwin and I are working on a unique *Quest for Love* film series, which will explore man's visual attempts from his earliest history—30,000 B.C.—to depict his and his woman's amazing sexuality and fruitfulness. We're not afraid to show man and woman copulating or worshipping their sex organs, but we'll never portray sexual ugliness as a part of our services."

Roje shrugged at his stunned listener. "On the other hand, we will not ignore the sexual degradation that is overrunning this country. We expect to offer special Tuesday evening programs which will show how men, fearing sex, have laughed at it, commercialized it, and devalued women through most of human history. Especially since the beginning of the Christian era when Adam and Eve and the Fall of Man was invented."

"God damn it!" Gallagher slapped Roje's desk emphatically. "I didn't come here to discuss sex or to hear about your crazy religion. I've been trying to reach Matt Godwin for the past week. Where the hell is he hiding out? He created this mess, and now he's left you holding the bag."

"He'll be here tomorrow for the opening night," Roje replied calmly. "If you read the papers, I'm sure that you know that Matt is battling with his father and the directors over who is going to run CPC. At the moment Gus Belshin, one of the big stockholders, is blaming Ike for the reduced dividends which he claims were caused by Ike's eighty-million-dollar memorial to himself—the new CPC building. Ike wants to get rid of Belshin, but he doesn't want Matt running the company either. Belshin is determined to get rid of all the Godwins, especially Matt. As you know, like many good Catholics and religious fundamentalists, Matt doesn't believe in Thomas Jefferson's 'wall of separation' between the church and state doctrine. Matt is convinced that all churches and synagogues must become a kind of third force in the internal and external politics of this country. Working together, we must try to create saner human moralities in all areas, including new approaches to the capitalistic system itself." Roje laughed. "And just to set the record straight, I am not holding the bag. I agree with Matt Godwin, and so do a lot of people. We're confident that in the next few weeks the First Church will reach its maximum membership goal of one thousand. We have already signed up 150 single members who are eighteen years or older and 200 family members who average three to a family. We expect that eventually our Sunday School will have 300 children in various age groupings. Our family and single membership fees, which entitle members and their families to use the recreational facilities in the new building, will cover all operating expenses. This will free our Foundation income for other purposes—hopefully, a national network of First Churches."

"In the meantime, you're building a bomb," Gallagher said coldly. "It's going to explode and wipe you out. What happens to CPC and your damned church isn't my problem, but Adamsport is. Every hotel and motel for miles around here is jammed either with Jesus followers or sex maniacs. They have all read about your clothing-optional swimming pool and basketball and volleyball courts and bowling alleys. Godwin's told reporters that you'll be showing movies and slides of men and women fucking."

Roje laughed, "I doubt if Matt said 'fucking.' Young men and women will occasionally dance nude as a part of our services, and we will show films of human beings making love."

Gallagher scowled at him. "You are not going to get away with it. You're only pretending to be a church, and you're not a private club. You've announced that non-members can attend your performances, after the free opening month, if they pay an admission fee of five dollars. That's not a church. It sounds like a profit-making organization to me."

"Eventually curiosity seekers will disappear," Roje said and, knowing that he was echoing Matt's words, he crossed his fingers. "We don't expect general admissions to average more than two or three hundred people a week. Non-members may provide an annual income of fifty to one hundred thousand dollars, which will help maintain our programs. And we will be very happy just to break even. Actually, you should be happy about the First Church, George. Eventually we'll become a popular tourist attraction on what is appropriately known in this area as the Freedom Trail."

"You'll be free all right—free in the county jail!" Gallagher suddenly realized that he was shouting, but he was totally shocked by this travesty on religion. "Tourists who come to Adamsport come to see the Adams Mansion and the Adams tombs—not a sex club. Now when they go home to Podunk, Idaho, they'll tell their friends that they visited Sex City, U.S.A. Eventually Adamsport will look worse than the combat zone in Boston ever did. You can bet your ass I'm not going to let that happen."

"I gather that you have not visited the remodeled tombs," Roje told him. "We charge no admission, and we provide tour guides. The entire basement of the former sanctuary has been turned into a fascinating historical museum. During the summer, three afternoons a week in the sanctuary, we will offer, for a modest admission charge, historical films covering the Revolutionary War and the lives of the Adams family."

"You're going to show Massachusetts history in a church filled with sex objects?" Gallagher demanded incredulously.

"I'll be happy to give you a personal tour of the church right now. You are obviously not aware of what's happening across the street from City Hall. The Adams memorial plaques and the busts of John and John Quincy are now in the entry of the church, and two side stairways on both sides of the entrance lead to the tombs and the museum."

Roje was getting a little bored with Gallagher. He rubbed his face wearily. "I can assure you there are no sex symbols in the sanctuary or in the parish building. We no longer have flags and crosses either. I'm really quite busy, George. I think before we talk any further you should take a tour of the building and attend our opening service."

Gallagher's face was bloodshot with anger. "I don't want a tour. I just want to go on record that I warned you, Lovejoy. All it takes is some of the rabble of this city to screw around, either on your side or against you, and sure as hell we'll have a riot on our hands. The city council is getting a lot of pressure from some pretty prominent people, including a few members of the former First Parish Church like the Belchers and the Hancocks. They claim that they have Ike Godwin's backing. If you are permitting naked kids to run around in the church or parish building, you could be arrested for corrupting the morals of minors. Or we can shut you down for offering sexual material that goes beyond this community's or any community's standards. The council has been working on a new bill which, despite the Supreme Court's mamby-pamby rulings, will eliminate so-called adult entertainment in this city. We got rid of the massage parlors last year. Only one so-called adult bookstore remains. And you can tell Mary Peachy, or Peachy Stein, or whatever the hell her name is now, that we are going to close Silly Willy's one of these days. And you can tell her I don't care who she goes to bed with, you or Godwin, Silly Willy's isn't going to reopen in the First Parish Church."

Roje had tried to terminate the discussion. "Just keep in mind," he said, "we're protected by the Constitution in the expression of our beliefs. While sex worship is something new in the United States, it has very ancient origins. If you take a trip to India, you will discover that on festival days, of which there are many, Hindu ladies happily carry huge reproductions of their various gods' phalluses through their towns and villages."

"Well, you'd better not try it in Adamsport, Lovejoy," Gallagher said. "You and Matt Godwin will get your pricks and balls shot off. I suppose you've heard that Mike Wilder is coming to Adamsport. He's going to make that damned First Church the butt of dirty jokes all over the country. Do me a favor, Lovejoy. The First Parish Church usually closes down in June. Move the date ahead a few weeks, and let's see if things will calm down during the summer."

"I'm sorry, George," Roje said. "The former UU Church closed down. We may eliminate one service during June, July, and August on Sundays, but we'll continue both services on Tuesdays and Thursdays. We also expect that eventually we'll have many summer weddings in the sanctuary, with outdoor receptions in the new Adams Mall. They'll be very popular since newlyweds will also have the opportunity to use our roof-top restaurant in the Parish Hall, or, if they can afford it, a new public restaurant on top of the CPC building, when it opens. Both restaurants overlook Adamsport and Boston Harbor."

Roje leaned back in his chair and smiled at Gallagher's growing dismay. "In many respects you should be with us. We are planning to make Adamsport a year-round night-time city with outdoor performances on the grounds of the church as well as a summer and winter evening series of plays and ballets in the sanctuary which will explore the entire history of religion from primitive man to the present. Since most religions, including early Christianity, in its Old Testament, were sexually quite honest, our presentations will obviously feature some nudity. We expect, given the hung-up nature of Christians and Jews, that they will be quite popular."

Gallagher finally gave up arguing, but his parting shot had been, "You won't get away with it, Lovejoy. The reason we have religion is to keep sex in its place. America may be sex crazy, but never on Sunday, or any other day in a church or synagogue."

35

Watching Irene and Father Tim in the crowded sanctuary, Peachy shivered. Within a few minutes, for the first time since her naked adventure with Roje in the belfry, she was going to face a live Adamsport audience in the sanctuary. She knew that there were several hundred mostly new UU's out there who had already become members of the First Church, but what about the rest of the audience? How hostile would they be? Tonight she wasn't preaching, but Sunday, at the first, more conventional UU service, she would be.

"There are some pretty grim faces out there," she said as Matt joined them. "Where have you been?"

"Carrying on where Roje left off." Matt pointed to George Gallagher, who was now standing near Roje in the sanctuary and shaking hands with Father Tim. "I convinced him to enjoy our opening services with us," Matt laughed, "but I don't think I made a convert."

"Aren't you nervous?"

Matt stuck out his hand. There were no tremors. "God is us. All we have to do is convince them that they are God, too."

"Right now your Peachy God and your Jill God are scared to death," Jill said.

"Don't worry." Matt hugged them both. "In those semi-transparent robes the spotlight makes you look erotically ethereal—everyone in the congregation will think they are in heaven with sexy angels." Matt left them to put on his own robe.

Peachy shook her head. "If this is a daydream, I don't want to wake up." But she was afraid that reality would cut them all down with a sharp scepter. The Foundation and the First Church were sitting ducks for the news media. Peachy was sure that by tomorrow some of the reporters now sitting in the sanctuary would insist that the lunatic fringe was alive and healthy in America. Matt told them that it really didn't matter; they needed publicity, good or bad. Mike Wilder, for example, might try to play judge and jury, but there were at least 40 million Americans who had no church, millions of people who didn't know whether they believed in God or not, and who needed something to cling to. If a few million of them dared to believe that man was God, and accepted the consequences in their day-to-day relationships, they could change the course of human destiny.

"Religion is like life insurance," Matt insisted. "It's an intangible product. You buy it now because someday you might be happy you did. But it's better than life insurance. At least you don't have to die to collect."

But both Peachy and Jill were sure that Matt was ignoring the real problem: the immorality of the means. If Wilder got on the trail of Grand Cayman and Sylvie's gold, it could lead back to Cuba and maybe even Sylvie's villa. Why Amir had partially paid Peachy for it was still a mystery.

They hadn't seen Amir Saud since. Nearly a year ago Matt had finally reached him by telephone in Jidda, but they had talked cautiously. He didn't ask Amir outright what had happened to the gold, or if by some miracle Nefwazi had actually got 11,000 pounds of it off Ramachanda's schooner before it sank. Instead he thanked Amir for his endowment to the Foundation and said he hoped that Allah had amply rewarded him for his generosity. He also managed to ask if Amir had visited Grand Cayman recently or planned to.

Amir had chuckled. "I'm sure that your friend Peachy told you that I made a down payment on her Daddy's villa. I'll complete the transaction as soon as Nate Billings advises me that she is the legal heir. Right now I'm very busy. I have many homes in various parts of the world, and I rarely stay long in one place. However, you can tell Peachy that if I had a woman like her to share the villa with, I'd most certainly get to Grand Cayman more often. In the meantime, I consider the villa a resource for my old age. As for your Foundation and my endowment, consider it gold cast upon the waters."

Matt told Amir that he hoped to be seeing him soon. "I'm in the process of changing the direction of Controlled Power Corporation. We're going to minimize our dependence on Pentagon contracts. Instead of destroying the world or making it uninhabitable, we're planning to use nuclear energy to make it fertile. Controlled Power is going to build off-shore, nuclear-powered, salt water distillation plants. We're going to turn Africa, Australia, and the Mid-East into agricultural gardens of Eden. We'll build the plants right here in Adamsport and in our Connecticut yard, and we'll float them to their ultimate destination." He told Amir that he was sure that Saudi Arabia could place an order for several billion dollars' worth of them.

Amir laughed. He wasn't sure that the Arabs could afford such expensive American friends. "Did you read about my friend Sheik Mohammed Fassi?" he asked. "Paying no attention to community property laws, he divorced his wife and came back here with his two children. But an American judge awarded his wife equal shares in Fassi's two Boeing 707 airplanes, and in a 150-foot yacht, 38 cars, including quite a few Rolls Royces, and 17 million dollars' worth of jewelry.

"I'll get to Adamsport one of these days and pay my respects to Jill and Peachy. I read about them in the *Wall Street Journal.* Your friend Gus Belshin evidently doesn't approve of polygamy," he said slyly. "Who knows? I may be interested in your distillation plants, but right now I'm glad that you're not a woman, Goddy. If I had married you, I might be even worse off than Mohammed Fassi."

Unable to certify that Sylvie was dead, Peachy had left her father's affairs in limbo. Guido Ponzello, who actually ran the day-to-day operation of Silly Willy's, kept asking if she had heard from him. He told her that he and her father had been trying to raise $10 million to launch a new franchise operation. They also were planning to open another Silly Willy's on the North Shore. Guido wondered if Sylvie might have taken a quick trip to Switzerland.

"I'm sure that he's got a boodle stashed away somewhere," Guido had said, staring speculatively at her. Peachy wondered if he had been waiting for her to come clean. She wouldn't have been surprised if he had suddenly revealed that he knew all about Sylvie's gold.

Guido insisted on going over the financial details of Silly Willy's with her. To Peachy's surprise, she discovered that in addition to averaging $20,000 a month income from two porno movies that they had recently financed, Silly Willy's was generating a profit of $15,000 a week, mostly from the sale of beer and wine. Together, Sylvie and Guido had been earning in excess of $500,000 annually. Sylvie's take was $300,000.

An interview that Peachy had had with Bill Walsh for the *Adamsport Chronicle* really upset Guido. "It sounds to me as if you're going to try to compete with Silly Willy's," he told her. "You can't mix tits and ass with religion. That's why you got religion—to keep the lid on sex. The cardinal doesn't worry about Silly Willy's. He knows that Irishmen need a little sin in their lives. They may worship pussy more than God, but they don't tell their priests about it."

Guido hadn't gone to church for years, but, he told Peachy, he'd die a good Catholic and God would forgive him. Peachy could see from the accounts that Silly Willy's paid the ladies plenty of money to shake their asses and boobs. "We don't exploit women," he told her indignantly.

Bill Walsh had asked Peachy whether porno stars from Silly Willy's would be stripping on the stage of the First Parish Church. Peachy had laughingly responded that they wouldn't have to pay porno stars—they could become UU's and do it free. She told Walsh that she was sure that many of the new female members, including herself, would be happy to reveal themselves as naked goddesses for the members.

That had worried Guido. Italian men might enjoy watching ladies of the evening stripping, but their wives better keep their asses well covered or they'd get their throats cut.

Peachy knew that Guido, who was in his sixties, had more than a fatherly interest in her. He was constantly fondling her with his eyes, and he was happy that she was finally rid of "that poop, Saul Stein." Guido insisted on calling her Mary, which, he told her, was his mother's name, too.

"One day," Peachy told Matt, "Guido is going to ask me to become *his* Ponzello. When I tell him no thanks, he'll probably tell me that I'd better or else, because he knows all about Sylvie's gold." But Matt told her to stop worrying. He was sure that Sylvie would never have been totally honest with a partner like Guido Ponzello, who according to rumor was related to the Mafia in Rhode Island.

But only yesterday Guido had told her somewhat cryptically: "Matt Godwin has a big surprise in store for him. Silly Willy's wouldn't have lasted this long without payola, and neither will your sexy First Church." Peachy thought that Guido meant that he and Sylvie paid the Mafia protection money, but Matt guessed that it was more likely that some of the city officials, including perhaps the mayor himself, were getting a little pay-off. Year after year they had threatened to close the strip club, but somehow they never got around to it.

Peachy suggested to Matt that maybe she should fly down to Grand Cayman and see for herself exactly what she had sold Amir, but Matt dissuaded her. He was convinced that Ramachanda hadn't actually found Sylvie's gold. "The villa isn't worth a half-million dollars—unless, of course, there's still a hundred million in gold bullion under the living room floor. The problem is, we don't know who might be guarding it—friend or enemy."

Roje had agreed. Peachy should let sleeping dogs lie. "If the First Church of Modern Moralities ever gets linked with Sylvie's gold," he said, "they won't just be picketing the church. They'll start a fire in Adams Mall and toss you and me and Matt into it. Remember, this is New England—years ago they burned witches for less."

Matt returned and jarred her out of her reverie with a big hug. "You're first on the firing line. You've got five minutes before the stage goes up. Get them all singing, and stop worrying. They'll love you!"

36

It was 7:30. The light-hearted music that had filled the crowded church and blended in happy revelry with the silent naked shadows on the screen slowly faded away. A soft fog of blue light suffused the dome and crept through the sanctuary, creating a mystical unity of a thousand upturned faces. Those sitting near the opening of the horseshoe tiers were dimly aware that the back stage had been retracted and now was slowly rising to a fixed position five feet above the floor of the sanctuary. As the lighting gradually became brighter it revealed a choir of twenty young men and women on stage wearing matching navy blue trousers and navy blue pleated skirts with white shirts and blouses.

Standing in front of them, wearing a shimmering white robe that revealed the motion of her body beneath it and a gold Yang and Yin circle hanging from a chain around her neck, Peachy heard a hum of recognition. "It's Peachy. Peachy Stein. Mary Peachy."

She smiled at the sea of faces. "Welcome to the First Church of Modern Moralities. As you have read in the *Adamsport Chronicle,* and in your program, for the next month this church is open to all—no charge for admittance. During this time, we hope that many of you will join us in a new kind of church fellowship. If you prefer not to become a member, after the second week in May, you may still attend any of our services for a nominal admission charge. Members, of course, can use our complete facilities, which include bowling alleys, a gymnasium, and swimming pool below the sanctuary, as well as our new parish building where many other activities will be available.

"Tonight, our opening night service is a get-acquainted potpourri, and is not typical of our future Thursday night services. On Thursday nights in the future, and at Sunday 9:00 A.M. services, we become a mystery religion. There will be no formal sermon. Using our total facilities we will offer music, film, and live drama. We will explore all the religious mythologies of the world and revel in the wonder of man and woman's search for God. We will rejoice in the never ending mystery of our bodies and our lives and our deaths. We believe that the sum total of all life—reaching its peak in human beings—is all the God there is, and the only God that we need to know and revere.

"We do not believe that anyone can blend his or her life into the never ending mystery of the universe through the use of drugs. We do not offer a hocus-pocus religion which depends on the use of secondary symbols to perpetuate itself. Many of these symbols are the fascinating by-product of a search for meaning and a dream of everlasting life. We will explore them in our services as we extol ourselves as God and the amazing mystery of all forms of life and our interdependence with each other.

"You as God . . . I as God . . . create a new kind of morality. If we accept the philosophy that God is good, you and I, when we act in ways that hurt each other, are no longer acting as God. Our search for new moralities will be guided by the nature and relativity of evil and the belief that modern men and women, acting as God, can define evils for ourselves better than we have done in the past.

"Tuesday evenings we will be more concerned with secular approaches to moral problems. I know that many of you already this evening have been a little shocked by the nudity in our pre-service film. . ."

"You can bet your ass on that!" a male voice yelled from one of the tiers.

Peachy stared into the darkened sanctuary and coolly replied, "Not until I know what I'm betting against."

Immediately, as Matt had planned, the man, now standing in front of his seat, was picked out on the fourth tier by a spotlight. Blinded for a second, he continued shouting as two ushers and an off-duty policeman whom Roje had hired moved toward him. "There's a lot of teen-agers in this church, and you're breaking the law showing them X-rated films! This is the most disgusting spectacle that I have ever witnessed!"

"How can your body or mine be X-rated?" Peachy asked. "You and I are God. Tonight we are celebrating ourselves. Please come to our services next Tuesday. If you have read our literature, you know that we are exploring many new approaches to human moralities. We believe that religion should offer a healthier understanding of human sexuality. Instead of being ashamed, we should rejoice over our naked bodies and sexual attraction to each other."

She was relieved when the man, although still shaking his head angrily, sat down and the spotlight went out.

"On Tuesday evenings," she continued, "we hope that all of you will come and express your own viewpoints. You don't have to agree with us. Asking questions, in and of itself, is healthy and human. While I know that many of you have questions and fears about our programs, I hope that tonight we can continue without further dialogue."

Peachy told Matt later that she had been shaking in her boots, but she continued without faltering. "On Sunday mornings at 10:30, if attendance warrants, we will offer a second, more conventional UU service for former members and new members who may prefer the old ways. Beginning next week we plan to offer two services on Sunday throughout the winter, and one during the summer months.

"We will offer a continuing series of drama, music, film presentations, modern dance and ballets, not specifically for entertainment but rather to express our never ending religious search for meaning and the inevitable mystery of life and death.

"After services tonight, you are invited to try red sumac punch, which was a favorite refreshment of the Indians who lived on this site 350 years ago, and cookies baked in our new parish building kitchen. Refreshment stands are set up throughout the new underground recreation area and also in the new Adams Museum, directly under the sanctuary, which is normally closed off from the recreation areas by sliding doors.

"The new recreation area includes an Olympic-size swimming pool, bowling alleys, and a gymnasium which will be available to our members for co-ed basketball, volleyball, and modern dance and ballet instruction. In keeping with our search for viable modern moralities, all facilities can be enjoyed, by members only, on a clothing-optional basis. In the former back balcony of the church you will find our new carillon organ, which will brighten your day with fifteen minutes of music at noon and at six o'clock.

"For those of you who remember the old Parish Hall, we invite you to inspect the new seven-story glass parish building. This building can be reached through sliding doors which will be opened on the left and right side of the stage after the services. Directly behind the retractable stage, on the first floor and below it, are the dressing rooms for actors and an area for stage scenery, much of which we plan to create on the premises.

"You may also wish to take the glass elevator to the other six floors in the new parish building, which by fall will be in full operation with a communal kitchen serving our members in a restaurant on the seventh floor. You will also see our day care center on the second floor; and on other floors you will find video rooms, a library, areas for small meetings, and the church offices.

"In the brackets under your seat, you will find our new hymn book. At the moment it is really a growing booklet as we pick and choose among thousands of songs which we believe are more suitable than the dreary hymns our ancestors sang. As you can see, we already have a choir to sing for us, but we need to sing songs together that express the various aspects of our lives. Occasionally we will offer specially guided sing-alongs conducted here or in the new parish building."

Peachy smiled. "And you may be sure that as God's children—hence God ourselves—we will offer gospel singing. Former First Parish members will be happy to see that we have saved a few UU hymns such as 'Morning Has Broken,' which has appealing words and melody, and we have modernized the music and words of quite a few others. Tonight our opening song will be #28, 'All My Life's a Circle.' I'm sure that the song is familiar to you. It will be danced, as we sing, by Lucy Bass and Tom Steele."

As the choir and most of the congregation sang the lyrics, Lucy and Tom swirled onto the center stage. Dressed in white matching togas cut high above their knees, they were followed by a pale green spotlight on the darkened stage, and their movements reflected the wry questioning of the words of the song. Then, as the congregation sang the last chorus, "All my life's a circle . . . but I can't tell you why," they let their togas drop to the floor. For a brief moment before the stage darkened, they were naked, clinging to each other.

Immediately following them on the center stage, which was now lighted only by the evening sky and a sliver of a moon overhead, Matt and Jill appeared, both of them wearing white robes similar to Peachy's. Only a few in the congregation were aware that the woman was Jill Godwin.

"Those of you who wish," Matt said, "may repeat with us a unison affirmation which is printed in your program. Unitarian Universalists will note that we in the First Church do not have the problem of addressing God as do theists who accept the existence of some vague but impersonal God; or as do deists, who believe that there is an active personal God somewhere up there; or as do humanists who find no necessity for God in the universe. Nor must we hedge, like some UU's, and begin our prayers with "To whom it may concern."

Matt smiled at the nervous laughter. "Nor do we have the problem of addressing God as he or she. Each and every one of us are God. This concept should not alarm most Unitarian Universalists, since UU churches have never been Christian churches in the formal sense of believing in the divinity of Jesus. The First Church of Modern Moralities is simply moving one step beyond most Christian churches and synagogues in the world.

"Especially so because we renounce patriarchal religion. None of our services will ever be conducted by a man alone. Whether it be a unison affirmation or readings and sermons, both the ministers and the lay people who will conduct the services will include both men and women. We worship together as God.

"Tonight Jill Godwin and I will alternately read the unison affirmation to each other. They are the words of a great Hindu seer, Vivekananda, who lived in the nineteenth century. The women will join with Jill and the men with me."

Smiling, Matt began: "'Above it is full of me. Below it is full of me. In the middle it is full of me.'"

"'I am in all beings, and all beings are in me,'" Jill read, and was pleased to hear a chorus of female voices saying the words with her. "'I am it. I am existence above mind.'"

"'I am the one spirit of the universe. I am neither pleasure nor pain.'"

"'My body drinks, eats, loves, dies.'"

"'I am not the body. I am not the mind.'"

"'I am Existence, Knowledge, Bliss.'"

"'I am the witness. I look on. When health comes I am the witness. When disease comes I am the witness.'"

"'I am the essence and nectar of knowledge.'"

"'Through eternity I change not.'"

"'I am calm, resplendent and unchanging. I am God!'"

As Jill spoke the final words, they were emphasized by three notes from Bach's Toccata and Fugue in D Minor on the organ, and now both she and Matt became more clearly focused in a hazy blue spotlight that gave them an ethereal appearance.

Speaking to Jill but turning slightly as he spoke so that the entire congregation could see him, Matt said, "As you have seen, using the techniques of our electronic age, we believe that without sermons we can help each other enjoy what has been called the 'oceanic experience,' our deep genetic identification with the sources of all life, which began in the oceans of the world. Coming together at least once a week, communing together in an atmosphere that evokes the wonder, the awe, and the everlasting mystery of our lives, we can regularly achieve what has been called 'a peak experience' and with it a sense of well-being and love and responsibility. In the process, discovering ourselves becomes the keynote of our lives.

"But tonight, as Peachy has told you, we are only giving you an over-view of our approaches. Some of you may prefer the spiritual experience in combination with a thought-provoking sermon. If so, I hope you will come to our first or second services on Sunday. Occasionally I will preach, but you will also hear many other men and women. Many of them will be invited from other religious affiliations to explain to us, if they can, why we need a God external to ourselves. Or you may prefer to join us on other nights when we will discuss what UU's call 'social concerns' and what we call modern moralities.

"While the First Church will try to influence public and political opinion, it will never be a one-man or one-woman show. We will provide a voice for millions of Americans who dare to dream a new American dream. Nearly three hundred of you who have read our literature and our proposals have already become members of our church club. You are at least in partial agreement with our search for new moralities.

"Tonight Jill Godwin, who some of you may have seen on Broadway in the long-running *Reverend Beecher and Mrs. Tilton*, will briefly review some of our new moral approaches to human sexual reality before and after marriage."

Matt smiled at Jill, and, as often happened, Jill's pre-stage nervousness vanished the moment she began speaking to an audience. She spoke in a warm, sexy, but reassuring voice. As one New York critic had said of her: "Sitting in an audience of thousands, you know Gillian Marlowe loves you and makes you feel as if she is telling you so personally."

"When Matthew asked me if I would tell you about our sex education and re-education program, I told him, 'Matt Godwin, you are a dreamer.' But I had to agree with him; impossible dream though this may be, without dreams and hopes and visions of a better way, this would be a dull, nasty, and brutish world.

"Most religions, whether they will admit it or not, tend to deny human sexual drives. Unless men and women make love to each other within clearly defined parameters, their sexual compulsions and needs are often labeled sinful or evil and dirty. Most religions believe that a naked woman excites lustful thoughts in men. Many religions believe that women are compelled by their natures to seduce men." Jill laughed softly. "Young women, of course! Most people believe that older women lose their power to control men sexually. But even watching naked people playing together and making love, as you have seen in the film this evening, is thought by many to be disgusting. Such movies are called dirty movies.

"As a by-product of these fears and religious and secular beliefs that human sexuality must be restrained—because otherwise civilization would come to a halt—we have created a sex-obsessed, sex-drenched, sex-frustrated society. By prohibiting and not recognizing that all men and women as God must express their creativity in a caring sexual release with one another, we have created a world where the sex tease substitutes for the joyous reality. We have created a world where young women, from their early teens until their mid-thirties, become fantasy sex objects. The underlying message that we learn from magazines, books, movies, and television is that love is pure but the sexual expression of it ranges somewhere between naughty but nice and sick and dirty. We agree that the human body is marvelous. But revealing one's buttocks, a woman's breasts, or, God forbid, a man's penis or a woman's vulva is disgusting.

"By contrast, we are proposing a new kind of religious world where young people of all ages will grow up seeing their peers and older people of all ages naked where it's convenient for them to be naked. In America today, this is considered immoral. It's against the law. But here at the First Church, as part of our religious belief that sex and the human body are sacramental, we will offer our members the opportunity to play together and laugh together naked.

"For many years Unitarian Universalists, realizing that their children received a very rudimentary sex education in public schools, have offered an outstanding course on the physiology of sex. We will also offer this course to all of our members and their children, but we plan to go a step further. The First Church of Modern Moralities will propose a new code of sexual values. One of these basic values is that all of us from birth are sexual creatures. But we fail to teach our young people that they can express their sexual compulsions and joy with each other in many ways, such as touching, kissing, and mutual masturbation.

"We believe that young people should not have sexual intercourse until they are seventeen or eighteen. Nor should they marry until they are in their mid-twenties. But we also believe that in all of their premarital years, they should have the opportunity for meaningful sexual relationships within the privacy of their own homes, with full responsibility, learned at home and in church, not to conceive children. This means that we will encourage our members to teach their younger children a new kind of sexual exaltation which permits mutual touching and mutual masturbation in their early teens. After their seventeenth birthday they should be able to enjoy sexual intercourse with a loving friend in the privacy of their own home.

"To explore this new kind of sexual caring and loving relationship, we will, at least once a month on Friday nights, discuss every aspect of human sexuality with all members over seventeen years of age. In the process we will show X-rated movies and all types of pornography and reveal to our members how a 'pornographic society' dehumanizes sex and how sadistic sex, sex with violence, is a by-product of a Judeo-Christian sex-repressed society.

"We believe in lifelong pair bondings, and we believe that this kind of religious thinking will make such pair bondings possible. But we do not believe that these lifelong pair bondings should of necessity be monogamous. Specifically, this means that we will try to educate our members that it is possible over a long marriage to experience parallel committed relationships with friends of the other sex without jealousy, but for the most part these parallel relationships should be with one other person at a time."

"What about you, Jill Godwin?" a woman in the second tier shouted, and was immediately spotlighted. "Aren't you fucking with old man Godwin and his son, too?"

The tension in the sanctuary was palpable. Although she was trembling, Jill managed to smile. "As Mary Peachy told you, tonight is not an open forum. If on one of the coming evenings, you wish to join me on this stage, I'll share my sex life with you, if you'll share yours."

Suddenly the congregation was on Jill's side. Released from embarrassment by her quick response, they broke out in cheers and laughter.

"In a few minutes," Jill continued calmly, "we will conclude our service this evening with a dance drama, *The Woman Caught in Adultery,* based on the Gospel story John 8:1-11. It will be danced by students from the New England School for the Dance to Stravinsky's *Agon* ballet music. Matthew Godwin will read the text from the Scriptures as they dance. Incidentally, Jesus' final admonition to the lady raises an interesting question of morality which we feel is no longer adequate two thousand years later.

"But over and above the specifics of human sexual relationships, sex worship is worship in utter amazement of each and every one of us as total human beings. We are in awe at the miracle of conception and birth. We sing the joy and wonder of the human brain and the human heart, the blood and the flesh and the bones that make us Gods.

"Young and old, we will forever be mystified by the beauty of youth and the lovely sexual compulsions of our teens and of our middle years. Young and old, we'll enjoy the sheer beauty of human flesh at play and in love. And rather than be ashamed of our gradual physical and sexual deterioration, we will be happily bemused that we are God. We may personally disappear from this earth, but we will return."

As she spoke she held out her hands to Matt and to Peachy as they joined her on center stage. They bowed to the audience and said together: "Thank you for coming. Enjoy the ballet. We hope that in future weeks we will see many of you as full-time members of the First Church of Modern Moralities."

37

Two days later, Irene knew that she must finally decide "what to do about Matt," as Becky put it. Despite all the publicity given to the fight for control of CPC, Ike grudgingly admitted to her that for the moment, at least, with Matt as president, the company was doing as well as it had in previous years. But Ike was sure that Matt was coasting on past performance. Ultimately his "no more Pentagon contracts" policy would wreck the company. Still, CPC headquarters was a reality in Adamsport. Ike was sure that it would cast a longer shadow into the future than Matt's goddamned First Church sitting smack in the center of the city.

After eighteen months of grueling, frustrating work, Ike told Becky that if it hadn't been for Irene's constant attention and loving care, he would never have learned to speak again. Right now, without Irene's faith in him, he'd be a doddering idiot.

"What I should have done, Renee," Ike had told her more than once while he patted her cheek or held her arm with more than fatherly affection, "was stolen you away from that stinking son of mine." Ike insisted that ministers, priests, and actors—including Father Tim and Jill—were all the same. "They don't know where the acting in the pulpit or the stage stops and reality begins." And as far as Ike was concerned, Sarah hadn't been much better. "I should have married a woman like you, Renee. You've got a head on your shoulders. You're smarter than any of those damned M.B.A.'s from Harvard, including my son."

Becky told Irene: "Matt may be my brother, but you're really a Godwin—not him, and not Sally. Matt's gone mad. He's turning Adamsport into a three-ring sex circus. You really haven't any choice. You should divorce him. Walk in on him tonight and tell him the carriage house is yours. Tell him to get out and take his harem with him!"

Irene didn't dare tell Becky that Matt, and especially Jill and Peachy, kept begging her to return to "Matt's seraglio," as Jill laughingly called it.

Strangely, although Becky, like Ike and Hendy, was a highly prejudiced anti-papist, she had never questioned Irene's consistent attendance at mass, nor Father Tim's frequent appearances at the Big House to see her. But Irene guessed that, like most of her Protestant friends, the family believed Catholic priests managed to have a regular sex life, and they probably wondered if she were providing it for Father Tim.

They were more than a little surprised, the day after the opening night at the First Church, to find Father Tim having breakfast with her at nine o'clock in the morning. Of course, they weren't sure, but the question was in their eyes. Had Father Tim stayed the night? Irene was living practically alone on the third floor of the east wing of the Big House, and Ink and Able were staying in the carriage house with Matt and his harem, so she had all the privacy she needed. But Irene glibly told them that Father Tim had arrived early because they were planning to play eighteen holes of golf at the club and they wanted to get an early start.

It wasn't true. It was a lie, and Irene reflected ruefully that her only confessor was the man she had lied for. Last night, walking with her up to the front porch of the Big House, after he had driven her home from the First Church, Father Tim had held her hand tenderly. In the subdued glow of the floodlights that illuminated the gardens and shrubbery of the Big House all through the night, Irene could see that Father Tim's eyes were misty with emotion. The caring smile on his lips reflected more than priestly concern. She was sure, as she had often been in the past, that Father Tim was steeling himself. He wanted to put his arms around her.

"Your husband is dangerous," he said quietly. "Tonight he made *eros*, sexual loving, so alluring that momentarily I forgot that it is secondary to *agape*, love of God, and *philos*, friendship."

Not knowing how, Irene dared to voice her thoughts. Needing a man's hand on her body after so many months, she squeezed his arm and whispered, "You told Matt about 'probabilism.' Probably the various aspects of love are equal." She looked at him questioningly. "Do you want to?"

"Want to what?"

"Forget about agape—for tonight?"

Almost sobbing with joy, he pulled Irene into his arms. "Forgive me, Renee, but I've loved you for a long time." He kissed her lips almost piously, as if he were embracing the Virgin Mary herself.

"A lot of people at the club think that we've been lovers for years," she told him. Tears were running down her cheeks. "Ink and Able are staying at the carriage house with Matt tonight." She was trembling. "If you want to come upstairs, we'll be alone. I may not be much fun. I haven't made love with Matt, or anyone, for over a year."

Following her up the wide circular carpeted staircase and down a long corridor, he whispered, "I haven't made love to anyone for ten years." In her bedroom, with the curtains fluttering in the warm April breeze and the lamps softly shaded, he looked sheepishly at Irene. She could see the bulge in his trousers. "But I guess that I still can."

Still dressed, she sat on the bed and he sat down beside her. For a long time, they lay beside each other and kissed and held hands. Lost in the sensual euphoria of each other's body, they didn't talk. Then, he leaned over her. Her eyes were closed, but she could feel that he was unbuttoning her blouse. He slipped her bra over her shoulders and released her breasts. She opened her eyes and smiled at the tears of joy in his.

"God forgive me. You are more beautiful than I ever dreamed." He kissed her nipples gently.

"You dream of me?" she asked.

He laughed. "Priests are men; even we have erotic dreams."

"But you said that you haven't made love for ten years. You've been a priest longer than that."

"A long time ago I was counselling an unhappily married woman. She had two children. Her husband was a confirmed alcoholic. I worried about her. He often beat her. She'd throw herself in my arms seeking consolation. I was at my wit's end. If I hadn't been a priest, I would have told her to divorce her husband. We made love many times for more than six months, but afterwards she always felt terribly guilty."

He watched Irene with a faraway expression in his eyes. She had gotten off the bed and undressed while he was talking. Standing naked beside the bed, smiling sadly at him, she asked, "Did you feel guilty? Are you remembering her?"

"I'm remembering her guilt and her unwillingness to stop. We had sinned and it tormented her." He took Irene's hand and kissed her fingers. "Strangely, I was more at peace with myself than ever before. She finally reconciled with her husband, but like that motion picture, *Days of Wine and Roses*, she eventually became a worse alcoholic than he was."

"Are you feeling guilty now? Do you want to leave?"

He shook his head and quickly shed his clothes. She noticed that although he was fifty-five, his body was lean and hard. "I think she was a better Catholic than I am," he said wryly. "I felt guilty that perhaps I drove her to drink, but not because I loved her." He surveyed his erect penis with a little grin. "God is forgiving."

"I hope so, Tim," she sighed.

Afterwards she was a little shocked at the intensity of her own passion. Was it because she hadn't had sex for such a long time? Or was it because it was the Devil's thrill of committing a mortal sin? She had asked Father Tim and encouraged him. She was worse than Jill, from what she had discovered about her. She had taken the initiative and seduced a priest, or, at the very least, had made it easy for him to break his vows. Would it have happened if they hadn't gone to the First Church together, had not been caught up in Matt's mad belief that loving was not sinful, but rather the ultimate beatitude? Even during the ballet, *A Woman Caught in Adultery*, Matt had tampered with Jesus' message. Instead of telling the woman to go and sin no more, he had concluded with Jesus' next to last words: "Neither do I condemn thee."

Whatever had motivated her sobbing need for Father Tim's body, she had been fully aware that she never had let herself go sexually to the pitch she had with him. Father Tim was both delighted and surprised to discover a moaning, scratching, biting, insatiable bucking mare beneath him. Inevitably he climaxed before she did. But before he could feel apologetic, she was murmuring soothingly over his deflated penis, and in a kind of love-making that she had rarely offered Matt, she slowly nursed him "alive" again.

Whether it would ever happen again, whether Father Tim was feeling guilty, Irene refused to indulge in self-recriminations. Actually, she didn't have time. The next day Sally telephoned from Big Sur. She had moved out of Gus's home in Santa Barbara and back to her studio to give Gus time to cool off.

"I'm really pissed off with him," she told Becky on the phone. "In case you haven't heard, Mike Wilder was out here last week. Gus agreed to be interviewed on Wilder's keyhole-watching 'Showdown.' Wilder knows that theoretically Gus has a majority vote of the stockholders and could have elected a new board of directors and ousted Matt as president. But Matt got a court injunction against him, and the judge agreed that Gus could only vote 50 percent of his shares because his wife, Miriam, claims that under their divorce settlement the other 50 percent belongs to her. She told the judge that she hates Gus so much she'd vote her shares for Matt Godwin."

Raving on, Sally told Becky, "The problem is that Miriam thinks that she still loves Gus. She thinks he's a little senile—robbing the cradle and all that crap—but she'd probably forgive him if he'd come back. Miriam is nearly fifty. I feel a little sorry for her. I'm almost young enough to be her daughter."

But Sally's real gripe was with Gus. On Gus's invitation, she had watched the filming of his interview with Wilder. Wilder got Gus to admit that he could have gotten around the problem of his wife's shares, if Sally had voted with him. Each of Ike's children had a half-million shares of CPC stock. "Sally's shares would have tipped the balance," Gus told Wilder grimly, "but she voted with her brother. I'm trapped between a vindictive ex-wife and Sally's commitment to her crazy family. Sally knows that if I had her proxies I'd toss the old man and her looney brother out on their ears."

Then Gus switched gears. He told Wilder that the real problem was the war between Ike and Matt. "Matt Godwin is sleeping with his old man's wife," he said."But you can't blame Matt or her. The old man is practically senile. On the other hand, his son is a wild-eyed dreamer."

During the interview, as reported by Sally, Gus said that the reason Matt was still president was because he had convinced the managers of several pension funds, who together controlled over eight million shares, that his plan to gradually move CPC out of its dependence on defense contracts was sound policy.

"They're not aware that it's all part of Matt Godwin's master plan," Gus told Wilder. "Ultimately Matt will be using Controlled Power to subsidize his damned Foundation. It's his insane belief that you can mix business with religion and straighten out the politicians in Washington at the same time. He's acting like these damned Mormons. The Mormon Church controls businesses doing billions of dollars in annual sales. No matter how you slice it, mixing business and religion is damned dangerous stuff."

Wilder got Belshin to admit that several CPC subsidiaries engaged in metal fabrication and heavy industry, including the Godwin shipyards and a submarine division in Connecticut, could be converted to build the nuclear-powered fresh water distillation plants that were part of Matt's crazy dreams. Belshin told Wilder that Matt was also pursuing the development of city sewage plants that could produce organic fertilizer and be powered by a combination of their own gases and solar energy. In addition, Matt was interested in a large bridge-building company. Matt was determined to get Controlled Power into the trillion-dollar refurbishing of the nation's bridges.

"I don't give a damn if they are all multi-billion-dollar projects," Gus had fumed to Wilder. "The problem is, who are the buyers? Third World governments and tax-poor communities who haven't got a pot to piss in. Who *pays*?"

Wilder asked Gus when CPC would finally move into its new headquarters building in Adamsport. "Never, if I can stop it!" Gus replied. "We didn't need to spend eighty million for that boondoggle. Matt Godwin insists it hasn't hurt our profits. He told the directors if CPC stockholders are against it, his Foundation will take over the building. Good. Let him do it! I don't plan to live in Adamsport."

In addition to putting the finger on her, Sally told Becky, Gus was going to stop Matt one way or the other. At the end of the interview, when Wilder asked Gus where Matt's Foundation got the money to buy the First Church and underwrite their upcoming Sunday morning television program, Gus had snorted, "Why don't you poke around Cuba? There's a guy down there named Torvo Vigilar who kept Godwin prisoner for three months. He probably knows the answer.

Ask him about the gold and a Hindu named Ramachanda. Matt probably stole it from him."

Before Sally hung up she calmed down enough to tell Becky to give Matt a big hug for her. She missed him. "I'm coming home Saturday," she said. "Someone's got to convince Daddy Ike to stop the Godwin war and listen to Matt." She chuckled. "Even if Daddy doesn't think he's God, he can pretend that he is."

38

Irene was sure that, sex circus or not, they were all walking a tightrope. In the tent below them, millions of faces were eagerly watching, anticipating their first misstep.

She certainly didn't condone Matt's sex life or believe it when Jill told her that Matt still loved her. No man could love two women and keep them happy. Certainly not three of them. Although she hadn't discussed it with Father Tim, she really felt a bit guilty about making love to him. She certainly wouldn't encourage him to do it again. She was vaguely aware that she loved Tim and he was no longer "Father" in her mind. An uneasy question kept popping into her head. What if she had surrendered to (seduced?) Tim before Matt got involved with Jill or Peachy? Certainly it would have been possible. Would she have tried to convince herself that she could love Matt and Tim, too?

Not knowing exactly what she wanted to say to Matt but using the excuse of Sally's impending visit and Ike's agreement that the Godwins should talk together, she telephoned the parsonage. Lovejoy told her that she would probably find Matt in the CPC building. He gave her the number and she telephoned him. She told him in detail and in a rather formal tone about the interview that Gus Belshin had given Mike Wilder. "I thought you should know," she said.

But Matt just laughed. "Until Gus solves his marital problems, and maybe even after, I have an enthusiastic admirer—Gus's wife, Miriam. She loves me better than Gus. She promised that she'd vote her some two million shares any way I wish."

It surprised Irene that Matt was talking to her so casually, almost as if he were oblivious to the fact that they hadn't spoken to each other for nearly a year.

"The furniture has just arrived for my new office," he said. "Why don't you come down and see it? Right now I am trying to decide whether to have 'Isaac Matthew Godwin, President', gold leafed on the door, or 'Reverend Matthew Godwin'," he chuckled.

"Why don't you just put I. M. God on the door?" Irene asked

sarcastically. "But maybe you don't have to advertise, since everyone knows it anyway."

"Oh, come on. Hop into the car and come on down. I'll meet you in the lobby. With the exception of a few painters and electricians putting the finishing touches on the building, the entire thirty floors and a million square feet of floor space is empty. We'll have it to ourselves. I'll meet you in the lobby."

Twenty minutes later he greeted her at the doors. He hugged her, but she pulled away from his enthusiastic embrace and scowled when he said, "I've missed you." She wanted to say, "I miss you too," but she couldn't. Confused tears were flooding her eyes as he guided her into the elevator.

"CPC will occupy only ten floors of the building," he told her. "The other twenty are sold out and will be occupied within the next two months, including the twenty-eighth floor for the Foundation. Roje is planning to move in next week."

On the twenty-ninth floor they stepped out of the elevator, and walked through a spacious reception area. He opened his office door, took her hand, and led her across the immense room on to a private balcony. A few miles away Boston and the Atlantic Ocean lay serenely in the sun.

Turning away from the view, Irene noticed that the office was furnished more like a penthouse apartment than a business office. In one corner was a well-stocked wet bar. Two sofas, a teak coffee table, several wing chairs and barrel chairs were tastefully arranged in the center of the room. Along one wall empty shelves waited to house several hundred books that would soon arrive. She examined an I.B.M. computer and monitor that sat on one edge of a long teak desk. "That's my contact with CPC reality," he said.

She gestured toward two huge Oriental rugs that looked like scatter rugs on the polished wood floor. "I like your Bokaras," she said.

Matt laughed. "I bought them for Ike, who hates broadloom. Incidentally, I'm looking for a secretary. A woman like yourself who has a business degree and can help me analyze the tons of information that this computer gives me access to." He grinned at her. "The one I have in mind has two kids named Ink and Able. She has nice warm tits and a pretty ass. With a secretary like that, when the going gets tough we can say 'the hell with it' and lock the door and make love on the balcony or on the rugs. Or, if you prefer, that sofa over there pulls out into a double bed." Standing behind the bar, he was mixing a pitcher of martinis. "It's a little too early to drink," he said, "but from the sardonic expression on your face, I think you may need one."

"How the hell many women do you need?" she demanded angrily. But she sat down on a leather bar stool and accepted the martini that he poured for her in a tall stemmed glass. She didn't wait for his answer. "Let's get things straight. I didn't come here to renew old acquaintances. I came here to talk about our sons. Among other things, Ink and Able have been pleading with me to join your crazy church. They want to run around in their birthday suits and look at all the little girls naked."

"They can look at older ladies, too," Matt said, "including their mother, if she joins."

Irene felt suddenly flushed. "I'm not so puritanical as you might think," she said, feeling a tingle of alcohol in her blood. "Maybe it's a good idea. If the boys grow up seeing women naked, they might not be so obsessed with them as their father is. But personally I'm not interested. I'm not so liberated as your other women friends." Irene didn't sound as certain as her words were. She remembered Father Tim ruminating with her that the clothing-optional area in the church had some good features. "Many Catholic countries are beginning to accept nude beaches as a normal way of life," Tim had told her.

As if he read her mind, Matt asked if Father Tim had been shocked by the opening night service.

Irene quickly wiped away a flashing memory of Tim lying in her arms. "He's worried about you," Irene said. "He's afraid that you may become chief guru of a crazy cult religion. He's not at all convinced that the First Church is offering any kind of sound theology. On the other hand, I'm sure that Father Tim is not so holy. He'd probably like to join your nudist club, if he dared."

Matt shrugged. "He's welcome any time. He doesn't have to believe that he's God. But he should realize that we're not a philosophical organization. Our theology is just as valid as the Catholic Trinity. Our religious and moral goals are as sane as any Christian's." Matt walked out from behind the bar and put his arms around Irene. "For example, you are God. I love God. I love you, too." He kissed her neck. "I especially love you," he said, cupping her face for a moment. "And I've missed arguing with you and occasionally seducing you in spite of yourself." Grinning at her, he refilled her glass.

"I didn't come here to get soused, or screwed," she said. Nevertheless she sipped the second drink. "I haven't had lunch, and I'm supposed to play golf with Emily Lovejoy—another one of your lady friends. Damn you, Matt Godwin, I don't even know why I'm here drinking with you. This is no celebration. I told you the reason I came—Sally is coming home. And you had better watch out for Gus Belshin. He really hates you. You've screwed up his financial life and his love life. When Becky told Ike about Belshin and the interview with Wilder, he agreed with Sally. He told me to tell you the time has come for a Godwin family conference."

Matt stared at her. "You mean that Ike wants to talk with me and Jill?"

Irene looked at him a little startled.

"Jill is a Godwin," Matt said calmly, "as much as you are. And who's going to speak for Ike? You or Becky or Hendy?"

Irene hadn't really expected that Jill would be at a family conference. "I really don't know whether he meant Jill. He hasn't even mentioned her name during the past eighteen months." Then, wondering what his reaction was going to be, she said, "Ike has a big surprise for you and Gus. He has regained almost full command of his tongue. Oh, he slurs an occasional word, but like it or not," she grinned at Matt, "big Daddy is going to try to move the pieces on the board. He's sure that the directors will elect him chairman and chief executive officer of CPC. Under his surveillance, you can continue as president, but Gus Belshin is going to have to take in washing."

Instead of being angry, Matt hugged her. "That's great! But Ike shouldn't tempt fate. If I were him, I'd elect *you* president. You know how Ike thinks better than he does himself."

Irene shook her head despairingly. "You're crazier than ever," she said, pulling away from him. "The big question is whether you and Ike can talk sensibly with each other about CPC and not let your weird moralities—including the fact that you are sleeping with his wife—screw you both up." She laughed a little sourly. "And I use the word 'screw' advisedly. If you do, despite his own sex problems, Gus Belshin will win the ball game."

Irene felt the zipper on the back of her dress sliding down. "Damn you!" she said angrily. "As usual you aren't listening to me!" With her loosened dress draped on her shoulders, she stared at him through tears in her eyes. She knew that she couldn't help herself. Two martinis had released memories of the loving part of their fifteen years together. She put her arms around him, forgetting momentarily their many arguments. "I can't help the way I am," she whispered in his neck. "I'm a person, too. I love you, but you've hurt me deeply."

As he edged her to the sofa, she sighed, "You've got two women. Why do you want me?"

"I told you, I love you."

"Then, promise me, when Sally comes home, let's all try to be friends." She let him lift her dress over her shoulders. He slipped off her bra and cupped her breasts and kissed them.

"You and I *are* friends," he said, "and always will be. I want you to come home, tonight." He kissed her salty lips. "The carriage house isn't a harem; it's a home. Jill and Peachy and I care for each other. They enjoy sex with me but not because they feel obligated. We make love when and if they want to. We don't own each other's minds or bodies. I'm sure that Jill has told you that. She and Peachy can leave any time they wish. If they find another man, or if they decide they prefer monogamy, I will still love them."

"I don't know what motivates Peachy . . ." Irene still hadn't made up her mind. How could she make love with a man—her husband, no less—who calmly told her that he loved two other women? But she let him remove her panty hose and her panties. "I know darn well that Jill would prefer you all to herself. And so would I," she said sadly, watching him undress. "What makes you so goddamned special that you should have three women at your beck and call?"

Sitting beside her naked on the sofa, Matt tried to put her hand on his erect penis. "I can talk better connected to you," he said, but she pulled her hand away. "I really don't think that I'm so special," he said. "I'm just lucky. I found three women who like me. You may not always love me, but deep down, like Jill and Peachy, I make your brain tingle. I bring excitement and new ways of looking at things into your lives." He bent over and kissed her breast. His tongue was shivery on her nipple. "You're a beautiful woman, Renee. I'm sure that you could find one man who would be faithful to you for the rest of your life, but he might not challenge you, like I do."

"Who says I want to be challenged?" Irene demanded. Yet she knew that basically the reason she had been so attracted to Matt many years ago, and had defied her Catholic upbringing by marrying him, was because he was not a follower. He would kneel before her but not before God or saints. She had read that some biologists believed that this attraction to the most powerful male was a natural female response to make sure that the best genes were perpetuated.

She opened her legs to accept Matt's gently probing fingers. "See," he said, grinning boyishly at her, "arguing with me makes your brain come alive. Your vagina can't help itself, it gets wet and ready. Neither you nor Jill or Peachy can surrender to a man who isn't on an intellectual par with them. Like the three of you, many women are getting better educated; they read more, think more than most men. You could have been a successful career woman, but even then your options would have been limited. Your kind of women outnumber the available men. Statistically your options are limited."

He grinned at her as she finally curled into his arms and began to play with his penis. "This is a hell of a way to woo any woman," she said. "You're trying to tell me that I have no choice. I have to accept a polygamous man." She couldn't help laughing. "My God—and I don't mean you as *my* God—you are cracked! What I'd like to know is whether the polygamous man would accept a polygamous wife?"

"Of course he would. At the interpersonal level we're talking about, my options are as limited as yours. I don't think there are very many Irenes, Jills, Peachys waiting out there with bated breath for me. Renee, come home. Today is Tuesday. If you'll come home for the next four nights and live with us as an experiment, I'll be a good boy. When we all get together at the Big House, I'll even give Ike a great big hug."

"What about Jill?"

"I hope that she'll come. She really likes Ike."

"But not Peachy—she's not family."

"Of course she is. Peachy knows everything that's going on. And she loves older men." Matt chuckled. "She'll love Ike. Can Ike still get it up?"

"Damn you, I haven't asked him!"

Matt released the spring on the sofa that brought out the bed. He pushed her back and spread her legs. Kneeling between them, he held her hands for a moment. "I really have missed you, Renee," he said softly. "You look so vulnerable and loving. I never want to hurt you," he sighed, "but I know that I do." He kissed her stomach, and snuggled his face into her vulva. "You taste nice, sweetie."

"Do you have to do that?"

"Don't you like it?"

Sobbing, she pulled him up to her face. "Oh God, Matt, I guess I do. The trouble is that I really don't know what I like. Anyway, I don't want to talk about it. I just know I love you. Come inside me." She arched her behind until she captured him deep inside her. "Maybe it's too late for me to get rid of my hang-ups; maybe I can't talk about sex." And then she laughed. "Maybe I don't have to. You've got two other women who never stop talking."

Joining Emily Lovejoy for golf an hour later, Irene told her that she had decided to move back to the carriage house. "But only until Sally arrives—until Saturday." She knew that she sounded a little grim. "To see if I can take it at close quarters."

Emily hugged her. "Honey, you can't lose," she said. "I'm glad you decided to do it. It's your territory. You got there first. You've got Ink and Able, and you've got just as good female parts as Jill and Peachy. I'll tell you a secret. After years of loving Roje, I learned that whenever I get jealous, not to let him know it. Be cool. Jealousy is like a bad cold: it makes you sniffle and feel miserable for a while, but it will go away." She laughed. "Another lover is a sure cure."

She stared at Irene quizzically. "Why not Father Tim?" Startled, Irene hoped that she wasn't blushing. "It's none of my business," Emily said, wondering if she could elicit a confession. "Even if he doesn't dare tell you, it's obvious Father Tim loves you." Anyway, he'd be a nice antidote for any neurotic feelings you might be having."

Irene laughed and hoped that it didn't sound like guilty laughter.

"You really don't have to worry about Jill or Peachy," Emily said, getting no response. "They love Matt and I'm sure that they enjoy him in bed, but they never kowtow to him. They could probably even live happily without him. They argue and disagree with him continuously. He and Roje love that kind of interaction with women. It eroticizes them. Matt never tries to control their thoughts. If Jill and Peachy frustrate him, he thinks it's amusing. Sometimes I think he really is God. He's so patient—even laughing—with people who don't agree with him. 'In the scheme of things,' he tells them, 'my ego is less than a wave on the beach. The waves you make are just as valid as mine.'"

Emily was silent a moment, then she made a perfect hundred-and-seventy-five-yard drive down the fairway. Jumping with excitement at her accomplishment, she hugged Irene. "Beat that, sweetie! And stop worrying! I've only been to bed with your husband twice since we nearly died in Cuba. Peachy rarely misses a month with Roje. She makes him think he's young again. It makes him nicer to live with." She grinned at Irene. "But at sixty-five, my age is pushing me back toward monogamy. Unless a miracle occurs and I could intrigue Ike Godwin or some other loving seventy-four-year-old man like John Codman."

To Irene's amazement, as they played the eighteen holes, Emily gradually told her not only about Sylvanus Williams but also several other men she had been in love with during the past forty years of marriage. "A few years after Roje and I were married," she said, "I discovered that he was a pushover for any female who 'adored' his novels. I was afraid that I was a moron. Roje put up with me, but no one else could love a woman like me. I wasn't a great armchair philosopher like the females Roje was attracted to. Then after a few years of terror and a conviction that Roje would run off with one of his disciples, I had the good fortune to meet a man who enjoyed a straight-out, caring female who liked to fuck and not make a religion out of it." Emily chuckled. "Not that I don't enjoy Matt's ideas, but I'm not completely on his wavelength. Religious fucking is great some of the time, but there's lusty pirates in the world, too, who like to conquer a woman and afterward fall into a blissful, snoring dreamland. I'm sure you know it better than I do. Sex with Matt is like a throw of the dice; you never know on a particular night whether you are bedding with a lusty pirate or Jesus come back to earth."

Before Irene left the club she was having second thoughts. Could she really go through with it? Could she live under the same roof—in her own home—with two women who were sleeping with her husband? Could she convince Ike and Becky, or herself for that matter, that she really didn't hate Jill and Peachy? Back at the Big House, after showering and changing clothes, she spotted Becky sitting on the verandah and waiting for Hendy. She told Becky that she had talked with Matt and that he would come for dinner Saturday. He wanted to see Sally and talk with Ike. "And he's bringing Jill."

"Oh Jesus—not Jill!" Becky said angrily. "I'm sure Ike doesn't want her in any family conference. He means close family. Controlled Power Corporation and Matt's First Church are enough of a problem. If Jill comes, instead of a discussion I'm afraid we'll have a family brawl. Damn it! I can't understand why Ike hasn't divorced her, or she him."

Irene had no solutions. "You might as well face it, Matt considers Peachy part of his family, too. He's planning to bring her."

Becky sighed. "He's quite mad. Maybe we'd better forget it. I'm sure that Ike won't be rational if Jill is around."

Becky was really astonished when Irene told her that she was planning to move back to the carriage house for a few days. "You're out of your mind," she said. "You're not really going to sleep in the same house with two women that your husband is screwing? For God's sake, Irene, don't do it! My brother must have softened your brain. You should kick them all out on their asses."

"I know it's crazy," Irene said, "but I've got to stop drifting. After a few days I'll probably convince myself that I can't take it, and I'll do what I have to do—file for divorce."

Becky hugged her. "You are a softie. But keep in mind, Ike's not like you. He's not accepting half a business or half a wife. What does Father Tim think about all this?"

Irene shook her head. "I didn't consult with him."

"You should. I'm sure he'll be as shocked as I am. You're a better Godwin than Matt. When the smoke clears, come back here. We'll nurse your wounds."

Later, when she told Ike that she had capitulated to Matt, he was astonished. "The pope should make you a saint," he growled at her. "If I were you I would have kicked those whores out of my home." He ignored her loving hug and her warning that he must keep cool. "I can't believe that you approve of my wife living down there with your husband, right under our noses. She's got more nerve than Gus Belshin. As for Peachy Stein, or whatever her name really is, everyone in Adamsport knows that she screwed her way through high school. Those kids of hers may be Walshes, but even Bill Walsh doesn't want that kind of grandchildren. She and Jill are evil, designing women. And my son is sick in the head to do this to you. All they want is a piece of the Godwin pie."

Irene surprised herself by taking Matt's side. "Your son isn't very rich," she said."His girl friends won't get that much. His biggest asset is the half-million shares of CPC that you gave him, and he can't sell those."

"Damned right, he can't!" Ike stormed. "He needs those shares and Sally's to stay in control. But you can bet that those ladies, if you can call them that, expect that he'll inherit my money. And don't tell me that Matt is poor. Becky gave me a pretty good idea of where he got the money to support his sexual merry-go-round. Maybe he never actually got his hands on Williams's gold, but maybe he did and refuses to admit it. Why in hell should some Arab support his Foundation? Why did the Cubans keep him prisoner for three months? There's a pretty smelly can of worms somewhere." Ike shook his head. "Becky is right. You should divorce him."

"Why haven't you divorced Jill?"

It was the first time Irene had dared to ask Ike that question. Even Becky treaded lightly and rarely mentioned Jill's name.

Ike stared at her for almost a minute, a faraway expression on his face and his eyes misty.

"Becoth . . . becoth . . ." He stammered, momentarily losing control. "Because, goddammit, I think that she still loves me. But thirty-two years difference was too much. I don't blame her if she wanted a younger man. But not my goddamned son."

"And you still love her?"

Unable to speak, Ike barely nodded. Then he said quite clearly, "Not just for sex. Even before this damned shock, Jill knew that I wasn't some twenty-year-old demon lover." He shook his head ruefully. "I guess, right from the beginning, I loved her the same way I love Sally. A cussed daughter who'll sit in your lap and give you a thousand Judas kisses. All the while she's conning you, and you both know that she needs to get her ass slapped. But you love her anyway, because deep down you know that she's a naive little moron and needs a protector."

Irene laughed, and squeezed his hand. "You really are a throwback to the days of chivalry, Ike. Jill is no moron, and neither is Matt. But Matt sure is naive. He really believes that he can save the world." She hugged him and kissed his cheek. "It begins with you as God," she said, aware that she was sounding a little like Matt. "A loving God can't hate anyone, and you're proving it."

"Bull shit," Ike snorted. "Matt better reread the Old Testament. I'm not God. God's up there somewhere and He'll get Matt yet. Hang him by his balls." He patted Irene's cheek. "Never mind. I love you. You're my third daughter and probably the most naive one of all."

Even as she drove the quarter of a mile to the carriage house, only dimly aware of the new spring canopy of leaves on the maples and elms that girded the secluded drive, Irene wasn't at all sure that she was really going to stay one night, let alone three. Thinking grimly how ludicrous it was to be packing a suitcase to go to her own home, she had tossed in underwear, panty hose, another dress, and a nightgown. She wondered if Jill and Peachy wore nightgowns. Not Peachy, probably; modesty wasn't in her dictionary. Would Matt try to convince them all to get in bed with him? How could one man screw three women? The women would have to take care of each other. Jesus, Mary, and Joseph . . . She was sure of one thing; she could never make love to another woman. She was no lesbian. Matt would learn one thing fast. She didn't care what *they* did, but *she* wasn't coming home for a sex orgy.

She knew that she was arriving early. It was only quarter of four, but making love with her husband for the first time in eighteen months in his office at ten o'clock in the morning, playing golf the same day with one more woman whom he had bedded, was confusing her sense of time. She had lived a month in one day. Ringing the door chime, she was thinking that the reason she was so early was that she couldn't stand the suspense of waiting for her own execution. She knew that Ink and Able wouldn't be home yet. They had spring baseball practice at the Academy. She never asked the boys what happened during the few nights a week that they slept at the carriage house, but Able told her that dinner was a noisy affair with everyone talking and all the kids being queried about schoolwork and being involved in discussions about everything from space travel to economics and "Pop's ideas about sex."

"It's all right to play around with girls and let girls play around with you," Ink told her with a big grin. "But absolutely no penises into vaginas. Not until we are seventeen, and not even then unless we really like the girl and we both know all about birth control."

She knew that Ink and Able were sleeping in one of the three attic rooms with David. Cheryl slept in her own room on the second floor, but Ink said she was "always up in the attic, and getting in our hair."

Jill and Peachy had separate bedrooms—the former guest rooms— and no one ever slept in Mom's bed "except Pop." Both the boys knew that Pop slept with Jill sometimes and Peachy sometimes, usually in the new bedroom overlooking the swimming pool. "It has a huge bed with the bounce of a trampoline," Able told her. "When you jump on it, your head nearly hits the ceiling."

While Ink didn't elaborate, she guessed that Matt must sleep there with one or both of his "wives." He was worse than a damned Mormon, she thought grimly. At least the more wealthy ones had provided their women with separate homes.

To her surprise, instead of the housekeeper, Jill opened the door. "Thank God," she said happily and hugged her. "And I mean God out there somewhere. You've come home. Matt needs you, and Peachy and I need you." Leading her into the living room, Jill told her that Roje had just telephoned. "Matt didn't know where to reach you. He had to fly to Chicago. He left about an hour ago in the company plane. He'll be back tomorrow."

Irene grimaced. She wondered if Matt had gone purposely. Was he assuming that without him to fall back on, she'd have to make a truce with Jill and Peachy?

"I really think he had to go," Jill said, reading her mind. "He's been trying to work out a friendly takeover of the Howell Bridge and Iron Company. The chairman, Bob Howell, seemed agreeable, but after Gus Belshin's full-page advertisement and the feature story on the Godwins in the *Wall Street Journal,* he got nervous. Matt flew out to try to calm him down."

"I really don't think I should stay," Irene said. "I think Matt hypnotized me this morning, but I'm coming out of it."

"That's silly," Jill said gently. "This is your house. We don't need him. I think we need a drink. Believe me, I'm more shaky than you are. When Matt called and said you were coming, much as I want you here, I kept thinking we should apologize. Peachy and I are the temporary interlopers."

Irene wondered what she meant by "temporary," but she didn't ask. "You don't have to apologize," she said. "Matt expected I'd divorce him. Knowing him, I could be certain that he wasn't going to live alone for the past year." She watched Jill nervously putting ice in a glass from a cooler on the living room bar. "Pour me a scotch," Irene laughed uneasily. "I think I need it."

"Peachy will be home in a little while," Jill said. "She's in charge of Tuesday night services along with Mark Vacchio, a new minister who has joined the church. It's open forum night, and several hundred people usually turn out. The majority rules on what moralities they will explore. We can go if you wish. If there's time after the discussion, they usually run a film." Jill laughed. "Sexy or controversial, but with a moral, of course."

Sitting uneasily on the sofa, Irene sipped her drink. "Two martinis this morning got me this far. I'm really not ready to appear in public with you or Peachy." She sighed. "I'm a pretty conservative person. I still go to mass once a week. I was taught that marriage is a sacrament. Obviously a lot of Catholics don't believe it anymore. But in the 1960s, when I was still in my teens, I was pretty shocked by the hippies and the flower children. My parents were very strict. No daughter of theirs would ever drink booze, let alone take drugs, and certainly she wouldn't go to bed with a man before he married her. They were pretty upset when I married a Protestant. Fortunately for them, they didn't live to discover that Matt wasn't even a Christian." Irene blinked away the tears in her eyes. "I was the perennial American good girl."

"So was I," Jill said. She wanted to reach out and touch Irene, and somehow assure her that they were not competitors. "I got married when I was twenty-two. Happily, I thought. But I was more career-oriented than you were. I was sure that I could have my cake and eat it. Steven, my first husband, believed that reading stories to our kids or my acting with the local repertory company was career enough. When I made it clear that it wasn't enough, he divorced me. I divorced my second husband because," Jill grinned, "to use a word that Matt detests, he was 'cunt happy'."

"Isn't Matt?" Irene demanded sarcastically.

Jill shook her head. "You know that's not true. Matt's a whole different ball game. He has a feminine super-sense, and he practices what he preaches. For him a woman is a whole person and he idealizes women. If he enjoys your body, it's because he sees in every curve and dimension of you a reflection of yourself as a special person—and something else beyond." She smiled. "You know as well as I do that Matt enjoys sex, and he's not always saintly either. You simply have to dare to have brain sex with him and be willing to shake off your old cultural conditionings and hang-ups. If you don't, you miss half the joy of it."

Irene stared at her hopelessly. She was feeling more at ease. It was impossible not to like Jill. "I'm sure Matt told you that's my problem. He was always telling me to let go. Be an abandoned woman. Take off my bra and don't wear any underwear. God forbid panty hose." She put down her glass, her hand shaking. "I love him, but I never could be a seductress. I'm afraid that in close confinement with you and Peachy, I'd feel so inferior that I'd be in tears half the time—or madly jealous." Irene couldn't help herself. She was suddenly sobbing.

Overwhelmed, Jill put her arms around her and stroked her face. "There's one thing you're overlooking," Jill said softly, and her eyes were glistening. "This isn't the sixties. None of us are young hippies. We're three middle-aged women. Peachy may be a few years younger, but she'll be forty next year. And Matt isn't a frustrated Playboy dreamer trying to prove his virility with younger women. He enjoys the very different style of woman that each of us is. He's aware of our infirmities—and we of his. None of us are too fat, but I'm plumper than you or Peachy. Neither Peachy or I can read a damned thing without glasses. We get colds and headaches, we get depressed, and we are occasionally constipated." She laughed. "Maybe it wouldn't work if we were younger and competing with each other or having a bunch of kids with one father. But we're past the child-bearing era. None of us have been deprived maternally. We might even still have time to squeeze out one more kid—but that would be a dumb thing to do."

Jill was holding Irene's hand, and her honesty was magnetic. "I guess what I'm trying to tell you is that I agree with Matt, that the four of us living together could be an experiment in love. We could be a variation on the monogamous middle-age family. We might even make it together until death do us part."

She tried to explain that she and Peachy had not turned the

carriage house into a total commune. "Matt provides the roof, and most of the food. Peachy earns plenty from the Foundation. She donates her time to the church. I have enough savings to support myself." She grinned. "Despite what Becky believes, I haven't stayed married to Ike because I want some of his millions. I don't want alimony, and I don't expect to inherit anything. I want Ike to live to be a hundred. I know I've hurt him, but I warned him when I married him that he could never own me." Jill was relieved to see that Irene was half smiling at her. "Anyway, I'm self-supporting. At the moment the First Church is paying me $35,000 a year as program director."

She poured Irene another scotch. "What it really shakes down to is that morally Peachy and I have been living beyond the pale of approved monogamous sexual behavior. But even a polygamous family has to have some rules. When we make love with Matt, each of us wants to be alone with him. When we're together we may tease him sexually and hug and kiss him, but there's no group sex. Peachy and I are totally heterosexual. We hug each other, we may even lie in each other's arms, but we're not bisexual. All of us, including the kids, get plenty of loving appreciation, but there is no overt sex-making in front of the children. Nudity at meals is forbidden, but there is plenty of casual nudity around the house." Jill chuckled. "As you know, Matt can't abide rooms heated much above sixty-two degrees, so ever since January, when I arrived, it's been so cold that we keep our asses covered most of the time."

"I suppose that I.M. God decides who he sleeps with," Irene said. She still couldn't believe they could all cope with the inevitable sexual jealousies.

Jill laughed. "No way! He gets us sequentially. For continuity each of us has been sleeping alone with him four nights in a row. But Peachy and I hope, if you come back to live with us, that you'll join the cycle." She looked at Irene a little apprehensively. "Obviously, Matt won't be here tonight, but tomorrow you and he could initiate a new three-night switchover."

Irene stared at her incredulously. "You mean that instead of sharing the master roughly 180 nights a year, you'll be reduced to 120 nights?" She couldn't help laughing. "God-almighty, even when I had him 365 nights in a row, I don't remember that he was ever that active!"

Jill laughed. "Matt told us that there's no compulsion or guarantee that he would climax on a particular evening." She was embarrassed, but she decided to be honest. "But he is very accommodating. He claims he learned how by reading ancient sex manuals. They were written by Chinese courtesans who convinced their lords and masters that the way to live a long life was to enjoy extended sexual intercourse and conserve their seed.

"Oh, Irene, Matt isn't like any other man that I've ever met, except perhaps Roje. He's not patriarchal. He's not the lord and master and he doesn't want to be. But he believes that new-style family groupings like this, and in many other combinations, are inevitable. Today there are more than eight million women with young children who somehow or other manage to function in fatherless families. Nearly 25 percent of them live in poverty. There are millions of other women, like us, who live alone because we can't find another man, or have given up searching. Matt calls us a TCC—a Temporary Committed Coalition. It's a moral experiment that millions of people would try if they had church sanction and approval." Jill looked at her timidly, wondering what Irene was thinking. "I'm sure that Matt hopes that the four of us have the nerve to try. Maybe we can become a PCC—a Permanently Committed Coalition."

"I'm not convinced," Irene insisted. "One pouting woman could wreck it. It's absolutely against human nature. I can't believe bigamy or polygamy could ever become a permanent way of life. Men and women are too possessive."

"You may be right," Jill said. "But fifty years ago, everyone thought that the lifetime nuclear family—a husband and wife and two or more children—was here to stay. Instead, only 7 percent of all monogamous families are a permanent way of life. Extended sexual coalitions may not be for everybody, but they may have a stability for many people that may be easier to maintain than monogamous marriage." She shrugged. "You may be different. At forty-five you may still think that you can find a guy who meets your standards and wants to live with you in a monogamous wonderland. But second marriages have a failure rate higher than the first ones. For me and Peachy, Matt's lovely daydream of a First Church and searching for new moralities is a lot more challenging than drifting in and out of strange beds looking for the one and only Mr. Right. And never forget, to coin a phrase, this is a 'floating crap game.' Peachy and I aren't promiscuous, but Matt never told us that we can't keep looking. Emily Lovejoy may have told you that Peachy sleeps with Roje occasionally, but that's the extent of her wanderings. As for me, at the moment, two Godwins are problem enough."

While they were talking, Peachy arrived with David and Cheryl. Without embarrassment she hugged Irene and kissed her cheek enthusiastically. "Gosh, I'm so sorry that I missed your discussion. But don't worry, talk is a way of life with us." Peachy looked at her watch. "It's five-thirty. I have to be back at church by seven. If it's okay with you, we usually help Mrs. Goodale prepare dinner."

Back in her own kitchen, although Mrs. Goodale seemed a little distant and disapproving, Irene felt her tenseness slowly disappearing, and she was glad that Matt wouldn't be home tonight. Whether she could ever swallow this happy, sexually polymorphous arrangement was still up for grabs. But she had to admit that she enjoyed the vibrant, laughing camaraderie that Peachy and Jill created and shared easily with the children.

At dinner, Peachy told them that the open forum tonight was going to consider genetic engineering. She was sorry that Matt wasn't going to be here.

"The Foundation's position is clear," she said. "We don't believe that we are on the brink of disaster with some mad Dr. Frankenstein purposely, or inadvertently, creating a monster, or cloning people. But if that should occur, or if we're dubious about the environmental effects of certain recombinations, hopefully we can deal with them better than we have with nuclear power." Peachy grinned at Irene. "I'm worse than Matt; I preach too much. Even Jill has to tell us to shut up every once in a while. Anyway, what I hope to get across tonight is that as God we are creative. We're searching to improve the quality of life, to understand it better and make life more fulfilling. Creating plant life that is more resistant to frost, or plants which extract their own fertilizers from the air, or creating genes that have greater longevity, allowing us to live longer and healthier lives, is really part of the evolutionary process. Man acting as God and bringing new human life forms into existence may raise many new moral problems, but it isn't creating monsters."

"I read *Frankenstein*," Ink interjected. "The monster wasn't really a bad guy. Not until people screwed him up and told him how ugly he was."

Ink had precipitated a discussion that not only included Mary Shelley's creation but the revelation that Mary's father was a Godwin. "His name was William Godwin," Peachy told them and sent the boys to the *Britannica* to see if they could find out more about a possible relative.

Irene listened in fascination as Jill and Peachy gradually led the children into thinking about "the beginnings of man and woman," "creationism," Genesis, and a comparison of the Old Testament with Greek and Hindu and Egyptian mythologies.

The conversation finally came to an end when Peachy told them that she had to get back to the church for the open forum. Before she did, Cheryl waved her hand and said that she had a question. "I still don't understand why God was so angry with Adam and Eve," she smiled mischievously at Irene, Peachy, and Jill. "After all, poor Adam only had one wife." Cheryl skipped off, leaving them open-mouthed to think about that.

Peachy agreed with Irene that until things settled down, they'd better not appear in public together. David's and Cheryl's grandfather, Bill Walsh, would be only too happy to compare Matt to Charles

Manson. She smiled at Irene affectionately. "You really are nice—and beautiful, too. I'm glad you don't hate me. Believe me, we're both as nervous as you are. The only thing that Jill and I are sure of is that if we can manage to suppress our egos a little and if we dare to take each other into our confidence and share our fears, we can not only live together, but we'll have more input and mind-boggling things to share than we'd ever have in a nuclear family."

After she had gone, Irene told Jill that she was "pooped" and retreated to her room to take a bath. Alone in her own bedroom, Irene tried to assimilate the events of a crazy day. Close to midnight she was still puttering around, renewing acquaintances with things she had left in the carriage house more than a year ago, when she heard a knock on the door. It was Peachy, wearing a nightgown.

"I just got back from church," she said nervously. "I hope I didn't wake you up. I noticed that your light was on. Jill told me that you and she had a nice talk. I just want you to know one thing. I really admire you. I think we could have a lot of joy together. But to make it work, the three of us have to run things. Not Matt."

Laughing, to Irene's surprise she flopped down on the bed beside her. "We have to dare to tell each other every bad feeling that we may be having about each other, and about Matt, and at the same time try not to be defensive but really try to be the other person. One thing you should know is that Jill and I are not in sexual competition. We never discuss how Matt does or does not perform with us. We've discovered that Matt is not orgasm-oriented. With him, making love is a natural consequence of conversation. When words finally become ineffable, you join bodies. His women always come first, literally and figuratively. If you're tired or just feel like hugging, or if you're passionate and need to climax, you can set your own pace with him."

Peachy looked at Irene a little embarrassed. "Good lord, this is ridiculous. I'm telling you things you must already know. I hope you're not angry with me." Before she left, she kissed Irene's cheek. "I hope that you like your husband as much as we do."

Staring at the door as it closed behind Peachy, Irene didn't know whether to laugh or cry.

39

To Irene's surprise, when Matt returned from Chicago she was less tense with him and on a friendlier level of communication than they had achieved in fifteen years. Was it because, as Matt laughingly told her, they had had a sabbatical from marriage and discovered that they missed each other? Or was it because there was no longer any question of monogamous ownership? Irene was tempted to tell him about Father Tim, but then decided she had no right to jeopardize Tim's life as a priest.

Wednesday, the first night, after the children were hugged and kissed good-night, and told "no television" but they could read in bed, Matt told her that she could have her choice of bedrooms. It was only nine-thirty. Irene shrugged, and smiled a little too sweetly, Matt thought. "When in Rome, I certainly don't want to change protocol," she said. "Jill told me that most nights, even after church services, during the week," Irene tried to conceal the nervous flutter in her voice, "you all talk together in the new bedroom. It's quite an addition to the house. I'll be interested to see how you handle your harem."

Taking her time undressing upstairs in her bedroom, knowing that they were already gathered in the bedroom overlooking the pool, Irene finally decided to arrive in a terry cloth bathrobe. Feeling a little trembly, she finally came downstairs and walked into the new bedroom. Through sliding glass doors on the far side she could see that the swimming pool in the background was lighted. The room was easily forty feet by forty feet, and, although it was out of character with the rest of the house, it provided an erotic background for lovemaking. She was a little shocked to see that Matt was lying on the bed wearing nothing but glasses as he read from a typewritten report to Jill and Peachy. At least Jill was wearing a nightgown, and Peachy, who had just showered, was wrapped in a towel. Matt pulled Irene down on the bed beside him into a heap of pillows, but she edged away from him.

"Don't worry," Peachy smiled reassuringly at her. "We have one rule that is never broken. If the King of Siam gets too excited when he's entertaining his half-naked ladies, the sleep-alone ladies depart and leave him to the lady of the night." Leaning on her elbows, she grinned at Irene. "The only change is that tonight there are two sleep-alone ladies—Jill and me. We'll leave before midnight, anyway, no matter what happens."

"In the meantime," Jill said, "all that really ever happens is that we forget our adult inhibitions and talk and play like kids." She got attention from Matt by yanking his big toe. "The biggest kid is Matt. He can't believe that we're a variation on the little girls next door, the ones he tried to undress in one of the parlors in the Big House." She laughed. "Now we're all middle-aged, but playing doctor and looking at each other naked and vulnerable is almost as much fun as when we were kids."

"The meeting will come to order," Matt said, and he grinned at Peachy, who had evidently decided that she was more comfortable without her towel. "The first order of the night is this report from Tom

Ferris. Ferris was Sylvie's lawyer," Matt explained to Irene. "He's a very conscientious guy and a specialist in First Amendment law. I hired him to represent the church and the Foundation. He keeps track of our opposition. He joined the First Church, not because we are a client, but because he finds us challenging. On the other hand, he's afraid that we may have a very short life in Massachusetts.

"According to Tom, George Gallagher, who, as you know, is a lawyer, has been consulting with the district attorney, Sam Hardman. Hardman is a devout Methodist. They think they can close us down. They don't believe that we're a religion in the constitutional sense of the word."

Matt shook his head. "When you challenge the tried and true mores, you evoke all kinds of strange ogres. Hardman told Ferris that the State of California is trying to prove that the Reverend Schuller, who runs the Reformed Church of America and who has a sanctuary called the Crystal Cathedral, has gone into the entertainment business. The Crystal Cathedral can hold three thousand people, and Schuller's church has an annual income in excess of $30 million from its members—plus a television audience of two and a half million people. The State has assessed the church for taxes of more than a half-million dollars. The State claims that a church loses its tax-free status when it gives aerobic dance classes, weight reduction seminars, Sunday brunches and breakfasts, etc. According to the State of California lawyers, when Schuller offers performances with Hollywood stars and chamber music groups and choral organizations, he is in the entertainment business, and this does not qualify as religious worship." Matt shrugged. "Tom Ferris insists that we're in the same boat. He's worried that I'm making an issue over it. I believe that the First Church, and all churches, have to learn how to compete with mass entertainment if they want to survive. If they do it on a non-profit basis, and the revenues are used by the members for church purposes, there should be no taxation. I told Tom that historically the church was the original source of community entertainment. Anyway, we'll cross that bridge when we come to it."

"I'm much more worried about Jeff Falconer," Jill said. She asked Irene if she had watched the "Falconer Gospel Hour" last Sunday on television. Irene knew that Falconer had created Moral America, a crusading organization to save America from the liberals, but she had never watched his program.

"With his big Bible," Jill said, "holding the word of God in one hand, he spent a half-hour excoriating Matt and the First Church. He told his listeners that he needs a million dollars to fight this latest invasion of Satan. He told anyone who was listening to him in Adamsport, Massachusetts, that they should revive an old Puritan custom—put us in stocks, or, better still, tar and feather us and run us out of town."

Matt admitted that Falconer was an effective and dangerous rabble-rouser. "Tom discovered today that Falconer telephoned George Gallagher. George promised him that the city council would vote favorably if Falconer wanted to set up a temporary headquarters for his Moral America in Adamsport. Falconer is planning to live in a mobile home in Morton Park during the month of June."

"He's going to preach up there every night," Peachy said. "He really scares me. According to Tom, he told Gallagher that Matt is the Devil incarnate. Falconer's even got his own college. He's the same breed as Bob Jones, the fundamentalist minister. Like Jerry Falwell, Jones has his own university in Greensboro, South Carolina. Like both of them, Falconer says his mission in life is to combat atheistic, agnostic, pagan, and so-called scientific adulterations of the gospel. That means us!"

Matt laughed. "We're not atheists or agnostics. Jeff Falconer's problem is that he's afraid to admit that he's God, too."

"He's a theonomist," Peachy said.

"What in the world is that?" Irene asked. She was aware that Jill, who was now listening on bended elbows with her breasts dangling, was no longer wearing a nightgown.

"It's a system of ethics—morals, if you wish—founded on God's revelation as given in the Bible, which 'in its far-reaching details,' according to the believers, 'is to be the source of all ethics.'"

Jill grinned at Irene. "I hope I'm not embarrassing you. It's a warm night. You might as well be comfortable. You've joined the company of evil, lascivious women. Lying here naked with Matt, we're defying God's law. Greg Bahnsen, a theonomist leader, believes that 'the Christian is obligated to keep the whole law of God as a pattern of satisfaction.' If they don't, á la ` Anne Hutchinson, some three hundred years ago, 'they should be banished by magistrates from all civil life.'"

Hesitating, unable to shake her feeling of embarrassment, Irene slipped out of her bathrobe. Cheering her, Matt kissed her bobbing breasts, and Jill and Peachy laughingly applauded her.

"Don't worry, Irene," Matt gave her an affectionate slap on her behind. "You and Peachy and Jill are all aging very beautifully. As for Christians, and Jeff Falconer, I refer them to Matthew 22, verses 22 to 30. The Sadducees tried to confound Jesus with a story about the seven brothers who, following Jewish custom, were supposed to marry their brother's wife if he died. They proposed as a problem a case in which the wife had outlived—" Matt chuckled, "—or worn out might be a better word, all seven brothers.

"'Whose wife was she?' they demanded. Jesus coolly juggled his answer and told them not to worry, 'for in the resurrection they neither marry nor are given in marriage, but are the angels of God in heaven.'"

"You're not resurrected yet," Irene said, ruffling his hair, "but I'm afraid you're getting closer to a crucifixion than you think. A lot of Catholics agree with Falconer. They're just as frightened by your secular humanist morality, and your beliefs in abortion on demand, euthanasia, termination of life of severely handicapped babies, gay liberation, pornography, and genetic engineering. Catholics are even more afraid of you than they are of Falconer."

"What do you believe?" Matt asked.

"Obviously, I'm a good Catholic. I haven't divorced you."

"But you're sure that right now you are sinning."

"Not me. You are. Oh, goddamn you—" she pounded his chest. "I'm so confused that I don't know what I believe." She smiled at Peachy and Jill. "Believe it or not, right at this moment, I'm not unhappy. But after all these years, Matt, I still don't know what makes you tick. Are you pleased now that you have the three of us naked and obviously in your control, all of us listening to your words with bated breath? Why do you want to own three women?"

"You're missing the point," Matt said. "I don't *own* you. I don't want to own any of you. I love all of you because I don't own you. I love all of you because each of you is God and utter mystery." He smiled at them with tears in his eyes. "You are so beautiful, so incomprehensible. I worship the essence of you. Relaxed, your flesh and bones reflect not only your moods but your natural eternal femininity. Seeing you warms my blood and makes me want to kneel down and kiss your breasts, your bellies, your vulvas—reverentially."

"We're not so verbose as you are," Peachy yelled, "but I think we feel the same way. We enjoy your body, too. Jill, hold his arms, I'll hold his feet. Irene, you go first. Kiss God from head to foot!" Peachy was doubled over with laughter.

"Peachy is playing with fire," Matt chuckled. "She wants to see if the God out there will strike us dead."

For a few minutes the three of them, giggling and laughing merrily, slithered over him and played pig-pile on top of him until he finally hollered uncle. Jill pointed at his erect, bewildered penis and said, "Time to leave, Peachy."

"Don't leave me with him yet!" Irene pleaded. "I'm frightened—not of you, silly," she gave Matt's penis a quick shake, "but of the world out there." She shivered. "God hasn't struck us dead, but he may be just biding his time. And I sure as hell don't believe that I'm God . . . or that any of you are, either.

"You think that you're going to convert everyone," she continued, "but so far you only have three hundred members of the First Church. There are almost that many picketing the place." She shook her head. "This may be a lot of fun, and somehow we might make it together without killing each other, but I'm sure that if the world out there could see us right now, they would be horrified. Even if men and women are God, they aren't loving Gods—not yet."

"Matt's got a couple of hundred feminists camped at Morton Park who adore him," Jill said, and she whacked his behind with a magazine. "But you're right, Irene. Women are the worst. When they find out about us, they'll hate Matt for loving more than one woman at a time. You'd better read Paul Kurtz's article in the *National Forum* that I just socked you with," she told him. "Kurtz is afraid that magical thinking isn't about to disappear from the world, or that secular humanism will ever take its place. Some 67 percent of the population still believe in life after death, 53 percent believe that there is a hell, 71 percent heaven. Thirty-five percent claim to be born-again Christians, and most of the others who can't identify with any ordinary religions believe in stuff like Scientology or ESP or UFO's, tarot cards, psychic healing, or, at a religious level, Yoga, Zen, transcendental meditation, or what have you."

"Kurtz wonders if secular humanism will ever satisfy man's existential quest," Peachy added. "Humanists believe that we can be self-reliant and willing to accept responsibility for our own actions. They believe that all of us are capable of freedom, autonomy, and rationality, and that we are all willing to live with uncertainty and ambiguity. I don't believe it. I keep telling Matt that we must be careful. We can't let our mystical belief that men and women are God become too intellectual."

"You're too intellectual for me," Irene sighed. "It's not easy to shake off everything you have ever been taught. Like right now. Are we really able to cope with this? I don't know whether I am." She shook her head in wonder. "I'm in bed naked with my husband and two other women. We're obviously fulfilling a daydream for him. Matt may believe in equal rights, but he's still the pivot on which we must all turn. But I'm not sure I can live with uncertainty and ambiguity. Can you, Jill? Peachy? Women are possessive creatures."

"That's the point," Matt said, then bounced up on the bed and swung Peachy and Jill around until they lay on each side of Irene. Kneeling over them, he swiftly kissed all their breasts and nuzzled their vulvas. Then, staring happily at their startled expressions and embarrassed laughter, he sat up on his haunches and smiled at them affectionately. "That's sex worship. It's not lust. I'm in awe at the very different beauty of each of you. Your eyes. Jill's are far apart, Peachy's open saucers, Irene's slightly almond-shaped. Four brown eyes and two deep blue eyes. Your noses. Peachy's upturned, Jill's with flaring nostrils, Irene's patrician. Irene's breasts big and maternal with pink nipples, Peachy's boyish perky with a flippant behind to match, Jill's with aureolas like chocolate pudding that smile at you sadly. Jill with hourglass hips and Irene with a firm, strong behind that matches her tits."

He laughed. "My joy with you is not intellectual—it's emotional, filled with awe and delight that you are not only beautiful and very different women but that your hearts are beating, your blood is flowing. I could never intellectualize my affinity with you as human beings. Individually and collectively you are miracles. I know that God exists because I can see Her and touch Her. And that's the problem with humanism—it's afraid of miracles."

"You're the miracle!" Irene said, gasping with laughter along with Peachy and Jill. In his enthusiasm as he spoke, Matt had jumped to his feet and his still engorged penis was pointing to heaven. "Do all preachers have an erection when they preach?" she asked.

"Of course," Matt laughed. "And that's a miracle, too—both intellectual and emotional. Keep one thing in mind. The reason that the First Church is crowded is that we are saying the words that millions of people have never dared to utter. We are revering human creativity and the amazing fertility of all life. Just think of one tiny wonder. Why, over millions of years, has the human female developed breasts and a prominent behind? Most female mammals have very small breasts, and very little flesh covering their pelvis. Human female breasts and behinds have just one evolutionary purpose—to arouse the male and make him want to copulate."

Marveling at his ability to keep preaching, Peachy grabbed Matt's wrists and pulled him down on the bed. "Come on, Jill and Irene, there's only one way to shut him up. Smother him."

But even with three ladies under and over him, poking at him and kissing him, Matt kept trying to make his point, and he was delighted to notice that Irene was laughing uninhibitedly.

"Sunday I'm going to preach that Jeff Falconer is right," he told them. "We all need to be born again. Not as Christians, but rather as Human Beings who are lifetime lovers and realize that love is man and woman sharing both their brains and genitals and never being ashamed of the profound and everlasting mystery of living, creating, and dying." His voice was occasionally garbled as his lips were pressed against unidentified breasts, but, choking with laughter, he continued. "Why does your flesh against mine feel so nice? Why does the curve of your breasts, your hips, your triangles pointing to the butterflies between your legs—why does your laughter, your words, the tears of joy and worry in your eyes—not only make me need to join my flesh with yours, but, even more, make it possible for me to transcend myself for a moment and become you? Why do I want to? That's not intellectual. That's one of the central mysteries of life. As God we should spend every minute of our lives celebrating Us. All of Us and the earth and the flora and the fauna are ultimate mystery."

"Matt's preaching a new sermon on the mount," Peachy said. "The sermon on the mount of Venus." She and Jill wiggled out of his arms.

For a moment they both jumped up and down on the bed over Matt and Irene, singing "Forward Through the Ages" to the tune of "Onward Christian Soldiers." After which—and Irene was sure that they had planned it that way—they sang "Good Night, Irene." Then they solemnly kissed her and Matt on the cheek, patted Matt's penis affectionately, and said, "Sweet dreams."

Alone, Matt leaned over Irene and kissed her tenderly. "Thank you for the new Irene," he said. "I love the old one, too."

"You've still got her," she sighed and arched her behind to receive him, and she was surprised at how very ready she was to have him inside her. "For better or worse."

"Are you happy, Renee?"

"I guess so." She hugged him fiercely, tears in her eyes. "I love you, but the competition is pretty scary."

40

Two days and warmly erotic nights later (including one dinner with Emily, Roje, and John Codman, who Emily asked if she could invite and who was obviously enamoured with her), Irene knew that she was laughing more than she had in her entire life. Unlike in the lonely Big House, or even the predictable environment of the Adamsport Country Club, here, for the first time in her life, she was living in the mainstream of conflicting and exciting ideas. Better still, she was listening and withholding judgment.

The carriage house was no placid harem. Along with Jill she often disagreed with Matt and Peachy and together with Jill tried to temper the hot cutting edge of their plans and ideas for the First Church without suppressing their enthusiasm. While she had to open the gates of prejudice and let their happy, mind-bending madness charge through her religious beliefs, she quickly discovered that she wasn't competing with Jill or Peachy, and her sexual inhibitions were rapidly disappearing. She discovered that she had an important place in the quintet. She knew more about the world of business and corporate finance than Peachy and Jill did, and she could organize a house, including the maid and Mrs. Goodale, better than they could. Jill was neat, but she was often lost in the dream world of theater and music, running wild with ideas for future programs for the First Church. Peachy, like Matt, was really an evangelist, and like Matt she was juggling so many balls that she often got herself in a nervous tizzy, especially when she couldn't keep them all in the air at the same time. And Peachy told Irene that as much as she loved Matt, she wasn't a one-man woman.

"I love to make love," she admitted. "Not with every man I meet, but I do enjoy my contrasting lovers. I'm not promiscuous, but unlike you and Jill, I prefer not to survive six days without a man. Emily doesn't miss Roje one night a week."

She told Irene that she hoped Emily found another man. "She misses Sylvie too much," Peachy sighed. "I really never knew my father. Maybe if he had lived, Emily would have made him easier to get along with." But Peachy was afraid that Sylvie's gold would come back to haunt them all.

And Peachy revealed to Irene why Jill had suddenly become moody and preoccupied. "Poor thing, she's all mixed up. She doesn't think she should be included in any family conference. She doesn't know how she should act with Ike, or what she should say to him Saturday when Sally arrives. Up until now, Ike's refused to see her." Peachy shook her head. "I asked her if she could sleep with Ike again after having been to bed with Matt, and she said, 'You sleep with Roje, don't you?'" Peachy couldn't help grinning. "But I don't sleep with Roje's son."

Irene was almost as nervous as Jill. She was afraid that Ike might get so enraged he might have another stroke. Although Ike had made it apparent to Irene that he was still interested in women, she had never consciously evoked the question that Peachy raised.

"Do you think Ike can still get it up?" Peachy asked.

Irene scowled at her. "I never asked him."

"Would you go to bed with him?"

"He's my father-in-law!"

"So what? He's not a blood relative." Peachy shrugged. "If I get a chance, I'll ask him."

"Ask him what?" Irene stared at her in alarm.

Peachy laughed. "Ask him if he's still interested in sex. Jill told me that he was a very affectionate old guy. Even if he can't get it up, there are lots of women, like me, who enjoy cuddling with a man who likes them, hugs them, talks to them. Screwing is not the alpha and omega of sex."

Friday night, during their usual pre-sleep conference in the big bedroom, Jill suddenly burst into tears. She clung to Irene and sobbed into her neck. "Oh, Renee, what should I do?" she asked as Irene, heedless that they were lying naked, breast to breast, tried to comfort her. "I told Matt today, I never could go back and live with Ike. It's not sex. I'm just not the same person I was a year ago." She looked at Matt across Irene's shoulder. "I've absorbed so many of your crazy ideas," she said to him, "that sure as hell, Ike and I would be arguing about you. Poor Ike, it would be almost as bad for him as my going to bed with you.

"I told you, Matt, I'm the *bête noire* in this drama. As a triangle situation you and Peachy and Irene are normal. Adultery is normal. They are part and parcel of life. Dramatists and novelists would stop writing if people were strictly monogamous. Even Roje agrees with me. I'm the problem. No author would ever tackle a third woman like me—married to the son's father! It makes the drama untenable. It has to end in suicide or murder. I should have been murdered on Grand Cayman."

"You're letting your stage sense run away with you," Matt said softly, stroking her behind soothingly. "Life isn't ever resolved in nice three-act packages. That's what makes it so interesting." He paused, reluctant to break bad news. "Speaking of Grand Cayman and of the Devil, a devil named Ramachanda telephoned me today."

"Oh, Jesus!" Frightened, Jill sat up and stared at Matt. "Is he in Adamsport?"

"No, he's in Florida, but he wanted to fly up to Boston tomorrow. I told him that I wouldn't be here, that I was on my way to Los Angeles. I also told him that he was quite mad to come here. I could have him arrested for murder. But that didn't frighten him. He's certain that he can implicate me in the greatest gold theft in history."

Jill explained to Irene and Peachy that Ramachanda was the Hindu who had been waiting in Sylvie's villa when they arrived. "Gus Belshin's advertisement and the story about us in the *Journal* brought him back to life," Matt said. "He's convinced that I've got Sylvie's gold. Ten percent—$10 million—will keep him quiet."

"I hope you told me the truth," Irene looked at him dubiously. "You told me that you only actually saw those three gold ingots, and I thought Amir Saud gave you the money for the Foundation."

"He did. But I still don't know why. Ramachanda can't prove anything, but I'll have to tell Tom Ferris and get his advice. Anyway, stop worrying. We have more important problems." He smiled at Jill. "Like Ike. We can settle that problem right now. Tomorrow tell him that I acquired you fair and square. Ike should be able to handle that. He took over Infinity Corporation. Gus didn't want him and it's been a very uneasy marriage. Quite a few of Ike's acquisitions in the past years didn't work out, and Ike had to get divorced from them." Matt laughed. "'Spin them off' is the corporate vernacular."

"Damn you!" Jill shouted, throwing a pillow at him. "I'm not an acquisition for any Godwin." But she couldn't help laughing, because she knew Matt was teasing her. "If you're not careful, I'll spin you off. Irene, you really are a saint. I don't know how you lived with Matt or why you have been so good to Ike."

Then Jill had an idea. She asked Irene if she could convince Becky that it would be easier to have an informal cook-out tomorrow right there at the carriage house. "Around the pool with steaks and hot dogs. The Big House is too formal," she said. "And there's no pool up there. Eight people can't relax together in any one of the sitting rooms. Down here, with the kids around, it will help keep the lid on things."

Irene shrugged. "It's all right with me. But please, no naked adults." Then she admitted that after three days of living with them it was getting easier—especially when there were no children around—to relax naked with them. She grinned at Peachy, who, completely uninhibited, was propped up against one side of the bed doing bicycle exercises. "I'm getting used to such sights, but believe me, Becky and Hendy would be shocked."

"So would Ike," Jill laughed. "But he wouldn't close his eyes in horror."

"Clothing optional," Peachy suggested. "All in favor say 'aye.'"

"Sally would love it," Matt agreed. He would be picking up Sally tomorrow at seven in the morning. "Who knows, maybe Ike will join us? None of us except Jill has ever seen Ike without his britches on."

It was ten o'clock, but Irene telephoned Becky to get her approval. "I don't give a damn where we eat, or what you have to eat, or if you're all bare-ass," Becky responded grimly. "But I just told Hendy that I'm in a cold sweat thinking about tomorrow. The trouble is that Ike is too gleeful. He's convinced that Matt is in so much trouble with his modern Babylon that he can make Matt walk the plank so far as CPC goes. As for Jill, I don't even want to think about her."

At breakfast Irene suggested that Jill go with Matt to meet Sally at the airport. "My three nights with the Lord are over," she grinned at Matt and Jill. "What's left is all yours—but first you've got to survive the cook-out this afternoon."

Reminding them that clothing was optional, Irene told them that she was going up to the Big House to get a bathing suit, and to see how Ike was reacting to the change in location of his family conference. Peachy said that she was going to enjoy a morning of peace and quiet in the minister's office at the new Parish Hall. She had to work on her sermon for tomorrow.

On the way to the airport, Matt noticed Jill's unusual silence. He put his arm around her and asked her why she was so morose. "I'm not an incurable optimist like you are," she answered with a hopeless shrug. "I'm scared to death about what Ramachanda may do. I worry about Irene, and I want to hug Ike and tell him that I'm sorry, but I don't dare."

"Why are you worried about Irene? In the past few days she's become a very different woman, much more relaxed than she ever was with me alone."

"You really are a complacent egotist, Matt Godwin," Jill replied. "For the past three days—and I hope that you made love to her every night—Irene hasn't had time to get jealous. But tonight and for the next five nights in a row, she'll have plenty of time to search her soul."

"What for?"

"To discover if she can really share you."

"Damn it, Jill!" Matt exploded. "Think about it! Any night that I'm alone in bed with any one of you, I'm only awake for about two hours at a maximum. The four of us spend more time together than that."

"For some women the only time they can really be naked with their man—and I mean mentally as well as physically—is when they are alone with him."

"Not Irene. That's the time she used to retreat into her shell the most. When there was just us, she was often in a panic that I might ask her to make love on top of the washing machine instead of comfortably in bed."

"If that's your hang-up, Matt Godwin, don't ask me either!" Jill kissed his cheek. "I doubt if any of us are good prospects for external vibration."

"You may never know until you try," Matt laughed and nearly sideswiped a car in the opposite lane as he ran his fingers along Jill's thigh. "Living with you and Peachy, I think Irene is discovering that both of you are very nice, average women. Not the boogieman that she thought you were."

"I should sock you," Jill said as he parked Irene's Cadillac, which he had taken because his Mercedes was too small, near the American Airlines terminal. "None of your women are average—especially me."

They discovered that the red-eye flight from Los Angeles had just landed. Running through the terminal, they arrived at the gate a minute before Sally emerged from the passenger tunnel. She saw them, but instead of the expected smile, she had a big frown on her face, and she kept glancing behind her.

"I'm sorry," she sputtered, hugging Matt and then Jill, "but that son of a bitch followed me. He didn't have a reservation, but he finagled a seat on the plane. He doesn't even have a bag. He tried to haunt me all the way to Boston. I never should have told him that I was coming. He tried to get his seat changed so that he could sit beside me, but I told the stewardess to strap him in as far back as she could get him. But he kept wandering by, hanging over me, telling me that if there is going to be a CPC stockholders' meeting in Boston, he is going to attend."

Matt didn't have to ask who she was talking about. Gus Belshin finally wandered out of the tunnel with a big grin on his face. "Sally and I are having a lovers' spat," he said and thrust out his hand at Matt. To Jill's surprise Matt showed no anger but greeted Gus with a cool smile.

"Sally is pissed off with me," Gus was saying. "She's mad because I took you over the coals with Mike Wilder. But, Jesus Christ, Matt, you can't blame me! I never thought I'd see you free and loose again. By this time you should be either in solitary confinement or in a strait jacket."

"Since you're indulging in homilies," Matt's face was still expressionless as he towered at least eight inches over Belshin, "it would seem as if you were cutting off your nose to spite your face."

Matt squeezed Jill's arm protectively. "In case you haven't recognized her, this is Jill Godwin. She's probably wondering why I don't beat the shit out of you."

Belshin backed away from Matt apprehensively. "Sorry about that, Jill. It was dirty pool. But Ike got me pretty aggravated. He was trying to foist Henderson Inch on me. He was so damned belligerent and puffed up that I decided to let the hot air out of him." He grinned nervously at her. "Maybe I did you both a favor. If I hadn't spilled the beans, you'd still be living with Ike and breaking your marriage vows. Adultery is a hard secret to keep. Look at me. If Miriam hadn't grabbed half of my stock and voted her proxies for Matt, I'd be running CPC now." Gus scowled at Matt. "Miriam only met you once, a couple of years ago. How in hell did you seduce her?"

"See what I mean?" Sally glared contemptuously at Belshin. "He thinks the only way to tame a woman is to fuck her."

"Stop shrying, honey," Belshin said. "I obviously haven't tamed Miriam or you. Your brother has C and C, I don't. If I did, I might have persuaded you and Miriam to share the wealth."

"What the hell is C and C?" Sally demanded.

"Chutzpa and charisma." He looked at Matt. "Only God has them."

Matt laughed. "You've got the first. The charisma takes a little practice. Anyway, there's no stockholders' meeting. You're on the wrong trip. And even if there were, unless Ike changes his mind and suddenly loves his 'beamish boy,' I don't control enough stock to get you out of my hair, either."

They were walking four abreast through the terminal to the baggage claim. "Anyway, I'm glad you came," Matt said. "I may have a better idea." He took Sally's arm. "It's about time that you both saw the new CPC headquarters, not to mention the First Church. From what Sally has told me, Gus, you're not a very religious man. When you move the headquarters to Adamsport, you may change your mind and become a member. In the meantime we're going to make things easy for you. Sally's going to telephone Ike and ask him if he'd be agreeable to having you come to our family cook-out this afternoon."

"Like hell, I am!" Sally said indignantly. "I'm not your patsy or Gus's. You've forgotten that the last time Ike talked with Gus he had a stroke."

"That was eighteen months ago," Gus said. "The reason that Ike was so angry with me was because I was backing Matt for president of

CPC. Now he knows that I have changed my mind and think that Matt should be under observation for incipient insanity." He grinned at Matt but stayed far enough away from him to duck a sudden attack. "Ike will probably love me now. And you really shouldn't be angry with me, Matt. If it hadn't been for me, you would have been on cloud nine playing God a year ago, and Henderson Inch would be president."

"Ike still wants Hendy to be president," Matt said calmly. "But I've got a better idea. If Sally can convince Ike to invite you to our family reunion this afternoon, maybe we can wrap it up."

Jill was listening to the conversation in amazement. "Honestly, Matt, I think Gus is right. You do have chutzpa. You're walking where angels fear to tread. I'm not speaking just for myself, but bringing *him* is adding insult to injury."

Sally finally agreed to make the phone call to the Big House. Irene answered, and she and Becky were vociferously against it. Ike evidently heard them arguing and picked up an extension phone. He greeted Sally affectionately. "So that rat-fink followed you to Boston," he said, sounding amused. "He's planning to screw a Godwin one way or the other. When and if he marries you, don't let that bastard make you change your religion. Better still, make him change *his* last name." Ike guffawed. "Augustus Godwin. That's a good name. I might have chosen it myself. Gus is no rose, but with a name like Godwin he might smell a little sweeter. I don't care what Becky says, if you want to bring him to our party, go ahead. And don't worry, I'm not going to have another stroke. I wouldn't give Belshin the pleasure. The way I figure it, the more skunks at the party, the merrier. Maybe we can air them all out. If not, I can always hold my nose."

After a tour of the new CPC building, Gus admitted that he was impressed, but he still wasn't enthusiastic about moving the headquarters to New England. He grinned at Sally. "Of course, if I were sleeping with a Godwin on a regular basis, I might change my mind."

But he was astonished when they took him on a tour of the First Church. The recreation rooms were filled with young people and quite a few adults; many of them were bowling, swimming, or playing volleyball, and most of them were happily naked. And he shook his head in amazement when Peachy climbed out of the swimming pool.

"Why ddidn't you tell me that you were bringing Sally here?" she asked Matt, and she grinned provocatively at Belshin, who was relishing her naked body with his eyes. "I'd have dressed for the occasion."

Matt introduced her as his co-minister. Peachy immediately invited Belshin to services tomorrow. "I'm giving a sermon series on the Worship of Priapus and the Worship of the Generative Powers. My sermons will be based on books written several hundred years ago by Richard Knight and Thomas Wright." She laughed at Bus's dubious expression and his obvious inability to concentrate on her face. "They'll give you perspective; you look as if you need it."

"I don't need perspective," Gus told Matt gloomily as they drove to the carriage house. "You and your friend Peachy may think sex worship is very moral, but most Americans will be scared shitless. Mixing sex and religion is a no-no. Mixing sex and religion and preaching your modern moralities while at the same time you're president of CPC is totally insane. You're living in a dream world, Matt. Maybe a few nuts in California would believe you're the Messiah, but good Jews and Christians will hang you upside down by your balls."

"Right now, I'm not worried about Matt's moralities," Sally told Gus as they were cleared at the sentry post into the Godwin estate. "The reality is that Becky thinks I'm pretty immoral. Even if she invites you to stay at the Big House, which I'm sure she won't, I'm not sleeping with you tonight. Not here or anywhere. Matt may think that he's God, but I don't think I am—so I can continue to hate you."

Gus shrugged. "So I'll find a hotel in Boston."

"From what I hear, all the hotels for thirty miles around here are sold out," Matt laughed. "There's no room at the inns."

"So I'll sleep on the sofa in your new office," Belshin said. "If by chance I come back for your crucifixion, I'll make my reservation in advance."

41

Wearing beach wraps and bathing suits, Irene and Becky, followed by Hendy, guided Ike, dressed in white linen trousers and a pale blue polo shirt, to a comfortable wicker chair near the pool. Shaking his head, he watched Ink, Able, David, and Cheryl, who, sans bathing suits, were happily diving and playing together in the water. Before he sat down he glared at Matt and Jill, and he immediately foiled Matt's attempt to embrace him. Backing away, he said gruffly, "I'm here, but I'm not ready for your Judas-style loving."

But then he accepted Jill's impulsive kiss on his cheek. "Hi, Ike," she said softly. "I'm glad that you're well. I've missed you."

"I don't know why." Ike stared at her grimly. "You're a smart lady. You traded death for life." Then, hearing Becky's "Oh, my God!" he followed her glance and saw Peachy and Sally emerging stark naked from the house with Gus Belshin. Trying to look casual, Belshin, wearing one of Matt's jockey-style bathing suits, waved at Ike, but he didn't join the group. He stood aloof watching the children.

"They told me this was a clothing-optional party," Sally laughed. Ignoring Ike's frown of disapproval, she hugged him and introduced him to Peachy.

Peachy bussed his cheek. "I've lived in Adamsport all my life," she said ecstatically, "but I never thought I'd get to kiss Isaac Godwin. I hope that Sally and I aren't embarrassing you. If we are, we'll put on bathing suits." She chattered away, telling him how handsome he was and how much she had loved Sarah. She was well aware that she was breaking the tension.

"When you've got one foot in the grave, it's too late to be embarrassed by anything," Ike responded gaily, totally entranced by her. "I have to admit you're the most interesting scenery I've looked at for some time." He kept surveying her body with unconcealed interest.

"You're going to live to be a hundred," Peachy told him. "And you'll see a lot more intriguing scenery than this before you die." She sat on a pool chair facing him with her legs perched over a plastic float and thus revealing her nether parts to him.

Grinning in spite of himself, Ike ignored Irene and Jill and told Matt that he wouldn't mind sipping a scotch on the rocks. He pointed to Gus on the other side of the pool. "And give him one. He's going to need it. And tell him to come over and enjoy the sights. I never thought I'd live to see my thirty-five-year-old daughter walking around bare-ass—or a UU minister showing me her womb." He grinned at Peachy, who blushed and closed her legs. "We didn't have it so good when I was a kid. We swam bollicky in Grandpa Zach's quarry, but there were no girls." He waved in the direction of Ink and Able and David, who were chasing Cheryl around the pool. "And sure as hell the kids never saw their mother naked."

"We're teaching children how to enjoy and respect their sexual drives," Peachy said, "not to be ashamed of them. Hopefully, they won't grow up so frustrated."

"You mean you're not frustrated?" Ike asked her.

Peachy shook her head. "Why should I be?"

"Sharing Matt with another woman." Ike scowled at her. "Whether you're frustrated or not really doesn't interest me, but advertising, not having sense enough to keep your mouths shut about your sex life—even preaching that it makes sense—is worse than playing with TNT. I hope Irene has sense enough not to get involved with you. You're driving a rocky road." He waved at Matt, who was putting steaks on a charcoal grill. "Before we eat and everyone gets half-crocked, I'll give you my proposition."

Ike glared at Gus. "I still don't like you, but I'm glad you're here so that you will know where I stand. If Sally marries you, that's her funeral. But I want you out of CPC's hair. If Matt, Sally, and Becky will vote their million and a half shares with me, I'm sure that I can pick up enough proxies to spin off Infinity. I'm going to give it back to you. I'm sure you can put together a group with enough cash to buy your CPC stock. After you have gone, we'll elect me chairman and Hendy president. Matt can remain on the board of directors, but we'll make an announcement that his religious activities are not approved or condoned by the corporation."

Ike smiled at Irene. "In view of your devotion to me over the past year, and your sound business sense, I think you should be on the board of directors, too. As for Gus and Infinity, I wish him luck. I'm sure we can put the money to work for better advantage."

Ike paused and smiled grimly at their silence. "As for Jill, it's about time she made up her mind. If she wants to live with me, she can come back—no recriminations. I forgive her. But I'm not like Irene," he scowled at Matt. "I'm not sharing my spouse with anyone, especially not my son."

"No dice!" Belshin smiled coldly at Ike. "You bought yourself a dybbuk. A few years ago, when you were after Infinity, I didn't want you, but now I like the total package. So you have an old devil sitting on your shoulder, and I'm not getting off until I'm directing the traffic."

Bewildered, Jill looked at Matt, wondering what he was going to say. To her surprise, and Ike's astonishment, he leaned over Ike, and finally managed to hug him. "You're a crafty old codger, but I love you," he said. "I always have. But that doesn't mean that I agree with you. First, I want you to know that I love Jill, and I love Irene, and I love Peachy. Who they love in addition to me, or instead of me, is strictly their own decision. But if I were Jill, I'd reject your offer. She's thirty years younger than you are. If you love her, don't ask for her love with conditions. Just consider yourself lucky that she loves you."

Sally nodded and clapped her hands softly. Becky raised her eyebrows with a hopeless expression.

"Next," Matt said, "and before any discussion, let's look at CPC. I'm willing to give up the presidency. But there are conditions." He paused and glanced at Henderson, who was listening impassively. "I really like you, Hendy, but I don't think you are tough enough to run the company. Ike is too old. As for Gus, I'm sure that he can run it, but not the way I envision it. I know you think that I'm playing God, Gus, but I'm not so naive as to think CPC can survive without a profit. I don't always like the way you think, but you are a tough bird, and I know you keep your eye on the bottom line."

Matt caught a water ball that bounced out of the pool in his direction. He threw it back to the boys. "One of our problems is that neither you nor Ike understand where I am coming from and, even more important, that I am totally committed. With or without you, I am going to make Americans aware that we can create a new kind of people's capitalism. Business and politics have a moral dimension that many Jews and so-called Christians overlook. If you accept the premise that you are God—each of us is God—then politicians, businessmen, and church leaders, acting as God, are one and the same with a similar moral responsibility. The concept of separation of the Church and State becomes academic. In God We Trust means we must trust ourselves. By contrast, living with the Judeo-Christian belief that God is out there somewhere and for the most part doesn't pay much attention to His creations has created a moral vacuum. Situation ethics opens the door to bedlam."

Matt laughed. "I know that you're a captive audience, but Gus and Ike are not likely to come and hear my sermons, so they'd better hear me out now. My belief is that the First Church and all religious sects must join together. We've got to put God—as Us—back into the Constitution of the United States. We've got to write new laws and offer new moralities to make humans believe in humans, and at the same time redefine evil and sin in our daily interactions with each other. We can't do this by leaning on the Bible or the Talmud or other religious ethical or moral teachings that no longer have meaning in a world where an external God doesn't care whether we destroy each other or not. It took hundreds of years to eliminate the sorry history of religious dictatorship and control over the affairs of men. In the process we have the equally sorrowful history of state and bureaucratic control and a hopelessly muddled democracy.

"Before it is too late, the church and the synagogue, which are closer to the people, must interject a new moral structure into the political structure. We must expose the governments that reward one section of society to the detriment of the other. By letting our politicians juggle our money and inflate the currency as they have in the past twenty years, we have demoralized Americans who have saved their money or bought insurance, and we have made millionaires and billionaires out of gamblers who bought real estate and gold. We have created a Las Vegas mentality in this country that even includes running for political office. It costs close to $300,000 to get elected to the House of Representatives, and over $2 million to the Senate. To raise that kind of money, and to pay off campaign debts, our elected representatives are forced to play fast and loose with sound moralities. Our government offices are filled with hundreds of thousands of incompetents who got their jobs by contributing money to the victor. After the men or women who spend the most money take office, they quickly become authorities on everything. They make speeches against the immorality of war. They deplore the situations in Central America, Afghanistan, the Middle East, or in African countries. Yet directly or indirectly they vote to subsidize the wars and the internal conflicts in these countries."

Matt grinned. "I hope I'm not boring you. What I am trying to tell you is that I am no longer a whimpering voice singing in the wilderness. The First Church and the Foundation can create a pretty loud bang. It will be even louder with the kind of leadership I have been giving CPC. What an appropriate name: Controlled Power. The company has annual revenues of $16 billion. We can challenge all the people and other corporations to search for new moralities and new approaches and root out the corruption and lack of brains in the capitalistic structure which erodes our political structure. We don't have to let a nitwit power elite annihilate the United States."

"God damn it, Matt!" Ike exploded. "If you could use all the $16 billion of our revenues, you couldn't stop wars. People love war. It's the only thing that unites them."

"Our family war isn't uniting us," Sally said. "Maybe we should listen to Matt." She smiled at him. "How is God going to stop war?"

"Maybe I'm not," Matt grinned at her. "But I think it's high time that we acted like the Christians we profess to be and immediately stop supplying armament and particularly ammunition of any kind to all Third World nations. We should demand that the Soviet Union follow our example, as well as France, England, and any other country who can manufacture ammunition. Selling bullets, torpedoes, grenades, and bombs to small nations—a way of testing their killing power without getting involved—is grossly immoral. Internationally we need a Modern Monroe Doctrine that stands up, even to the point of direct confrontation, if necessary, to those nations who won't go along with us. The sale of bullets or armaments between nations is immoral. When there is no international traffic in bullets and bombs, no more merchants of death selling them, the peoples of Iran and Iraq, Lebanon, Chad, Israel, Afghanistan, Nicaragua, Cuba, El Salvador, Guatemala, Honduras, you name them, will have to return to primitive warfare. Let them fight with bows and arrows and slingshots."

"That's pretty utopian." Henderson finally broke his silence.

"Like hell it is," Matt said. "More than a hundred thousand lives have been lost so far in a ridiculous war between Iran and Iraq. Who supplies them with arms? France, the United States, and the Soviet Union. Take a country like Chad in Africa. In 1979, Defense Minister Hissene Habre rebelled against Goukoni Quedi, the chairman and dictator of Chad. Libya's Colonel Quadhafi sent 10,000 well-armed troops into Chad. These arms were supplied to him by the Soviet Union and probably indirectly even by America and France. With them he reduced the capital, N'Djamena, to rubble and killed thousands of people. A year later Habre found reinforcements and drove Goukoni out again. Nothing was solved. But as a result of these weapons being supplied by the major countries, hundreds of thousands of Chadians are starving or dying. Providing the weapons so people can kill each other is the ultimate immorality. It's not utopian to challenge the death merchants—or the politicians who condone them."

To Ike's astonishment, Irene sided with Matt. "The National Council of Churches sponsors the Interfaith Center on Corporate Responsibility," she said. "Quite a few mutual funds, like Calvert Social Investment Fund, the Working Assets Fund, the Shearson American Fund for Balanced Investment, the Dreyfuss Third Century Fund, and several others, won't invest in companies with bad labor relations records or unequal opportunity employers. They even blacklist South African investments." She smiled seriously at Ike. "If I were on your board of directors, I wouldn't be afraid of establishing CPC's belief in corporate responsibility, and it may be worth trying. Maybe we can establish saner, newer moralities."

"Damn it, Irene, Matt has you brainwashed." Ike frowned at her. "I can't believe that you—a Catholic—believe in sex worship, not to mention abortion on demand and euthanasia. You've had a good business education. The purpose of business is to turn out a product efficiently or offer an exceptional service, find customers, and make a profit. It can't get involved with its customers' sex lives or their religious beliefs. I'm sure that you know that we have a division that manufactures rifles and army field weapons. Our two shipyards will build battleships and landing ships and submarines for whoever wants to buy them. Altogether they represent at least five or six billion annual sales dollars. What's more, they are cost-plus contracts, and they are more profitable than any damned sewerage, distillation, or bridge building contracts that Matt is trying to dream up."

"I'm sure that we'll never be in total agreement," Matt said. "But the time has come to stop preaching. I'm going to broil the steaks. Before I do, no matter what other decisions we may arrive at today, I think Ike should agree to make out a check to the Foundation for $2 million." He grinned at Ike's shocked expression. "Let's say it's the money that Sarah asked him to give to the UU's before she died."

"God damn you!" Ike stood up angrily. "You're going too far."

"Listen to him, Daddy," Becky said, praying that her father wouldn't drop dead on the spot. "You promised that you could take it and not blow your top."

"He's God! I'm not."

"Think about it, Ike," Matt said gently. "Sarah would be proud of you." He smiled at Hendy. "I know you think that I'm against you and I'm always putting you down. But you are a very important guy in CPC. My proposal is that we should make you president in charge of penny pinching. I'm not kidding. You are very good at it. If CPC doesn't conform to the money-making system, I will never be able to prove my point. On the other hand, you need someone over you—your bosses. They would not be publicized; they would only be known to the other directors of the company. I propose a triumvirate." Matt grinned at Ike and Gus, who were now listening to him attentively. "If you're not familiar with what a triumvirate can do, I refer you to Roman history. Caesar, Pompey, and Crassus formed the first triumvirate. It worked out so well that later Octavius, Lepidus, and Mark Antony created an even more powerful one. Alone they were sitting ducks. Together they controlled every aspect of Roman life. Three of us, in today's lingo a top executive committee, will run CPC. We'll not only direct the policy of the company, accelerate its growth, but we will also, *by prior written agreement*, oppose any national policy or national legislation and any moral beliefs that are unsatisfactory to any one of us."

He smiled at Gus and Ike, letting the idea sink in.

Ike shook his head in complete disbelief. "You're a complete ego maniac. You make Hitler look like small change." Ike was gritting his teeth and trying not to yell at his exasperating son. "What you are asking is that Gus and I endorse your Foundation and your insane moralities."

Matt shrugged. "They may be insane, but they represent alternatives to corruption and blowing ourselves off the face of the earth. Whether either of you privately agree with me or not, it doesn't mean that I would have carte blanche. We're in agreement that CPC is first and foremost a profit-making organization. But it does mean that I could publicly excoriate any lack of corporate responsibility that you or any other corporate leaders may be guilty of. And keep in mind, despite my critics, I don't want the First Church or the Foundation running the government. On the other hand, the directors may decide to encourage the Foundation with a large annual donation. In the meantime, I'm simply going to try to get more sex worshippers, more people who know that they are God, running the government than Bible lovers."

After a steak and a second scotch, Ike reluctantly admitted that Matt was the most persistent con artist he had ever known. Nevertheless, if Jill had any doubt before, she told Matt later that she had confirmed one thing during the family get-together: "My two Godwins, deep down—and although Ike may never admit it—admire each other." After a lengthy discussion of the impossibility of a three-way management functioning together for more than an hour, Gus finally agreed that if Ike could swallow his Jewish prejudices and if Matt would turn the burners down and keep CPC far removed from the sexual aspects of the First Church and the Foundation, he "would consider it."

Gus also agreed to recommend the quick move of the headquarters to Adamsport. "I may not personally decide to move back here," he said, "but it is obvious that I'm going to have to spend a lot of time in this city to keep a handle on the Godwins. And if Sally finally decides to marry me, you're going to have to give us a bedroom in the Big

House."

Lying on top of Matt that night, kissing his eyes and nose, but not quite totally blended with him, Jill wondered if they had really solved anything that day. "Watching the three of you and listening, even though Ike went home happy and Gus is sleeping with Sally at the Big House, I keep thinking it's the calm before the storm."

Matt cupped her face gently and kissed her. "Out of conflict comes harmony. The see-saw is never in balance." He laughed. "It would be boring if it were. Right now Irene is still living with us and sleeping blissfully alone. I really don't think that she's worried about you or Peachy—or jealous. In fact, before she left with Peachy, she whispered to me, 'I hope you realize that Jill is still dangling. Ike wants her, too. Be nice to her.' Irene knows that you can't live with Ike day in and day out."

Jill was silent a long time. "Ike told Irene that he still loves me. I suppose if I want to keep peace in the family, I may even have to sleep with him." She hugged Matt and kissed him passionately. "It won't be as nice as this. But I am a good actress."

Matt grinned at her. "Maybe Peachy will help you. I heard her telling Ike about the benefits of gerecomy."

"What's that?"

"In ancient times, when the king got old and his wives were too plump or bored from high living, he'd commandeer young women to sleep with him, not for sex, but to breathe their young air into his lungs." Laughing, Matt slowly merged with her. "The idea was to increase the king's longevity when he no longer could do it this way."

Jill slapped his buttocks. "Damn you," she chuckled. "Anyway, that lets me out. I'm too plump and not young enough." She rolled out from under him and, still joined, hunched over him so that her breasts were caressing his face.

He snuggled in them for a minute and whispered, "Sometimes I think the best solution would be to buy a desert island and just disappear with all three of you."

"You'd be bored silly with us in a week."

Matt laughed. "Well, don't ask me how I'm going to please Gus and turn the burners off."

42

By the last week in June, Matthew Godwin's "devil's cauldron," as Jeff Falconer labelled it, had become a bubbling inferno. Falconer announced that on Sunday, the night before the Fourth of July, his television crew would be on hand for a live broadcast on the "Falconer Gospel Hour." Direct from Sex City, Adamsport, Massachusetts, he would give an epoch-making sermon. He was going to challenge the State of Massachusetts to arrest Matthew Godwin and put him in prison for promulgating filth under the depraved delusion that everyone was God. He told reporters that the First Church was corrupting the morals of minors. Matthew Godwin was promoting a blasphemous, obscene, and evil religion that was merely a cover for immoral behavior—a cover for filthy Hollywood and New York City pornographers.

"In addition," Falconer advised his listeners, "rumors abound that Godwin has either brainwashed the three women who are living with him on the Godwin estate, or they are all on drugs. I'm warning Matthew Godwin that if he's actually cohabiting with three women, whether he's married to them or not, he's not only breaking the laws of the State of Massachusetts, but he's also committing a federal crime. In 1892, the Congress of the United States outlawed bigamy. Godwin's citizenship and his franchise to vote can be revoked."

Roje was in a bit of a panic. Mike Wilder had finally arrived in Adamsport, and his cameramen were expending miles of film covering Falconer. Roje knew that Wilder was interviewing the UU First Parish Church members who were trying to put together a majority of the former members.

"We're going to use our new resources and build a small New England church for sane UU's," Henry Hancock told Wilder. "Nearly forty years ago, we had a UU minister who lost his moorings the same way as Godwin. His name was Reverend Stephen Fritchman. At the time he was editor of the *Christian Register*. He was a troublemaker like Godwin. The General Assembly of the American Unitarian Association got together and by a majority vote excommunicated him. Among other things, Fritchman condemned the Truman Doctrine for aiding military dictatorships in Greece and Turkey. We got rid of Fritchman, and we'll get rid of Godwin."

Mike Wilder confirmed to Roje that he had tried to interview Gus Belshin again. Wilder knew that Belshin was living on the Godwin estate, temporarily marking time, and that he might even be relenting toward the move of CPC headquarters to Adamsport. But Belshin had refused to talk with Wilder.

"I'm sorry, but I can't give you any details," Roje told Wilder. "There was a family conference, but I wasn't there. If things work out, you can forget CPC. There is no longer any conflict between the company and the First Church. In the meantime," Roje asked, feeling a little belligerent and irritated at Wilder's incessant prying, "when are you going to wrap this up? Just being around here with your 'Showdown' crew is adding fuel to the fire."

"It may not be a four-alarm fire, yet," Wilder responded, "but it sure as hell is a smoking volcano. I can't hurry things. I can't take a chance that the top might blow off after we have left. Especially when it may happen tomorrow. I have a feeling that the curtain is rising on the final act. I want to be around for the finale."

"God damn it!" Roje exploded. "That's all you're looking for—a nice tight drama for the television viewers who watch your show. It isn't going to happen that way. Last week Falconer got rained out twice. He can't keep tilting at windmills forever."

"Don't count on it," Wilder laughed. "So long as Jeffrey is getting television coverage and plenty of publicity, he'll keep ranting until his throat gives out." Then he asked Roje what Matt thought of God's Avengers, a group of ten or twelve men, and possibly a few women, who wore white sheets and peaked pillow cases, Ku Klux Klan style, and arrived every night that Falconer spoke at Morton Park. Carrying luminescent crosses, they waved them silently at the crowd. "They don't say a word," Wilder said. "I think they are afraid that people might recognize some of them. But they are dangerous. The other night they were swinging their crosses like machetes at a group of Feminists For Godwin who were showing their tits and jeering at them. It was touch and go for a while until the police broke it up."

Two days later, Wilder telephoned Roje and asked him what Peachy was going to do about Silly Willy's. Roje thought he was referring to an ordinance that the city council had just passed rezoning the adult entertainment area in the city. "It's a *post facto* law," Tom Ferris had told Peachy. "They can't use it to shut down Silly Willy's. It's been there for years."

But Wilder thought it might be an undercover way of getting at the First Church. "They've zoned downtown Adamsport against adult entertainment," Wilder told Roje. "For my book, that's just what the First Church is providing."

But Wilder hadn't called Roje for that reason. "I guess you haven't heard the news. Last night Guido Ponzello, the manager of Silly Willy's, was arrested. They were serving liquor to Billy Salter and his girl friend. She's twenty, but Billy is only sixteen. What's more, he's the son of one of the city councilors," Wilder chuckled. "I just wondered what Mary Peachy is going to do about that?"

Roje told him that only Peachy could answer his question. He knew nothing about Silly Willy's. Of course, it wasn't the truth; Peachy loved to talk to him in bed. All Roje had to do was to let his own brain relax, and he could actually think and emote just like Peachy . . . or Emily, for that matter.

Wilder located Peachy before Roje could warn her. Peachy knew about the police raid an hour before it happened. "My lawyer, Tom Ferris, is handling it," she told Wilder. "It's a put-up job. Billy Salter is a hundred-and-eighty-pound Adamsport High School football halfback. He looks as if he were at least twenty-five. We're betting that his father, Frank Salter, is behind it along with four or five others on the city council. He told Bill Walsh that they were going to close down the First Church but they would take on Silly Willy's first because of me." She laughed. "It doesn't matter. Silly Willy's is obsolete. All the sex-starved guys who live in Adamsport have to do is join the First Church. They can see naked women of all ages here. Some of us will even dance erotically for them."

"What about your father? Where is he?" Wilder demanded. "Ponzello told me that Sylvie wouldn't be very happy about this. Since your old man disappeared, you're *de facto* owner of the place. I can't believe that you don't care. Silly Willy's used to be pretty lucrative. I heard that you're paying some of those porno stars as much as three thousand a week."

"I don't know where my father is." Peachy was getting impatient with Wilder. "As for profits, a year ago, when it looked as if my father might never come back, I assigned all profits from Silly Willy's to the Foundation for Modern Moralities." She chuckled. "You can tell your TV audience that naked women—and men—can be erotic and moral at the same time."

"What about Nikki Holmes, the porn actress?" Wilder asked. "She's supposed to appear at Silly Willy's next week."

"I talked with her yesterday," Peachy said. "If Silly Willy's is still barricaded by the police, Matt and I have decided to let her dance right here at the First Church. We've scheduled her for Friday before the Fourth of July weekend. In addition to the various acts she would have done at Silly Willy's, Nikki has agreed to discuss her natural empathy with men. In case you do not know it, she has a master's degree in psychology. It's going to be very educational. We expect that she will discuss the female's role as a sex object and why she personally went into so-called adult filmmaking. Nikki will even reveal what it does emotionally to a woman when she de-sacralizes sex." Peachy laughed. "Presumably she has screwed at least a hundred different guys; yet somehow she maintains a private sex life. She has two children, a girl and a boy, who are aware of her working sex life. She feels sorry for American males who are so deprived sexually that they have to pay to see women fucking. She's very interested in Matt's new moralities." Peachy invited Wilder to come and hear her at the First Church. "You can bring your television crews if you wish. I'm sure it will be saner than anything Jeff Falconer is offering."

Peachy didn't tell Mike that Tom Ferris was very much against Nikki's appearance at the First Church. "You're not only pitting a porno star against Jeff Falconer on the Fourth of July weekend," he told Matt, "but you're charging admission! I've warned you over and over again, any religious institution is playing with fire when it crosses over into the entertainment industry. You've been doing that for the past month with your porno film showings. I know that you're using them to kick off discussions on sexual devaluations, but you do charge admission to non-members." Tom shook his head. "Offering Nikki Holmes in a live performance is even worse."

"We have to charge admission to non-members for the same reason the Cape Cod Police closed the nudist camps. The voyeurs were ruining the sand dunes. You keep forgetting," Matt told him, "we're offering a new religion and a theology based on the belief that Man is God. Sex worship, properly understood in its original sense, is a hymn of praise and adoration. One of the many 'bibles' of this church is a book written by Richard Payne Knight several hundred years ago, *A Discourse On the Worship of Priapus*. Knight points out that all early religions were based on the worship of the male and female genital powers. He asks: 'In an age, therefore, when no prejudices of artificial dignity existed, what more just and natural images could they find, by which to express their ideas of the beneficent power of the great creator, than organs which endowed them with the power of procreation, and made them partakers, not only of the felicity of the Deity, but of His great characteristic attribute; that of multiplying His own image, communicating His blessings, and extending them to generations as yet unborn.'"

Matt had smiled and hugged his doubting Thomas. "I know that we're walking on thin ice, Tom. But Christianity corrupted sexuality. The First Church is trying to undo that terrible sin against man and woman. Enjoying Nikki Holmes naked, responding erotically to her as God—who even in the Christian sense is an exhibitionist and demands that men and women celebrate him—is an act of worship."

Peachy tried to get rid of Wilder by telling him that she couldn't talk on the phone with him any longer.

"At two o'clock I'm playing volleyball in the First Church gymnasium. The Women's Alliance against the Men's Chowder Society. You can come and watch us if you wish. But no cameras."

"Are you all playing in the nude?" Wilder asked incredulously.

"Of course."

Later, a bemused Wilder discovered that the ladies, ranging in ages from thirty to fifty, also showered in the locker room with their male contenders. They had held their male opponents to a tie score.

"Do all the ladies of the First Church show their cunts to the male members?" Wilder asked after the game. "This damned religion is more dangerous to public welfare than those snake handlers and poison drinkers in Tennessee. Despite Jesus telling them in the Bible that it was better to worship snakes than evil men, the Supreme Court issued an injunction against them."

"I don't know anything about snake worship," Peachy said sarcastically as she sat down naked beside him on a gymnasium bench, "but unless you lie down on the floor, it's pretty difficult to see a lady's cunt. You should have been watching them playing volleyball."

"I stand corrected. What about Irene and Jill Godwin? Are they here today?"

"I don't think you are ever going to get Irene, Jill, and me here together."

"Okay," Wilder said, "I'll take you alone. A bird in the hand is worth two in the bush." He was finding it difficult to keep his eyes off Peachy's body. "One of my men is outside waiting with a camera. I'll call him in."

Peachy shrugged. "It's okay with me, but there is one stipulation. You must ask me the question you just asked. I can't wait to hear you use the word *cunt* on national television." She grinned at him provocatively.

"You know that I can't do that."

"Then why did you ask me with such a snide expression on your face? We don't like the word *cunt*. It's demeaning—a male way of denigrating a woman." Never at a loss for words, Peachy rambled on, telling him coolly that in any interviews he managed with her, Irene, Matt, Jill, or Roje, he'd better not take a holier-than-thou attitude. "We'll fry you in your own oil. Jill told us that she slept with you for about six months a few years ago. From what I've heard, your ego is bigger than your penis."

Wilder grinned in embarrassment. "Touché. Change the subject." He didn't tell her what Peachy already knew. Despite several phone calls, Jill had told him that she wasn't interested in reliving the past. She would talk with him only as a trio with Irene and Peachy—if they ever finally agreed to appear on "Showdown."

Wilder tried to probe into Jill's dual relationship. "Is she sleeping both with Matt and the old man?" he asked.

But Peachy only grinned at him. "Sorry, Mike, I'm not a Godwin. You'll have to ask the Godwins about their marital relationships."

Wilder had already done that. A week ago he had managed to get Ike on the telephone, but Ike told him bluntly, "My private life is none of your goddamned business. You're a moron—catering to all the little morons in the world who listen to your show and read all those slimy so-called people's magazines. My son may be immoral, but you and your ilk are a damn sight worse. Someone should put the finger on all of you."

Although Mike Wilder was sure that Matt Godwin was a charlatan and that if he kept digging he'd find the soft, wormy spot, he couldn't stomach Jeff Falconer, either. Mike had tentatively entitled his upcoming fall show "The Last Heretic," and he was convinced that

Matthew Godwin *was* a heretic equal to, or worse than, any who had preceded him on this planet. But Godwin wasn't a heretic beyond belief. Despite Falconer, and the crowds that Falconer was drawing twice a week at Morton Park, more than a thousand people jammed the First Church to hear Matt Godwin or Mary Peachy at every service. Some of them might have been coming as sexual voyeurs, but many of them left, in Matt's words, "bashful believers," praising Matt and Peachy with tears in their eyes at the joy they had experienced.

God wasn't dead! They were God! It was an idea that embarrassed them at first, and they could even laugh or joke about it. But deep down the belief was comforting and more realistic than a remote God "out there somewhere" that millions of people could no longer pray to. According to Matt, if you told any man or woman that they are God, though at the moment they may or may not be acting like God, you helped give them a point of reference with their conscience that was hard to deny.

But there wasn't any question in Wilder's mind that Matt lacked credibility because of his relationship with Irene, Jill, and Peachy, and his incessant prying made Roje nervous. He kept telling Matt that none of them should discuss their intimate sexual lives with Wilder. "He thinks that you've got Irene, Jill, and Peachy hypnotized, or you're feeding them some kind of drug that gives you a svengali power over them. He keeps hoping that he can interview them in the clothing-optional area of the church. He told Peachy they could be naked if they wished; no genitals or breasts will be showing in the final cut."

Roje shook his head disgustedly. "Wilder knows damn well that your marital philosophy, discussed in the environment of any church, will shock hell out of millions of Americans."

"I know it," Matt said. "And I know that both he and Falconer are sensationalists. But if Jill, Irene, and Peachy want to talk with Wilder, it's okay with me. I have a written agreement with him that I can respond to any of the final interviews which are going to be shown. One thing that Mike will discover is that they are modern American women. They are not members of my harem. No man could ever hypnotize them or brainwash them or make them do what they don't want to do."

But Tom Ferris admitted to Matt that he was worried too. "You're breaking too many rules at once," he said. "Even my wife wonders what motivates you and your women. She thinks that a guy who needs three women is just as flaky as a homosexual. How can you take care of three women sexually? Why would you want to?" Bewildered, Tom rubbed the thinning hair on his head. "If you were monogamous and your personal sexual life was above suspicion—straight arrow— then you might get away with the return to sex worship philosophy that you're preaching. We both know that the First Church is extolling human sexuality and trying to restore sexual wonder, but there's millions of people out there like Falconer who are positive that a guy who sleeps with three women is indulging in sex orgies. Americans are basically monogamous."

"No, they're not," Matt said. "The dream goes on, but the reality is quite different. The divorce rate is close to 50 percent. On top of that, half of the men who are still married have had at least one adulterous relationship, and their mates aren't far behind them. I don't believe that tandem polygamy—divorce and remarriage—is a sound way of ultimately finding a suitable marriage partner. Like a lot of women who have been through divorce, Jill and Peachy don't want to marry again. Together with Irene, we've created an extended family. We are just as religious and caring of each other as the families of any hell-and-damnation fundamentalist. I'm sure that one difference between me and Falconer is that I really enjoy competitive women. They are much more exciting to live with than competitive men. And I'm not afraid of human commitment or involvement with people I love, as distinguished from Falconer's commitment to Jesus. I enjoy the vagaries of the human mind, and I don't care whether a woman (or you, or any man) disagrees with me. Disagreement is the leaven that makes the dough rise."

But Tom kept hoping that he could convince Matt to keep a lower profile. "You don't seem to realize that you're outnumbered. I know that the response to your first Satellite Network broadcast on Saturday evening was phenomenal. But you're never going to outnumber the Catholics or the Jesus-believing Protestants, or even the Jews. Even if you gradually pick up a few million believers, the First Church will still be a minority religion."

"Falconer doesn't think secular humanists are a minority," Matt countered. "He fulminates against humanism every time he preaches. He thinks humanists are a threat to our national survival."

"That's the point," Tom insisted. "You're probably the first humanist who ever offered a mystical religious philosophy to go with humanism. In the process you may become nationally famous—or infamous, if you prefer—but you have given Falconer just what he's been looking for: a prominent target. Like Khrushchev, he claims he's going to bury you. And you can be sure it won't be a crucifixion. Falconer doesn't want any competition in that area."

Thursday, before the holiday weekend, Ramachanda gave the target an even bigger dimension. Matt had stayed at church later than usual, working with Jill and Bill Ramey, who were developing a film series on Visual Sex: man's never ceasing need, from 30,000 B.C. to A.D. 2,000, to express the mystery of fertility and his polarity with women in all forms of art. Peachy had gone home early in her car, to help prepare for Emily and Roje, who were coming to dinner, and Jill, who had told Matt that she really didn't need an automobile with three others in the family, was planning to drive home with him. They were alone in Matt's parish office, just getting ready to leave, when the phone rang.

Matt recognized the cultured English accent as soon as he picked up the phone. He stared grimly at Jill as Ramachanda told him that he had just arrived from Florida in a fifty-foot ketch, which right now was tied up at the Adamsport Marina. "I've been reading *Time* and *Newsweek* about your Foundation and your church, Reverend," he said smoothly. "I've discovered that the famous Mike Wilder is doing a fall show on your new religion, and that Jeffrey Falconer is very unhappy with you. As for me, I'm still searching for El Dorado." Ramachanda told him that if he wanted to avoid any unpleasant publicity, he must talk with him immediately. "I'll meet you here in a half-hour on my boat."

Matt knew that he couldn't tell Ramachanda that he was leaving town. He decided that the only way he could defuse him was to know exactly how Ramachanda was going to expose him. He heard Ramachanda chuckle when he told him that under no circumstances would he meet him on a boat. "I don't want to find myself somewhere in the Atlantic wearing cement shoes."

"I'm telephoning you from a restaurant, the Harbor View, which is right here in the marina," Ramachanda said. "I don't drink, but I'll buy you a cocktail on the verandah."

"It's know-your-enemy night," Matt told Jill. He wanted to drive her to the carriage house first, but Jill insisted on coming with him. "If anything happens to you, the show is over," she said nervously. "I don't know who in hell is writing this drama—if I did, I'd kill him—but whatever happens, I'm part of the plot. Remember? Ramachanda damned near killed me too." Jill was frightened, thinking that Ramachanda might try to kidnap them again. She thought that Matt should try and reach Tom Ferris. "A lawyer might scare him to death," she said.

But Matt was sure that the whole scenario would shock hell out of Ferris. "When I decided that I needed a lawyer, I thought that Ferris was the logical guy. He's got at least six other partners, and they're all skilled in handling Sylvie's affairs. Strangely, although Tom obviously read about Grand Cayman and the stuff that appeared in the newspapers, he never questioned me. Maybe he knows about Sylvie's gold and he doesn't want to be involved, or maybe he prefers not to know too much." Matt shrugged. "It looks as if Sylvie's gold is going to haunt me the rest of my life."

Wearing a T-shirt, white ducks, and a captain's yachting cap, evidently trying to appear less conspicuous by abandoning his Sikh-style dress, Ramachanda was waiting at the far end of the Harbor View outdoor cocktail lounge when they arrived. Seated at a table shaded by an umbrella, near the railing, he recognized Jill and greeted them both with a sly smile. "I'm glad to see that you both survived Grand Cayman," he said. After he had ordered a Coke and a scotch on the rocks for them, he said coolly, "I know that you both have every reason to hate me. I'm not at all sure that the Reverend isn't carrying a gun." He opened his coat. "But I can assure you that I'm not. The only way that we can proceed together is to forget the past. I'm sure that we agree that often moral ends may be achieved by immoral means. But most Americans wouldn't understand that philosophy. I'll come to the point immediately. On board my ketch—and I'll be happy to show it to you—is fifty kilos of cocaine. It's worth several million dollars. I haven't paid for it, and the sellers aren't willing to wait until I turn it over. I need a million dollars. Actually, so that we can avoid continuing contacts, I'll be honest with you. I need $10 million."

"I'm sorry, I haven't got it," Matt said. "And if I did have, I'd see you in hell first."

Ramachanda laughed. "Don't be so hasty, Reverend. I'm sure that you'll change your mind. First let me tell you a little story. Forty years ago, when I was twenty-two, I had a job in a bank in Calcutta equivalent to what you might call a teller in America. One day, a few weeks after Japan surrendered, I met an American soldier who was wearing a master sergeant's uniform, but he asked me to call him Colonel Gamble. He was changing dollars into rupees, and since we were about the same age and he was very interested in Indian banking, I had dinner with him and told him all that I knew about foreign exchange. I won't go into details, but about twenty years later, Colonel Gamble returned to India and made me a proposition that involved a substantial amount of gold. To cement the deal he gave me three ingots, and I, rather than try to cash them into rupees, helped myself to enough of the bank's money to get the colonel's cargo on a freighter bound for the Caribbean. My reward was to be substantially more than three gold ingots. Unfortunately, I never heard from Colonel Gamble again. I spent the next fifteen years searching for El Dorado. But I no sooner located the end of the rainbow, on Grand Cayman, when Colonel Gamble himself, now very much older, and his lady friend arrived. I told him I was still willing to share with him on a 50-50 basis, but he insisted that the gold wasn't in his villa. But of course it was. My guess is that it's still there. For some reason your friend the sheik hasn't sold it. Probably because gold prices are depressed and he's waiting for a rising market. But I'm sure that he has paid you very well for it."

"You're wrong," Matt said coldly. "I never sold any gold to Amir

Saud." Jill wondered how he could be so calm. "Why don't you contact him?"

"I tried to," Ramachanda said. "I'm sure that you remember our friend Torvo Vigilar?"

"I wouldn't call him a friend."

"Agreed. And he's not a Castro Communist either. He guessed correctly that if I were released, I might lead him to the gold. Unaware that he was following me, I returned to Grand Cayman. Your sheik wasn't there, but he had turned the villa into a kind of rest camp fortress with his own private army. Vigilar and I were not welcomed, and we were greatly outnumbered." Ramachanda smiled. "We may return, but not until we can get reinforcements. In the meantime, a man has to live. Vigilar went into cocaine smuggling. Unfortunately, he doesn't trust me. I left Florida without him. He refused to take any of the risks, but he wants half of the pie."

"Whatever your pie is," Matt interrupted, "I'm not interested."

"I read in *Time* magazine that you believe that drugs should be legalized," Ramachanda said. "I need some quick financial backing. I don't want something for nothing. You could participate in the profits."

Matt couldn't help smiling. "I believe in government-controlled legalization of drugs, which would quickly put you and all the drug smugglers out of business." Matt looked at his watch and stood up. "I'm sorry. We're late for a dinner engagement."

"Like it or not, you'd better listen to me," Ramachanda said coolly, restraining him with one hand. "I think you should know there's one ingot of Colonel Gamble's gold left. It's in a safe deposit vault in a Florida bank. With it there's a letter to the FBI, telling them where I think the rest of it is." Ramachanda was drumming on the table as he spoke. "It would help them solve a forty-year-old mystery. The trail, of course, leads right here to Adamsport."

Matt wondered if he were bluffing. One ingot was worth close to $200,000. If Ramachanda were actually smuggling cocaine and needed money, he'd have found a buyer for that ingot a long time ago. Matt was about to tell him to go ahead and give the ingot to the FBI—he didn't give a damn—when Jill screamed, causing a sudden flutter of sea gulls that were perched on the roof of the restaurant.

A heavy-built, swarthy man had climbed up the pilings that supported the porch. He was poised on the outer edge and was pointing a gun at them. A second before he fired, Matt grabbed Jill and toppled them both to the floor. They heard Ramachanda yell: "Don't shoot, Torvo! It's half yours!" They were his last words. Two shots cracked off. The man disappeared, jumping at least twelve feet down into the soft ocean mud below. Ramachanda crashed to the floor, splattering Matt and Jill with his blood, and flesh, and shattered brain.

Three hours later, after extended questioning, Al Zurda, Chief of Adamsport Police, released them to Tom Ferris, who was grimly waiting. "We told him the truth," Matt said, trying to alert Ferris. "Ramachanda, the man we were with, was murdered by a Cuban, Torvo Vigilar. Ramachanda was evidently double-crossing him in a cocaine smuggling deal."

"Godwin insists that he's not involved," Zurda said sarcastically, "but I sure as hell don't believe him. I should toss him in the tank. But since he's a Godwin, I'm letting him go—temporarily. We searched every nook and cranny of the Hindu's ketch. There's not a sniff of coke anywhere. Godwin's probably got it buried under the First Church. Or maybe his friends Lovejoy and Mary Peachy are hiding it in the belfry."

Zurda glowered at Jill. "I'm damned sure your husband, Isaac, isn't going to be very happy about this publicity. If you know something that you're not admitting, my advice to you is to get your own skirts clean fast. If we don't get your boy friend for smuggling or murder, we'll get all of you for lewd and obscene behavior."

It was midnight, but Tom followed them back to the carriage house where Irene, Peachy, Roje, and Emily were waiting. For the first time Matt told Ferris in detail about Sylvie's gold, and was surprised to discover that Sylvie had never mentioned it to him.

"It's the goddamnedest story I ever heard," Ferris said, flinging questions at both Jill and Emily and trying to absorb the details. "If any of this comes out, you won't need a lawyer to save you, you'll need God."

"You forget," Irene said with a half-smile on her face, "he *is* God."

"Then God had better contact Amir Saud immediately and convince him to tell everyone that he gave God $45 million out of the goodness of his heart."

"Maybe Amir didn't," Matt said warily. "I can't believe that he's an altruist. If you've been reading the papers lately, you know that the Saudi Arabians have just reactivated a gold mine called the 'Cradle of Gold.' King Fahd presided at the ceremonies. Oil Minister Ahmed Zaki Yamani expects it to yield thirty tons of gold, at the very least." Matt shrugged. "Why should Amir expose himself? Arabian gold mining could provide a nice cover for Sylvie's gold. I think the only solution is to be honest. I'll preach a sermon next week and admit that even though I never saw or touched forty million dollars' worth of stolen gold, on one count at least, I *am* the immoral Reverend."

Tom scowled at him. "If you do anything as stupid as that, you'd better find yourself another lawyer. You've been playing havoc with the First Amendment. Only the Fifth Amendment is going to save your neck. Hopefully, some people will believe that you're innocent and that Ramachanda interpreted your modern drug morality incorrectly. Maybe he was bluffing about the gold ingot. Your only hope is to keep your mouth shut and pray. But don't ask me to whom!"

43

Two days before Nikki Holmes arrived, Matt showed Tom Ferris copy for an advertisement that he was planning to run in the *Adamsport Chronicle*. Scanning it with disbelief, Ferris finally read it aloud: "'Friday and Saturday evening at 8 o'clock, Nikki Holmes, star of many adult films, will appear with members of the New England School of the Ballet in a modern dance drama based on the *Song of Solomon*. Admission to non-members is $6.'

"For Christ's sake, Matt!" Tom tossed the typewritten sheet at him angrily. "Don't do it! The whole damned town is in an uproar over the murder of that Hindu. Many people—even members of the church—are wondering if you're lying. Some people are sure that you're involved in drug smuggling or worse." Tom had also heard rumors that the top brass at Unitarian Universalist headquarters on Beacon Street in Boston weren't too happy about the First Church, either.

"Horace Belcher told me that at a meeting this week they referred to your members as Mo Mo's. They're proclaiming that Modern Moralists aren't following the principles and purposes of the church as approved by UU members. They believe that UU's should think for themselves and no Pope Godwin should tell them what to believe. Mike Wilder and Falconer have already picked up the tag. Mo Mo's. It sounds like a sick cow, but I'm afraid that you're stuck with it."

Matt laughed. "It's no worse than Jehovah's Witnesses or Christian Scientists, not to mention Moonies. Tell Horace that the UU's need a few heretics. They're an endangered species. Who knows? The Mo Mo's might save them from extinction."

Tom sighed hopelessly. "Some people think that you're getting too smart for your britches. They're comparing you to DeLorean, the former General Motors whiz kid. Al Zurda swears that when they get their hands on that Cuban, Vigilar or whatever the hell his name is, that he'll put the whammy on you. Please, I'm begging you. Let things cool down. Sponsoring a porno actress at the First Church is adding insult to injury. At least postpone her until after the Fourth weekend."

He reminded Matt that Falconer had been telling reporters for the past week that Sunday at 7:00 P.M., on the "Falconer Gospel Hour," with the Lord's help he was going to reveal the truth: Matthew Godwin was really Satan in disguise.

"And don't get any ideas that you're going to the stadium to hear him in person," Ferris warned Matt. "All of you, stay home! And that includes Irene, Jill, and Peachy—your wives, as everyone is calling them—along with Roje and Emily. You can all watch Falconer on television. And for God's sake, don't let Nikki appear in church on Sunday. Don't go head to head with Falconer, or try to take away his audience. He'll murder you."

Matt admitted that he wasn't happy about the growing tension in the city, but, he reminded Ferris, "Jill and I had nothing to do with Ramachanda's death. If he actually wrote a letter to the FBI, I'll have to cross that bridge when I come to it. There's a moral somewhere in the story of Sylvie's gold." Matt grinned at the dubious expression on Tom's face. "Don't worry, I'll try not to make it a Requiem Mass. As for Falconer, he's been going head to head with me for the past month. I didn't invite him to Adamsport to harass me or the First Church. The truth is, Falconer needs me. If he didn't have me to fight, he'd have to invent me."

Matt told Ferris that he had made several attempts to be friendly with Falconer. "I even offered him the First Church for his Fourth of July sermon. I tried to convince him that in many areas we're not so far apart as he might think. I don't agree with the politicians who would confine ministers, priests, and rabbis to the spiritual aspects of religion. All churches should be constantly examining the morality of governmental decisions and old and new laws. Morality has many dimensions. Whether man and woman are God, or God is out there somewhere, our president, senators, and congressmen need a watchdog constantly yapping at their heels. But unlike Falconer, I think that religions which try to legislate their moralities need a watchdog, too. I think abortion is a sad commentary on the lack of sex education provided our young people. If all denominations, including Catholics and fundamentalists, would offer a sane approach to sex education, the problem of abortion would disappear. If they would advocate a loving, caring environment for premarital sex and a thorough knowledge of birth control for all young people, very few abortions would be necessary."

"You're preaching," Tom interjected.

Matt laughed. "I'm a preacher. The same applies to pornography. Like Falconer, I'm fighting against any portrayal of human sexuality that is sadistic, domineering, uncaring, degrading, or treats women as sex objects. But I don't believe in state censorship. The Church should dare to use sexual devaluation of any kind as a teaching tool, and expose its lack of sound human values. Despite Falconer, I firmly believe that all children should grow up seeing, in life and in the arts, naked human beings enjoying each other in the act of caring sex. But enough of preaching. Falconer is a one-dimensional man. He stalked away from me as if I were a poisonous snake. The last time I talked with him, he responded with Paul's advice to the Romans, Galatians chapter 8: 'For the good you will do, you do not do, but the evil you will not do, that you practice.'"

Irene agreed with Tom. "The best place to watch Falconer is at home on television. Sunday night I'm going to be right here in bed. And I'll be thankful that George Orwell was wrong—we haven't gotten two-way television yet." She laughed. "Thank God Big Brother Falconer can't see us right now."

They had all gathered in the big bedroom. Irene grinned at Jill, who, stark naked, was making horrible faces at herself in a full-length mirror and at the same time was doing a fair imitation of Falconer preaching on his "Gospel Hour." "And Tom is right about something else," Irene said to Peachy, who was immersed in a book entitled *Religion and Sexism*, "the less publicity we give our personal lives, the better. Six weeks ago, I never thought I'd be sharing God's bedroom with his two other female apostles. But here I am, and I care for all of us. But I'm not like the rest of you. I'm not trying to change the world or trying to convince people that what works for us will work for them, or that three women and one man are behaving just as morally together as any monogamous couple."

She paused. Jill slid down beside her on the bed and gave her behind a loving smack. "In a nutshell," Irene couldn't help giggling, "if Ike or Becky or Gus Belshin could see us, the three of us, they'd be as horrified as Jeff Falconer."

"Maybe," Jill said. "But maybe not. I think Ike is changing his mind. Peachy convinced him that gerocomy isn't such a crazy idea. Ike would probably be happy to snuggle in bed with any one of us."

Jill nudged Peachy as Matt wandered into the bedroom and flopped on the bed beside them. "You're not reading," she accused Peachy. "Your eyes are closed. Wake up and tell us what you think. Personally, I think Nikki Holmes is the bomb that could blow us all to kingdom come. I don't think she should appear in church until Falconer leaves town."

Peachy smiled. "I wasn't sleeping. I was thinking. It's too late. We're committed for Friday and Saturday night. But Falconer's big night isn't until Sunday night, the Fourth. So I think we should go ahead with Nikki and let her do *The Song of Songs*. Then Sunday night, she could appear for members only. We could invite members only to watch Falconer on the sanctuary screen. Three times life size. We've got the equipment to project his television broadcast. He'll be finished by eight o'clock, then Nikki can do some of the acts she would have performed at Silly Willy's. Afterwards the members can have a dialogue with her. Maybe, in addition to *The Song of Solomon*,

Nikki would do a Salome dance for us with a simulated head of Jeff Falconer." Peachy chuckled. "If she won't, I might even try it myself."

"Rather than putting on a strip show Silly Willy style," Matt said, "maybe Sunday night we could convince Nikki to be her own critic. I'm sure she knows the difference between performances where she's being a naturally erotic woman and when on stage and in films she's being manipulated as a temptress and sex object."

Jill and Irene were still a little dubious. Jill wasn't sure that Nikki was that talented or whether she understood—or whether Matt understood, for that matter—the difference between erotic female behavior and just plain sexiness. "If she does," Jill grinned at them, "then she can teach me."

Irene didn't think that they should publicize the members-only night. If they did it quietly and the church weren't opened to the public, she thought, Father Tim might even come.

"I'm sure that he's going to listen to Falconer." She smiled a little self-consciously. "But he told me personally he's quite curious about porno actresses and how a woman ever gets involved in such a sad, unfulfilling life." Leaning on one elbow, she stared at Matt. "Like me, Father Tim wonders what makes you tick, too. He's afraid that you're a dreamy idealist who refuses to admit there's evil in the world."

Matt kissed her dangling breasts, which he insisted were frowning at him, and then he swiftly kissed Jill's and Peachy's, too. Grinning at them, he finally responded, "You're all asking the same question with nine separate expressions on your faces and breasts. Is loving three women evil? Obviously, Tim and I simply do not agree on what the particular evils are. Neither Tim's God, nor any one of us as God, is always rational. If Tim's God really cared about His creations, would He let them destroy each other or give them the power to do so? Would he let them die in childbirth or before their time? Would He create floods, hurricanes, volcanoes, and earthquakes and kill thousands of His creatures in one blow? Would He have made so much of the world arid and ridden by drought? The truth is, Father Tim's God is irrational. When men and women realize that *they* are God, and act like God, they have the potential to be more rational toward each other and more loving than any God out there that man has ever conceived."

Matt had tumbled between Peachy and Irene while Jill straddled his thighs. "No doubt Tim thinks that it is evil for a priest to snuggle in the arms of beautiful women, but he might learn more about God from them than from Matthew, Mark, Luke, and John."

Happy that Matt couldn't read her mind, Irene smiled at the memories of her night with Tim, memories which she had not shared with any of them yet. She had promised herself that she would never take the initiative with Tim or indicate that she might enjoy a reprise.

During the past month they had played golf together at least once a week, but always in a foursome. His first allusion to their love-making had been, "Do you have any regrets?" She had shaken her head no and asked, "Do you?" He had answered, "How could I? I love you."

Irene hoped that their night together had been a joyous experience for him. But she guessed that close to the surface of his mind, his need for her was constantly prowling and tripping over his religious commitments to the Father, Son, and Holy Ghost. Yesterday, while they were playing the eighteenth hole with another couple but finally found a chance to be alone for a few minutes, he remarked that during the past twenty years, more than twelve thousand priests had resigned from the church, many to get married. He left his statement dangling, and Irene wondered if he might be considering abandoning the church. She hoped not. How could a fifty-year-old ex-priest adjust to secular life?

She knew she must reveal her new relationship with Matt, which she did in some detail. "It's crazy, I know," she said, "but sleeping with Matt only a third of the time . . . we're actually closer than we were before Jill and Peachy."

Reflecting on her confession, Father Tim drove a golf ball nearly two hundred yards down the fairway. Then he turned to her with a pixieish smile and left her speechless. "You are a remarkable woman," he said. "I love you. Perhaps you might enjoy a friend and lover occasionally on your nights off."

At breakfast, before Peachy left for the airport to meet Nikki, Irene surprised herself and all of them by wondering aloud if it wouldn't be better if Nikki stayed in the carriage house with them rather than in the Holiday Inn where she had reservations.

"She won't attract so much attention if she stays here," Irene said. "No one can get by our security guards at the front entrance. One of us could drive her back and forth to the church."

Last night they had watched one of Nikki's films on video tape called "The Love Explosion." Irene had never seen a porno film before. Jill and Peachy had seen "Deep Throat." Matt had seen a few others, and he reminded them that several thousand X-rated films had been made in the past ten years, and several million Americans—mostly men—watched them every week, at home or in so-called adult theaters.

At first they were all a little embarrassed, but then the continuous "fucking and sucking" became both funny and sad.

"It's orgasm gymnastics," Matt said. "There's no love or laughter."

Irene wondered why such a beautiful woman would let herself be used by so many men. "She can't be over thirty years old."

"She's an actress," Jill said, "or tries to be. Thin as the story line was, she did try to be the woman in the story, not herself."

"Could you screw with so many different men in front of a camera?" Peachy asked her.

"No way." Jill shook her head. But she admitted that on stage she had passionately kissed quite a few men. "In the theater or on camera you learn how to depersonalize yourself. Your body is there, but your mind momentarily has become another person. Anyway, it's all right with me if she stays here. Maybe we can find out what makes her tick." She grinned at Matt. "Or maybe she can teach us all some new tricks."

"Assuming that she hasn't got VD," Irene said. "She can bunk with me, or, if she prefers, since Peachy will be sleeping with Matt, and if Peachy doesn't mind, Nikki can sleep in her bed."

Before she left for the airport, Peachy hugged Irene. "You really are an angel." She grinned at Matt. "But I think your wives should warn you. You've got enough trouble already. Even though Nikki is ten years younger, you'd better tell her this territory is staked out. Three women are a happy crowd, and anything she can do, the three of us can do better!"

44

Driving back to Adamsport from the airport, Nikki told Peachy how excited she was that she was going to dance in a church rather than at Silly Willy's. 'I can't wait to tell my mother," she grinned happily. "My stepfather will never believe it. He sends Jeff Falconer at least ten dollars a week. He's convinced that I am a totally diseased and evil slut. The last time I saw my mother, she had to come down to the hotel where I was staying. I'm not allowed in his house."

Nikki was even more astonished and delighted when Peachy told her that she was God. "Of course you have to understand we believe that man and woman as God are in a process of continuous evolution," Peachy said. "Matt will tell you that you are denying your divinity when you screw without love."

"I screw for love," Nikki laughingly assured her. "Love of money. Last year, from films and personal appearances I earned $65,000. It's not a fortune, but it's a hell of a lot more than I earned teaching." She explained that five years ago she had been teaching psychology in a Nashville high school and had repeatedly plunged into hot water as she wandered into areas of sex education that went beyond the limits of "Daddy's seed impregnates Mommy's egg." "Especially when I established a source of supply for the pill for some of my fifteen-year-old girls who were playing Russian roulette with their boyfriends."

Nikki shrugged. "Anyway, I was dating a guy who was studying filmmaking. He shot a 16-millimeter film of me. It was very artsy and romantic and naked. He called it *Veronica, My Love*—Veronica is my birth name. It won an amateur filmmaking prize. A guy named Villis Ricci saw it, and he called me from California and offered me $4,000 for five days' work—mostly on my back or on my knees." Nikki grinned. "I had been screwing and sucking since I was fourteen. I loved all the boys, and I loved to tease them and watch them go ape when they got me undressed. But no one had ever paid me."

From the moment she arrived at the carriage house, Irene and Jill, along with Peachy, were completely captivated by Nikki's total lack of sophistication. None of the crass ugliness of the mechanized sex she had performed on film had rubbed off on her. With silky brown hair, almond-shaped blue eyes, a sprinkling of freckles, a bony jaw line, provocative turned up nose and full lips, and no make-up, she had a girlish beauty that was irresistible. At twenty-eight she was still the zesty all-American girl who lived next door and maybe even sang in the choir, and wouldn't dare to admit that she liked to make love as much as any guy.

"This is really me, Veronica Butz," Nikki told Irene, who wouldn't have recognized her. "What you see on the screen—make-up, mascara, false eyelashes, and occasionally blonde wigs—is Nikki Holmes. She's a fantasy. The poor guys who have no women to hold their cocks wouldn't get an erection if they knew what I really looked like or the kind of person I am. In reality, I'm the kind of girl they marry, after which they dream about Nikki Holmes."

"Tomorrow night, if you're agreeable, we're going to transform you into a bride of Solomon," Jill told her. "You're going to be the Shulamite woman in the 'Song of Songs.' You'll love your Beloved, Ashley Moore. He's a handsome guy about your age. He's a student at the New England School of the Ballet. While you and Ashley bring the 'Song of Songs' to life, Peachy and Irene will be offstage reading the words of the Daughters of Jerusalem. Matt will read the Beloved's lines from offstage, and I the words of the Bride. Our voices will be amplified in the sanctuary. The music will be Tschaikowsky's Serenade in C Major."

Nikki laughed. "Are you sure you have the correct scenario? My stepfather thinks that I'm the whore of Babylon." She shook her head worriedly. "I love to dance, but I'm not a ballet dancer. I was a go-go dancer once, and I'm a sensational stripper."

Later, when Matt arrived home to get a quick lunch and meet Nikki, to his amusement all four ladies were splashing naked in the pool and playing water ball with the children. Nikki stood on tiptoes and kissed him reverentially and said in smiling awe, "You really do look like God ought to look." To Matt's amazement, she was blushing.

"You are probably making a mistake casting me as a virgin," she sighed. "What's more, I'm not sure I dare to do my 'raincoat crowd' routines while God is watching."

"Don't worry," Irene laughed. "Matt isn't like any God you learned about in Sunday School."

Matt explained to Peachy, Jill, and Irene that the "raincoat crowd" categorized men of all ages who watched women performing erotically and presumably wore raincoats for easy access to their genitals. "You can do your regular show Sunday night," Matt said, admiring Nikki's lithe body. "In the meantime, I hope Jill has told you that all day tomorrow she and Max Dashow, who runs the ballet school, are going to work hell out of you. I expect that you will be the most lovely and erotic Shulamite in biblical history." He explained that in addition to watching the dancers live, the audience would be able to see them simultaneously televised on the sanctuary screen from many different perspectives. "For an hour and a half, every man in the congregation will imagine that he is your beloved, and every woman will be you."

By Friday afternoon, after twenty hours of rehearsals in the church, Nikki proved that she was, in Jill's words, a real trouper. She fascinated them all with her ingenuous, loving portrayal of a Palestinian woman and her ability to float across the stage into her Beloved's arms.

An hour before Nikki's first appearance in the First Church, Tom Ferris left City Hall with Roje. They had just suffered through a last-minute, two-hour conference with George Gallagher and Al Zurda and several members of the city council. Gallagher had been insistent. "I don't give a shit whether she's in good taste or not. We're not going to let any porno star strip right across the street from City Hall in a church where the Adams family are buried. I don't give a damn if she's appearing in a biblical story. What are you trying to do? Make me and Adamsport the laughingstock of the nation? You tell Godwin to cancel Nikki Holmes. He can give a sermon, or you can show one of those fucking sex-worship movies that you've cooked up. Ultimately, you're not going to get away with showing porno movies in a church or letting young kids run around bare-ass together either. That's not a religion. It's a sexual side show."

Roje told Tom that it was too late. The six hundred seats in the sanctuary which they had made available for non-members were sold out for both nights. Now, as they crossed the square to enter the church the back way through the new parish building, they were dismayed to see, parked along the street, six or more cruising cars with blue lights flashing ominously. Twenty or more policemen were leaning against the hoods of the cars or wandering through the crowd of two hundred or more people already milling around the church. The front doors wouldn't open for a half-hour, but the protesters had arrived already. Firecrackers were exploding, creating a sulphureous odor in the sultry Fourth of July twilight. Several people, carrying signs, begged them not to pay money to watch a whore. "The lust of the flesh, the lust of the eyes is not the Father," one sign read. Other protesters poked their signs at them: "Walk in the spirit and you shall not fulfill the lust of the flesh," "If one loves the world, the love of the Father is not in him," "Let the Lord come into your heart," "Trust Jesus as your Savior."

Inside the church, Tom located Matt talking with Peachy, Jill, and Irene. They were all backstage with the dancers, going over bits and pieces of the dance and music sequences. Everyone was bubbling with pre-performance jitters. "I don't know what in the hell is going to happen tonight," Tom said, "but Zurda, Gallagher, and even Sam Hardman, the district attorney, have bought tickets. They're out to get you, Matt, on one charge or another."

In angry astonishment he stared at Nikki and Ashley, whose diaphanous costumes accentuated the lines and curves of their bodies. Nikki's breasts were bare, and her pubic hair and Ashley's penis were vaguely visible. "For Christ's sake, Matt," he hissed, "this isn't New York City. Is that all they're going to wear?"

"Halfway through, not even that." Matt grinned at him. "Keep in mind that they're lovers right out of biblical times. If you could read an unexpurgated translation of the Song of Solomon, I'm sure that you'd realize that the ancient Jews weren't as inhibited as we are."

"You'd better warn them," Ferris said grimly. "My contact in the police department told me that Zurda and a couple of his lieutenants will be carrying high-speed cameras. They're going to get the evidence. Before you finish, you could all be arrested for indecent exposure."

Matt shook his head wearily, then waved his hands and asked for everybody's attention. "Tom Ferris is afraid that we might be arrested tonight for putting on an obscene performance. It's your choice. We can cancel *The Song of Songs* and offer a panel discussion with Nikki exploring the subject of pornography and explicit sex. Or with Ashley properly attired in a jock strap and Nikki in a bra and panties, we can brave it out."

"Why not?" Ferris demanded. "If they were properly dressed, that would confound Zurda and Gallagher."

"Will you bail us out if we're arrested?" Mark Dashow, the bearded impresario, speaking for the ballet school, asked. "Will you pay our fines?"

Matt assured them that he'd personally bail them out. Ten minutes later they unanimously agreed to dance as they had planned. Laughing, Nikki told them not to worry, even if they were arrested. "I spent several nights in jail," she said. "It's an interesting experience. You'll look at life a little differently when you come out."

Roje shook his head and told Tom to brace himself and look through the two-way mirror at the audience. "The Mass Bay Colony of judges has arrived already. Gallagher may be Irish, but he looks like a reincarnation of Governor John Winthrop. Jeff Falconer and Mike Wilder are sitting next to him. Tomorrow we'll all be banished."

"For God's sake," Ferris gasped. "It's only seven-thirty and the place is damned near filled. I told you that Zurda is out to get you. He's taking pictures already. What the hell are they watching so glassy-eyed on the screen?"

Matt laughed. "You'd better take a seat in the sanctuary and watch it. It's a half-hour film we just produced, called 'The War Between Baal and Jehovah.' Long before the Israelites were united by Elijah, one of the tribes, the Canaanites, worshipped a loving, mysterious God they called Baal. Baal presumably slept with Astarte, Goddess of the Earth. Baal never stopped making love to her, and thus the earth was impregnated and the crops grew. Very sensibly, the Canaanites worshipped Baal and erected huge phallic statues commemorating his joyful work. They prayed to the sexual images of Astarte and Baal as they happily copulated together. Baal and Astarte were not only responsible for their own fertility, but for the joy their worshippers had when they were making love.

"Alas, then a spoilsport called Elijah arrived. He was worse than Jeff Falconer. Elijah confronted some four hundred and fifty priests of Baal on Mount Carmel and challenged them to prove that Baal was greater than his God Jehovah, who would permit no graven images."

Noticing that Tom was slightly aghast, Matt patted his shoulder. "You can read the details in I Kings 18. It's obvious that Elijah was a better meteorologist than the sex-loving priests, and a better con man. The priests invoked Baal, but he was happily exhausted from a loving night in bed with Astarte and paid no attention to them. It took Elijah all night, but he had picked the right evening. The clouds gathered and Jehovah obligingly hurled a few thunderbolts and lightning in the direction of Mount Carmel. While that was happening, and no one was looking, Elijah's troops knocked over a few statues of Baal, whose marvelous erection was pointed toward heaven. Alas, Elijah and Jehovah had won. Thus began the twelve tribes of Jacob, who worshipped the new sex-denying God of Israel." Matt shrugged. "Even after Adam and Eve betrayed him, Jehovah expected his creations to love him more than they loved each other. It was a sad turning point in history. The First Church and the Mo Mo's are trying to straighten things out."

Ferris was shaking his head helplessly. "If you still believe in Baal, you'd better pray to him. Gallagher's got reinforcements. He's getting ready to hurl more than thunder at you."

"I am Baal," Matt said, and Tom couldn't tell whether he was joking or not. "Our services define our sacraments. Human sexuality and human creativity stemming from the same source is our religion."

He handed Ferris a program. "You'd better read it."

Inside was a brief biography of Nikki Holmes, nee Veronica Butz, and the listing of the cast of *The Song of Songs*. On the opposite page was a printed explanation of Thursday night services and special services like tonight's performance: "We believe that religion must provide both a sense of the mystery and the mystical experience in human existence, and at the same time celebrate the awe and playfulness and our total dependency on each other as separate Gods. Us—a multi-billion-member aggregate on this planet. Us—the only God that we will ever know. Because much of this sense of one-ness with creation, life, and death is ineffable, we invite you at least one evening a week, without sermons or secular concerns, but in an atmosphere of music, drama, motion pictures, and ballet, and in loving community, to bridge your personal island existence and revel in the joy of knowing that you are not alone."

"Sixty seconds to go!" Dashow called, waving to the group. "Nikki, Ashley, and the Daughters of Jerusalem, take your places on the rising stage!"

Watching through the one-way look-out, Jill knew that the story of Baal on the sanctuary screen was concluding. For a moment, at the curve of the horseshoe tiers, she could see the grim face of Al Zurda. Beside him Jeff Falconer was talking angrily to George Gallagher and Mike Wilder. Then, as the moving figures on the screen faded away, the dome was suffused with the early evening, star-lighted sky. It was the Middle East more than 2,500 years ago.

Invisible to the audience, Jill's warm contralto voice filled the sanctuary: "Around 200 A.D., Rabbi Akbar, defending the inclusion of the Song of Songs in the sacred scriptures, said, 'The entire world from the beginning to the end does not outweigh the day on which the Song of Songs was given to Israel. A better title would be the Best of all Songs.' Like the ancient Hebrews, Modern Moralists believe that exalting human love, as this poetry does, offers a beautiful religious expression of man's and woman's sexual affinity with each other. So now, to the music of Tschaikowsky's Serenade in C Major, we invite you to wonder, and to enjoy with our dancers and with us, your readers, this hymn to human love."

Jill paused, and Nikki, wearing a jeweled headdress, her youthful breasts proud and uplifted, her hips, stomach, and pubic hair clearly visible under her pale silk gown, followed by the Daughters of Jerusalem, similarly attired, glided off the backstage into the center of the congregation. Jill could hear an audible gasp of surprise from the audience as the Daughters, dancing erotically around Nikki, provided a contrapose to her own naively sensual movements, expressing in dance the words that Jill was now saying:

"'Kiss me with the kisses of your mouth, for your love is better than wine . . . Your name is ointment poured forth. Therefore virgins love you . . . Oh, lead me away.'"

Peachy and Irene spoke the words of the Daughters together: "'We will run after you.'"

"'The king has brought me to his chamber,'" Jill said for Nikki, as the screen momentarily became a backdrop for a three-dimensional sultan's palace. She continued speaking as three television cameras, monitored by students, followed the dancers and intercut various aspects of their bodily movements onto the screen. The pulsating montage of breasts, faces, pubes, and behinds created an almost tactile eroticism before the screen once again faded into the palace interior.

To Tom Ferris, Roje, and Emily, who had slipped into seats reserved for them, it was apparent that many people in the sanctuary were experiencing via the music and lighting a total sexual identification with the dancers. But in the shadowy light it was also obvious that some of them, including Al Zurda and Jeff Falconer, were shifting uneasily in their seats and trying to contain their rage.

Then, as Jill spoke for Nikki—"'Who is this coming out of the wilderness like pillars of smoke?'"—the Daughters appeared carrying a billowy air cushion center stage. Ashley, tall and kingly, followed by a soft purplish spotlight, leaped onto the stage. With sensuous dance movements, he adored the Shulamite woman while she swayed beguilingly with a charming invitation to love.

Finally, they danced an extended pas de deux, during which Ashley's toga and Nikki's flimsy skirt floated to the floor. Unseen by the audience, Matt said for the Beloved: "'Behold you are fair, my love . . . You have dove's eyes . . . Your breasts are like two fauns . . . You are all fair, my love.'"

Wide-eyed, the audience watched the naked lovers respond to the music in a fleeting flesh contact as Matt continued: "'You have ravished my heart . . . You are a garden enclosed . . . a spring shut up, a fountain sealed . . .'"

Trembling, Nikki swooned into Ashley's arms, and he kissed her lips and breasts while he lightly caressed her. Momentarily magnified and projected on the sanctuary screen from different perspectives, Nikki's vulva was a shadowy butterfly, and Ashley, despite the exertion of his dance, was pointing at her with his penis.

Then, as the Beloved slowly danced away, Nikki collapsed tearfully on the cushion.

"'I have taken off my robe. How can I put it on again? I have washed my feet. How can I defile them? Oh my beloved, you touched the latch of my door and my heart yearns for you. I arise to open for you . . .'"

Jill's words were cut short by the blast of a police whistle. Twelve or more policemen, guns bared, charged into the sanctuary. On his feet, a bull horn in his hands, Al Zurda was yelling like a storm trooper at the congregation, which had suddenly become a frightened, shouting, screaming bedlam.

"This is a police raid! Everyone not connected with this obscene performance please leave immediately. Clear this church!" he bellowed. "Matthew Godwin and everyone connected with this performance are under arrest. You're charged with corrupting the morals of this community, endangering the public welfare with lewd and obscene behavior, and breaking the zoning laws of this city for adult entertainment."

45

Matt, Roje, Jill, and Peachy spent the night in jail. When the cruising cars and a paddy wagon, filled with the dancers from the ballet school as well as Irene, Nikki, and Emily, arrived at the Adamsport police station with sirens screeching, Al Zurda was waiting. They were all fingerprinted and booked. Then Zurda finally listened to Tom Ferris, who kept shouting that he couldn't do this.

Zurda agreed with him. "The criminals in this case are Matthew Godwin, Robert Lovejoy, Mary Peachy, and Jill Godwin," Zurda said, scowling at all of them. "The rest of you, including Nikki Holmes and Ashley Moore, were being paid to do a job. You're free to leave." He frowned at Irene Godwin and Emily Lovejoy. "That includes you, but I'm warning both of you; if you continue to associate with these men, you'll be in criminal violation of the law, too."

"You're a stupid ass, Al Zurda," Irene said, surprising even Matt with her cold anger. "There was nothing lewd or obscene about the performance, except in your filthy mind."

Zurda shook his head sorrowfully. "You'd better get the hell out of here." He gestured to a policeman and told him to drive them back to the church or to the Godwin estate if they wished. "I'm afraid that your husband has brainwashed you. Nikki Holmes and Ashley Moore were naked. They were practically screwing on the stage. I've got pictures to prove it. You may call it modern morality, but I call it an obscenity."

Before Matt, Jill, Roje, and Peachy were led away to cells, Zurda told them angrily: "I know damned well that you'll be out in the morning, but this will prove to you that the people of Adamsport aren't kidding. You're in criminal violation of city and state ordinances. If the courts decide that I'm wrong and Judge Gravman lets you off with just a reprimand, I'll hand in my badge."

"I warned you," Tom Ferris told Matt, shaking his head sadly. "I can probably get you out before noon, but unless I can get the charges dropped, you may have to face criminal charges."

"Good," Matt said cheerily. "I'm not the first minister to take on the State of Massachusetts. Just make sure Roje, Peachy, and Jill are not included in any charges. I'm solely responsible for their actions."

The next morning, more than a little bedraggled after spending the night in a police station cell with Roje and listening to Peachy and Jill, who began to think it was all very funny (especially when Peachy, stark naked, waved at one of the male guards through the iron bars), Matt tried to convince Judge Gravman that Modern Morality was a religion.

"We are not ashamed of human nudity, or human loving. We have as much right, under the First Amendment, to our beliefs and our ways of worship as any religious sect," he told Gravman. "Freedom of religion is one of the reasons we celebrate this Fourth of July weekend."

Judge Gravman wasn't so sure. Staring down at Roje in particular from behind the bench, he said ominously: "The Constitution doesn't protect flashers, even if they try to make their occupation a religion. I've been expecting to see you again, Mr. Lovejoy. You may think it is your constitutional right to run around the Prudential Tower naked, but I don't. As for this complaint, Mr. Ferris, it's not my place to agree or disagree with this arrest and whether your clients' incarceration was legitimate or not. I'm sure that Captain Zurda believes that he has acted within the law. In any event, the problems raised by your church and its religious beliefs are now at the State level. District Attorney Samuel Hardman informed me this morning that he has entered a cease and desist injunction against the First Church. The State of Massachusetts will prosecute you on the grounds that the First Church of Modern Morality is not a legitimate religion and therefore so-called Modern Moralists are not entitled to special protection under the First Amendment." Gravman stared grimly at Matt. "It's the district attorney's conviction, Mr. Godwin, that your church and your beliefs represent 'a clear and present danger' to the State."

Then, speaking to Al Zurda and several attorneys for the City of Adamsport, Gravman said: "You and I may be repulsed by the morals of the First Church and what has been occurring on its premises, but I will not invoke any cease and desist order against it. Matthew Godwin and Mary Peachy have evidently convinced four hundred or more citizens of this city that their moralities are not obscene. Among them are John Codman, president of the Adamsport Trust Company, and several otherwise sober citizens whose names I will not mention. Under the circumstances, I have no choice but to let them continue to operate the church according to their beliefs until the people of this state, in a jury trial, decide otherwise."

Matt hugged Roje and grinned at Jill and Peachy. "Thank you, Judge Gravman, for being God," he said warmly. "If you'd like to watch an uninterrupted performance of the *Song of Songs*, we'd be delighted to have you with us tonight."

Gravman scowled at him but couldn't conceal a tiny smile. "If you promise me that Mr. Lovejoy is not one of the dancers, I might come."

Al Zurda was disappointed and angry. "Just for the record," he told Gravman, "the police department of this city is no longer responsible. Keeping the church open, especially on the Fourth of July weekend with Jeff Falconer in town, is an invitation to riot."

To Jill's consternation, when they were finally all back in the carriage house, Irene told her that Ike wanted to talk with her—alone. Scarcely awake after a sleepless night on a prison cot, Jill looked at her despondently. "What next?"

Irene hugged her. "He knows that you spent the night in jail. I don't think he's angry. He's just worried about you."

Ike greeted her on the front porch of the Big House and led her around to the back verandah. "It's been three weeks since we had our family meeting," he said. "I had hoped that by this time we might have talked. I hoped we might be friends, at leath." He grinned at her weakly. "As you can hear, I still lithp a little, and I gueth my mouth will always be a little out of kilter." He gazed at her affectionately. "I want you to know that I'm sorry. I never should have hit you."

Tears flooding her eyes, Jill impulsively kissed his cheek and hugged him. "Oh, Ike. I'm the one who's sorry, and to blame. I never wanted to hurt you." She shook her head pathetically. "I just couldn't help myself, but I love Matt, too." She sobbed into his shoulder. "I love him very much, and I'm frightened and worried about him."

Putting his arm around her shoulder, realizing suddenly that she needed him and that he could have her love, too, if he didn't reject her, Ike tried to soothe her. He sat beside her, stroking her hair for a long time.

"Gus Belshin telephoned me this morning," he said somewhat reluctantly. "He's very unhappy about the news stories. The president of Controlled Power in jail for obscene behavior could raise hell with the price of our stock when the exchange opens next Tuesday. I realize now that Matt is both our problem. You probably know better than anyone what kind of devils are driving him."

"There's a Unitarian hymn that Matt sings when I ask him that," Jill said. As she had often done when she talked with him, she played with Ike's hand and his fingers. "It's called 'Unrest': 'A fierce unrest seethes at the core of all existing things. It was the eager wish to soar that gave the gods their wings. But for the urge of this unrest these joyous spheres are mute. But for the rebel in his breast had man remained a brute.'" Jill smiled at him. "You should understand that, Ike. You and Sarah wound your little boy-toy up together. You as the Calvinist father who was determined that a man should prove his worth and seek his salvation through good works, and Sarah convincing him that he was guided by an 'inner light,' a belief that God is within you."

"What's salvation for Matt?" Ike asked.

"Your love, Irene's love, Peachy's love, my love, and our belief in him," Jill said softly.

Matt was delighted when Jill told him that Ike had decided to come to church tonight and see what the fuss was all about. "But I think the real reason," Jill laughed, "is that you're what they used to call a chip off the old block. Ike wants to see Nikki in her birthday suit."

Despite the headlines in the *Adamsport Chronicle* and the Boston newspapers blaring "Godwin and his Mo Mo's Arrested for Indecency," "Matthew Godwin versus the State of Massachusetts," "Is Modern Morality a Religion?" and many more protesters than usual trying to dissuade people from entering the church, the Saturday night performance of *The Song of Songs* was completed without incident with an audience of more than a thousand.

At the conclusion, Matt appeared on stage and thanked the performers. Ignoring the advice of Tom Ferris, who had begged him not to throw fuel on the fire, he said, "Tomorrow evening, after Jeff Falconer's Fourth of July sermon, which we will televise on the sanctuary screen, we will show an X-rated film in which Nikki was featured. She will also perform live one of her strip club acts. Afterward she will discuss with us so-called adult films and her own views on women's roles in intriguing and exciting their lovers into the act of loving. Nikki is a feminist who believes that women do not devalue themselves by offering sexual enticement to the male. She also feels that the female sexual devaluation that occurs in most so-called adult films is instigated by males who do not believe in equal sexual rights."

Matt paused. "In view of the fact that the First Church is on the verge of a showdown with the State of Massachusetts that may even resolve many questions being asked by Mike Wilder, who, as many of you know, is in the audience right now, I'm sorry to tell you that tomorrow night is a members-only night." He grinned at the audience. "On the other hand, it's not too late. If you are interested in becoming a member, ushers wearing the Flaming Chalice insignia will be happy to sign you up. Otherwise, tomorrow night I hope that you will listen to Jeff Falconer. Even though he doesn't believe it, Jeff is God, too."

On Sunday morning, the Fourth of July, using Becky as the intermediary, Ike invited Nikki, and whoever else in the Godwin ménage might be interested, to go swimming with him in Grandpa Zach's quarry. Although Becky's opinion of the idea was "ugh," she told Irene and Jill that it was really a command invitation. Like it or not, they should all go with Ike.

Wearing a 1930s style, two-piece bathing suit with belted blue trunks and white top, Ike arrived at the sandy beach that old Zach had created on the one accessible edge of the two-hundred-foot deep hole. Here, more than one hundred years ago, Adamsport granite had been sawed out of the earth. Opposite the man-made beach, a twenty-foot granite cliff towered over the clear cold spring water, making an excellent diving platform. Jill, Becky, and Irene agreed that the water was too cold for comfortable swimming, and, like it or not, they were wearing bathing suits. To Ike's delight, Peachy and Nikki joined the kids. Naked sylphs, they dove from increasingly higher elevations into the clear water.

Matt arrived wearing a jockey-style suit, which he quickly shed. Then to everyone's surprise, Hendy, who had already drunk several glasses of champagne, told Ike that many years ago he had swum in Grandpa Zach's quarry bollicky. Rawboned, looking like a reincarnation of one of his Puritan forebears, Hendy slid out of his trunks and into the water and later began playing a hard and driving game of frisbee with Nikki and Peachy, delighting in making them reach and bend for the flying plaque. Irene finally decided that, since they were all having so much fun without clothes, she would doff her bathing suit. Ike applauded enthusiastically, and Jill, not daring to watch Ike's expression, joined her.

Becky stared glumly at her father and said, "Oh shit . . . I will if you will."

46

Later that evening, as they drove to church, Matt happily recalled Ike's joyous return to childhood. After a half-bottle of champagne to wash down his picnic lunch, Ike had become a bubbling seventy-three-year-old Bacchus, frolicking naked with his naked ladies and wearing a crown of leaves that Jill had woven for his head. Patting Nikki's fanny, his arm around Peachy, Ike had guffawed, "I hope Grandpa Zach can see me now!" as he waved enthusiastically toward heaven. "It's a damn sight more fun swimming naked with girls than with boys."

But now, as they emerged from the underground garage and walked through the Adams Mall to the front entrance of the church, their laughing memories were suddenly erased. It was 6:45. The humid ninety-degree temperature had dropped to the high seventies. In fifteen minutes, less than two miles away in Morton Park, Reverend Jeff Falconer would be giving his Fourth of July sermon on the "Falconer Gospel Hour." They passed a dozen or so protesters who waved "Jesus Saves" banners at them dispiritedly and implored them not to enter the church. Otherwise the square seemed unusually deserted.

And then they saw it. A twelve-foot-high stuffed effigy, dressed in the garb of a preacher, was dangling on a gallows rope from the front portico of the church. Across its chest a sign read: "The Immoral Reverend." Roje and a few late arrivals were clustered around the front entrance. "Some of your friends put it there," Roje told Matt grimly. "I can't figure out how they got it up there. Bill Blake, the custodian, is looking for an extension ladder to take it down."

Roje told Irene that Father Tim had arrived and was waiting inside for them. "He's with Tom Ferris and his wife. Everyone is pretty jittery. Mike Wilder told Ferris that he had heard rumors that the crazy group called God's Avengers would like to hang us all from the church. Ferris thinks that you should call it off . . . or at least we should evacuate immediately after Falconer's sermon."

Tears of worry in her eyes, Irene squeezed Matt's arm before she walked inside the church with Jill, Peachy, and Nikki. "Please, Matt, do call it off. Tom is right," she said. "I'm sure Nikki won't care."

Matt told her and Roje to stop worrying. "If there's going to be a demonstration, they might as well have their straw man." He looked at his watch. "Come on, Falconer will be speaking in a few minutes."

"We can't leave you dangling there," Roje said. He was relieved to see Blake finally arriving with a ladder. "Some of those crazies might torch it and set the church on fire." He pointed to a pickup truck across the street. A few hundred yards north of City Hall, two men were dumping a huge pile of kindling wood in the middle of the street. "I'm damned sure the city didn't give them permission, but it looks as if they're going to have a bonfire right in the middle of Adamsport." And burn us at the stake, Roje thought, though he didn't say it.

"Bring it over to them," Matt told Blake, who had managed to yank the straw man down. Propped against Blake's knees, its clown's face wore a clerical collar and was smiling happily at them. "If they are going to have a voodoo ceremony and burn me in effigy, they might as well do it where there's plenty of room."

Roje gestured around the square. "You're too damned complacent. Haven't you noticed anything different? Every other night there's been at least a half-dozen policemen around. Tonight there's not even a cruising car in sight. Zurda probably told them to stay away. He practically warned Gravman that if trouble came, he'd let us fry."

"All the fuzz are probably up at Morton Park guarding Falconer," Matt said casually, "and hoping the feminists don't start a riot. Aren't you sorry that you ever got involved with UU's? Don't you wish that you had stayed quietly in Happy Shores and never discovered that you were God?"

Roje chuckled. "I didn't need you or the UU's. I've been trying to convince Emily for years that I am lord and master. The trouble is that she never believed me."

Making their way into the sanctuary, greeting people and waving at others, Roje and Matt found Peachy, Nikki, and Jill sitting with Tom Ferris and his wife a tier behind Irene, Father Tim, and Emily.

"I count about two hundred and fifty people," Peachy told Matt. "Pretty good turnout for a midsummer night on a holiday weekend, when Jeff Falconer is in town." Her saucer eyes held a nervous question. "But everyone is a little shocked, seeing you hanging from the portico. You can feel the tenseness. Do you think we should call it off?"

Nikki heard her and said, "I don't know about you, but I'm a little scared. Stripping at places like Silly Willy's is a hell of a lot easier than this. At least I know what the horny guys are thinking when they watch me."

Matt hugged her. "It's easier to tell what the Reverend Falconer and his fundamentalist friends are thinking. Purgatory, hell, and damnation for all of us. Anyway, I guess we should bring it out in the open."

The church television monitor was already receiving a prior broadcast from the Christian Broadcasting Network, and the closing minutes of the previous telecast were being silently projected on the sanctuary screen. Smiling reassuringly at Irene and Jill, Matt walked up to the center stage. "It's nice to see so many members here tonight. As UU's and Mo Mo's, I know that you want me to be honest with you. Are we going to be under siege tonight? I really don't know. Probably, after Jeff Falconer's sermon there will be a bigger demonstration outside the church than usual. If you wish, we can all quietly leave now, or we can listen to Falconer and then leave. We might have time to evacuate before the demonstrators can get downtown from Morton Park. We can reschedule Nikki for Tuesday night services. Or we can go ahead and try to ignore them."

"Are you afraid of Jeff Falconer?" someone yelled.

"No, but I don't want any physical confrontation with those who may disagree with us."

Matt acknowledged Ada Bass, who was waving her hand indignantly. "This is our church," she said angrily. "Let Falconer stew in his own juice. I'm an old lady; I certainly don't agree with Falconer that Jesus is coming back and going to save me. I'm not sure that I approve of Nikki Holmes, but I'm not afraid to hear what she has to say." She pointed to the screen where the credits for the "Falconer Gospel Hour" were now emblazoned in three-foot-high letters. "Turn on the sound, Matthew Godwin. Let those who want to leave, leave. I want to hear Mr. Hellfire tell me how I'm going to squirm in the fiery pit."

She was greeted with enthusiastic applause, and no one left.

On the screen, a voice-over was announcing that Reverend Jeffrey Falconer, Baptist minister, head of Moral America, and founder of Falconer College, would deliver his nationwide sermon this evening from Morton Park in Adamsport, Massachusetts. Following the sermon, Jeff Falconer would provide, at his own expense, a half-hour fireworks spectacular. As the announcer faded away, the Falconer Chorale, accompanying a Kate Smith look-alike, began singing "God Bless America." The Falconer television crew panned the stadium to reveal more than three thousand people waving flags and joining in an enthusiastic rendition of "This Land is My Land."

"Okay, Jeff," Matt said. "Give the Immoral Reverend hell!"

Falconer, a dark-haired, heavy-set man with an infectious smile, carrying a huge Bible, walked onto the special platform that had been erected on the stadium playing field. Three times life size on the sanctuary screen, he seemed to be looking into the heart and soul of everyone in the congregation.

"O Heavenly Father," Falconer said with the cameras closing in on his sincere, imploring face. "Thank you that we have faith. Thank you for the Bible. Thank you for Jesus Christ. Thank you for the promise of the Second Coming. Thank you for America! And thank you for Old Glory and this Fourth of July commemorating our Declaration of Independence, and giving us the endless benefits of private property, free elections, and freedom of speech." He paused. "Before I continue, please, everyone stand and pledge allegiance to our flag, a flag and a nation blessed by God and his Son Jesus Christ."

Following the Pledge of Allegiance, the Falconer band swung into a rousing version of "The Star Spangled Banner," and the camera revealed Falconer and many in the stadium singing with tears of joy in their eyes.

"I hope all of you know," Falconer continued as the music faded away, "that I believe in the Second Coming of Jesus. I can't tell you the day and the hour, but the time is imminent. He wants to help us in a spiritual revival, a harvest of faith that is spreading across this great land. But Jesus warned us: 'Take heed that no man deceive you.' And the Lord has blessed us with God-fearing, God-loving forefathers who created this great nation, where not only do we have freedom of speech but also freedom to blast out the false prophets." Falconer thumped his Bible portentously. "'Many false prophets will rise up and deceive many,' Matthew 24:11, 'and because lawlessness will abound, the love of many will go cold.'

"Thank you, Lord, for Freedom of Speech, and thank you for Freedom of Religion—a freedom that allows Jeff Falconer to exercise his constitutional rights and lay the truth on the line to you.

"And that's why I'm here tonight, and that's why I have spent the entire past month in Adamsport, Massachusetts. The Lord knows that there is a false prophet here in this city, turning it into a sinkhole of depravity and corruption that he's trying to spread across our nation. I am here to extirpate, uproot, and cast back this evil man into Hell and give him back to Satan who sent him here.

"There's a book in sacred literature that I believe should have been included in the Scripture. It details the fall of Adam and Eve *after* their expulsion from the Garden of Eden, and it reveals that Satan continued to try to tempt Adam and Eve many times. He even assumed the heavenly light of angels to betray them. It's a never ending war against the Devil. Right now Satan is trying to turn Adamsport, Massachusetts, a city where the roots of democracy flowered, into a modern Babylon. A quicksand of iniquity and fornication. And Satan has reappeared using the holy name of Jesus' greatest disciple, Matthew. But this Matthew, with a name that lures believers as well as sinners, is no apostle of the Lord. Matthew Godwin is a sower of sleazy lust, of vile and obscene teachings. Guided by Satan, he preaches immorality and dares to call it 'modern morality.'

"The Lord warned me. He told me to expose Matthew Godwin, and the Devil's Disciple, Robert Lovejoy, and those modern Liliths, those seducers of men, Mary Peachy and Gillian Marlowe, the harlot sisters. 'Son of man, there were two women,' Ezekiel 23, 'Obolah, the older, and Obolibah her sister. And Obolibah told the Lord God, behold I will stir up your lovers against you, from whom you have alienated yourself, and I will bring them against you on every side.'"

Falconer glared sternly from the sanctuary screen. "Sometimes when I'm speaking, I get so enthusiastic when I'm saying the words of the Lord that I spit. But that's a loving spit. Now I spit in contempt." Shaking his fist, Falconer actually spat into the air. "I spit in righteous anger at these unclean, foul, swinish people who call themselves humanists and Modern Moralists—Mo Mo's. Beware of the Mo Mo's! They are mowing down all of our sane moralities with their sex-ridden, lewd beliefs.

"Right now, tonight, instead of coming down here to Morton Park and facing me in person and listening to the word of God under God's sky, they are hiding in air-conditioned comfort in that venerable old church in the middle of this city, a church that they have purchased with their death money.

"We all know that Matthew Godwin is the son of a God-fearing man, Isaac Godwin. By the sweat of his brow, Isaac Godwin, in the great American tradition, created a billion-dollar corporation that Americans can be proud of, a company that produces ships and arms and many of the weapons we need to keep the Soviet Union under control. But many of you do not know that Isaac Godwin has publicly denounced his son's ambitions. He knows that Satan—disguised as his own son—is trying to stop Controlled Power from manufacturing armaments which could be used for the defense of this country and is advocating—under the guise of religion—a policy that would make the United States a second-rate nation.

"You may have noticed that I said, 'Satan and his disciples purchased the former First Parish Church with death money.' I know for a fact that, although Matthew Godwin is trying to tap the vast resources of Controlled Power Corporation to fund his church and promote his satanic moralities, at this point neither the corporation nor his father have given one *dime* to this vile and immoral purpose. Where did the money come from? Where is it still coming from? How many people have died to convince an Arab oil billionaire to give $60 million to Godwin's Foundation?

"Last week, in the presence of Gillian Godwin and Matthew Godwin, a Hindu named Ramachanda was shot to death in this city. Was he involved with Matthew Godwin in cocaine smuggling? What was Matthew Godwin doing in Grand Cayman nearly two years ago, not with his own wife, Irene, but with his father's wife, Gillian? Was he smuggling gold? When the truth comes out and we discover the kind of modern moralities that Matthew Godwin is really preaching, Almighty God will demand retribution. God always exposes Satan's work. Don't ever forget it. The good Lord keeps an accurate, immaculate set of books. He knows that the so-called First Church and this travesty on religion is not a church gathered to worship Him. He knows that right now Nikki Holmes, a self-proclaimed whore of Babylon who freely admits that she has fornicated with more than a hundred men, is sitting in that church. Soon she will take off her clothes and teach women how to seduce men."

Falconer pointed his fingers so that it almost seemed as if he were picking Nikki personally out of the congregation. "Get out of Adamsport, Massachusetts, Nikki Holmes! Go back to the sex slums of Los Angeles or New York City. Go back to Sodom and Gomorrah where you belong!

"And I warn you, Matthew Godwin, read Galatians, chapter 5: 'The works of the flesh are evident . . . adultery, fornication, uncleanness, licentiousness, idolatry, sorcery, hatred, heresies . . . murder, drunkenness and revelries. Those who practice such things shall not inherit the kingdom of God . . . . Whatsoever a man soweth that shall he reap.'"

Falconer thumped his Bible. "God *knows* the evil this false prophet is sowing. Do *you* know? Matthew Godwin's moralities are nothing less than deadly sins. He defies the tradition of the monogamous family. I have it on sworn testimony that Matthew Godwin not only fornicates with his father's wife, Gillian Godwin, but he's a polygamist and also has sexual relations with his co-minister, the former Peachy Stein, a lady—and I hesitate to call her lady—who was found naked in the belfry of the former First Parish Church with that libertine, Robert Lovejoy."

Matt grinned at Peachy and Jill, both of whom gave his ankles a swift kick, and Jill whispered, "You're a nasty false prophet. No wonder we've had trouble with you. But really, it's not funny. Who gave him sworn testimony? Mrs. Goodale?"

"Take pity on poor Irene Godwin," Falconer was continuing, lips curled with rising vehemence. "Surrendering to his satanic powers over her, this poor Catholic woman, the former Irene Ferruzi, also helps alleviate his abnormal carnal desires. Sitting with Irene Godwin in the First Parish Church listening to me right now is a well-known Catholic priest. I pray that Father Timothy Sullivan will save her from a man who no doubt also consorts with whores like Nikki Holmes."

"My God," Irene turned to whisper to Matt, "are you sure you haven't got two-way television?"

"And that's not all!" Falconer's anger, conjured up or not, looked worse than any Jehovian wrath. "Matthew Godwin and his Mo Mo's advocate the murder of unborn babies. They defy God's word, 'Thou has covered me in the womb,' Psalms 139:12-16, which proves that the fetus from the time of conception is the child of God. Defying Leviticus 20:13, Godwin approves of the gays and lesbians, and he laughs at God's ordination of one man and one woman for a lifetime. 'Therefore shall a man leave his father and shall cleave unto his wife; and they shall be one flesh.'

"In the sanctuary of a historic church he preaches the worship of the human sex organs, and he shows pornographic films filled with all the rotten horror of perverted sexual acts—movies that would turn your stomach. Poor John Adams and his wife, Abigail, and their children! They must be shifting in their graves, imploring God to crumble this temple on the heads of its deluded members.

"And that's not all. Godwin extols premarital sexual relations, legalized prostitution, legalization of drugs, and euthanasia. He even advocates adultery as a postmarital way of life. Within the walls and under the roof of a church, with roots that extend back three hundred and fifty years to our Declaration of Independence on the Fourth of July, he encourages his members to parade around the church naked, inciting each other to lust with a constant sexual display of their bodies.

"And he insists that we stop trying to contain the Soviets. He wants us to withdraw our missiles from Europe and our advisors from Central America and Lebanon, and let the Russians run amok all over the world."

Unable to continue for a moment, Falconer shuddered, his face contorted with dismay. The television cameras swept across the thousands of horrified faces in the stadium and picked up the roar of crowd anger.

"I think we'd better leave right now," Roje turned to Matt. "He's building to a charge that will make the Light Brigade look like small change."

"He's really pretty good," Matt said calmly. "Who knows, maybe we can convert him."

Falconer waved for silence and continued. "This monster believes that he can trample the Lord and his son Jesus into the oozing slime of his apostasy. In the second tempting of Adam, 'Satan, the hater of all good saw how many commanded in prayer, and how God communed with them and he made an apparition.' Adam and Eve, chapter 27. He began with transforming his hosts. In his hands was a flashing fire, and they were in a great light. And he tried to convince Adam that he was God.

"Never forget it. Satan never quits! Matthew Godwin is his emissary. Defying God's commandments, Godwin doesn't care whose light he travels under. Like the secular humanists, he's determined to keep God from our schools, where, with the help of the Supreme Court, prayer to the almighty God has been outlawed. Godwin gloats over the 50 percent divorce rate, the breakdown of the family, and the drug epidemic. He's plunging millions of dollars into a religion that aids and abets our sex-obsessed, anti-free-enterprise society and followers of the Devil.

"Every day he defies God. He tells you that *he* is God, that *you* are God. He tells you that any other God is an illusion. But Jesus himself said that we are all the Sons of God."

With tears rolling down his cheeks, Falconer held his hand high over the heads of his audience. "'Violating a nation's principles brings a nation to shame.' Proverbs 14:34. 'Let no one deceive you, by any means, for that day will not come unless the falling away comes first, and the man of sin is revealed, the son of perdition.' II Thessalonians 2. 'Who opposes and exalts himself all that is God, or that is worshipped so that he sits as God in the temple of God, showing himself that he is God . . . the Lord will consume him with the breath of his wrath and destroy him with the brightness of His coming.'

"Paul told the Thessalonians: 'The coming of the lawless one is according to the work of Satan . . . with all power and signs and lying wonders.' And Paul told them: 'God will send them a strong delusion so that they may believe in the lie, and those who will not believe the truth will be condemned.'

"And Paul said for them and for us: 'Stand fast, brothers and sisters, against the lawless one, for he is Satan himself come to destroy you.'

"And Jeff Falconer warns you. Today in America you must not only stand fast against those who would destroy our country. You must march against them, singing hymns to the Lord, and with the determined sound of marching feet trample the degenerate sinners in the mud of their iniquitous, depraved blasphemy against God and our Savior Jesus Christ.

"Three hundred and fifty years ago, the founding fathers of the Massachusetts Bay Colony knew how to combat those who denied God and his words in the Bible. The first president of Harvard College, who preached against infant baptism, was indicted by a grand jury and publicly shamed. William Penn, the governor of Pennsylvania, proclaimed: 'Only persons who believe in Jesus Christ, the Savior of the World, shall be capable to serve this government in any capacity.' Anne Hutchinson and John Wheelwright were banished from Massachusetts by Governor John Winthrop and the ministers of Boston because they denied the only covenant God gave to Adam and Eve. And Mary Dyer was hanged from the gallows because of her lack of faith.

"Thank God that today the good Lord, in His Majesty, has made us more tolerant of sinners. But He does not expect us to lie down and be conquered by Satan. Tonight, I call upon the people of Massachusetts and their legislators to put an end to this travesty on religion called the First Church of Modern Morality and let the people know that sex worship, and the belief that you are God, is the work of the Devil.

"A few minutes from now, in a famous historic church, less than two miles from here, the Archenemy of God, Isaac Matthew Godwin—who often writes his name I. M. God—together with his deluded followers and the lascivious women he has brainwashed, will be watching Nikki Holmes, a whorish playmate of the Devil, dancing naked for them and inciting them to unspeakable orgies. Don't wait for the fireworks. You can watch the rockets of God bursting in the air over Adamsport, Massachusetts, as thousands of you march into downtown Adamsport. Surround this temple of lust that is inhabited by pagans and heathens, and with a thousand voices let Matthew Godwin hear you say together as one voice the Lord's Prayer. Jesus our Savior, help us destroy this new apparition of Satan! Help us send him and his disciples back to the nether world from which they came!"

47

As Falconer finished, television cameras rolled over the stadium, filling the screen with a churning sea of cheering faces. Waving flags and chanting "Jesus is our Savior," they were (at least momentarily) a united army against lust and the Devil. Finally, with the Falconer choral group singing "Onward Christian Soldiers," the "Gospel Hour" ended. The sanctuary screen faded into a soft blue.

Without waiting to consult with Roje or Peachy, Matt quickly walked up on the stage and stood smiling at the dazed faces of his congregation under the first stars of night, visible through the clear dome. "I'm sure that we all agree that Jeff Falconer is a very persuasive rabble-rouser. I hope that he hasn't convinced you that people like us—humanists, UU's, Modern Moralists—are all in league with the Devil and the communists, or that we are trying to destroy America. But I am afraid that tonight the better part of valor will be for all of you to leave the church before the angels of God engulf us."

"Are you afraid of that bastard, Matt?" someone yelled.

"Not at all. I plan to stand on the steps of the church and listen to his followers pray for me. Don't worry, one man can't create a battlefield. The reality is that tonight, we as loving Gods are outnumbered by those who pray to a wrathful God out there who punishes sinners. Sadly, the history of the world revolves around men killing each other while they implore their God to help them."

By this time Irene, Jill, and Peachy had stepped onto the stage, and Peachy, waving her hands for attention, said, "I think Matt is right. I think we had all better leave here as quickly as possible."

"You're not staying here alone either," Irene and Jill said to Matt almost simultaneously. "You're coming with us."

But they were too late. Just as the congregation, shouting their approval of Matt, began snaking their way along the tiers toward the aisles and the front entrance, twenty white-hooded figures shoved through them and swarmed into the sanctuary. Half of them leaped onto the stage and grabbed Matt. The leader pointed angrily at Peachy, Jill, and Nikki. "Godwin's whores!" he yelled. Then he spotted Emily and Roje. "Bring those two up here too; they're the Devil's disciples." Six of the menacing hooded figures on the stage were scanning the congregation with sawed-off shotguns and revolvers. Four others, who, judging by their height, were probably women under their Klan-style disguise, waved luminescent crosses.

"Keep your seats—all of you," their leader, waving a gun, bellowed through a bull horn that he was carrying. "If you do what we tell you, no one is going to get hurt." His amplified voice crackled with a doomsday echo as it reverberated against the domed ceiling.

"Get the hell out of here," Tom Ferris yelled at five of them who were dragging Peachy, Jill, and Nikki screaming back to the stage. "You and Jeff Falconer will all end up in jail!" He tried to pull the sheet off one of them but was quickly knocked back into his seat. Four others had corralled Irene, Emily, and Roje, pushing aside Father Tim, who cried angrily, "*You* are the devils, not this woman. Don't listen to Jeff Falconer."

"Sit down in your seat, Father. Falconer did not send us." Standing at the edge of the stage, the leader pointed his gun menacingly at him as he spoke through his bull horn. "I'm really surprised to see you here among these infidels. You'd better read your Bible, Father Tim. We're God's Avengers. 'If thy brother . . . or thy son . . . or the wife of thy bosom, or thy friend which is as thine own soul entice thee saying, let us go serve other Gods . . . thou shalt not consent unto him nor hearken unto them.'"

Glaring at the congregation through the slits in his pointed hood, he looked like a vengeful archangel. He watched imperiously as the women were dragged onto the stage, Irene struggling, tears running down her cheeks; Peachy snarling between two of her captors, kicking and calling them filthy bastards; Jill not struggling but letting herself be led with a hopeless expression; Nikki disdainful; and Emily shrieking, "Let go of me, you dirty monsters!" Roje, shaking his head in disbelief at Matt, was pushed beside him. The seven of them were now a pitiful cluster in the center of the stage.

Shouting, Father Tim tried to wrest himself free from one of the hooded figures. "Let Irene Godwin go! She's not active in this church!"

"I'm staying with Matt," Irene screamed. She clutched Matt's arm. "I don't care what they do to me. I love you."

Joined by many voices in the congregation, Father Tim kept pleading, "Let them go. Stop this insanity immediately. God is merciful. He does not ask man to mete out his justice."

"You're wrong, Father Tim." The leader's voice was disguised by the bull horn, but Matt was sure that he was a New Englander, not one of the Southern out-of-town protesters. "God has sounded his trumpet," the leader bellowed. "He warned Matthew Godwin and his perfidious friends. 'Thou shalt have no other Gods before me.' And if you do, the Bible tells us, 'Thou shalt surely kill them.'"

Ignoring the shocked moan of the congregation, he waved his gun at Father Tim. "We know that Irene Godwin is your special lady friend, Father," he said belligerently. "Don't try to stop us. We're not going to hurt Irene Godwin or anyone. We're here to remind them that this is God's country. We don't need any sex-worshipping pagans here. We're just going to shame them a little so they'll never forget it. We're going to give these sinners a choice. It shouldn't be too difficult for them. Lovejoy and Peachy Stein have already flaunted their naked bodies all over this city." He pointed his gun at the seven of them. "All of you strip down to your skin right now—or we'll do it for you!" As he spoke, ten of his silent cohorts, many of whom suddenly flashed long knives, moved in menacingly. They were obviously quite willing to cut off their clothes, if necessary.

"For Christ's sake, if you really believe in Christ," Matt pleaded, "let the women and Robert Lovejoy go. I'm responsible for this church." But the leader ignored him.

"He's a crackpot," Matt whispered to Irene and Jill. "I'm sorry. Just hope they haven't got gas chambers waiting for us outside."

The leader heard him. "We're Christians, not Nazis, Matthew Godwin. Acknowledge that Christ is your savior and we will take pity on you."

Boldly Nikki unzipped her dress and let it fall to the floor. Except for panties, she was naked. "If Jesus loves us, he'd better save us," she murmured grimly.

"I told you, you were a dreamer," Irene sobbed as one of the men nudged her and told her to hurry up. "Man is a long way from being God."

Undressing, dropping his suit coat and pants in a heedless pile, Matt saw Irene hopelessly lift her dress over her head and undo her bra. Awkwardly, she finally removed her panty hose. "Oh, please God, help us," she said, as Jill, with a haughty expression on her face, dropped her skirt and unbuttoned her blouse and exposed her sorrowful breasts. Peachy and Nikki, naked, stared defiantly at the hooded figures, one of whom prodded Emily and threatened to cut off her bra and panties.

Within a few minutes, while the congregation watched with glazed eyes and almost silent horror, the seven of them stood naked and shoeless, their clothing a confused heap on the stage. The women clung dejectedly together, pathetic in their exposure. Matt looked ruefully at Roje and at the paralyzed congregation, who kept moaning to let them go but were powerless to save them.

Blaming himself, Matt wondered how men and women—and he was sure that some of the hooded figures were women—could degrade other human beings and force them into such abject submissiveness. Should he have gone down fighting against them? Was it better to fight hopelessly than to be herded as the Jews were into concentration camps and gas chambers? Roje was muttering and calling them "Fucking Jesus-demented bastards." Hearing him, one of the hooded figures slapped him across the buttocks and pushed a knife perilously close to his stomach until Roje fell silent.

Bewildered, wondering what in the hell they were going to do with them, Roje saw three of them approaching with dangling handcuffs. Realizing that they were going to be chained together and dragged out of the church, Matt lunged furiously at the leader. He knocked him off balance for a moment but was unable to elude a handcuff that was snapped around his left wrist. In seconds they were linked together in a snake line. Matt's left hand was fastened to Irene's right, Irene's left to Jill's right, Jill's to Peachy, Peachy to Nikki, Nikki to Emily, Emily to Roje. Then they were dragged, pushed, goosed, fumbled at, and pulled down off the stage and out of the front door of the church into a screaming, jeering, howling mass of people who filled the square and Hancock Boulevard as far as they could see.

Yanked by his free arm, dragging the screaming six behind him, and followed by the members of the church, who yelled at the crowds to stop these insane guardians of God's justice, Matt could not believe his eyes. Ahead of them a twenty-foot bonfire blazed in the sultry, foggy night. At the top of it the straw preacher was engulfed in flames.

"They're going to burn us!" he heard Irene moan. For a moment Matt wondered if they had all climbed into a time machine and had been transported back to some medieval town where burning heretics at the stake was a way of life. But now, the hooded figures began pushing the crowd back, clearing a circle. Two of them grabbed Matt's free arm, dragged him toward Roje, and snapped the dangling handcuff on his right arm onto Roje's left wrist.

The seven of them were linked together back to back. Facing a sea of sneering, jeering male and female faces yelling obscenities, they were being turned in a slow circle as the crowd pushed and jostled them and the men grabbed at the breasts and genitals of "Godwin's whores." If there were any sympathetic faces, they couldn't see them.

Stunned, wondering if she were going to faint, Jill staggered through the hooting, grasping crowd. Five hundred or more people had become one, and with the mad hum of a demented person, they were almost orgasmic with the thrill of their impending torture. Struggling to escape a man who was fondling her breasts, she tried to butt him with her head. He laughed lasciviously and shifted his attention to Irene.

Trying to escape his probing fingers between her legs, Irene tripped and fell to her knees. Matt and Jill, with one hand each, tried to lift her to her feet, but they didn't have any leverage. To save her from being dragged on the pavement, Matt dropped down beside her. At that moment, tugged and hauled by God's Avengers, they were all forced to lie down with their backs on the street. Formed into a seven point star with their linked arms, they were unable to see each other's faces. Matt stared grimly into the foggy night. A solid curve of relentless witch-hunter faces, like an incarnation of a Hieronymous Bosch painting, jeered and hooted at them. Where had his followers gone? An image of Anne Hutchinson, being excommunicated from her Boston church, flashed through his mind. Denouncing her as a leper, a whore, a daughter of Satan, none of the hundreds of men and women who had attended her meetings and praised her stood up to save her.

"For Christ's sake, hurry up!" a hooded figure yelled. "Let's get it over with before someone gets hurt."

Matt could see the headlights of a pickup truck as it honked a path through a shouting, cursing mass of people who refused to get out of the way. In the distance he could hear the wail of police sirens, and he wondered why they had taken so long to arrive. "They'll never get through the crowd," he heard Peachy sob. Although he could only see her profile, he knew Irene was crying. He squeezed her hand and muttered, "I'm sorry. I love you."

Then, as some of the hooded figures pushed the crowd back, the rest of them climbed into the open truck. The driver slowly circled them, within inches of their heads, while those standing in the back of the pickup splashed gallons of warm brown stuff over them, followed by a deluge of feathers. The crowd was screaming a gutteral approval: "Tar and feather them! Ride them out of town on a pole!"

Less than a minute before the cruising cars, with sirens blasting, began inching through the crowd, the truck loaded with God's Avengers, with horn honking and hooded figures threatening to shoot anyone who didn't get out of their way, disappeared down Hancock Boulevard.

Blinded by the stuff, sputtering as he inhaled a mouthful of feathers that sprouted from his body, Matt struggled to his knees and with Roje's help lifted Irene to her feet. Sobbing, she fell into Father Tim's arms. Heedless of her slippery naked body, he put his arms around her and gently wiped her face with his handkerchief.

"It's only molasses," Matt heard Jill confirm what he had already discovered. But trying to lap the sticky stuff from their lips, they all choked on feathers.

Cooled by the arrival of the police, the taunting crescendo of anger and derision had dissipated into sighs of shame and pity. The naked women were suddenly surrounded by sympathetic men and women commiserating with them and trying to wipe the oozing treacle and gluey feathers from their eyes and mouths with Kleenex and paper napkins. When Matt was finally able to open his eyes, he didn't know whether to laugh or to cry. His chicken-feathered ladies and Roje looked like slithering, partially plucked escapees—two roosters and five hens—from a barnyard.

Al Zurda pushed through the crowd and stared belligerently at Matt. "I hope to fuck you're satisfied," he shouted. "You damned near got yourself and your harem slaughtered." He pointed at two television cameramen whom Matt recognized as part of Mike Wilder's team. With floodlighted cameras and obvious enthusiasm, they were videotaping the naked, feathered ladies and the solidly packed crowd who were shuffling about, wondering how to cut them apart. "You brought that asshole Falconer to Adamsport," Zurda said. "Tonight he told the whole damned country about Sex City, USA, and now Mike Wilder's crew is immortalizing you for 'Showdown.'"

Still unable to open his eyes, Roje yelled, "Where in hell have you been? It took you long enough to get here! I suppose you loaned these handcuffs to God's Avengers."

"Like hell I did." Zurda was examining the handcuffs angrily. "They probably bought them in some damned joke store." He waved at one of his men. "There's a metal cutter in the trunk of my car. Get it."

"Instead of standing around here, why don't you go after them?" Emily demanded. She scowled at John Codman, who was surveying her nakedness with compassionate but helpless interest.

"Don't worry; we'll find them," Zurda said grimly. "What charges do you want us to bring against them? Disturbing the peace?"

"Why don't you arrest us instead?" Matt asked sarcastically. "We're as guilty as they are. We not only made them disturb the peace, but here we are naked with friends and enemies." Getting a grip on his anger, Matt grinned at the crowd. "It's a nice warm night. Why don't you all take off your clothes and join us? We'll give you a slippery hug."

"You're forgetting one thing," Zurda said in exasperation as several young women started to undress. "You're already under arrest. Judge Gravman made one goddamned mistake; he should have locked you all up yesterday." Zurda pointed toward the foggy sky. "Up there somewhere, their God must be chuckling in his whiskers. I don't know how in hell you can live with your God. Whoever he is, I'm sure as hell he isn't me or any one of those bastards who did this."

Several policemen arrived with metal cutters and within a minute had them all cut apart. An ambulance with its siren u-rahing crept toward them. Zurda gestured at the white-coated attendants. "Take them all to the hospital. Give them a bath, and see if they have any bruises that they're going to blame on the police."

"I'm not going to any hospital," Irene said emphatically. She clung to Matt, her slippery breasts rubbing against his chest. "I'm not hurt, physically, anyway."

"There's a shower in the recreation area," Peachy said. "Why can't we all wash there?"

She had instant approval. Followed by Father Tim and a contingent of First Church members, Peachy insisted that they enter the church the back way through the parish building. "We don't want molasses stains on the carpets," she said, and Jill, shaking her head in amazement, complimented her on her pragmatic response.

Roje was complaining that he still couldn't see a goddamned thing, so Nikki took one arm and Peachy his other, while Emily muttered to him: "You were better off writing about it than doing it." She clung to his neck, her sticky bare breasts and feathery pubic hairs bumping against his back and behind, as they headed for the parish building.

They showered in the big co-ed shower next to the gymnasium with the solicitous help of twenty or more members of the First Church, including John Codman and Ada Bass (who were careful to keep beyond the spray). But to everyone's surprise, Father Tim shed his soiled priestly collar and suit and joined them. With tears in his eyes, he helped Irene wash the muck out of her hair, and he said sadly so they could all hear him, "It's much easier to live with a God who is external to you than to believe that everyone on earth is a loving God."

Matt tried to cheer them up. "Whoever they are, God's Avengers have some compunctions," he said as he merrily plucked feathers off Nikki's behind and Jill's pubic hairs. "They could have used tar instead of molasses. Tonight we have another Mo to add to Modern Morality: Mo-lasses."

Peachy shook her head at him in loving amazement. "It may be sweetness, but it's not light," she said. She wanted to ask Matt, is it worth it? Is it worth being a Michael Servetus with three Joans of Arc? But she didn't. She knew his answer and probably theirs, too.

Epilogue

We are concerned about the future of humankind. We do not believe that traditional religious and political orthodoxies are adequate to solve the problems that face us.

> Paul Kurtz, announcing the
> Academy of Humanism,
> September 1983

"Ladies and gentlemen of the jury, during the past three weeks District Attorney Hardman has not only cross-examined Irene Godwin, Gillian Marlowe Godwin, and Mary Peachy, exploring in nauseating detail the sex life of Matthew Godwin, with whom these ladies live, but he has also attempted, with no apparent success, to prove that Matthew Godwin has been involved in drug smuggling and the theft of gold bullion. He has intimated that without the income from these nefarious activities, the Foundation for Modern Moralities and the First Church would never have come into existence.

"He has also implied, more than once, that if Matthew Godwin continues as president of Controlled Power, in a proxy battle that is still unresolved, he will try to bleed the corporation for the benefit of the church. He has tried to convince you that, to the detriment of the stockholders, Matthew Godwin wouldn't hesitate to destroy one of America's largest corporations, because Matthew Godwin believes that business in America should be more closely aligned with our religious beliefs, and that no matter what our daily pursuits may be, we all have a common interest in creating modern moralities.

"To leave no stone unturned in the State's effort to prove that the First Church and Modern Morality is not a religion, Mr. Hardman has spent several hours trying to prove to you that when the First Church, or any church, sells tickets to its members or non-members to see performances and uses the profits to support the church, it should no longer have protection from taxation as a non-profit institution.

"While the district attorney was unable to subpoena Sheik Amir Faisal Saud to appear in this courtroom, Sheik Saud, who is a billionaire, did send a cablegram to Matthew Godwin stating that he had personally endowed the Foundation for Modern Moralities with $40 million to assist his good friend Matthew Godwin and to help forge new moralities for America and the world. Whatever compensating arrangements may or may not have been made between Matthew

Godwin and Sheik Amir Saud are not at issue here. Nevertheless, the district attorney has tried to leave you with the impression that the Foundation and the First Church are a cover for a Soviet-Arabian plot to demoralize America with godless immoralities that are inimical to the defense of our country.

"Throughout this trial, I have constantly reminded the district attorney that Matthew Godwin is not on trial for polygamy. He actually has only one legal wife. Nor is he on trial for grand larceny, or running a business in which there might be a conflict of interest between his objectives and the stockholders. Nor is the First Church on trial for trying to realize a profit from its entertainment activities, although this raises an interesting problem, and Matthew Godwin has made no bones about his belief that all churches must be allowed to compete on a non-profit basis against the entertainment industry, if they are to survive.

"The State of Massachusetts versus I. Matthew Godwin is based on the State's cease and desist injunction against the First Church and revolves around one issue and one issue only: Does the theology, the beliefs and practices, of the First Church qualify it for protection under the First Amendment of the Constitution? Is the First Church and its beliefs in Modern Moralities a valid religion?

"During the past weeks you have learned that Matthew Godwin and members of the First Church believe in new approaches to morality, especially in the sexual areas, which are shocking to old-line Christians. Just as important, they have a theology—based on the belief that you and I are God—which equates all human creativity with sexual activity. They offer religious services which trace the roots of all religion back to fertility worship and primitive man's awe and reverence of seed and life itself generating in mother earth. Their sexual morality exalts human sexuality. It does not degrade the human body or the act of love. But it does offer members and their children a continuing value-laden sex education during which young people may see their peers, parents, and other adults of all ages naked within the church environment.

"As has been shown in this courtroom, their members and the general public, past the age of eighteen, have been shown films in the sanctuary of the church which are considered by many people to be pornographic. But as Matthew Godwin stated in this courtroom: 'Only the church and the synagogue can combat the degradation of sexual loving and sexual joy and sexual communion, not by censoring it, but by daring to meet it head on and compare shoddy, sleazy sex, wherever it appears in any of the media, with the romantic, caring, joyous, rapturous, mysterious, soulful, awe-inspiring wonder of a man and woman losing themselves and finding God in each other's naked embrace.'

"But unfortunately the district attorney is personally rooted in the Judeo-Christian belief that the love of God is primary and that our love of each other is a secondary relationship that God has given us only because He wants to multiply His glory. As a result, Mr. Hardman has tried to overwhelm you with past Supreme Court decisions which prove, if nothing else, that 'the wall of separation between the church and State,' as we approach the twenty-first century, is still a very 'uneasy alliance.'

"Obsessed with Matthew Godwin's relationship with his women and shocked that the women associated with him seem to be perfectly happy with their multiple relationship, Mr. Hardman has gone back to the Mormons and cited the *United States* v. *Reynolds, Davis* v. *Beason*, and the Statute of Congress of March 1882, which finally outlawed bigamy in the United States. He is especially fond of Justice Field, who stated more than a hundred years ago, and I quote: 'Bigamy and polygamy are crimes by the laws of all civilized countries. They tend to destroy the purity of the marriage relationship, to disturb the peace of families, to debase women and degrade men. To call their advocacy a tenet of religion is to offend the common sense of mankind.'

"According to Justice Field, 'It was never intended or supposed that the First Amendment could be invoked as a protection against the punishment of acts inimical to the peace and good order and morals of society.'

"Justice Field also fulminated against any religious sect 'which denies as a part of their religious tenets that there should be any marriage tie, and which advocates promiscuous intercourse of the sexes.'

"Ladies and gentlemen of the jury, it's important that you understand that in some areas Matthew Godwin agrees with Justice Field. But beliefs about what is moral and what is immoral and inimical to society have changed considerably in the past hundred years. Today bigamy and polygamy have been legalized in a new moral context called divorce and remarriage. More than 50 percent of those who marry monogamously will have another spouse or several other spouses in their lifetime. Of those who remain legally married, half of the men and close to half of the women will experience a sexual relationship with another person. Today we have a benign attitude toward people who live together unmarried, especially in their premarital years. Premarital sex and cohabitation have become a social norm. But, as Modern Moralists point out, most churches are still living in a moral backwater. They are doing nothing to create new marriage forms and new sexual commitments with a foundation of sound moral and caring value relationships for our time. In the context of their religious beliefs, and at their time of life, Matthew Godwin, Irene Godwin, Gillian Godwin, and Mary Peachy, creating a family and living together happily, may be living a more fulfilling life than many strictly monogamous couples.

"Despite District Attorney Hardman's beliefs, their lifestyle is not 'in violation of peace and good order,' a phrase that was used in the Mormon trials to eliminate the Mormon religious practice of bigamous marriages. Bigamy was probably outlawed in this country, not because these marriages were in violation of peace and good order or because the women were held in subjection, but because the Mormons at that time were more financially successful than their Christian adversaries, and Christians were afraid of them politically.

"The district attorney has also raised the spectre of 'a clear and present danger to society,' which has been used in the past to disqualify particular religions under the First Amendment.

"The Supreme Court of Tennessee issued a permanent injunction against the Holiness Church of God in Jesus' Name. These worshippers fully believed that they were empowered by God to handle poisonous snakes and use poisonous drinks in their religious practices. The court ruled that such a religion not only presented a clear and present danger but also was 'a public nuisance,' which the court defined as 'everything that endangered life or health, gives offense to the senses, violates the laws of decency,' and offers 'beliefs and practices that are out of harmony with contemporary customs, mores, and notions of morality.' Mr. Hardman has relished these words and repeated them over and over again in his attack on the First Church.

"Although Modern Moralists believe in the federal legalization of all drugs as the only way to control the horrendous, high-profit crime element trafficking in illegal drugs, they do *not* advocate the use of any drugs inside or outside the church. Nevertheless, the district attorney has drawn upon the words of the Supreme Court in the case of *Timothy Leary* v. *United States*: 'If religious conviction permits one to act contrary to civic duty, public health and the criminal laws of the land, then the right to be let alone with all the spiritual peace it guaranteed would be destroyed in the resulting breakdown of society. The vital significance of Constitutional protection of religion will be diluted by the degree of tolerance that accepts the practice of acts which leave society helpless to protect itself.'

"Despite Mr. Hardman's allegations, nothing that is occurring or has occurred in word or deed within the confines of the First Church constitutes a clear and present danger to the city of Adamsport or to the nation. The real clear and present danger for all of us is that men like Mr. Hardman and Jeffrey Falconer may ultimately force upon the public their moral beliefs, such as right to life, the right to prayer in public schools, and the right to destroy ourselves in nuclear war—all of which they would be happy to make the *modus operandi* of this country.

"There is one other test of religious belief that the Supreme Court has invoked to disqualify certain religious practices from protection under the First Amendment. Mr. Hardman has spent much of the court's time challenging 'the sincerity of religious belief' of the First Church and Modern Moralists. This is perhaps the most dangerous weapon that the State has against the church. It is important for your decision, ladies and gentlemen of the jury, to understand that even the best judicial minds can stumble against their own moral beliefs as they apply this test to others with whom they may disagree.

"In the case of the *United States* v. *Ballard*, 1944, the court stated: 'Men may believe what they cannot prove. They may not be put to the proof of their religious doctrines or beliefs. Religious experiences which are as real as life to some may be incomprehensible to others. Man's relation to his God was made of no concern to the State. He was granted the right to worship as he pleased, and to answer to no man for his religious beliefs.'

"But then in 1965, in the case of the *United States* v. *Seeger*, the court created a worm of doubt. 'We hasten to emphasize,' the court stated, 'that while the "truth" of belief is not open to question, there is a significant question whether it is truly held. This is the threshold case of sincerity which must be resolved in every case.'

"Following this thinking, in the case of *Scientology* v. *United States*, 1969, the district attorney has made much of the court's decision, which stated: 'We do not hold that the Founding Church is for all legal reasons a religion. Any prima facie case made out for religious status is subject to contradiction by showing that . . . the forms of religious organization were erected for the sole purpose of creating a secular enterprise with the legal protection of religion.'

"On top of that, Mr. Hardman has tried to disqualify the First Church by quoting other court decisions such as *Wisconsin* v. *Yoder*, in which the court stated: 'The concept of ordered liberty precludes allowing every person to make his own standards on matters of conduct in which society as a whole has important interests.' And he has made much of *Theriault* v. *Carlson*, 1975, in which the court stated: 'such difficulties have proved to be no hindrance to the denial of First Amendment protection of so-called religions which tend to mock established institutions, and are obviously sham and absurdities and whose members are patently devoid of sincerity.'

"Thus we come to the nub of the problem. Do the practices and religious beliefs of the First Church represent a clear and present danger to the State? Are their practices in violation of good order? Do they violate the laws of decency? Are they out of harmony with contemporary customs, mores, community standards and notions of morality? Do they go beyond 'the threshold of sincerity'? Or, as the district attorney has tried to convince you, are they simply a devious way of the Devil himself to destroy the foundations upon which this country stands?

"Let's examine the First Church's sexual beliefs. They believe that within the walls of their church, and in the privacy of their homes, they may, if they so choose, regardless of age, play together naked. They advocate that YMCAs and YWCAs and public swimming pools and beaches be available on a clothing-optional basis. They advocate a society which accepts public nudity where it is convenient to be naked, but they do not practice public nudity and will not until it is legal under the law. There are no sexual orgies between the members within the environs of the church, and they do not advocate promiscuous sexual relationships. But within the parameters and structures of their new moralities, they believe that wider sexual experience and sexual caring, both premaritally and postmaritally, would create sounder lifelong pair bondings.

"Although many members of the First Church are monogamous, they do not believe that sexual fidelity is a condition of a happy marriage. Unlike fundamentalists, Catholics, and most Protestants, they believe that either partner in a monogamous marriage may be involved in caring sexual relationships with members of the other sex.

"In these areas as well as in other areas, such as legalized prostitution, acceptance of homosexuality, and in the uncensored portrayal of explicit human loving in all the arts, they are actively trying to change the law in their belief that sounder moralities, more in keeping with the realities of human existence, would make a better and more self-fulfilling world possible.

"Despite millions of Americans who may be horrified by the Mo Mo sexual beliefs, none of them violate sane human values as much as the horror and violence and sick, sleazy human sexuality that is a staple of many of our novels, movies, magazines, and newspapers.

"Obviously sex worship and the belief that each and every one of us is God, offered within the confines of a church that is unafraid of naked human Gods, is frightening to Christians who believe that the Word of God was written for all times in the Holy Bible.

"District Attorney Hardman has spent many hours in this courtroom trying to establish that a religion with the central concept that each man and woman is God cannot be a religion in the accepted definition of the word, which, according to him, entails the recognition of some Supreme Power. He has tried to equate the beliefs of the members of the First Church of Modern Moralities with the Supreme Court of Chautauqua County's decision against the Religious Society of Families in which the court stated: 'Relying on examination of the actual tenets and beliefs of this society, as set forth in its constitution and bylaws, which include a denial of the existence of God, and in total reliance upon human reason, the society is not a religious organization.'

"If this decision had been rendered in Massachusetts Bay Colony in 1636 instead of the last half of the twentieth century, it might be more believable. We have not come very far in 350 years. We still give lip service to religious freedom and the First Amendment, but we fear a church like the First Church of Modern Moralities, which flies in the face of Christian beliefs and Judeo-Christian moralities and our underlying Protestant Calvinistic belief in 'good works' as the route to salvation. Most of us still believe in a powerful, remote, austere Old Testament God who loves his children but is quick to punish sinners, and often we revert to the horror of a Puritan morality which states: 'I'm right. You're wrong. There's no room for you in my world.'

"In the 1630s, the Puritans who came to America to practice religious freedom quickly proved that it was a freedom to practice their religion only. They passed the first alien and sedition act, which effectively kept out so-called papists. They banished John Wheelwright and Anne Hutchinson from the Mass Bay Colony for a slightly different interpretation of Genesis. They hung Mary Dyer, a Quaker, for her belief in an inner light. They paraded women naked, publicly whipped men, put both sexes in stocks, burned their hands, and cropped their ears—all for entertaining beliefs different from the official beliefs of the Colony.

"Less than a month ago, proving that this kind of thinking is still rampant in Massachusetts and elsewhere in the United States, Matthew Godwin, Robert Lovejoy, Mary Peachy, and three responsible women, whom you've listened to in this court, were symbolically tarred and feathered for their religious beliefs, and consequently brought to trial here.

"Yet the truth is that their belief that each man and woman is God is far saner than a belief in a patriarchal, vindictive God who loves those who believe in him and hates their enemies.

"District Attorney Hardman has practically admitted that he believes that unless there is an ultimate creator out there somewhere who passes judgment on men and women, there can be no ultimate moralities. He has tried to frighten you with the vision of poorly educated, demented men and women who believe they are God and who will be walking the streets with machine guns blatting, exterminating people at random. He has tried to equate Matthew Godwin with Genghis Khan and Adolf Hitler. He refuses to believe that children raised in the belief that they are loving Gods are not as likely to be hateful and vengeful as those who imitate an Old Testament Judeo-Christian God. He does not understand that the greatest sin for a person raised in the belief that he or she is God is the failure to act like God.

"Twenty years ago, a great Catholic priest, Bishop Fulton J. Sheen, a man of God who had the same kind of charisma as Reverend

356 THE IMMORAL REVEREND

Godwin, wrote a book called *These Are the Sacraments* in which he described the symbolism of the seven Catholic sacraments. The Sacrament of Baptism, the Sacrament of Confirmation, the Sacrament of Eucharist, the Sacrament of Penance, the Sacrament of Anointing of the Sick, the Sacrament of the Holy Orders, and the Sacrament of Marriage.

"In the introduction to the book, Bishop Sheen explains: 'No one can understand the sacraments unless he has what might be called a divine sense of humor . . . Our Lord had a divine sense of humor because he revealed that the universe is sacramental . . . A sacrament in a very broad sense combines two elements; one visible, the other invisible—spiritual. One that can be seen, or tasted or touched or heard; the other unseen to the eyes . . . Thus a handshake is a kind of sacrament, a kiss a kind of sacrament.' Bishop Sheen pointed out that the word *sacrament* in Greek means 'mystery'.

"Matthew Godwin is offering you—yourself as God—and your birth, your sexual loving, your creation of new life, and your death, as a never ending mystery that you can share with each other directly without any saintly intermediaries. He's proposing that we search for saner moralities that make the joy and sacrament of your life and your death meaningful and filled with hope and love. That is religion, and it needs no Christ, Buddha, Mohammed, or Sacred Tabernacles as a mediator between God and you.

"Ladies and gentlemen of the jury, it's your decision. I know that, like fifty million or more Americans, most of you watched Mike Wilder's 'Showdown' a few weeks ago, on television. You must not let Wilder's rightist leanings toward men like Jeffrey Falconer, nor his hyped-up interpretation of events in Adamsport, nor his unsubstantiated implication that Matthew Godwin was associated with some unsavory business dealings, influence you. Nor should you question why an Arab oil billionaire would endow a church whose beliefs are so foreign to Christian and Mohammedan thinking.

"The question here is the First Amendment right to worship God according to one's own beliefs. If you believe in a Kingdom of Heaven ruled by a loving God, I am sure you'll agree that there is room in America for a religion which celebrates the mystery and wonder of men and women, God's creatures, in the act of loving each other and daring to be a reflection of a loving God who has given us the power and the glory of creation."

Rimmer, Robert H.
    Immoral reverend.   1985 $23

10/85   85-43080
        86 C

T   **CY**
      BALTIMORE COUNTY   0879752998
         PUBLIC LIBRARY
      COCKEYSVILLE AREA BRANCH